D0827116

CHICAGO WORKS:

A Collection of Chicago Authors' BEST Stories

THE MORTON PRESS

CHICAGO · 1990

ACKNOWLEDGMENTS

The pieces in this collection are reprinted by permission of the authors and originally appeared in the publications as listed herein: "The Beach Umbrella" in *The Beach Umbrella*, "Pet Milk" in *The New Yorker*, "The Journal of a Wife Beater" in *Harper's Bazaar*, "The Rock Garden" in *Southwest Review* and *The Calling*, 1980, copyright 1973 by Mary Gray Hughes, "Re-entry: Chicago" in *Story Quarterly*, "Sartre is a Cold Fish" in *Cimarron Review*, "Julie" in *The Literary Review*, "The Waning of the Middle Ages" in *Chicago Magazine*, "What We Learned in Vietnam" in *Other Voices*, "Coming Back a Star" in *Chicago Magazine*, "Last Rights" in *Other Voices*, "From Treemont Stone" in *TriQuarterly* and *Treemont Stone*, "Noble Rot" in *Chicago Times* and also *Noble Rot, short stories*, "James Jeans (not James Dean) and the Jiffy Lube Man" in *Formations*, "Papageno" in *Playboy Magazine*, "Vanishing Point" in *Saints* published by Persea Books, copyright 1986, "He Read to Her" in *Iowa Woman*, "Risk" in *Atlantic Monthly*, "Gallagher's Old Man" selection from *Paco's Story*, copyright 1984, 1986 by Larry Heineman, originally in *TriQuarterly*, reprinted by permission of Farrar, Straus and Giroux, Inc., "City Dogs" in *City Dogs*, Harper & Row, "Coming Around the Horn" in *Other Voices*, "Twenty Questions" in *Chicago Magazine*.

Cover design by Linda Lee, Design 1, Oak Park, IL
Typesetting by Typeset Offset, Inc., Chicago, IL

Published in 1990 by
The Morton Press
Chicago, Illinois

Copyright © 1990 The Morton Press

Printed and bound in the USA
No part of this book may be reproduced in any form
without the express written permission of the publisher.

Library of Congress Catalog Card Number: 89-064304
ISBN: 0-9625446-1-2

PUBLISHER'S NOTE

The publisher would like to thank the editor of this anthology, Laurie Levy. In spite of being a busy Chicago freelance writer who also writes fiction (she has had many short stories published and has a novel in progress), she worked tirelessly suggesting stories and contacting the final 22 authors we chose from the 40 she recommended. Without her taste, knowledge, professionalism, great care and generous efforts, there would be no book.

—The Morton Press

Scott Turow

FOREWORD

I remember, when I was ten or eleven, reading, in the midst of some childhood illness, certain novels of Dumas — *The Count of Monte Cristo* held me like an illness itself — a remarkable tale of revenge and adventure — and in this experience, I learned about the transporting power of fiction and longed, at once, to somehow replicate that — a sort of natural child's wish, the way my kids always want to hold the steering wheel. I knew this was preposterous. The idea of being a writer is as romantic as *The Count of Monte Cristo.* It is no job for a normal person. A writer is an aesthete, a bohemian, someone living solely by his wits.

And yet, the ambition persisted and so did my thinking about this strange calling. I was lucky enough in college to study with gifted professors of literature, from whom I naturally learned literary aesthetics. This can all be very high flown and complex, but most of what I decided as a result of all this instruction can be summarized in a single word: authenticity. The writer, the artist, I came to believe, searches to find that small uniquely personal grain in our own experience that expresses our truest self and which can be enlarged and shared, and thereby achieve the eternalness of art.

In those years, the world of letters to me was like some mansion at the edge of town to which common folk were only rarely admitted. I regarded established writers as nobler types than the rest of us, who lived higher, better lives. But I noticed one thing about the writers I admired — they shared one attribute — they all had been published. And with that recognition the first element of adult practicality forged its way into my fantasies. I wanted, poor thing, to be published too. And yet, if the purpose of art is simply self-expression — to dredge the writer's soul in search of treasure — who cares about being read?

Over time I realized that as writers we long for our audience. We are lovers looking for a mate. Writers may despise their audience or disregard it; many are too fearful of rejection to write for anything but the drawer. And yet, I must confess that I suspect even the most private poet must have momentary fantasies of the wonder his written work will someday inspire. We yearn for the embrace of those we seek to inspire.

My own belief is that the stories that have stood the ages have not been preserved by a literary elite, but by their ability to continuously stir a broad range of readers. That in the end was the audience I wanted to try to reach — the community of readers who cared enough about a book to recall it.

I have commented elsewhere that the experience of *Presumed Innocent* has made me no less cynical about American publishers. I have watched not only my own experience over the years but that of my friends. They have labored with remarkable stubbornness, dedication and skill to produce works of real beauty. And all of them have had a number of earlier works that have never seen the light of day. All of this leads me to say what all of us know: there is a lot of junk published, and much worthwhile writing that gets rejected, or published and ignored. Most publishers do not attempt to edify or cultivate public taste — and they do that because they do not want to lose their shirts.

Much as we writers want to blame publishers, we must accept the fact in a market economy public tastes determine what gets published, and that is still not a bad thing. I would rather have had that than some Brahmin elite of new novelists take it upon themselves to tell the rest of us what is to be published. We have to accept the fact that there are many fine books which are not destined for an audience of millions of readers, that are too difficult, or static, or which do not strike enough of the chords in people who do not live daily with literature. And of course, on the other side, there are books that could be much better read that get ignored. Moreover, there are voices that simply deserve to be heard, whether or not they command a wide audience, because they instill so much and so deeply inspire the smaller audience they may attract.

Having said all of that, it should be clear that I feel some ambivalence about the success of my first novel. When I walk into a store and find 20% of the shelf space given over to *Presumed Innocent,* as was the case in the first weeks of the paperback display, I know what is not appearing there as a result. I know about the good books that will never find the readers they deserve. But I also must tell you that I do not wish for one less reader. I wish there was more good reading, more space, more time, but I am grateful for every person who has read my book.

None of this of course was expected. When I wrote *Presumed Innocent,* I had in mind a determination not to go through one more battery of rejection slips ... but no greater commercial ambition than to see the book sold. That is my last observation. That we are all powerless to determine what will happen when our works leave our hands. The only audience that matters is the one that is imagined, that perfect reader who is out there waiting for the work we labor to create. By our own internal barometer we tend to know whether he or she is pleased. But there is never any telling.

In the end, our task is merely to do our best, to produce the real thing, so that we have the courage to raise our hands, and with whatever longing, ambivalence, or sheer hope, to reach outward for the embrace.

The stories that follow are their authors' best work, the real thing. They ignite and inspire. They illustrate both the transporting power of fiction and the writer's mission: to reflect, refine, to find in the smallest details and the grandest struggles the common tale of our species' survival.

CONTENTS

Cyrus Colter

THE BEACH UMBRELLA

(from *The Beach Umbrella*)

T he thirty-first street beach lay dazzling under a sky so blue
that Lake Michigan ran to the horizon like a sheet of sapphire
silk, studded with little barbed white sequins for sails; and the heavy
surface of the water lapped gently at the boulder "sea wall" which had
been cut into, graded, and sanded to make the beach. Saturday
afternoons were always frenzied: three black lifeguards, giants in
sunglasses, preened in their towers and chaperoned the bathers—
adults, teenagers, and children—who were going through every
physical gyration of which the human body is capable. Some dove,
swam, some hollered, rode inner tubes, or merely stood waistdeep
and pummeled the water; others—on the beach—sprinted, did hand-
springs and somersaults, sucked Eskimo pies, or just buried their
children in the sand. Then there were the lollers—extended in their
languor under a garish variety of beach umbrellas.

Elijah lolled too—on his stomach in the white sand, his chin
cupped in his palm; but under no umbrella. He had none. By habit,
though, he stared in awe at those who did, and sometimes meddled in
their conversation: "It's gonna be gettin' *hot* pretty soon—if it ain't
careful," he said to a Bantu-looking fellow and his girl sitting near by
with an older woman. The temperature was then in the nineties. The
fellow managed a negligent smile. "Yeah," he said, and persisted in
listening to the women. Buoyant still, Elijah watched them. But soon
his gaze wavered, and then moved on to other lollers of interest.
Finally he got up, stretched, brushed sand from his swimming trunks,
and scanned the beach for a new spot. He started walking.

He was not tall. And he appeared to walk on his toes—his
walnut-colored legs were bowed and skinny and made him hobble
like a jerky little spider. Next he plopped down near two men and two
girls—they were hilarious about something—sitting beneath a big
purple-and-white umbrella. The girls, chocolate brown and shapely,
emitted squeals of laughter at the wisecracks of the men. Elijah was
enchanted. All summer long the rambunctious gaiety of the beach

1

had fastened on him a curious charm, a hex, that brought him gawking and twiddling to the lake each Saturday. The rest of the week, save Sunday, he worked. But Myrtle, his wife, detested the sport and stayed away. Randall, the boy, had been only twice and then without little Susan, who during the summer was her mother's own midget reflection. But Elijah came regularly, especially whenever Myrtle was being evil, which he felt now was almost always. She was getting worse, too—if that was possible. The Woman was money-*crazy*.

"You gotta sharp-lookin' umbrella there!" he cut in on the two laughing couples. They studied him—the abruptly silent way. Then the big-shouldered fellow smiled and lifted his eyes to their spangled roof. "Yeah? . . . Thanks," he said. Elijah carried on: "I see a lot of 'em out here this summer—much more'n last year." The fellow meditated on this, but was noncommittal. The others went on gabbing, mostly with their hands. Elijah, squinting in the hot sun, watched them. He didn't see how they could be married; they cut the fool too much, acted like they'd itched to get together for weeks and just now made it. He pondered going back in the water, but he'd already had an hour of that. His eyes traveled the sweltering beach. Funny about his folks; they were every shape and color a God-made human could be. Here was a real sample of variety—pink white to jetty black. Could you any longer call that a *race* of people? It was a complicated complication— for some real educated guy to figure out. Then another thought slowly bore in on him: the beach umbrellas blooming across the sand attracted people—slews of friends, buddies; and gals, too. Wherever the loudest-racket tore the air, a big red, or green, or yellowish umbrella—bordered with white fringe maybe—flowered in the middle of it all and gave shade to the happy good-timers.

Take, for instance, that tropical-looking pea-green umbrella over there, with the Bikini-ed brown chicks under it, and the portable radio jumping. A real beach party! He got up, stole over, and eased down in the sand at the fringe of the jubilation—two big thermos jugs sat in the shade and everybody had a paper cup in hand as the explosions of buffoonery carried out to the water. Chief provoker of mirth was a bulging-eyed old gal in a white bathing suit who, encumbered by big flabby overripe thighs, cavorted and pranced in the sand. When, perspiring from the heat, she finally fagged out, she flopped down almost on top of him. So far, he had gone unnoticed. But now, as he craned in at closer range, she brought him up: "Whatta *you* want, Pops?" She grinned, but with a touch of hostility.

Pops! Where'd she get that stuff? He was only forty-one, not a day older than that boozy bag. But he smiled. "Nothin'," he said brightly, "but you sure got one goin' here." He turned and viewed the noise-makers.

"An' you wanta get in on it!" she wrangled.

"Oh, I was just lookin'—"

"—You was just lookin.' Yeah, you was just lookin' at them young chicks there!" She roared a laugh and pointed at the sexy-looking girls under the umbrella.

Elijah grinned weakly.

"Beat it!" she catcalled, and turned back to the party.

He sat like a rock—the hell with her. But soon he relented, and wandered down to the water's edge—remote now from all inhospitality—to sit in the sand and hug his raised knees. Far out, the sailboats were pinned to the horizon and, despite all the close-in fuss, the wide miles of lake lay impassive under a blazing calm; far south and east down the long-curving lake shore, miles in the distance, the smoky haze of the Whiting plant of the Youngstown Sheet and Tube Company hung ominously in an otherwise bright sky. And so it was that he turned back and viewed the beach again—and suddenly caught his craving. Weren't they something—the umbrellas! The flashy colors of them! And the swank! No wonder folks ganged round them. Yes . . . yes, he too must have one. The thought came slow and final, and scared him. For there stood Myrtle in his mind. She nagged him now night and day, and it was always money that got her started; there was never enough—for Susan's shoes, Randy's overcoat, for new kitchen linoleum, Venetian blinds, for a better car than the old Chevy. "I just don't understand you!" she had said only night before last. "Have you got any plans at all for your family? You got a family, you know. If you could only bear to pull yourself away from that deaf old tightwad out at that warehouse, and go get yourself a *real* job . . . But no! Not *you*!"

She was talking about old man Schroeder, who owned the warehouse, where he worked. Yes, the pay could be better, but it still wasn't as bad as she made out. Myrtle could be such a fool sometimes. He had been with the old man nine years now; had started out as a freight handler, but worked up to doing inventories and a little paper work. True, the business had been going down recently, for the old man's sight and hearing were failing and his key people had left him. Now he depended on *him*, Elijah—who of late wore a necktie on the job, and made his inventory rounds with a ball-point pen and clipboard. The old man was friendlier, too—almost "hat in hand" to him. He liked everything about the job now—except the pay. And that was only because of Myrtle. She just wanted so much; even talked of moving out of their rented apartment and buying out in the Chatham area. But one thing had to be said for her: she never griped about anything for herself; only for the family, the kids. Every payday he endorsed his check and handed it over to her, and got back in return only gasoline and cigarette money. And this could get pretty tiresome. About six weeks ago he'd gotten a ten-dollar-a-month raise out of the old man, but that had only made her madder than ever. He'd thought about looking for another job all right; but where would he go to get another white-collar job? There weren't many of them for him. *She* wouldn't care if he went back to the steel mills, back to pouring that white-hot ore out at Youngstown Sheet and Tube. It would be okay with *her*—so long as his pay check was fat. But that kind of work was no good, undignified; coming home on the bus you were always so tired you went to sleep in your seat, with your lunch pail in your lap.

Just then two wet boys, chasing each other across the sand, raced by him into the water. The cold spray on his skin made him jump, jolting him out of his thoughts. He turned and slowly scanned the beach again. The umbrellas were brighter, gayer, bolder than ever—each a hiving center of playful people. He stood up finally, took a long last look, and then started back to the spot where he had parked the Chevy.

The following Monday evening was hot and humid as Elijah sat at home in their plain living room and pretended to read the newspaper; the windows were up, but not the slightest breeze came through the screens to stir Myrtle's fluffy curtains. At the moment she and nine-year-old Susan were in the kitchen finishing the dinner dishes. For twenty minutes now he had sat waiting for the furtive chance to speak to Randall. Randall, at twelve, was a serious, industrious boy, and did deliveries and odd jobs for the neighborhood grocer. Soon he came through—intent, absorbed—on his way back to the grocery for another hour's work.

"Gotta go back, eh, Randy?" Elijah said.

"Yes, sir." He was tall for his age, and wore glasses. He paused with his hand on the doorknob.

Elijah hesitated. Better wait, he thought—wait till he comes back. But Myrtle might be around then. Better ask him now. But Randall had opened the door. "See you later, Dad," he said—and left.

Elijah, shaken, again raised the newspaper and tried to read. He should have called him back, he knew, but he had lost his nerve—because he couldn't tell how Randy would take it. Fifteen dollars was nothing though, really—Randy probably had fifty or sixty stashed away somewhere in his room. Then he thought of Myrtle, and waves of fright went over him—to be even thinking about a beach umbrella was bad enough; and to buy one, especially now, would be to her some kind of crime; but to borrow even a part of the money for it from Randy . . . well, Myrtle would go out of her mind. He had never lied to his family before. This would be the first time. And he had thought about it all day long. During the morning, at the warehouse, he had gotten out the two big mail-order catalogues, to look at the beach umbrellas; but the ones shown were all so small and dinky-looking he was contemptuous. So at noon he drove the Chevy out to a sporting-goods store on West Sixty-Third Street. There he found a gorgeous assortment of yard and beach umbrellas. And there he found his prize. A beauty, a big beauty, with wide red and white stripes, and a white fringe. But oh the price! Twenty-three dollars! And he with nine.

"What's the matter with you?" Myrtle had walked in the room. She was thin, and medium brown-skinned with a saddle of freckles across her nose, and looked harried in her sleeveless house dress with her hair unkempt.

Startled, he lowered the newspaper. "Nothing," he said.

"How can you read looking *over* the paper?"

"Was I?"

Not bothering to answer, she sank in a chair. "Susie," she called back into the kitchen, "bring my cigarettes in here, will you, baby?"

Soon Susan, chubby and solemn, with the mist of perspiration on her forehead, came in with the cigarettes. "Only three left, Mama," she said, peering into the pack.

"Okay," Myrtle sighed, taking the cigarettes. Susan started out. "Now, scour the sink good, honey—and then go take your bath. You'll feel cooler."

Before looking at him again, Myrtle lit a cigarette. "School starts in three weeks," she said, with a forlorn shake of her head. "Do you realize that?"

"Yeah? . . . Jesus, time flies." He could not look at her.

"Susie needs dresses, and a couple of pairs of *good* shoes—and she'll need a coat before it gets cold."

"Yeah, I know." He patted the arm of the chair.

"Randy—bless his heart—has already made enough to get most of *his* things. That boy's something; he's all business—I've never seen anything like it." She took a drag on her cigarette. "And old man Schroeder giving you a ten-dollar raise! What was you thinkin' about? What'd you *say* to him?"

He did not answer at first. Finally he said, "Ten dollars is ten dollars, Myrtle. *You* know business is slow."

"*I'll* say it is! And there won't be any business before long—and then where'll you be? I tell you over and over again, you better start looking for something *now*! I been preachin' it to you for a year."

He said nothing.

"Ford and International Harvester are hiring every man they can lay their hands on! And the mills out in Gary and Whiting are going full blast—you see the red sky every night. The men make *good* money."

"They earn every nickel of it, too," he said in gloom.

"But they *get* it! Bring it home! It spends! Does that mean anything to you? Do you know what some of them make? Well, ask Hawthorne—or ask Sonny Milton. Sonny's wife says his checks some weeks run as high as a hundred twenty, hundred thirty, dollars. One week! Take-home pay!"

"Yeah? . . . And Sonny told me he wished he had a job like mine."

Myrtle threw back her head with a bitter gasp. "Oh-h-h, God!

5

Did you tell him what you made? Did you tell him that?"

Suddenly Susan came back into the muggy living room. She went straight to her mother and stood as if expecting an award. Myrtle absently patted her on the side of the head. "Now, go and run your bath water, honey," she said.

Elijah smiled at Susan. "Susie," he said, "d'you know your tummy is stickin' way out—you didn't eat too much, did you?" He laughed.

Susan turned and observed him; then looked at her mother. "No," she finally said.

"Go on, now, baby," Myrtle said. Susan left the room.

Myrtle resumed. "Well, there's no use going through all this again. It's plain as the nose on your face. You got a family—a good family, *I* think. The only question is, do you wanta get off your hind end and do somethin' for it. It's just that simple."

Elijah looked at her. "You can talk real crazy sometimes, Myrtle."

"I think it's that old man!" she cried, her freckles contorted. "He's got you answering the phone, and taking inventory—wearing a necktie and all that. You wearing a necktie and your son mopping in a grocery store, so he can buy his own clothes." She snatched up her cigarettes, and walked out of the room.

His eyes did not follow her, but remained off in space. Finally he got up and went into the kitchen. Over the stove the plaster was thinly cracked, and, in spots, the linoleum had worn through the pattern; but everything was immaculate. He opened the refrigerator, poured a glass of cold water, and sat down at the kitchen table. He felt strange and weak, and sat for a long time sipping the water.

Then after a while heard Randall's key in the front door, sending tremors of dread through him. When Randall came into the kitchen, he seemed to him as tall as himself; his glasses were steamy from the humidity outside, and his hands were dirty.

"Hi, Dad," he said gravely without looking at him, and opened the refrigerator door.

Elijah chuckled. "Your mother'll get after you about going in there without washing your hands."

But Randall took out the water pitcher and closed the door.

Elijah watched him. Now was the time to ask him. His heart was hammering. Go on—now! But instead he heard his husky voice saying. "What'd they have you doing over at the grocery tonight?"

Randall was drinking the glass of water. When he finished, he said, "Refilling shelves."

"Pretty hot job tonight, eh?"

"It wasn't so bad." Randall was matter-of-fact as he set the empty glass over the sink, and paused before leaving.

"Well . . . you're doing fine, son. Fine. Your mother sure is proud of you . . ." Purpose had lodged in his throat.

The praise embarrassed Randall. "Okay, Dad," he said, and edged from the kitchen.

Elijah slumped back in his chair, near prostration. He tried to clear his mind of every particle of thought, but the images became only more jumbled, oppressive to the point of panic.

Then before long Myrtle came into the kitchen—ignoring him. But she seemed not so hostile now as coldly impassive, exhibiting a bravado he had not seen before. He got up and went back into the living room and turned on the television. As the TV-screen lawmen galloped before him, he sat oblivious, admitting the failure of his will. If only he could have gotten Randall to himself long enough— but everything had been so sudden, abrupt; he couldn't just ask him out of the clear blue. Besides, around him, Randall always seemed so busy, too busy to talk. He couldn't understand that; he had never mistreated the boy, never whipped him in his life; had shaken him a time or two, but that was long ago, when he was little.

He sat and watched the finish of the half-hour TV show. Myrtle was in the bedroom now. He slouched in his chair, lacking the resolve to get up and turn off the television.

Suddenly he was on his feet.

Leaving the television on, he went back to Randall's room in the rear. The door was open and Randall was asleep, lying on his back on the bed, perspiring, still dressed except for his shoes and glasses. He stood over the bed and looked at him. He was a good boy; his own son. But how strange—he thought for the first time— there was no resemblance between them. None whatsoever. Randy had a few of his mother's freckles on his thin brown face, but he could see none of himself in the boy. Then his musings were scattered by the return of his fear. He dreaded waking him. And he might be cross. If he didn't hurry, though, Myrtle or Susie might come strolling out any minute. His bones seemed rubbery from the strain. Finally he bent down and touched Randall's shoulder. The boy did not move muscle, except to open his eyes. Elijah smiled at him. And he slowly sat up.

"Sorry, Randy—to wake you up like this."

"What's the matter?" Randall rubbed his eyes.

Elijah bent down again, but did not whisper. "Say, can you let me have fifteen bucks—till I get my check? ... I need to get some things—and I'm a little short this time." He could hardly bring the words up.

Randall gave him a slow, queer look.

"I'll get my check a week from Friday," Elijah said, " ... and I'll give it back to you then—sure."

Now instinctively Randall glanced toward the door, and Elijah knew Myrtle had crossed his thoughts. "You don't have to mention anything to your mother," he said with casual suddenness.

Randall got up slowly off the bed, and, in his socks, walked to the little table where he did his homework. He pulled the drawer out, fished far in the back a moment, and brought out a white business envelope secured by a rubber band. Holding the envelope close to his stomach, he took out first a ten-dollar bill, and then a five, and, sighing, handed them over.

"Thanks, old man," Elijah quivered, folding the money. "You'll get this back the day I get my check .... That's for sure."

"Okay," Randall finally said.

Elijah started out. Then he could see Myrtle on payday—her hand extended for his check. He hesitated, and looked at Randall, as if to speak. But he slipped the money in his trousers pocket and hurried from the room.

The following Saturday at the beach did not begin bright and sunny. By noon it was hot, but the sky was overcast and angry, the air heavy. There was no certainty whatever of a crowd, raucous or otherwise, and this was Elijah's chief concern as, shortly before twelve o'clock, he drove up in the Chevy and parked in the bumpy, graveled stretch of high ground that looked down eastward over the lake and was used for a parking lot. He climbed out of the car, glancing at the lake and clouds, and prayed in his heart it would not rain—the water was murky and restless, and only a handful of bathers had showed. But it was early yet. He stood beside the car and watched a bulbous, brown-skinned woman, in bathing suit and enormous straw hat, lugging a lunch basket down toward the beach, followed by her brood of children. And a fellow in swimming trunks, apparently the father, took a towel and sandals from his new Buick and called petulantly to his family to "just wait a minute, please." In another car, two women sat waiting, as yet fully clothed and undecided about going swimming. While down at the water's edge there was the usual cluster of dripping boys who, brash and boisterous, swarmed to the beach everyday in fair weather or foul.

Elijah took off his shirt, peeled his trousers from over his swimming trunks, and started collecting the paraphernalia from the back seat of the car: a frayed pink rug filched from the house, a towel, sunglasses, cigarettes, a thermos jug filled with cold lemonade he had made himself, and a dozen paper cups. All this he stacked on the front fender. Then he went around to the rear and opened the trunk. Ah, there it lay—encased in a long, slim package trussed with heavy twine, and barely fitting athwart the spare tire. He felt prickles of excitement as he took the knife from the tool bag, cut the twine, and pulled the wrapping paper away. Red and white stripes sprang at him. It was even more gorgeous than when it had first seduced him in the store. The white fringe gave it style; the wide red fillets were cardinal and stark, and the white stripes glared. Now he opened it over his head, for the full thrill of its colors, and looked around to see if anyone else agreed. Finally after a while he gathered up all his equipment and headed down for the beach, his short, nubby legs seeming more bowed than ever under the weight of their cargo.

When he reached the sand, a choice of location became a pressing matter. That was why he had come early. From past observation it was clear that the center of gaiety shifted from day to day; last Saturday it might have been nearer the water, this Saturday, well back; or up, or down, the beach a ways. He must pick the site with care, for he could not move about the way he did when he had no umbrella; it was too noticeable. He finally took a spot as near the center of the beach as he could estimate, and dropped his gear in the sand. He knelt down and spread the pink rug, then moved the thermos jug over onto it, and folded the towel and placed it with the paper cups, sunglasses, and cigarettes down beside the jug. Now he went to find a heavy stone or brick to drive down the spike for the hollow umbrella stem to fit over. So it was not until the umbrella was finally up that he again had time for anxiety about the weather. His whole morning's effort had been an act of faith, for, as yet, there was no sun, although now and then a few azure breaks appeared in the thinning cloud mass. But before very long this brighter texture of the sky began to grow and spread by slow degrees, and his hopes quickened. Finally he sat down under the umbrella, lit a cigarette, and waited.

It was not long before two small boys came by—on their way to the water. He grinned, and called to them, "Hey, fellas, been in yet?"—their bathing suits were dry.

They stopped, and observed him. Then one of them smiled, and shook his head.

Elijah laughed. "Well, whatta you waitin' for? Go on in there and get them suits wet!" Both boys gave him silent smiles. And they lingered. He thought this a good omen—it had been different the Saturday before.

Once or twice the sun burst through the weakening clouds. He forgot the boys now in watching the skies, and soon they moved on. His anxiety was not detectable from his lazy posture under the umbrella, with his dwarfish, gnarled legs extended and his bare heels on the little rug. But then soon the clouds began to fade in earnest, seeming not to move away laterally, but slowly to recede into a lucent haze, until at last the sun came through hot and bright. He squinted at the sky and felt delivered. They would come, the folks would come!—were coming now; the beach would soon be swarming. Two other umbrellas were up already, and the diving board thronged with wet, acrobatic boys. The lifeguards were in their towers now, and still another launched his yellow rowboat. And up on the Outer Drive, the cars, one by one, were turning into the parking lot. The sun was bringing them out all right; soon he'd be in the middle of a field day. He felt a low-key, welling excitement, for the water was blue, and far out the sails were starched and white.

Soon he saw the two little boys coming back. They were soaked. Their mother—a thin, brown girl in a yellow bathing suit—was with them now, and the boys were pointing to his umbrella. She seemed dignified for her youth, as she gave him a shy glance and then smiled at the boys.

"Ah, ha!" he cried to the boys. "You've been in *now* all right!" And then laughing to her, "I was kiddin' them awhile ago about their dry bathing suits."

She smiled at the boys again. "They like for me to be with them when they go in," she said.

"I got some lemonade here," he said abruptly, slapping the thermos jug. "Why don't you have some?" His voice was anxious.

She hesitated.

He jumped up. "Come on, sit down." He smiled at her and stepped aside.

Still she hesitated. But her eager boys pressed close behind her. Finally she smiled and sat down under the umbrella.

"You fellas can sit down under there too—in the shade," he said to the boys, and pointed under the umbrella. The boys flopped down quickly in the shady sand. He started at once serving them cold lemonade in the paper cups.

"Whew! I thought it was goin' to rain there for a while," he said, making conversation after passing out the lemonade. He had squatted on the sand and lit another cigarette. "Then there wouldn't a been much goin' on. But it turned out fine after all—there'll be a mob here before long."

She sipped the lemonade, but said little. He felt she had sat down only because of the boys, for she merely smiled and gave short answers to his questions. He learned the boys' names, Melvin and James; their ages, seven and nine; and that they were still frightened by the water. But he wanted to ask *her* name, and inquire about her husband. But he could not capture the courage.

Now the sun was hot and the sand was hot. And an orange-and-white umbrella was going up right beside them—two fellows and a girl. When the fellow who had been kneeling to drive the umbrella spike in the sand stood up, he was stringbean tall, and black, with his glistening hair freshly processed. The girl was a lighter brown, and wore a lilac bathing suit, and, although her legs were thin, she was pleasant enough to look at. The second fellow was medium, really, in height, but short beside his tall, black friend. He was yellow-skinned, and fast getting bald, although still in his early thirties. Both men sported little shoestring mustaches.

Elijah watched them in silence as long as he could. "You picked the right spot all right!" he laughed at last, putting on his sunglasses.

"How come, man?" The tall, black fellow grinned, showing his mouthful of gold teeth.

"You see *everybody* here!" happily rejoined Elijah. "They all come here!"

"Man, I been coming here for years," the fellow reproved, and sat down in his khaki swimming trunks to take off his shoes. Then he stood up. "But right now, in the water I goes." He looked down at the girl. "How 'bout you, Lois, baby?"

"No, Caesar," she smiled, "not yet; I'm gonna sit here awhile and relax."

"Okay, then—you just sit right there and relax. And Little Joe"—he turned and grinned to his shorter friend—"you sit there an' relax right along with her. You all can talk with this gentleman here"—he nodded at Elijah—"an' his nice wife." Then, pleased with himself, he trotted off toward the water.

The young mother looked at Elijah, as if he should have hastened to correct him. But somehow he had not wanted to. Yet too, Caesar's remark seemed to amuse her, for she soon smiled. Elijah felt the pain of relief—he did not want her to go; he glanced at her with a furtive laugh, and then they both laughed. The boys had finished their lemonade now, and were digging in the sand. Lois and Little Joe were busy talking.

Elijah was not quite sure what he should say to the mother. He did not understand her, was afraid of boring her, was desperate to keep her interested. As she sat looking out over the lake, he watched her. She was not pretty; and she was too thin. But he thought she had poise; he liked the way she treated her boys—tender, but casual; how different from Myrtle's frantic herding.

Soon she turned to the boys. "Want to go back in the water?" she laughed.

The boys looked at each other, and then at her. "Okay," James said finally, in resignation.

"Here, have some more lemonade," Elijah cut in.

The boys, rescued for the moment, quickly extended their cups. He poured them more lemonade, as she looked on smiling.

Now he turned to Lois and Little Joe sitting under their orange-and-white umbrella. "How 'bout some good ole cold lemonade?" he asked with a mushy smile. "I got plenty of cups." He felt he must get something going.

Lois smiled back. "No, thanks," she said, fluttering her long eyelashes, "not right now."

He looked anxiously at Little Joe.

"*I'll* take a cup!" said Little Joe, and turned and laughed to Lois: "Hand me that bag there, will you?" He pointed to her beach bag in the sand. She passed it to him, and he reached in and pulled out a pint of gin. "We'll have some *real* lemonade," he vowed, with a daredevilish grin.

Lois squealed with pretended embarrassment. "Oh, *Joe!*"

Elijah's eyes were big now; he was thinking of the police. But he handed Little Joe a cup and poured the lemonade, to which Joe added gin. Then Joe, grinning, thrust the bottle at Elijah. "How 'bout yourself, chief?" he said.

Elijah, shaking his head, leaned forward and whispered, "You ain't supposed to drink on the beach, y'know."

"*This* ain't a drink, man—it's a taste!" said Little Joe, laughing and waving the bottle around toward the young mother. "How 'bout a little taste for your wife here?" he said to Elijah.

The mother laughed and threw up both hands. "No, not for me!"

Little Joe gave her a rakish grin. "What'sa matter? You *'fraid* of that guy?" He jerked his thumb toward Elijah. "You 'fraid of gettin' a whippin', eh?"

"No, not exactly," she laughed.

Elijah was so elated with her his relief burst up in hysterical laughter. His laugh became strident and hoarse and he could not stop. The boys gaped at him, and then at their mother. When finally he recovered, Little Joe asked him, "Whut's so funny 'bout *that?*" Then Little Joe grinned at the mother. "You beat *him* up some-times, eh?"

This started Elijah's hysterics all over again. The mother looked concerned now, and embarrassed; her laugh was nervous and shadowed. Little Joe glanced at Lois, laughed, and shrugged his shoulders. When Elijah finally got control of himself again he looked spent and demoralized.

Lois now tried to divert attention by starting a conversation with the boys. But the mother showed signs of restlessness and seemed ready to go. At this moment Caesar returned. Glistening beads of water ran off his long, black body; and his hair was un-processed now. He surveyed the group and then flashed a wide, gold-toothed grin. "One big, happy family, like I said." Then he spied the paper cup in Little Joe's hand. "Whut you got there, man?"

Little Joe looked down into his cup with a playful smirk. "Lemonade, lover boy, lemonade."

"Don't hand me that jive, Joey. You ain't never had any straight lemonade in your life."

This again brought uproarious laughter from Elijah. "I got the straight lemonade *here!*" He beat the thermos jug with his hand. "Come on—have some!" He reached for a paper cup.

"Why, sure," said poised Caesar. He held out the cup and received the lemonade. "Now, gimme that gin," he said to Little Joe. Joe handed over the gin, and Caesar poured three fingers into the lemonade and sat down in the sand with his legs crossed under him. Soon he turned to the two boys, as their mother watched him with amusement. "Say, ain't you boys goin' in any more? Why don't you tell your daddy there to take you in?" He nodded toward Elijah.

Little Melvin frowned at him. "My daddy's workin'," he said.

Caesar's eyebrows shot up. "Ooooh, la, la!" he crooned. "Hey, now!" And he turned and looked at the mother and then at Elijah, and gave a clownish little snigger.

Lois tittered before feigning exasperation at him. "There you go again," she said, "talkin' when you shoulda been listening."

Elijah laughed along with the rest. But he felt deflated. Then he glanced at the mother, who was laughing too. He could detect in her no sign of dismay. Why then had she gone along with the gag in the first place, he thought—if now she didn't hate to see it punctured?

"*Hold the phone!*" softly exclaimed Little Joe. "Whut is *this*?" He was staring over his shoulder. Three women, young, brown, and worldly-looking, wandered toward them, carrying an assortment of beach paraphernalia and looking for a likely spot. They wore scant bathing suits, and were followed, but slowly, by an older woman with big, unsightly thighs. Elijah recognized her at once. She was the old gal who, the Saturday before, had chased him away from her beach party. She wore the same white bathing suit, and one of her girls carried the pea-green umbrella.

Caesar forgot his whereabouts ogling the girls. The older woman, observing this, paused to survey the situation. "How 'bout along in here?" she finally said to one of the girls. The girl carrying the thermos jug set it in the sand so close to Caesar it nearly touched him. He was rapturous. The girl with the umbrella had no chance to put it up, for Caesar and Little Joe instantly encumbered her with help. Another girl turned on a portable radio, and grinning, feverish Little Joe started snapping his fingers to the music's beat.

Within a half hour, a boisterous party was in progress. The little radio, perched on a hump of sand, blared out hot jazz, as the older woman—whose name turned out to be Hattie—passed around some cold, rum-spiked punch; and before long she went into her dancing-prancing act—to the riotous delight of all, especially Elijah. Hattie did not remember him from the Saturday past, and he was glad, for everything was so different today! As different as milk and ink. He knew no one realized it, but this was *his* party really—the wildest, craziest, funniest, the best he had ever seen or heard of. Nobody had been near the water—except Caesar, and the mother and boys much earlier. It appeared Lois was Caesar's girl friend, and she was hence more capable of reserve in the face of the come-on antics of Opal, Billie, and Quanita—Hattie's girls. But Little Joe, to Caesar's tortured envy, was both free and aggressive. Even the young mother, who now volunteered her name to be Mrs. Green, got frolicsome, and twice jabbed Little Joe in the ribs.

Finally Caesar proposed they all go in the water. This met with instant, tipsy acclaim; and Little Joe, his yellow face contorted from laughing, jumped up, grabbed Billie's hand, and made off with her across the sand. But Hattie would not budge. Full of rum, and stubborn, she sat sprawled with her flaccid thighs spread in an obscene V, and her eyes half shut. Now she yelled at her departing girls: "You all watch out, now! Dont'cha go in too far.... Just wade! None o' you can swim a lick!"

Elijah now was beyond happiness. He felt a floating, manic glee. He sprang up and jerked Mrs. Green splashing into the water, followed by her somewhat less ecstatic boys. Caesar had to paddle about with Lois and leave Little Joe unassisted to caper with Billie, Opal, and Quanita. Billie was the prettiest of the three, and, despite Hattie's contrary statement, she could swim; and Little Joe, after taking her out in deeper water, waved back to Caesar in triumph. The sun was brazen now, and the beach and lake thronged with a variegated humanity. Elijah, a strong, but awkward, country-style swimmer, gave Mrs. Green a lesson in floating on her back, and, though she too could swim, he often felt obligated to place both his arms under her young body and buoy her up.

And sometimes he would purposely let her sink to her chin, whereupon she would feign a happy fright and utter faint simian screeches. Opal and Quanita sat in the shallows and kicked up their heels at Caesar, who, fully occupied with Lois, was a grinning, water-threshing study in frustration.

Thus the party went—on and on—till nearly four o'clock. Elijah had not known the world afforded such joy; his homely face was a wet festoon of beams and smiles. He went from girl to girl, insisting she learn to float on his outstretched arms. Once begrudging Caesar admonished him, "Man, you gonna *drown* one o' them pretty chicks." And Little Joe bestowed his highest accolade by calling him "lover boy," as Elijah nearly strangled from laughter.

"At last, they looked up to see old Hattie as she reeled down to the water's edge, coming to fetch her girls. Both Caesar and Little Joe ran out of the water to meet her, seized her by the wrists, and despite her struggles and curses, dragged her in. "Turn me loose! You big galoots!" she yelled and gasped as the water hit her. She was in knee-deep before she wriggled and fought herself free and lurched out of the water. Her breath reeked of rum. Little Joe ran and caught her again, but she lunged backwards, and free, with such force she sat down in the wet sand with a thud. She roared a laugh now, and spread her arms for help, as her girls came sprinting and splashing out of the water and tugged her to her feet. Her eyes narrowed to vengeful, grinning slits as she turned on Caesar and Little Joe: "*I* know whut you two're up to!" She flashed a glance around toward her girls. "I been watchin' both o' you studs! Yeah, yeah, but your eyes may shine, an' your teeth may grit . . ." She went limp in a sneering, raucous laugh. Everybody laughed now—except Lois and Mrs. Green.

They had all come out of the water now, and soon the whole group returned to their three beach umbrellas. Hattie's girls immediately prepared to break camp. They took down their pea-green umbrella, folded some wet towels, and donned their beach sandals, as Hattie still bantered Caesar and Little Joe.

"Well, you sure had *yourself* a ball today," she said to Little Joe, who was sitting in the sand.

"Comin' back next Saturday?" asked grinning Little Joe.

"I jus' might at that," surmised Hattie. "We wuz here last Saturday."

"Good! Good!" Elijah broke in. "Let's *all* come back—next Saturday!" He searched every face.

"*I'll* be here," chimed Little Joe, grinning to Caesar. Captive Caesar glanced at Lois, and said nothing.

Lois and Mrs. Green were silent. Hattie, insulted, looked at them and started swelling up. "Never mind," she said pointedly to Elijah, "you jus' come on anyhow. You'll run into a slew o' folks lookin' for a good time. You don't need no *certain* people." But a little later, she and her girls all said friendly goodbyes and walked off across the sand.

The party now took a sudden downturn. All Elijah's efforts at resuscitation seemed unavailing. The westering sun was dipping toward the distant buildings of the city, and many of the bathers were leaving. Caesar and Little Joe had become bored; and Mrs. Green's boys, whining to go, kept a reproachful eye on their mother.

"Here, you boys take some more lemonade," Elijah said quickly, reaching for the thermos jug. "Only got a little left—better get while gettin's good!" He laughed. The boys shook their heads.

On Lois he tried cajolery. Smiling, and pointing to her wet, but trim bathing suit, he asked, "What color would you say that is?"

"Lilac," said Lois, now standing.

"It sure is pretty! Prettiest on the beach!" he whispered.

Lois gave him a weak smile. Then she reached down for her beach bag, and looked at Caesar.

Caesar stood up. "Let's cut," he turned and said to Little Joe, and began taking down their orange-and-white umbrella.

Elijah was desolate. "Whatta you goin' for? It's gettin' cooler! Now's the time to *enjoy* the beach!"

"I've got to go home," Lois said.

Mrs. Green got up now; her boys had started off already. "Just a minute, Melvin," she called, frowning. Then, smiling, she turned and thanked Elijah.

He whirled around to them all. "Are we comin' back next

Saturday? Come on—let's come back! Wasn't it great! It was *great!* Don't you think? Whatta you say?" He looked now at Lois and Mrs. Green.

"We'll see," Lois said, smiling, "Maybe."

"Can *you* come?" He turned to Mrs. Green.

"I'm not sure," she said. "I'll try."

"Fine! Oh, that's fine!" He turned on Caesar and Little Joe. "I'll be lookin' for you guys, hear?"

"Okay, chief," grinned Little Joe. "An' put somethin' in that lemonade, will ya?"

Everybody laughed . . . and soon they were gone.

Elijah slowly crawled back under his umbrella, although the sun's heat was almost spent. He looked about him. There was only one umbrella on the spot now, his own; where before there had been three. Cigarette butts and paper cups lay strewn where Hattie's girls had sat, and the sandy imprint of Caesar's enormous street shoes marked his site. Mrs. Green had dropped a bobby pin. He too was caught up now by a sudden urge to go. It was hard to bear much longer—the lonesomeness. And most of the people were leaving anyway. He stirred and fidgeted in the sand, and finally started an inventory of his belongings . . . . Then his thoughts flew home, and he reconsidered. Funny—he hadn't thought of home all afternoon. Where had the time gone anyhow? . . . It seemed he'd just pulled up in the Chevy and unloaded his gear; now it was time to go home again. Then the image of solemn Randy suddenly formed in his mind, sending waves of guilt through him. He forgot where he was as the duties of his existence leapt on his back—where would he ever get Randy's fifteen dollars? He felt squarely confronted by a great blank void. It was an awful thing he had done—all for a day at the beach . . . with some sporting girls. He thought of his family and felt tiny—and him itching to come back next Saturday! Maybe Myrtle was right about him after all. Lord, if she knew what he had done . . . .

He sat there for a long time. Most of the people were gone now. The lake was quiet save for a few boys still in the water. And the sun, red like blood, had settled on the dark silhouettes of the housetops across the city. He sat beneath the umbrella just as he had at one o'clock . . . and the thought smote him. He was jolted. Then dubious. But there it was—quivering, vital, swelling inside his skull like an unwanted fetus. So this was it! He mutinied inside. So he must sell it . . . his *umbrella.* Sell it for anything—only as long as it was enough to pay back Randy. For fifteen dollars even, if necessary. He was dogged; he couldn't do it; that wasn't the answer anyway. But the thought clawed and clung to him, rebuking and coaxing him by turns, until it finally became conviction. He must do it; it was the right thing to do; the only thing to do. Maybe then the awful weight would lift, the dull commotion in his stomach cease. He got up and started collecting his belongings; placed the thermos jug, sunglasses, towel, cigarettes, and little rug together in a neat pile, to be carried to the Chevy later. Then he turned to face his umbrella. Its red and white stripes stood defiant against the wide, churned-up sand. He stood for a moment mooning at it. Then he carefully let it down and, carrying it in his right hand, went off across the sand.

The sun now had gone down behind the vast city in a shower of crimson-golden glints, and on the beach only a few stragglers remained. For his first prospects, he approached two teenage boys, but suddenly realizing they had no money, he turned away and went over to an old woman, squat and black, in street clothes—a spectator—who stood gazing eastward out across the lake. She held in her hand a little black book, with red-edged pages, which looked like the New Testament. He smiled at her. "Wanna buy a nice new beach umbrella?" He held out the collapsed umbrella toward her.

She gave him a beatific smile, but shook her head. "No, son," she said, "that ain't what *I* want." And she turned to gaze out on the lake again.

For a moment he still held the umbrella out, with a question mark on his face. "Okay, then," he finally said, and went on.

Next he hurried down to the water's edge, where he saw a man and two women preparing to leave. "Wanna buy a nice new beach umbrella?" His voice sounded high-pitched, as he opened the umbrella over his head. "It's brand-new. I'll sell it for fifteen dollars—it cost a lot more'n that."

The man was hostile, and glared. Finally he said, "Whatta you take me for—a fool?"

Elijah looked bewildered, and made no answer. He observed the man for moment. Finally he let the umbrella down. As he moved away, he heard the man say to the women, "It's hot—he stole it somewhere."

Close by, another man sat alone in the sand. Elijah started toward him. The man wore trousers, but was stripped to the waist, and bent over intent on some task in his lap. When Elijah reached him, he looked up from half a hatful of cigarette butts he was breaking open for the tobacco he collected in a little paper bag. He grinned at Elijah, who meant now to pass on.

"No, I ain't interested either, buddy," the man insisted as Elijah passed him. "Not me. I jus' got *outa* jail las' week—an' ain't goin' back for no umbrella." He laughed, as Elijah kept on.

Now he saw three women, still in their bathing suits, sitting together near the diving board. They were the only people he had not yet tried—except the one lifeguard left. As he approached them, he saw that all three wore glasses and were sedate. Some school-teachers maybe, he thought, or office workers. They were talking—until they saw him coming; then they stopped. One of them was plump, but a smooth dark brown, and sat with a towel around her shoulders. Elijah addressed them through her: "Wanna buy a nice beach umbrella?" And again he opened the umbrella over his head.

"Gee! It's beautiful," the plump woman said to the others. "But where'd you get it?" she suddenly asked Elijah, polite mistrust entering her voice.

"I bought it—just this week."

The three women looked at each other. "Why do you want to sell it so soon, then?" a second woman said.

Elijah grinned. "I need the money."

"Well!" The plump woman was exasperated. "*No*, we don't want it." And they turned from him. He stood for a while, watching them; finally he let the umbrella down and moved on.

Only the lifeguard was left. He was a huge youngster, not over twenty, and brawny and black, as he bent over cleaning out his beached rowboat. Elijah approached him so suddenly he looked up startled.

"Would you be interested in this umbrella?" Elijah said, and proffered the umbrella. "It's brand-new—I just bought it Tuesday. I'll sell it cheap." There was urgency in his voice.

The lifeguard gave him a queer stare; and then peered off toward the Outer Drive, as if looking for help. "You're lucky as hell," he finally said. "The cops just now cruised by—up on the Drive. I'd have turned you in so quick it'd made your head swim. Now you get the hell outa here." He was menacing.

Elijah was angry. "Whatta you mean? I *bought* this umbrella—it's mine."

The lifeguard took a step toward him. "I said you better get the hell outa here! An' I mean it! *You thievin' bastard, you!*"

Elijah, frightened now, gave ground. He turned and walked away a few steps; and then slowed up, as if an adequate answer had hit him. He stood for a moment. But finally he walked on, the umbrella drooping in his hand.

He walked up the gravelly slope now toward the Chevy, forgetting his little pile of belongings left in the sand. When he reached the car, and opened the trunk, he remembered; and went back down and gathered them up. He returned, threw them in the trunk and, without dressing, went around and climbed under the steering wheel. He was scared, shaken; and before starting the motor sat looking out on the lake. It was seven o'clock; the sky was waning pale, the beach forsaken, leaving a sense of perfect stillness and approaching night; the only sound was a gentle lapping of the water against the sand—one moderate *hallo-o-o-o* would have carried across to Michigan. He looked down at the beach. Where were they all now—the funny, proud, laughing people? Eating their dinners, he supposed, in a variety of homes. And all the beautiful umbrellas—where were they? Without their colors the beach was so deserted. Ah, the beach . . . after pouring hot ore all week out at Youngstown Sheet and Tube, he would probably be too fagged out for the beach. But maybe he wouldn't—who knew? It was great while it lasted . . . great. And his umbrella . . . he didn't know what he'd do with that . . . he might never need it again. He'd keep it, though—and see. Ha! . . . hadn't he sweat to get it! . . . and they thought he had stolen it . . . stolen it . . . ah . . . and maybe they were right. He sat for a few moments longer. Finally he started the motor, and took the old Chevy out onto the Drive in the pink-hued twilight. But down on the beach the sun was still shining.

Stuart Dybek

PET MILK

(from *The New Yorker*)

Today I've been drinking instant coffee and Pet Milk, and watching it snow. It's not that I enjoy the taste especially, but I like the way Pet Milk swirls in the coffee. Actually, my favorite thing about Pet Milk is what the can opener does to the top of the can. The can is unmistakable—compact, seamless-looking, its very shape suggesting that it could condense milk without any trouble. The can opener bites in neatly, and the thick liquid spills from the triangular gouge with a different look and viscosity than milk. Pet Milk isn't *real* milk. The color's off, to start with. There's almost something of the past about it, like old ivory. My grandmother always drank it in her coffee. When friends dropped over and sat around the kitchen table, my grandma would ask, "Do you take cream and sugar?" Pet Milk was the cream.

There was a yellow plastic radio on her kitchen table, usually tuned to the polka station, though sometimes she'd miss it by half a notch and get the Greek station instead, or the Spanish, or the Ukrainian. In Chicago, where we lived, all the incompatible states of Europe were pressed together down at the staticky right end of the dial. She didn't seem to notice, as long as she wasn't hearing English. The radio, turned low, played constantly. Its top was warped and turning amber on the side where the tubes were. I remember the sound of it on winter afternoons after school, as I sat by her table watching the Pet Milk swirl and cloud in the steaming coffee, and noticing, outside her window, the sky doing the same thing above the railroad yard across the street.

And I remember, much later, seeing the same swirling sky in tiny liqueur glasses containing a drink called a King Alphonse: the crème de cacao rising like smoke in repeated explosions, blooming in kaleidoscopic clouds through the layer of heavy cream. This was in the Pilsen, a little Czech restaurant where my girlfriend, Kate, and I would go sometimes in the evening. It was the first year out of college for both of us, and we had astonished ourselves by finding real jobs—no more waitressing or pumping gas, the way we'd done in school. I was investigating credit references at a bank, and she was doing something slightly above the rank of typist for Hornblower & Weeks, the investment firm. My bank showed training films that emphasized the importance of suitable dress, good grooming, and personal neatness, even for employees like me, who worked at the switchboard in the basement. Her firm issued directives on appropriate attire—skirts, for instance, should cover the knees. She had lovely knees.

Kate and I would sometimes meet after work at the Pilsen, dressed in our proper business clothes and still feeling both a little self-conscious and glamorous, as if we were impostors wearing disguises. The place had small round oak tables, and we'd sit in a corner under a painting called "The Street Musicians of Prague" and trade future plans as if they were escape routes. She talked of going to grad school in Europe; I wanted to apply to the Peace Corps. Our plans for the future made us laugh and feel close, but those same plans somehow made anything more than temporary between us seem impossible. It was the first time I'd ever had the feeling of missing someone I was still with.

The waiters in the Pilsen wore short black jackets over long white aprons. They were old men from the Old Country. We went there often enough to have our own special waiter, Rudi, a name he pronounced with a rolled R. Rudi boned our trout and seasoned our salads, and at the end of the meal he'd bring the bottle of crème de cacao from the bar, along with two little glasses and a small pitcher of heavy cream, and make us each a King Alphonse right at our table. We'd watch as he'd fill the glasses halfway up with the syrupy brown liqueur, then carefully attempt to float a layer of cream on top. If he failed to float the cream, we'd get that one free.

"Who was King Alphonse anyway, Rudi?" I sometimes asked, trying to break his concentration, and if that didn't work I nudged the table with my foot so the glass would jiggle imperceptibly just as he was floating the cream. We'd usually get one on the house. Rudi knew what I was doing. In fact, serving the King Alphonses had been his idea, and he had also suggested the trick of jarring the table. I think it pleased him, though he seemed concerned about the way I'd stare into the liqueur glass, watching the patterns.

"It's not a microscope," he'd say. "Drink."

He liked us, and we tipped extra. It felt good to be there and to be able to pay for a meal.

Kate and I met at the Pilsen for supper on my twenty-second birthday. It was May, and unseasonably hot. I'd opened my tie. Even before looking at the dinner menu, we ordered a bottle of Mumm's and a dozen oysters apiece. Rudi made a sly remark when he brought

THE JOURNAL OF A WIFE-BEATER

(from *Harper's Bazaar*)

OCTOBER 2: Today I beat my wife, Nitsa, for the first time! I preserve this momentous event for future generations by beginning this Journal and recording this first entry with some pride.

I did not beat her hard, really not hard at all. I gave her several clouts across her head with my open palm, enough to make her stagger and daze her a little. Then I led her courteously to a chair to show her I was not punishing her in anger.

"Why?" she asked, and there were small tears glistening in the corners of her eyes.

"Nothing of great significance," I said amiably. "The coffee you served me was not hot enough this morning and after the last few washings my shirts have not had enough starch. Yesterday and the day before you were late in arriving at the restaurant. All of these are small imprudences that display a growing laxity on your part. I felt it was time to suggest improvement."

She watched me with her lips trembling. How artfully women suffer!

"You have never struck me before," she said thoughtfully. "In the year since we married, Vasili, you have never struck me before."

"One does not wish to begin correction too soon," I said. "It would be unjust to expect a new bride to attain perfection overnight. A period of flexibility is required."

Her big black eyes brooded, but she said nothing.

"You understand," I said consolingly. "This does not mean I do not love you." I shook my head firmly to emphasize my words. "It is exactly because I do care for you that I desire to improve you. On a number of occasions in my father's house I can remember him beating my mother. Not hard you understand. A clout across the head, and a box upon the ear. Once when she left the barn door open and the cows strayed out, he kicked her, but that was an exception. My mother was a happy and contented woman all her life."

The conversation ended there, but Nitsa was silent and meditative as we prepared for bed. She did not speak again until we were under the covers in the darkness.

"Vasili," she asked quietly, "will you strike me again?"

"Only when I feel you need it," I said. "It should not be required too often. You are a sensible girl and I am sure are most anxious to please me by being a good wife and a competent homemaker."

She turned away on her pillow and did not say another word.

OCTOBER 3: I slept splendidly last night!

OCTOBER 5: Since I have a few moments of leisure this evening, I will fill in certain background information about Nitsa and myself so that future generations may better understand this record of an ideal marriage relationship.

First I must record my immense satisfaction in the results of the beating. Nitsa has improved tremendously the past two days. She has taken the whole affair as sensibly as any man could have wished.

Her good sense was what first impressed me about Nitsa. I met her about a year ago at a dance in the church hall, sponsored by the daughters of Athens. I drank a little beer and danced once with each of a number of young ladies whose zealous mothers beamed at me from chairs along the wall. I might add here that before my marriage a year ago I was a very desirable catch for some fortunate girl. I was just a year past forty, an inch above average height, with all of my own hair and most of my own teeth, a number of which have been capped with gold. I had, and of course still have, a prosperous restaurant on Dart Street and a substantial sum in United States Savings Bonds. Finally, I myself was interested in marriage to a well-bred young lady. My first inclination was to return to Greece and select some daughter born to respect the traditions of the family; but as our parish priest, Father Antoniou, pointed out with his usual keen discernment, this would have been grossly unfair to the countless girls in our community who hoped for me as a bridegroom. Although marriage to any one of them would dismay the others, it would be better than if I scorned them all for a wife from overseas.

Nitsa impressed me because she was not as young as most of the other girls, perhaps in her late twenties, a tall athletic-looking girl who appeared capable of bearing my sturdy sons. She was not as beautiful a girl as I felt I deserved, but she made a neat and pleasant appearance. Most attractive young girls are too flighty and arrogant. They are not sensible enough to be grateful when a successful man pays them attention. Bringing one of them into a man's home is much the same as bringing in a puppy that has not yet been housebroken. Too much time is spent on fundamentals!

Imagine my delight when, in inquiry regarding Nitsa's family that night, I learned she was the niece of our revered priest, Father Antoniou, visiting him from Cleveland.

I danced several American dances with her to demonstrate I was not old-fashioned and spoke to her at some length of my assets and my prospects. She listened with unconcealed interest. We sat and drank coffee afterward until a group of my friends called to me to lead one of the old country dances. Conscious of her watching me, I danced with even more than my usual grace and flourish, and leaped higher off the floor than I had in some time.

A day or two later I spoke seriously to Father Antoniou. He was frankly delighted. He phoned his sister, Nitsa's mother in Cleveland, and in no time at all the arrangements were made. As I had accurately surmised, the whole family, including Nitsa, were more than willing.

Several weeks later we were married. It was a festive affair and the reception cost a little over a thousand dollars which I insisted her father pay. He was a housepainter who worked irregularly, but in view of the fact that Nitsa brought me no dowry I felt he should demonstrate the good faith of the family by paying for the reception.

Nitsa and I spent a weekend at the Mortimer Hotel for our honeymoon, so I could return to count the cash when the restaurant closed each evening. As it was, God only knows what the waitresses stole from me those two days. During our absence I had the bedroom of my apartment painted, and after considerable deliberation bought a new stove. I write this as proof of my thoughtfulness. The stove I had was only twelve years old, but I am worldly enough to understand how all women love new stoves. If permitted by weak and easily swayed husbands they would trade them in on newer models every year.

In recalling our first year together, while it was not quite what I expected, I was not completely disillusioned. There was a certain boldness and immodesty about Nitsa which I found displeasing, but one must bear with this in a healthy young woman.

As time went on she spent a good part of the day with me in the restaurant taking cash. She became familiar enough with my business so that when the wholesale produce and meat salesman called she could be trusted to order some of the staple items. But I noticed a certain laxity developing, a carelessness in her approach to her responsibilities, and remembering my father's success with my mother, it was then I beat her for the first time.

I am pleased that it seems to have prompted unreserved improvement. Bravo, Vasili!

OCTOBER 7: It is after midnight and I am alone in the restaurant which is closed until morning. I am sitting at the small table in the kitchen and can hardly bear to write the shameful and disgraceful episode which follows.

Last night after returning from the restaurant I went to bed because I was tired. Nitsa came into the room as I was slipping under the covers. I had noticed a rather somber quietness about her all that day, but I attributed it to that time of the female month. When she had donned her night clothes and gotten into bed beside me, I raised my cheek for her to kiss me goodnight. She turned her back on me and for a moment I was peeved, but remembering her indisposition I turned off the lamp and said nothing.

I fell asleep shortly and had a stirring dream. I fought beside Achilles on the plains before Troy. I carried a mighty shield and a long sword. Suddenly a massive Trojan appeared before me and we engaged each other in combat. After I brilliantly parried a number of his blows he seemed to recognize he was doomed. He retreated and I pressed him hard. While we slashed back and forth, another Trojan rose beside me as if he had sprung from the earth, and swung his weapon at my head. I raised my shield swiftly but not quite in time and the flat of his sword landed across my head. The pain was so terrible I shrieked out loud, and suddenly the plains of Troy and the helmeted warriors were all swept away and my eyes exploded open to the sight of Nitsa bent over me, calmly preparing to strike again!

I bellowed and clawed to sit up, and tried desperately to flee from the bed. The stick she swung bounced again across my head and the pain was ferocious. I fell off the bed in a tangle of sheets at her feet; then I jumped up frantically and ran to the other side of the bed, looking back in desperation to see if she followed. She stood dreadfully calm with the stick still in her hand.

"Are you mad!" I shouted. My nose seemed to be swelling and my head stung and I tasted blood from my cut lip. "You must be mad or in the employ of the devil! You have split me open!"

"I owed you one," she said quietly. "A debt that had to be paid."

I looked at her in astonishment and rubbed my aching head. I could not comprehend the desecration of a wife striking her husband. "Your senses have come apart," I bellowed. "You might have broken my head!"

"I don't think so," she said. "You have an unusually dense head."

I was horrified. On top of my injuries her insolence could not be tolerated. I ran around the bed and pulled the stick from her hands. I swung it up and down. When it landed across her shoulders she winced and gave a shrill squeal. Then I went to bathe my swollen head. A harrowing and terrible experience indeed!

OCTOBER 11: Plague and damnation! Blood and unspeakable horror! She has done it again.

That wench of evil design waited just long enough for the swelling of my nose to recede and my lip to heal. All week she had been quiet and reserved. She came to work promptly and performed her duties efficiently. While I could never forget that night in bed when she struck me, I was willing to forgive. Women are by nature as emotionally unstable as dogs under the mad light of a full moon. But I am a generous man and in this foul manner was my generosity rewarded.

It happened shortly after the rush at lunch was over. The restaurant was deserted except for Nitsa at the register and the waitresses chattering beside the urns of coffee. I was sitting at the small table in the kitchen, smoking a cigar, and pondering whether to order short ribs or pork loins for lunch on Thursday. Suddenly I was conscious of an uneasy chill in the center of my back. A strange quick dread possessed me and I turned swiftly around and Nitsa was there. Almost at the same instant the pot she was swinging landed with a horrible clatter on my head. I let out a roar of outrage and pain, and jumped up holding my thundering head. I found it impossible to focus my eyes, and for a frenzied moment I imagined I was surrounded by a dozen Nitsas. I roared again in fear and anger, and ran to seek sanctuary behind the big stove. She made no move to follow me but stood quietly by the table with the pot in her hand.

"You must be mad!" I shrieked. "I will call the doctor and have him exchange your bloody head!"

The dishwasher, who had come from the back room where he had been eating, watched us with his great idiot eyes, and the waitresses, cousins of imbeciles, peered through the porthole of the swinging door.

"I owed you one," Nitsa said quietly. She put down the pot and walked from the kitchen past the awed and silent waitresses.

As I write this now, words are inadequate to describe my distress. Fiercer by far than the abominable lump on my head is the vision of chaos and disorder. In the name of all that is sacred, where is the moral and ordered world of my father?

OCTOBER 15: Disturbed and agitated as I have been for the past few days, tonight I decided something had to be done. I went to speak to Father Antoniou.

Nitsa, that shrew, has been at the restaurant for several days now acting as if nothing had happened. She joked with the customers and took cash calmly. Heartless wench without the decency to show some shred of remorse!

Last night I slept locked in the bathroom. Even then I was apprehensive and kept one eye open on the door. While it was true that by her immoral standards we were even, she could not be trusted. I feared she would take it into her stony soul to surge into a shameful lead. Finally tonight, because I knew the situation had become intolerable, I visited the priest.

He greeted me courteously and took me into his study. He brought out a bottle of good sherry. We sat silent for a moment, sipping the fine vintage. "You may speak now, my dear friend," he said gently. "You are troubled."

"How can you tell, Father?" I asked.

He smiled sagely. He was indeed a fountain of wisdom.

"Well, Father," I struggled for the mortifying words. "It is Nitsa. To put it plainly, she has struck me not once, but twice, with a stout stick and a heavy pot."

He sat upright in his chair.

"May God watch over us!" he said. "Surely, Vasili, you are jesting!"

I made my cross and bent my head to show him the hard lump that still dwelt there. He rose from his chair and came to examine it. When he touched the lump, I jumped.

He paced the floor in agitation, his black cassock swirling about his ankles.

"She must be demented," he said slowly. "The poor girl must be losing her mind."

"That is what I thought at first," I said seriously. "But she seems so calm. Each time she strikes she merely says, 'I owed you one.'"

"Aaaaah!" the priest said eagerly. "Now we approach the core of truth." His voice lowered. "What did you do to her for which she seeks revenge?" He winked slyly. "I know you hot-blooded Spartans. Perhaps a little too passionate for a shy young girl?"

"Nothing, Father!" I said in indignation, although I could not help being pleased at his suggestion. "Absolutely nothing."

"Nothing?" he repeated.

"I have clouted her several times across her head," I said. "My prerogative as a husband to discipline my wife. Certainly nothing to warrant the violence of her blows."

"Incredible," the priest said. He sat silent and thoughtful, then shook his head. "A woman raising her hand to her husband in my parish, and that woman my niece. Incredible!" He wrung his hands fretfully. "A stain upon the sacred vows of marriage." He paused as if struck by a sudden thought. "Tell me, Vasili, has she been watching much television? Sometimes it tends to confuse them."

"Our picture tube is burned out now several months, Father," I said. "They want a fantastic price to fix it."

"Incredible," the priest said.

"Perhaps if you talk to her, Father," I said. "Explain what it is to be a dutiful wife. Define the rights of a husband."

The priest shook his head sadly. "When I first entered the priesthood," he said somberly, "I learned never to attempt to reason with a woman. The two words should never be used in the same sentence. The emancipation of these crafty scheming descendants of Eve has hurled man into a second Dark Ages."

I was impressed by the gravity of his words and had to agree I had spoken hastily.

"My son," the priest said finally, a thin edge of desperation in his voice. "I confess I am helpless to know what to advise. If you came to seek counsel because she drank to excess or because she had succumbed to the wiles of another man . . . but for this! I will have to contact the Bishop."

I sipped my sherry and felt anger coming to a head on my flesh as if it were a festered boil pressing to break. I, Vasili Makris, subjected to these indignities! Humiliated before my own dishwasher! Driving my parish priest to consult with the Bishop!

"There is only one answer, Father," I said, and my voice rang out boldly, a call to battle. "I have clouted her too lightly. There is nothing further to be done but for me to give her a beating she will not forget!" I waved my hand. "Rest assured I will remember my own strength. I will not break any bones, but I will teach her respect." I became more pleased with that solution by the moment. "That is the answer, Father," I said. "A beating that will once and for all end this insufferable mutiny!"

We watched each other for a long wordless moment. I could sense that good man struggling between a moral objection to violence and an awareness there was no other way.

"They who live by the sword," he said dolefully, and he paused to permit me to finish the quotation in my mind. "This cancer must be cut out," he said, "before it spreads infection through the parish."

Father Antoniou raised his glass and toasted me gravely.

"Consider yourself embarked on a holy crusade," he said in a voice trembling with emotion. "Recapture the sanctity of your manhood. Go, Vasili Makris, with God."

I kissed his revered hand and left.

OCTOBER 17: The promised retribution has been delayed because a waitress has been sick and I cannot afford to incapacitate Nitsa at the same time. But I vow her reprieve will be brief!

OCTOBER 19: Tonight is the night! The restaurant is closed and we are alone. I am sitting in the kitchen making this entry while she finishes cleaning out the urns of coffee. When the work is all done I will call her into the kitchen for judgment.

Nitsa! Misguided and arrogant woman, your hour of punishment is here!

OCTOBER 23: In the life of every noble man there are moments of decisive discovery and events of inspired revelation. I hasten with fire and zeal to record such an experience in this Journal!

That epic night when Nitsa came to the kitchen of the restaurant after finishing her work, without a word of explanation I struck her. Quick as a flash she struck me back. I was prepared for that and hit her harder. She replied with a thump on my head that staggered me. I threw all hesitation to the winds and landed a fierce blow upon her. Instead of submitting, she became a flame of baleful fury. She twisted violently in search of some weapon to implement her rage, and scooped up a meat cleaver off the block! I let out a hoarse shout of panic and turned desperately and fled! I heard her pounding like a maddened mare after me, and I made the door leading to the alley and bounded out with a wild cry! I forgot completely the accursed stairs and spun like a top in the air and landed on my head. I woke in the hospital where I am at present and x-rays have indicated no damage beyond a possible concussion that still causes me some dizziness.

At the first opportunity I examined myself secretly for additional reassurance that some vital part of me had not been dismembered by that frightful cleaver. Then I sat and recollected each detail of that experience with somber horror. A blow now and then, delivered in good faith, is one of the prerogatives of marriage. Malevolent assault and savage butchery are quite another matter!

However, as my first sense of appalled outrage and angry resentment passed, I found the entire situation developing conclusive compensations. I had fancied myself married to a mortal woman and instead was united to a Goddess, a fierce Diana, a cyclonic Juno! I realized with a shock of recognition that one eagle had found another, perched on Olympian peaks, high above the obscure valley of pigeons and sheep.

O fortunate woman! You have gained my mercy and forbearance and have proven to my satisfaction that you deserve my virile love and are worthy of my intrepid manhood!

Nitsa, rejoice! You need no longer tremble or fear that I will ever strike you again!

Mary Gray Hughes

THE ROCK GARDEN

(from *Southwest Review*)

I t was necessary to say that millions died in the concentration camps in Germany. And millions before that in the Belgian Congo. Or in slave ships on the Atlantic. Children terrified and adults worked to death. Mothers frantic, holding too thin babies. Firm-bodied young men with terror in their faces. She could have been one of them, could be one of them now in Vietnam, dying any day, every day. This day. It was necessary to remember, never to forget.

So she spoke to herself each morning as she woke in the midst of the luck of her life, aware of its preciousness. Sixty-eight and with a husband living. Well-off to rich, depending on the viewer's finances. Traveled. Healthy. Even having aged well, staying slim, handsome, with the clearest round blue eyes of the sort that never fade.

"We have been considering Australia again for the next trip." Her voice. "Doing it more thoroughly, to see the rare birds. We have been so interested in birds."

How do the rich pay their debts? she wondered. All this luck, this money, this health. This free, and freeing, time so there could be the music and birds, the travel, the beautiful presents. Courtesy. Great courtesy. ("You were so extremely kind when we were there last summer we did want to send you this little remembrance of our good times together. We had such fun selecting it.") Constant courtesy.

He was retired. Was cleverer than she, but less humane. Was vain, hurt by age, stranded in some limbo between solitude and company, some battlefield of loss where the half-deaf go. He tried, retried, bought, repaired hearing aids. "It has the most minute battery invented," he said. "Transistorized. No, no, you have to look much more carefully than that. Try. There are three of them, see? No, you haven't looked really close. Now try again."

"If we were meant to fly, the Lord would have given us wings, my mother used to say. Oh, she *was* old-fashioned. She taught me how to do this," braiding flowers for a teenaged granddaughter and her young friend, "and how to blow on a blade of grass to make it hoot. She showed us both, me and my brother. Dear Tag." He had been killed in the war, World War I, that was. Her greatest, only, grief, that bitter death. "My mother preferred him, and I am glad she did, you see, because he had so little time." Meant what she said, too, braiding flowers into a colored stream, eyes blue under her bright straw hat. So human, so courteous. So good, remembering in the morning the tortured dead, blue eyes to the familiar ceiling, trying not to be only rich and lucky, but rich and lucky and good.

"Don't you think we owe them remembering?" she had asked him.

"It can't matter to them," he said. Logic.

"But it does matter. At least, it matters to me."

In September they traveled all the way to south Texas to see the whooping cranes. She rose at four and touched his shoulder (he could not hear the alarm) and they went out in the wet predawn on land flat as a mirage and watched the sun bring the birds up, watched the birds run out of the reeds with a machine's clumsiness, the flap and stretch of wings pounding the cold air for support and then, as slowly as if the air were a stairway, rising up, forward, up, and gone.

Later, in Florida, they saw the flamingos. And the threatened alligators. They saw and appreciated all the endangered species.

"We *should* see them since we are among those fortunate enough to be able to do so, and it is such an opportunity. We feel we ought to," she said.

The species did not know they were dying. They had that gift, were dying unawares. She longed for that, to die sleeping, in bed, unknowing and unafraid. For wasn't that the worst, she thought, knowing? To see the horror coming day by day, closer and closer, to know it and not be able to help. She read that the camp inmates knew, denied in their minds they knew, did know, admitted, wept, cried, begged, and still were tortured, still died, all the same. There had been those just like herself. She had read about them—Bruno Bettelheim's family, dying in concentration camps. They who had been lucky all their lives until their ends. Which did not mean it had to happen to her. It did not do, she understood that, to be morbid. But could not stop trying to imagine the unimaginable, could not understand the luck of her life, could make no sense, and no use, of having been one to survive.

"Alan and I found each other before I knew he might inherit money," she had said, a burst, outburst, of confidence made beside a crystal lake. Quite true. All the good that had come to her had been uncalculated and unearned. "We never worked for this money, we both know that." But kept it, spent it, nonetheless.

"The lions were so wonderfully arrogant." Talking to a friend's listening children. "And terribly healthy, but so arrogant. Thank heavens, they had *no* ticks. A scientist friend told me they would be covered with ticks, and I had dreaded that, but these were so clean. Our driver, such a funny man, insisted on going right off the road and into the brush. My poor spine, pancaked ... but I have been doing exercises, just the way you children are supposed to, and I'm so much better."

The lion account was from Africa. Their second trip, to do it better. Avoiding the Union of South Africa, for reasons of conscience. Sorry for the poverty. Overtipping. But loving the animals. Rolls of film taken of the animals and none of the people.

She had been afraid in Africa. Afraid of the poverty. Afraid of the blacks. Afraid she would not recognize the ones she knew as their features melted in the blackness of their skin. "Look at the spring-boks leap up for no reason," she had said. "Why do they do that?" The guide answered in his tongue, and all the natives laughed.

She had turned her face, eyes straight ahead, one arm pointing determinedly at the animals, her face smiling. She knew sex in a laugh when she heard it. Yet it was the same guide who sat half-hour after half-hour beside her, begging for please one more bracelet made from the brilliant flowers he brought her and loved to wear on his beautiful black background of skin. And she, showing him her ways, told herself that not even in her secret heart must she think she was improving him, for surely she was learning from him, too.

"But the little koalas in Australia," she went on, and the children came closer, "they were my favorites. They put up their paws like this," doing it herself, herself a cunning little blue-eyed koala, so willing to be funny, such a good sport and companion, so charming with little children who did not breathe in order to watch her better, "just like this they do it, and rub rub rub their noses. Rub rub rub. They are enchanting little creatures, and not extinct at all. But it is a very smug country," turning to the adults for this, "and so very comfortable. We rather did *not* care for that."

She thought. She thought behind her smiles, her courtesy, her concert-going, behind her carefully chosen gifts and cards of thanks or condolence, her notes at Christmas (always nondenominational, always UNICEF to help poor children). She thought with helpless honesty that she had no special courage or strength, that she hated pain and feared fear, that she was not worth her long life's many gifts, and still with all this allowed her, still she wanted peace, health, her end to come some long space of time away and in her sleep and she unknowing and unafraid. She thought, calling herself foolish, that the only anguish in her life was that she had no anguish, and no reason for that sparing.

She kept on being delightful for her own grandchildren and her friends' grandchildren; cheerful for her sons and her daughter, her son-in-law, her daughters-in-law. She remained the best of friends for her troubled friends ("How it would please us if you would join us this Thanksgiving and make it so much warmer for us both . . . ."), consistently generous to poor musicians, consistently charming to all. "The little koalas put up their paws, just like this, and rub rub rub . . . ."

She read the digest of the Nuremberg Trials by Lord Russell of Liverpool, the British prosecutor. Read all the details, looked at all the pictures. Resisted the pressure to read further volume after volume about it. "Don't you think," she said, "that to read so much in such detail about it is, I don't like to use the word but I will, voyeurism?"

Yet the stories of horror came at her, puncturing the floor of her consciousness in the same way she had seen anti-aircraft flak, in films, come up at the photographing airplane and burst through its floor of safety in strange and dangerous flowers. They were unavoidable, the stories of people suffering, straining uselessly, knowing. One, just a photograph, from Vietnam, of a man running, his mouth clothes-hanger shape with fear and strain, running, a child in his arms (the child dead, blood seeping from its ear, quite dead, but he did not know and how could she tell him?), running across a rice field, mud on his thin muscled thigh, one foot raised forever. His wife behind him running also, a child shielded against her breast, a younger child, living perhaps. Both adults terrified, running, and nothing stopping it, one foot always raised. She saw it when she did not sleep, saw it with no need to look at the picture she had cut out and slipped between the programs from the winter's concerts. Visiting her son, she saw it in the dark in the slightly unfamiliar room, the others in the house near her and all sleeping, and in her mind that frozen running, the distorted mouth, the soft rice plants, the child, the foot raised, the terror, the child, and nothing ever helping.

"Would you let us," she wrote, "take the family's youngest Alan to the coast this summer? He has never seen it, and the birds are a marvel there. And more, we have not yet had the pleasure of taking him on a special trip, all alone, with us, and we would love to do so." She and the child collected shells. "That one's too small to hear the sea in," the boy said to her. "You need a conch for that. Or any old thing that's big and hollow. A jug."

"But I like the small ones because they are so sweet," she said.

"I like them because they are easy to find," he said. They laughed; his teeth were like the crests of tiny waves. A darling, darling boy. She was so lucky.

They had their own cabin, their beach, their own ocean, it seemed, its roar filling up the air. Deaf, did he hear the ocean in his own ear's whorls? She had taken to asking silly questions in the sleepless dark. Got up instead. Read. And when the grandson rose, went swimming with him in the warm dawn. In her psychedelic suit and flowered cap, dipping in on her long crane's legs, careful, enjoying, sensible. She thought (oh, I am a silly woman, I surely am) the salt water on her cheeks might be the tears she had not needed to weep.

Sitting on the beach chairs beside the cabin, the boy at their feet on the ground, watching the water burn at sunset, she jumped as her husband touched his hand slowly to the side of his neck and brought it away with blood. It's starting, she thought. But he was studying on his palm a mosquito crushed in his usual careful way, and was commenting to the boy on the blood transfused from his body and now spread on his hand. Then he leaned to the side and wiped his hand clean on the thin grass coming up through the sand.

They returned home, northward, at the end of summer. "Oh, we could never give up the season's concerts," she said in answer, "and we are used to the cold, when it comes."

They decided to make a rock garden. He made the design, taking days to perfect it. They would do it all themselves. He would search for rocks, from their acres or those of friends, or even sometimes buy them. He would drive out in the car going at slow speeds, the car no sound to him, his eyes going back and forth from the highway to the countryside for forms or colors of rocks that he wanted. She did the carrying and placing. She learned how she could squat and rise straight up, a rock cradled in her arms. She found she could carry heavier stones than he. Nothing daunted her. "Aren't we lucky," she said, "that we didn't do it before?"

And she learned to lever and how to roll rocks down planks, always shielding him from the fact that she managed the heaviest ones. She would kneel and roll the big round ones, tumbling them end over end to the approved position. But best of all she liked the middle-sized rocks she could carry in her arms, the ones which on warm days (for she had given up work gloves) she would stand holding with their sunbaked surface against her bare arms and hands. Her unshed tears, she called them, shaking her head at her silliness, her unshed tears she had been spared.

She learned to make borders. Learned to shape unexpected designs from the combinations of different shapes. Learned how to brace against the slope and how to save her toes from being crushed. "I must have New England in my blood," she said. "I sleep so well."

In fall, in the cooler weather, he tired of it. She hesitated to show disagreement, lest it seem her strength was outlasting his and he be wounded. So she sat, her long spine curved over a book, reading beside him on the glassed-in porch. But when he was absorbed inside the house, she returned to the garden and her rocks. She arched over them to find just the one she wanted next, her eyes alert for the right size and color, for the little stones she would need for bracing, the big ones she would have to lift slowly and carry in her arms to their new homes. She loved to stand above the empty space when she had raised a rock, holding it close, her breath coming well earned and cold into her working lungs.

She feared the winter. Feared the bad weather, but when it came the rocks did not freeze and split, only became coated with ice and snow, though over and over again she would go out and sweep them clear with a soft broom and see their shapes again.

"You've forgotten to feed the birds," he said.

"Oh, shame on me," she said. "Aren't I silly? I've gone over entirely to stone." She cut lard in pea-sized pieces, crumbed bread, and cast both for the whirlpool of birds descending.

"Charming," she said. But her smile moved her lips only. "Charming. Birdie, birdie."

"Why," she asked him, "with the resurgence of German literature, is there no book on the triumph over France, or a journal of the life of a concentration camp guard?"

He had not heard. Like a reading lamp, his concentration was turned only in the direction he faced. She moved within his line of sight so he could see she spoke.

"There's all this talk of a new German literature," she said firmly. "It's all about Germany's defeat. Why not the joys of an SS guard, or the victory march into Paris?"

His intelligence was sharpened on her. She had caught his interest; he was not being polite.

"An excellent question. As a rule our time favors the criminal over the victim. Capote's book, for example. So in all logic we should focus on the SS. Someday, yes, I envisage an entire literature on this untouched subject. Memoirs of an SS guard's youth. Pseudo-fiction, of course, in the best modern. Then pornography—Sex outside the Gas Chambers."

She said, "There was one job, a guard searched the clothing women had to hang on pegs outside the gas chamber because sometimes mothers tried to hide their children in the clothes."

"Presumably the world of serious literature is not ready for that as art yet. The fall of the Wehrmacht, that's what's selling now."

"I wonder about them."

"Who?"

"The guards who searched the clothes for children."

When it was very cold the snow hardened. Across the tops of the rocks and the sides facing west the snow melted in the daytime and froze again at night until layer after layer sheeted over the rocks. The fresh snow fell on ice then, and thickened, and was pressed down itself by icy rain, which formed a light crystal glaze at first, but froze hard later, at night, or on colder days, covering all the rocks so there was no longer any way to see their shapes. She would walk out, carefully, on crane's legs, and bend over them, searching for her favorites. They no longer had a separate color but were a single mass of the bleached gray, mud-textured white of winter. She curved over them, looking closer. The cold blazed her ears and face, but she would not leave them. She crouched down, shivering and shivering, and pressed her ungloved hands against them, holding the outlines of some as best she could under the thickness of snow.

"Oh my darlings," she said to them. "My darlings."

"What are you doing?" His voice. The essence of him coming down to her. "You've got no coat."

He pulled her up. His hands were warm manacles circling through her cold-stiffened blouse (long sleeves always to cover age's shrinking flesh). He was leading her back to the house, up the steps to their back door, into the kitchen where bands of stainless steel and birch shot out around them.

"Are you unwell?" he demanded of her.

"No," she said, "no." She tore out of his hands. "I'm perfectly well, God forgive me," and she smashed with her fists into the cabinets level with her face once, twice, three times, saying, "I'm perfectly, perfectly well."

The sound was shattering in the room, and she saw him gape, saw a mask fall from him and under it an unfamiliar, startled, alarmed old man.

"So clumsy of me," she said. And let herself lean forward against him, her hands supporting him while seeming to support herself. "So clumsy. Do excuse. The cold must have . . . . Aren't I silly?"

He was too polite to question, or to fuss hard. Just led her, quite unnecessarily but she let him because she wanted to, into the living room and had her lie stretched full length on the couch beside the fire. He set an extra log in the flames, and the warmth melted into her where she lay with her head resting back on a soft pillow and the white and heavily beamed ceiling overhead. They were old beams, carefully chosen and unusually thick, and the adz marks into them made soft shallows softened further by the firelight's shadows. They ran in great parallel rows above her body, and she saw in them the freight cars she had read about last summer. She had been flipping through the pages of the book review section of a Sunday paper, glancing, flipping, and the paragraph leaped off the page and burst into her mind. The siege of Stalingrad. Freight cars outside, filled, packed, with Russian prisoners, then abandoned (how long? forever?), left completely, left on a siding and in the bright sunlight feces and urine dripping down through the cars' wide boards onto the railroad tracks beneath.

He was stirring the fire steady for her, caging it. He brought a red wool blanket they had bought in Norway and placed it the wrong, heavy way across her knees. He left to heat soup for lunch, but returned unexpectedly to throw a handful of sea salts into the misshapen mouth of the fire. The ceiling became vibrant with colors, and the room was streaked with the sounds and smells of the salts burning. She turned her face toward the fire.

"Charming," she said. "Charming. Aren't we lucky, that we have them?"

Michael Anania

RE-ENTRY: CHICAGO

(from *Story Quarterly*)

"**N**ow, as I said, the way to the Celestial City lies just through this town where this lusty fair is kept; and he that will go to the city, and yet not go through this town, must needs "go out of the world."
Pilgrim's Progress

Portland, Oregon. Cold November rain the whole weekend, all the green and pleasant sublimity of the Northwest foreclosed. Toward the airport the highway begins to ice over, and the water on the car windows lingers in slowly descending baguettes. Along the way, motels and massage parlors, their neon signs running like candle wax—the free parking, fast service, color TV in all rooms, polyester fray of every city in America, even more garish at night in the rain-water on the streets and along the car's windows catches the colors like tinsel or spins them into angel-hair circles around streetlamps and headlights. McDonald's Golden Arches have an airy thinness about them, and the fluorescent lights of the food service area shine from their glass enclosure like the facets in a diamond solitaire. The Earthly Pleasures Salon glows like a pinched cheek. Suddenly, the airport, with its uniform blue signs and high ticket counters. A quick farewell and a dash to the departure gate.
"Chicago. Smoking. Thank you."
Wet snow and no jetway in Spokane. Snowflakes in the landing lights, a moment of tension from *Airport* as we all descend the aluminum gangplank—they call it deplaning—and cross into the low terminal, drip awhile, then file out to a 707 waiting in the snow. Airborne, I chat with a woman from Pullman, dressed head to foot in Pendleton. In a dream over Montana she reveals herself to me as an Indian princess. The Pendleton, she says, is a disguise. Awake, I decide that she is the spirit of the Northwest, all woodsy heartiness, her bright eyes nestled in piney wrinkles. She sleeps the sleep of the just, the unfretted sleep so many Haight-Ashbury refugees have gone to Oregon and Washington to find, a sleep as green as a sunlit

haze over the San Juans. The Princess says that she is a direct descendant of Sacajawea and that it is her task to guide me back from the mouth of the Columbia.

Minneapolis for an hour's layover. I de-plane into a great gallery of departure lounges. In the center are several rows of cushioned steel chairs with swing-away, coin operated television sets. It is 1:30 am, and a dozen or so passengers are scattered along the first row, each watching the same late show on his own screen. It's like the dogwatch at Mission Control. A hard rain beats against the dark glass that encloses the gallery. Outside, a rhinestone and sequined light swirls over the ground crews. On all the television screens Charleton Heston in buckskin shouts silently at Fred MacMurray.

The last time I flew from Minneapolis to Chicago was the Saturday after Martin Luther King's assassination. In the landing pattern to O'Hare we could see the west side of the city burning, as though it had been bombed by a squadron of planes just ahead of ours. Tonight, the city has a chilly clarity. Streetlights pillow suburban streets. The expressways pump slowly. It's past four in the morning, and O'Hare is as quiet as it ever gets, empty enough to seem like some newfangled monument. The fixtures protrude, or rather, obtrude: light fixtures, suspended television screens flicking arrivals and departures, empty check-in counters, water fountains and fire hoses in bas-relief, red coin-operated newspaper vendors, a stand-up cocktail bar closed for the night. A gallery of unnoteworthy objects thrust into view—an exhibition, of sorts. I think of the Auditorium Theatre's celebration of the electric light bulb, Louis Sullivan's coherent faith in technology and its continuousness, the way the light bulbs are pearled along its heavy arches, a delicacy that diagrams its classic lines of stress. The airport's array of gadgets is mere accumulation against minimal surface. The junk is more substantial than the walls. It is the primary surface of O'Hare, monument to a surfeit of hardware. That's why all airports seem so much alike; the essential parts are interchangeable. Portland, Spokane, Minneapolis, Chicago—half a continent's worth of the great American airline terminal—terminal, now, in the contemporary sense, something you plug into.

The concourse ends in a maze of security gear, two clutters of leftover Holiday Inn parts and electronic debris. None of it seems particularly secure in itself—an appropriately awkward setting, I suppose, for seeing the insides of an overnight bag in X-ray, shadowgrams of shaving cream, razor, toothbrush, books, soiled underwear. The attendants have a boredom about them that must go with such godlike vision. I pass it all by. You don't have to be checked on the way out. I am leaving America's last Arcadia, that fractured pastoral made up of the departure concourses of hundreds of airports and their little jet-propelled canisters of sky—the fifty-first state, freed by metal detectors and high-speed gamma rays from guns, knives and cudgels, the ultimate suburb. Where else in America can you be so sure that the person sitting next to you is not carrying some kind of deadly weapon? Leaving this otherworld, as tinny and insubstantial as it is, you return home, quickly putting on all the protective paranoias that get you by day to day. The chumminess of your fellow skysailors begins to collapse almost immediately; by the time you reach the baggage carrousel, the jostling competition of buses and subways has returned. You also pass into a period of special vulnerability. You are markedly, now, someone without a weapon. However meek and mild you may be, it is otherwise possible for your thousands of potential attackers to think that you might be carrying a gun.

I heave my bag, then myself into the back seat of a taxi—no airport buses this time of night. The driver is a woman with a moon face and hair up in blond woodshaving curls. It's the Ford City Shopping Center up-do, just out of enormous plastic curlers and uncombed. She is heavy and fits rather too snugly under the steering wheel, so turns it with short gestures at the sides. We move out past the O'Hare Inn and onto the highway, flanked with still more inns, O'Hare's very own transient's paradise of restaurants, bars and show lounges. Businessmen now travel to Chicago and never enter the city itself, loitering here, instead, in an underbrush of doubleknits waiting for morning meetings in their hotels or out among the hundreds of regional offices that spread from the airport, drab low structures mostly that sport their corporate logos like boutonnieres. The driver asks where I've been. I answer. Am I in business? I tell her that I teach. High school? No, college. That's her cue.

"You know I read all that stuff once. I was really good at it, too. In high school, I was in college prep . . . read all that stuff, books and everything. Everybody said I should go to college."

Out the window the hotels and regional offices subside to the tidiness of the north-west side, an orderliness of red and green asphalt roofing above textured brick house fronts.

"Got married instead. And my husband? He was one of them guys don't want his wife to know nothin. He'd come home, find me readin a book and get mad as hell. He kept me down, know what I mean? I mean he didn't want me readin or nothin. And what could I do? Cause I got pregnant right away. Three kids—damn good kids too—before I got my divorce. You know what I regret most?"

There's not really time to say, what?

"Not going to college, like everybody said I should. But you know when I was coming up, everything was marriage, everything! You went to a movie and it was all sweetness and light, you know what I mean? Everybody'd fall in love and get married and go off into the sunset. And the comics? They was just the same . . . love and marriage and sunsets. Boy, was I ever dumb. All of us, all of us was dumb. Go steady, get engaged, get married. That's what all of us did back then. This here *new morality*? Whatever you say about it, it's all right with me cause girls ain't so dumb."

She pauses, and I consider saying something about movie sunsets and the sexual revolution, then think better of it. "Sweetness and light. What a laugh! You get married and you find out real quick. First time you see that thing of his you find out. Five years, three kids—that's how long it took me to get out. I only stayed that long cause I thought I was supposed to ... just like my mother. She never had it no better. You think she'd tell me anything? No, just more sweetness and light. My oldest girl? She's goin' on sixteen, and I'll tell you, she wants to go to one of them X movies, I'll give her the money myself. Honest! Better to see it that way, better than all that Debbie Reynolds crap we used to go to. Sweetness and light. How dumb can you get?"

We are into the junction of the Kennedy and the Edens expressways. At the top of the rise you can see the Loop, skewed slightly because of the highway's odd angle so that the Hancock building and the Sears Tower seem quite close together. *Kennedy, Edens, the Loop, Hancock, Sears*—entering Chicago is like coming upon the shuffled remnants of an allegory you are supposed to understand and reassemble. My blond familiar is talking about her daytime job as a receptionist for a plumbing company. There's this guy, a real gentleman, who comes in every week for one of the suppliers (Why not Royal Quiet Flush, my all-time favorite?), and she's been seeing him. It sounds sylvan, almost like "keeping company". Then suddenly, she's back at her marriage, her husband's lack of respect for her and "that thing of his," which has become thematic to her monologue. Each time it enters one of her sentences something more is said. Like a composer, she's working by carefully plotted steps toward a full-fledged description.

"That thing ... just like the church says, I came to my marriage pure ... That thing ... like the church says ... I didn't have the slightest idea ... Course I had brothers, but it ain't the same ... That thing ... like the church says ... I always wanted kids." No doubt about it, if the ride lasts long enough, she'll describe her whole wedding night, but there are diversions, embellishments, perhaps—her plumbing supplies salesman, a good restaurant on south Harlem Avenue, her kids, and for tympani, regular verbal assaults on the few other drivers on the highway. She returns to "that thing," then veers away. I forget the terrain, and quite abruptly, we're in my driveway. She hasn't done it yet. I say something about things working out for the best and hand her a twenty-dollar bill. She has no change, she says, and suggests we head over to Bridgeport to an all night gas station, one of those big discount places with milk by the plastic gallon and cut-glass premiums. But after 10:00 it's correct change only according to the sign over the pumps.

AFTER 10 P.M.
ATTENDANT HAS NO MONEY
MONEY KEPT IN SAFE
ATTENDANT HAS NO KEY
EXACT CHANGE SALES ONLY!

I tell her to drive on to Halsted Street, and she begins her polyphonic confession once again. We reach Ed's Snacks—Breakfast Anytime, and I run in for change.

As I start back into the cab, someone screams at me from the middle of the intersection. Incredible, the corner is dark; David's across the street is closed; Ed's has only one customer, and suddenly, from the middle of the street there's a woman screaming at me. She's wearing glittered, three-inch platforms, a bright dacron dress and one of those Ginger Rogers fur jackets—tall and very thin, with a hairdo of frosted Dynel, running, or rather, spindling toward me. "That's my cab!" Close up, she looks like a Charles Addams version of a hooker; her mascara is smudged over her eyelids, and her face is extremely pale. The snags at the corners of her mouth are alcoholic, but her eyes are pure Dexadrine. I explain that it's *my* cab and tell her about stopping to get change. I even show her the change.

"Well, what the hell am I supposed to do. I'll never get another cab out here." Somehow, it's all my fault, and without knowing quite why, I accept the blame, finally agreeing to let her ride back home with me, then take the cab herself. The driver is displeased by the whole thing but gives in. We start back, and the driver takes up her story, somewhat desperately now. At the same time, my fellow passenger decides that stopping for a while at my place would be better than keeping the cab.

"Well, I don't see why we couldn't have just one drink."

"Ain't none of my kids gonna be as dumb as I was, I can tell you that for sure."

" . . . really, no hurry at all . . ."

" . . . like the church says . . ."

" . . . cause, I mean, you really helped me out of a jam back there . . ."

" . . . that thing, the first time I saw it . . ."

" . . . I didn't know what to do."

" . . . I didn't know what to do."

At my door again, I pay the driver what is by now a ridiculous fare. The driver keeps talking as she takes the money; my new companion has her hand on my arm. In the light from the lobby I can see both their faces—one round, the other almost skeletal, both circled by outrageously unreal auras of hair. The one in back slouches into the seat, the matted fray of her wig scraping the textured vinyl loudly. The driver says, "What I'll always regret is that I didn't go to college like everybody said I should," and pulls herself under the steering wheel. They back out of the driveway together and drive off into the sunrise, somehow meant for each other.

June Rachuy Brindel

SARTRE IS A COLD FISH

(from *Cimarron Review*)

Every morning there is a knife above Ms. Koven, cutting a hole in the ceiling, then hovering as though ready to drop. She wakes, clutching the smooth sheet. It has been this way since Sam's death. But the instant she makes this measurement, time melts like a jammed slide and she shudders out of bed groping for things to start it up, a faucet, a lamp, scizzors pointed sharp into the palm. By the time she looks again the knife has faded. It has always faded as the windows grow lighter. It has never been visible in daylight until this morning.

It is, the rational mind concludes, an illusion. A dream or the afterlife of a dream. Or the forecast of dreams to come. A Phallic Symbol, no less, penetrating the virginity of her chaste room. "We must analyze this, students," she says aloud.

The lights are all on, and the sun is flaring across the bed. Shower water rages hot down her back. Her eyes are closed, but she is perfectly aware that this morning the knife has followed. So this is the way the wind blows? A ghost on the parapet.

Where in hell are you now, Sam? She looks up and confronts. The knife is withdrawing, convexity merging into concavity, the without becoming the within or the within the without, as you like it. She is left with a hole in the sky or an inside view of a phallus probing.

A stiffness materializes in her now as if the spine had sensed its destiny. More likely, she mutters, rubbing briskly, the bones have sensed calcium deposits. The unmasked face in the mirror hints at the likelihood. And of course, there is no sign, suddenly, of the phenomenon, as one would expect. An emotional plaything. The hallucinatory dildo of a widow lady, Sam, forgive me. And time begins to rip past again in its usual fashion, the projector speeded up beyond anyone's control, her head throbbing at the pace.

All the same, the coffee shop is frozen as though her order has been a heinous demand: Your skin, miss. I need it for a lamp I am making. It's really for myself, she explains silently.

The aging waitress stares at her briefly, Nefertiti's hairdo rising above her caked makeup. Ms. Koven murmurs an incantation of sorts and Nefertiti disappears.

The air is tingling with pain. With smoke, rather. With words, too, with words. The very wordy gentleman is there again, across the counter. How he has come there this morning she is not sure. The words have touched her before the image. They burn into her ears like spots of napalm. It is something about his wife and how she has died retching blood in a kind of Eleusinian rapture and he can't help it, he is relieved, he hates to say it, may she rest in peace, but she drove him crazy in those last days, in all the days, if the truth be known, she was a hellcat, a shrew, a nag, a witch, but he loved her, he never left her, not once, even though many a man would have . . .

Ms. Koven bolts from the coffee shop a good half hour earlier than she needs to get to the college. Already the car is hot, baking in Indian summer sun. She feels the heat flowing into her scalp, penetrating hair roots and sinking heavily down the spine. Her headache subsides. It is a cautery. The key nerve severed, as with Sam. The first thing he had whispered after the surgery was, "No more pain." Which of course was the point of the whole thing. She had known that his legs would be still, no more thrashing from side to side in the tangled sheets, but this was a stillness of the pores. And when he spoke it was as if his breath were involuting, like the condensation of stars.

It was the weight of a star that she had carried around with her as he withdrew, though she had tried to follow, not knowing what to say besides a ritual I love you over and over until he was completely lost inside. And now she seemed to be caught forever in a howling space which she must not mention to others. "You're too young!" they shout. "Go out! Meet people! Live!"

In the car, the steady traffic noise wraps her around without need of response, other drivers harrying only the edges of the wound, unlike friends with their do's and students with their why's torturing the skinless state. Better drive around awhile before facing them all. Bathe in anonymity for a half hour and grow scabs.

She turns off into the forest preserve. A man washing his car looks up directly into her eyes as if he had been expecting her. In another car, a woman sits in the passenger seat, reading a paper, waiting, perhaps, for a driver. If the truth be known, Sam, we are all waiting. She drives farther along into the woods and they close around her; the trees toss sunlight back and forth; leaves drop silently. She feels a stillness of the mind as if her thoughts were involuting.

Above her yawns a cavernous hole.

• • •

Ms. Koven is at the college with no memory of how she has got there. Suddenly the classroom is in focus, every eye spearing her.

She feels undressed in a public place as in a dream. It seems she has said something, but she cannot remember what it was. Have I shocked them again, Sam? Shall I apologize? This dirty old radical teacher lady doesn't really want to knock your buggies out of the ruts. You look so safe.

But the hole has followed her and looms above the entire room. She wonders if they see it. Most of them are still staring at her as if anesthetized, and she hears her voice continuing to explain in a rational tone that they should write whatever enters their heads. "For ten minutes," the voice says. "Work fast. Try to catch all your ideas, feelings, sensations. Don't let anyone see your paper. Don't put your name on it. Don't be inhibited. Say anything." From a distance she is aware of a few smirks and snickers before they settle into silence. Not the worst idea, Sam, she thinks. Don Judson uses it all the time, claims revolutionary results. Besides, the silence is like a swathe, the jabbing reality muted to pen whispers. No more thrashing from side to side. She feels as if she has killed them.

The heads are bent as if praying, here and there a hand covers the eyes and there is the dead stillness of a chapel over all. Sacrifice performed by high priestess as delineated in ancient text. How in hell had Judson justified it to the Department, his limp prophet hair damp with enthusiasm? "Gives value to their unconscious! Recognizes their pain! Their joy!" Followed by a loud scathing snort from the line of occupationalists. This isn't Harvard. What profiteth it a mechanic to gain his own soul and lose a job? Better teach them to shut up and spell right. March in step and collect the pension at the seventh stage. Don't hold up the line.

But Ms. Koven is ready for Fresh Approaches, Extended Perceptions. "I'm winging, Sam," she says daily to the mirror. "You did it. You catapulted me into a New Dimension." She has plans for taking transient lovers, hallucinogenic drugs, and sabbaticals in ashrams, though none of these has yet materialized. She takes copious notes as Judson flings his shining, evanescent ideas into the stifling office. But she has not used them before today. And even today she is not sure how it has come about. The experiment does not appear in the Rhetoric syllabus for this date.

She is aware that the hole is expanding and lowering above the students' nice lower-middle-upper-working-class, mainly Caucasian heads. When will it engulf them, she wonders. Most of them still live at home. Will that save them? Icons and elders hovering, clouding over the bald harsh shapes of Ideas, from the vision of which they scurry into hiding. Not all of them. Not Lynne Giovani, immersed in Sartre fresh out of the baptismal font, eyes boldly piercing the existential moment, the terror of freedom flapping about her like (ah) black wings.

It occurs to Ms. Koven that she has performed this rite for

Lynne's sake as much as her own, but she knows instantly that this is a lie, that she is not the helper here, not today, if ever. She is hanging onto the students, to their youth, over emptiness, with emptiness above. Not just Lynne, all of them. Chuckie Evans, his eager nose racing along after his racing hand, covering every inch of paper, straining to be a good boy, do what teacher wants, the others laughing at him, but he himself too embedded in mother fat to feel the pain, a tender of the queen ant, happy in his slavery. And Harvell Jackson, defiant in the farthest seat. "You don't know who I am, do you?" he had said to her in the hall the second week. "Why, Mr. Jackson," she had replied smugly, "do you think all Blacks look alike?" And Mary Jacek, immobile, staring at her paper, her father on her mind again, no doubt. Daddy drunk running from Mom's nagging, Daddy working nights to get away from Mom, Daddy letting her (Mary) nurse him, undress him, hide him from Mom, Daddy and Mary. And the boy whose name she can never remember, the mute one, blinking when questioned and moving his lips without sound, writing nothing, staring now at the chalk-board, one word on his paper.

The knife has reappeared. What am I doing, thinks Ms. Koven. The swathe has become a band of flame. She cuts the time short, and her abrupt words startle the students. "Place the papers upside down," says the voice, "so that anonymity can be preserved." Salve, salve. Preserve us from the wound of knowing. Oh, Machiavellian Judson. It has been the snake's advice. Or is it the testing of the Lord?

As the papers gather in her hands she is tempted to hide them away, but apparently she has made a promise. The eyes are fixing her in a formulated phrase. She sprawls on her pin and wriggles. That is not what I meant at all. But the rational voice is already presuming. She shuffles the papers, hoping not to identify them, and begins to read hurriedly, misgivings scuttling in her ragged voice. "Logic doesn't work in life." "What a shitty world." "I feel as if I'm being slowly embalmed." "Nothing."

What have I said to them, thinks Ms. Koven. Have I told them about the knife or do they see it too? The air around her seems sharp with agony, thrashing from side to side. She wants to stop reading, but their eyes are fixing her. When she lifts the next paper, Lynne Giovani stirs. The handwriting is unmistakable even if the words were not. They rise from the page through Ms. Koven's voice like an offering. "I want out from death," she whispers. "Sartre is a cold fish."

A school of cold fish swarms about Ms. Koven, nibbling at her liver. In short, they say, we are all afraid. Yet she seems to be riding seaward on their fear, a wave in the cries flooding through her, pulsating with a familiar needful primeval throb. She lends herself to it. Incoherent phrases merge in her mind without thought and come forth again through her lips into the ears of the students, through her eyes into theirs, and through them (oh, she knows it is true!) into someone else somewhere, who can tell how many? Over and over again into and out of the current of momentary being, like the earth itself. Back into her furrows they plough the dead and from them the living arise in spirals uncurling upright into the air, making paths out of the depths, angling into space.

"All phalluses, all wombs," Ms. Koven murmurs aloud. The eyes of the students glisten with understanding. "Male and female, drawing upward the deep deep power that rises from the hot center," she declares firmly, feeling warmth wriggle in and around her as though Life Itself had moved of a sudden. "Receiving and giving are one!" She is shouting now, her voice shaking but strong. "Good old Hermaphrodite, begetting as you are begot! Dying in birth and erupting out of death into life, Oh Joy! Can you hear me, Sam?"

The students are transfixed. Ms. Koven's arms are thrown upward, her eyes lifted. She is watching the world rise through the hole above the room. "Here we are, here we are!" she shouts. "Here I am!"

Andrew M. Greeley

JULIE

(from *The Literary Review*)

"Roberta, who's that woman by the table at the end of the pool?"

"You mean the handsome one with the red hair and the green swim suit?"

"Uhm."

"That's Julie Lyons. Her husband is an oil company vice president type up at Kuala. They have a cottage on the Strait and usually come down on weekends. Lovely woman."

"Uhm."

We were at the Port Dickson yacht club, once the symbol of white imperialism and now as racially mixed a place as you could find anywhere in the world. Indians, Malays, Chinese, Dutch, English, Swedes, and an occasional south side Chicago exile like Roberta bumped elbows at the bar without a second thought. Under the clear tropical sky, children of black, brown and white colors and lots of mixed hues jumped in and out of the delightfully cool waters of the pool. Others scampered across the wide beach to watch the scores of shining sails crisscross the gleaming blue wavelets of the Straits of Malacca. British imperialism was gone, but the good life on a Sunday afternoon at Port Dickson was better than it had ever been in the days of the Empire if, of course, you had the money to join the Club. Almost as good as an American country club, I reflected, and a lot more colorful.

Roberta sipped her gin and bitter lemon and noticed that my eyes were still fixed on Julie Lyons. "Would you like an introduction?" There was a frown in her voice.

"Not necessary, Berts, the lady and I have known each other for a long time."

"Old friends?"

"I didn't say that."

I saw Julie against a very different waterside background, much less romantic than the carnival colors of the Straits of Malacca: a small Wisconsin lake, a tiny fringe of beach, an old pier, a few drab trees. She was wearing a green swim suit then to match her eyes, I guess, and with her was Terry Dunn. For one frightening moment I saw Terry Dunn standing beside her now, here at Port Dickson, then that disorienting mixture of past and present quickly faded away.

We were sophomores in high school. Terry and Julie were recounting with great glee his religious experience at the Baptist church the previous week. In that pre-ecumenical era our Protestant neighbors were fair targets for anything. The little redhead was no longer little and now filled her swim suit quite adequately. Even though we had a big fight that day, I felt kind of sorry for her. She would soon leave Terry behind. It was the end of her childhood. She and Terry came to a parting of ways in September, she insisting that it was time for her to "grow up" and Terry solemnly swearing that he would never grow up.

Terry Dunn. Terry Dunn. How can I make him real for you? His lightness, his grace, his contagious laughter, his manic imagination. We used to say of him with some defensiveness that he didn't have a mean bone in his body. His mischief, we argued, never really hurt anyone, not so long as you didn't mind an occasional broken window or a couple of hours rearranging your house after you were a victim of one of Terry's raids. Our parents thought he was terrible, but even they had to laugh at the "Gray Ghost's" exploits. Terry Dunn, at that age, was the kind of person who made you laugh even when you wanted to be angry at him.

His pranks started in the last year of grammar school when we had tired of summer softball. He suggested to the rest of us that it might be fun to break into Kraus's grocery store on Division Street and "rearrange" the place. I resisted, but the others went along. When Herr Kraus as Terry called him came in the next morning, he saw that his canned goods were as neatly arranged on shelves as they were the previous night but on different shelves. The poor man thought he was losing his mind, sat down at his counter and wept for an hour. Then he got furious, and then Herr Kraus, who was a good guy, laughed for three straight days.

On his cash register, he found a neatly printed card: "Compliments of the Gray Ghost." The era of the Gray Ghost and his band had begun.

They took dangerous chances. "Breaking and entering" was a crime; however benign their intent, they could have all ended up in reform school. They never were caught. The victims were not people who would be told by those of us who knew.

Apartments were raided and furniture rearranged. Vacationers came home to find that clothes had moved to different closets and drawers. Statues from the church appeared in the vestibules of private homes. The pastor found St. Joseph waiting for him inside the sacristy door one morning. The organist encountered dead mice on her keyboard. Scanty underwear (well, by 1940 standards) showed up on convent clotheslines. St. Teresa appeared on the altar of the Lutheran church. Democratic posters blocked the windows of the Republican ward office and vice versa. Sister Superior wrote obscene notes to the pastor and vice versa. Hearses pulled up at parties. Singing telegrams came in the middle of the night. Christmas cards arrived from the king, the pope, and the president. The oddest people sent each other valentines.

The Gray Ghost was on the loose.

Mostly, the Gray Ghost was four people. Terry, Tony McCarthy, Ed O'Connor, and Julie Quinn. At that time a tiny, grim-faced red head, she was the worst of the lot because she egged the others on. I was left out; Julie decided I was a coward, which I was.

She was the driving force, Terry the imagination. I can still see him, his pinched, little face, framed by wiry, black hair, his darting leprechaun eyes, his wickedly grinning mobile mouth. The Gray Ghost's raids were the high point of Terry's life. I was useful, I guess, because I was the appreciative audience he could share it with afterwards.

It went on for three years; they were not greedy, a raid every couple of months, carefully planned and daringly executed. Many of their victims were not amused. I guess there was a touch of cruelty about some of what they did. Most of us thought that they made up for it by their flair, their wit, and their imagination. They danced lightly through the neighborhood, dangerously close to the flame, perhaps, but at least they danced.

The police must have found a pattern. I suspect that some of the neighborhood cops were sufficiently plugged into the grape vine to know who was involved. They laid off, doubtlessly figuring that there were worse criminals on the loose. Certainly the Protestant church raids did not offend the police one bit.

One of the congregations of what we now call our separated brothers had a revival tent on Division Street in the summertime, with prayers, preaching, conversion, and tongue-speaking going on every night. We used to hang around in the back some of the time because it seemed great entertainment, little realizing that we would live to see the same kinds of goings on in Catholicism in twenty years. One hot sticky evening with the acrid smell of the stockyards riding strong on the south wind, Terry decided to "get converted." At the personal testimony time of the prayer meeting, he rushed down the aisle, and in a thick Irish brogue announced to all that he had been a terrible sinner and had lived a life of drunkenness, lechery, blasphemy, and idolatry. Our separated brothers and sisters were so delighted that it never occurred to them that this fifteen year old couldn't have had much time for all the sinfulness he confessed, unless he had started out at two-and-a-half. Terry then led them through a session of hymn singing, shouting out in his rich off-key Irish tenor voice their favorite songs with enough caricature to send us into peals of laughter, but not enough to make them anything more than slightly uneasy.

At the end of the service, after the preacher gave thanks for the conversion of this "papist sinner," Terry grabbed the microphone one final time, shouted to the multitude, "God damn you to hell, all you Protestant bastards. Long live the Pope!" and ran full speed for the door of the tent and the safety of the summer night. In the back, we all scattered with equal speed. Our separated friends followed vigorously, but they were not nearly fast enough. After that, there was hardly a minister in the neighborhood who didn't have a sincere questioner or a loud heckler or several off-key singers in his congregation. Apparently, the ministry didn't communicate with each other because none of them were prepared to give chase when Terry and the gang took to their heels.

It was this unecumenical activity which finally brought the career of the Gray Ghost to an end. There was some very important function at the local Missouri Synod Lutheran congregation. Terry and Julie got a chorus of thirty papists to stand across the street singing hymns to the Blessed Mother all evening long. The police were called but, in 1942, what Irish cop was going to put kids in jail for praising the Blessed Mother?

The Lutheran pastor went to see the monsignor in solemn high procession, an unheard of event, and the monsignor, who knew nothing of the exploits of the Gray Ghost, gave the young curate strict instructions to "stop that blasphemy." The young curate knew all about the band of the Gray Ghost, but had minded his own business. Now, he laid down the law.

Though Julie wanted to go on, soon afterwards, she decided that it was time to be a dignified young woman instead of a tomboy. Terry was not a presentable boyfriend she could bring to school affairs. She was now at the stage of adolescence (junior year) when she was three or four years older than her male contemporaries in poise, sophistication, and interests. There never had been anything "romantic" between her and Terry as far as we know, so it was not a "break up," but the passing of a phase in life.

Now, Julie was a tall, strikingly beautiful girl with long red hair and flashing green eyes. She and the others were on their way to adulthood. Terry was still a kid, hanging around the pool hall, the softball field, the basketball courts. They worried about dances, parties, proms; he worried about getting a couple of bottles of beer. He found a group of older guys who were interested in the same kind of thing and settled down to the life of the permanent adolescent, which was possible in those days before you went into the service. He managed to make it through high school, though only barely. The war came to an end. While Tony and Ed and Julie went off to college and I to the major seminary, Terry started to work for the city like his father before him, caught in a swamp of failure before he had a chance at anything else in life. Terry's family were slovenly shanty Irish; his father, a huge, fat, brawling character, worked for the sanitation department and was drunk every night of the week. His mother, from whom Terry inherited his physique, was a shrewish, wispy little woman who sighed in every second sentence. There were vague, slatternly grandparents, aunts, and four younger sisters hanging around the back of their house. In grammar school, kids don't notice those sorts of things, but in high school they got finely tuned into social class distinctions. We knew that Terry didn't quite belong and never would. The Gray Ghost exploits were the peak of his career. He drank more and more and drifted out of our lives. A soul in purgatory.

He was in church every Sunday, dressed uncomfortably in the suit and tie his mother made him wear though sneaking out early for the cigarette which he desperately needed. He played softball and bowled in the parish league and helped the young priest at all the carnivals. He even worked at night as a janitor when Mr. King, our perennial parish janitor, (they had not yet been promoted to engineers) was on vacation. Being part of the church was, I guess, some sort of compensation for being excluded from the crowd of his old friends. "He'll die young," my mother predicted. He usually came by our house when I was home on vacations. I was something of an outcast. Julie never liked me much and was abusively angry that day on the beach at Twin Lakes when I foolishly suggested that Terry belonged in the seminary. In those days in our neighborhood, if Julie wrote you off, you were written off.

One summer night, I remember it quite well because it was the strange, haunted week when both the old monsignor and the young priest died within two days of one another, Terry and I were sitting on our back lawn in a long, aimless conversation (we lived on the corner, so the back lawn was an ideal gathering place).

"Terry, you should go to college."

"Ah, they'd never let a dumbbell in, besides what's the point, I'll get my union card next year and I'll make good money."

"You're not dumb. You just didn't study at Philip's (St. Philip the Servite high school, now defunct)."

"It's too late," he chewed nervously on his cigarette. "If I had thought two years ago that we weren't going to have another depression right away, I might have given it a whirl. With some of the mutts that are getting higher learning, though, sure, someone has to do the plumbing," and he went into the Irish brogue to which he always fled when he was uneasy.

My mother had long ago foretold that "Terry Dunn will have a nervous breakdown some day." He had always been "high strung," but you didn't notice that sort of thing when you're a kid. Now, the nervous movements of hands and feet, the chain smoking, and the puffing of his face from too much beer told you there was something a little different about Terry.

"The world is changing, Terry. There isn't going to be another depression and everyone is going to go to college. You should give it a try, even in night school."

He was silent in the warm darkness of the night. "You worried about me trying to soak up the beer on the west side?"

"I'm worried about your talent going to waste!"

Again a long silence in the patient night. "I guess you're right. Maybe the Gray Ghost ought to go to Mayslake this weekend and get his life squared away." He had gone to the retreat house every year since he was sixteen. After each retreat, he went on the wagon for a while. In those days, Mayslake offered a brisk, locker room masculine Christianity. "That's a heck of a good idea," I said, though I had seen this therapy fail before. There was yet another silence in the night then an embarrassed, "You're a great pal to worry about me." I'd swear that there was a sob in the Gray Ghost's voice.

Terry came home from that weekend and announced that he was going to be a priest. He joined the Franciscans and was off to their college within a month. I knew the strains of life in the seminaries in those days and wondered why the Franciscans had not done any checking on Terry's psychological background. At that time a lot of us didn't believe in psychology.

He lasted longer than I thought he would, eighteen months; and then he came home with a bad ulcer, trailing behind him rumors of a "nervous breakdown," just as my mother had predicted. He kept away from me in our January vacation. By summertime, he was back working for the city and seriously pursuing his campaign to dispose of all the beer on the west side. I didn't hang around the ball field much that summer, mostly because I didn't want to embarrass him. I was not far enough in life to smell doom. At twenty-two, Terry already had the stench of it.

Then, he went to Mayslake again, took the pledge and tried once again to get "squared away." He enrolled full-time at Loyola, worked an evening watchman job for the city, gave up drinking and smoking, lost weight, kept his hair cut, and acted like a bright young man in a hurry. I saw him briefly during our January vacation; the light was back in his eye. He looked better than he had since the sophomore summer at Twin Lakes and was getting "A's" in all his courses. He was already talking about law school and a career in politics. His fingers were reaching eagerly for his passport to suburbia. The word was out in the neighborhood that Terry Dunn had finally "straightened himself out." Even my mother admitted that he had really "pulled himself together." He went to double semester summer school so that he could make it into law school a year from September. I barely saw him at all that summer. He was dating Julie Quinn, much to everyone's amazement and to the anguished dismay of Dr. Quinn and his wife. The Quinns hated to see the daughter of the neighborhood's richest family waste herself on an alcoholic shanty Irishman. The neighborhood said they were great for each other. They drove by one night when I was walking home from church in her white convertible; in those days, even college types rode the bus on dates, unless they were well off. "The Gray Ghost rides again," he shouted. We talked for a few moments, Julie impatient and not liking me anymore than she ever did.

They were engaged at Christmas, the wedding was scheduled for June. He had a law school scholarship and a job. She was going to teach school at St. Ursula's. My mother thought they were both crazy.

I was invited to the wedding. I half suspected that Terry would turn up on the door step one night with cold feet. Better, I thought, for him to take the initiative.

It was Julie who came. Two weeks before the wedding, I was in the house alone, reading Joseph Conrad; the doorbell rang and to my dismay, the white convertible was in the front and the redhead at the door. She was cool and elegant in a white dress with a thin red belt at her waist, tall and slender on her high heels.

"Can I come in and talk?" she asked shyly, then groping for confidence. "The one night I hoped to find you in your damn throne on the yard, you have to be inside."

"Beautiful women can always come in," I said gallantly.

Her green eyes flashed at me. "You've changed."

I didn't offer her anything to drink, mostly because I forgot to.

"I have to talk to someone."

"Cold feet?"

"I'm scared silly. I love him so much and yet . . ." Tears began to pour out of those green waterfalls. She fumbled for a handkerchief.

"Julie, it's great to see the band of the Gray Ghost together again."

The impish grin from the old days came back. "We're really so good together. I steady him down and he makes me laugh. He's such a great person . . . of course, I don't have to tell you that, so kind and gentle and..and . . ." Now she was sobbing. For an errant moment, I thought it would be very nice to have such a woman sobbing for me. I made a big leap, much more than I would do in later days in the rectory.

"You're not sure that saving a man is a good enough reason for marrying him." She fought the sobs.

"Is that what the neighborhood thinks? My mother says that's what I'm doing... I don't know... whether... What do you think?"

I chose my words as carefully as I could. "I haven't heard anyone say that. I'm not sure you're the martyr type, Julie. He is a reformed alcoholic, that's a big risk."

She flushed with anger. "You call yourself a friend?"

"I'm simply stating the facts. You're taking a bigger risk than if he didn't have his record. If you win, you win big... if not... anyhow, you wanted to know what I think."

"I'm sorry. You're right. I know it's a big gamble. That crude, vulgar family of his..."

"Shanty Irish," I said.

"If only I could know the future. I care about him. I love him. I want to be with him forever. I'm frightened. I don't want to hurt him."

"And hurt yourself in the process."

"I don't care about me."

"Sure you care about you. What happens in church next week might ruin your life."

"I don't want people to say that I'm a spoiled, selfish brat."

"Better to say that than to say five years from now that you were a blind fool."

The tears stopped. She was cool and composed. Those shrewd green eyes glinted at me. "Are you telling me not to marry him?"

I felt very tired. "No, Julie."

"The side for him..." she leaned forward intently from the edge of her chair, hoping for some sign from heaven.

"He loves you. You've given him a new hope in life. He's been on the wagon for almost two years. You're happy whenever you're with him. And, cold feet come before every marriage."

Our old living room lit up in the radiance of her smile. She stood up. "Thanks, you've been a darling. See you at the wedding." As she left in a swirl of white dress, she gave me a hasty kiss on the cheek. Lucky man, Terry Dunn, I thought.

At 11:00 a week from the following Saturday, I was in the old basement church with a thousand other people, the altar awash in roses, the sanctuary filled with clergy for the solemn high nuptial mass of Julie Anne Quinn and Terrance Michael Dunn. The twelve men in the wedding party looked uncomfortable in their stiff summer formals. The ladies of honor were awkward, if lovely, in their tight rose dresses chosen, I'm sure, to match Julie's hair. All of us were eagerly awaiting the march of the lovely bride down the red-carpeted aisle.

Only she never came.

Terry went on a two week binge, did not graduate from college, never tried law school, and went back to work for the city. He soaked up all the beer on the west side and began to work on the north side supply. He was a chronic alcoholic by the time of my first mass to which he was not able to come because he was in the hospital drying out.

The Quinns moved out of the neighborhood in disgrace and bought a home in Lake Forest. I never saw Julie again.

Terry was dead at thirty of a liver ailment, they said. I didn't have a car (we couldn't own one for five years after ordination in those days). I made it to the wake on public transportation the final night. I knew I would not be able to get from Beverly to the west side for the requiem mass the next morning.

His mother, now white-haired and frail, gripped my hand tightly when I offered my sympathies. I didn't recognize the Gray Ghost in the casket; he looked as though he were sixty years old.

"It was that redheaded bitch who did it to him," she screeched at the top of her voice, causing everyone in the funeral home to jump with dismay.

While a cold November rain fell on the tiny knot of mourners, the Gray Ghost was laid to rest in Mt. Carmel cemetery the next day. None of his band were at the grave side.

Derek came back with the children. The sun was sinking toward Sumatra. The expatriates at the swimming pool were clinging to the last splendid hours of a Port Dickson weekend.

Eugene Wildman

THE WANING OF THE MIDDLE AGES

(from *Chicago Magazine*)

When Jonathon applied for the apartment, Mr. Perlberg, the realtor, informed him matter-of-factly what the rent would be. It was somewhat steeper than he had expected. Then Perlberg smiled, softening the blow, and said, "So, you write pieces for the newspapers, for the supplements? Do I know your work? No? That's too bad. Well, who knows, maybe you'll get lucky like the other fella who lived there. I suppose you know who I mean."

Jonathon knew. The "other fella" was Saul Bellow and he had written *Herzog* while living in that same apartment. The book had come out the year that Jonathon arrived in Chicago to begin graduate work in English. The following year he had interviewed Bellow for a piece in a magazine. It was his first published work and he was paid $250 for it, a small fortune at the time.

"This was the actual apartment?" he asked, attempting to show a discreet uncertainty when Perlberg gave him the tour.

"The very one. Come on, let me show you around. It's got plenty of room, got lots of closet space, and could you ask for more light? And look at those leaded windows. Those alone are worth the price. You'll get plenty of inspiration here." Perlberg looked at him with large, dark, understanding eyes.

Jonathon signed the lease.

"The apartment has *mazel*," Perlberg said, shaking Jonathon's hand.

"I can certainly use some," Jonathon said.

He and Alice used to fantasize about what it would be like to live there. That was when they were newlyweds and had come upon the building by chance one day. It was like an archaeological discovery. They could not get over the architecture. It was modeled after the Cloisters in New York, Jonathon's absolute favorite museum. How perfect, given its illustrious former tenant, that behind the Christian and medieval facade a smooth-talking Yid, who might have come straight from his pages, should turn out to be the rental agent.

Jonathon declared that the building was like a beehive of prayer cells with plumbing. Alice announced that the only way anyone could hope to live there would be to read the obituaries every day. "Nobody who's still moving would ever be moving," she said. In those days they read books about the Holy Grail and held hands and listened to *Carmina Burana* together. Now they had gone their separate ways.

Until recently Alice had lived in their old apartment, sharing it with a series of lovers. Jonathon could not keep up with who they all were; she had gone crazy after their breakup. He had been living for a year in a residence hotel, a decaying structure called the Harper Arms, in a room with cracked and yellowed window shades and horrid brown wallpaper that tore itself loose from the walls at night; with a television set in the lobby that went on at six in the morning and stayed on until the late late late show was over, the sound seeping in through the rents in the wallpaper. He lived there because he felt like a failure and thought he did not deserve any better.

He and Alice had signed the lease on a larger place only a month before they separated. "We need *lebensraum*," Alice had said. "Who can fight that," he agreed. When he left, he spent their first night apart sleeping on the bare floor of what would have been his study, huddled for warmth in his overcoat. It was the only night that either of them spent at the new apartment.

Jonathon was the one who had walked out, but he was convinced that Alice would come back to him, that they could pick up the pieces and start over again. He believed it in spite of the fact that even to think it panicked him so that he knew he would run again if it happened. He was probably not the marrying kind, he figured, though he was lonesome without women around and there were times when he craved Alice's presence.

The knowledge that he had abandoned her plagued him, yet hardly had they separated than she began sleeping with all his men friends. Friends were only the beginning.

"This is one marriage that ended with a bang," he complained when they met in the street one day.

"I rather thought it petered out," she said with a tight-lipped smile.

He had been too wrapped up in his work, the old story. She was making up for it with a vengeance. It was true that one night he had insisted the television stay on while they were making love. But he was not altogether culpable. The program he had insisted they leave on was a documentary about the Galapagos Islands, about which he had a travel article due. Alice had never let him live it down. "You kept turning your head," she said. "What else could I have done?"

he asked. "Oh, go stick your head in a vat of turtle soup," she said.

Her biggest complaint was not his neglect or his distractions. Alice was convinced that he had had an affair with her best friend and maid of honor, Ellen Grace. When Jonathon swore up and down that no such thing had ever occurred, she said, "Then it's even worse because you were thinking of it, you were lusting for her in your heart."

One time in bed, while they were locked in an embrace, he had had his eyes closed. Alice had forced herself up on her hands and asked, "Who are you thinking about, her or me?" "You," he said, looking at her with wide-eyed dismay. "I'm with you, not her. And I didn't go to bed with her." "What's the difference," Alice said. "She'll always be intangible. A real woman I could compete with, but not an ideal or a fantasy."

He ended by confessing to the affair even though it had never happened. He thought it would bring peace, resolution; that it would derail her obsessive imaginings. Besides, it was true, he admitted to himself, it was true in his heart. Confessing was a mistake. Alice never forgave him for it.

Most of her women friends treated him like a pariah, and he would not have anything more to do with the men he knew who had affairs with her. After a year of breaking off relations with almost everyone he knew, Jonathon persuaded himself that he deserved a change of luck. And now, ironically, an apartment in their dream place had opened up.

Perlberg was not alone in not knowing Jonathon's work. How could anyone know? Twice a week he ghosted an entertainment column for one of the darlings of the Chicago press. Occasionally he did articles or interviews, but most of those were sold out of town, to papers in Toronto or Boston or San Francisco. He got slightly better rates. Part-time he taught a class in writing for the media at one of the community colleges. It was a life, it kept him in food and shelter; but the thought of his future made Jonathon wince.

Jonathon's novel was likewise going nowhere. It was bogged down in what seemed to be an endless middle. It was a lengthy episodic affair, loosely based on his own marriage, about a couple who keep drifting apart but who stave off divorce by moving into larger and larger apartments. He could not think how to end it, so he kept proliferating incidents. Every Tuesday he went to his therapist and talked about his difficulties with the plot.

"Well, how's it going this week?" Dr. Griggs would ask.

"They moved again," he would answer.

"Moved again. My oh my, what was it this time?"

"Another argument. He criticizes her in public, she's had it. I don't know how to end it. I want them to stay together, but I don't know how to make it come off."

Dr. Griggs would slowly remove a package of Life Savers from his pocket, dig one loose with his thumb and fastidiously place it in his mouth, always omitting to offer Jonathon one. Jonathon was uncertain whether these omissions were deliberate, but he generally felt angry anyway, though he was never able to express his anger.

"How do you want it to come off with Alice?" Dr. Griggs would usually ask at that point, rolling the Life Saver around in his mouth.

"I don't know that either," he would answer, wondering if he would ever be able to ask Dr. Griggs for one.

His first night in the apartment he called Alice up. It was about midnight and she was out. He kept calling at five to ten minute intervals and finally at two-thirty she answered.

These calls were a habit he had lately gotten into. There was nothing he had to say but he needed to know she was there, hear her pick up the phone. His ears would strain to catch background noises or something in the tone of her voice that would tell him if she were there with someone else. "Where were you, a movie?" he would ask sometimes, trying to sound casual. She would not hang up but would wait silently, as if the question were an aberration she need not concern herself with. At his end he could faintly make out her breathing, sense her exasperation, judge how close to the edge he had pushed.

"This is a time to call?" she said now.

"Do you have any idea where I'm calling from?"

"All right, I'll bite. Where?"

He had not let on to anyone where he was looking.

"From my own apartment in our old dream place, the same apartment in fact where Bellow wrote *Herzog*. What do you have to say to that?"

"Congratulations, I'm glad you're finally in comfortable surroundings. Because I have some news to tell also. I've met somebody I like and you can't be calling me at all hours anymore."

"You have the same wonderful timing you always did. Don't you remember that this was the place where you and I were going to live together?"

"Poor picked on Jonathon. You called me, remember? But since now I'm such a bitch, why don't you not call at all anymore. And oh, I hadn't wanted to break the news quite this way, but I've seen a lawyer. So you can talk to him from now on."

Living in the apartment made Jonathon's failures seem even worse. He walked through the rooms and the aura of Moses Herzog was everywhere. Here Bellow had looked out the window and contemplated Herzog's agonies over the infidelities of his wife. There he had sat in his easy chair pondering the erotic delights of Ramona. Even the bathroom was no escape. There he imagined Bellow composing the letters to Nietzsche and to God that Herzog became famous for; while he, Jonathon Cutler, merely did the obvious. The steamy shower produced vaporous likenesses of Herzog and his creator, like ghostly presences of the fatherly spirit that Hamlet was haunted by. True to her word, Alice had stopped taking his calls.

"Do we really have anything to talk about?" she had said and hung up the last time he tried. He had stared into the empty receiver, unwilling to acknowledge that the line had gone dead.

He brooded about it. He added a new episode to his novel. The couple, who had long since retreated to separate bedrooms, now added phones of their own. Living in the same house, they talked to each other on the phone every day.

"Art inverts life?" Dr. Griggs asked when Jonathon described the latest development.

"My life is its own inversion," he said.

He became suddenly possessed with an urge to call all the people he knew from childhood, his classmates in elementary and junior high school. Especially the girls. Eleanor Hausman from the first grade, who sat next to him and whose dresses used to come up to her thighs, the sight causing in him a tingling sensation that he loved without any understanding of it. Sandy Shell from the seventh grade, who had a crush on him but whose unusually tiny feet were just too small for his finicky taste. After she moved away he was haunted by the thought of those feet. Rhoda Carlin from the sixth grade, who looked like Ruth Roman and whom he could never have the courage to talk to.

He wondered why he had this need to make contact with his past. Why were these girls, now women verging on middle age, suddenly so important? They would be married, with children and overweight, possessive husbands. Eleanor Hausman might be Eleanor Klotsky now. She might, for all the world, be living in Sioux City, Iowa or Racine, Wisconsin. Who knew where. The same with the rest—the Rhodas, the Sandys. They would go jogging every morning or work out at their health clubs in an effort to hold on to what they were.

And that was just it. What he was. In his mind these women existed like Balthus's girls, caught in a moment of unconscious eroticism; or, like the snapshot someone had once described of his grandmother and two of her girlfriends at about the age of twelve, posed in old-fashioned striped bathing suits, their hair hanging nearly to their waists. Jonathon longed to be with them and all that early, frozen possibility.

Because something had gone wrong. He had gone off somewhere and if he could contact the past and correct the orbit of his life, a life that was shooting off into space and time, it still might not be too late. Otherwise what was there? Emptiness and absence. In the entire city of Chicago, on the entire planet for that matter, not one woman missed him, not one woman would be going to bed wishing that he could be with her. As he wished to be with all of them.

The only number he could think of calling, the only one whose name would be the same and whose address he was sure he could pinpoint, was his old-time chum Bucky Hoffer. They had played hundreds of hours of ball together and after high school they had never seen each other again. But Bucky would never stray from the ancestral haunts; he knew his old schoolyard pal that well.

"Bucky," he said, after getting the number from information, "is this Bucky Hoffer?"

"Yes, this is he. This is Buckman Hoffer."

"This is *he*? This is *Buckman*?"

"May I ask who is calling please?"

"This is *he*. Bucky, you're the same old shlump you always were." He hung up.

Again he dialed New York information. Did they have an Eleanor Hausman listed in any of the boroughs? No? Well what about Eleanor Klotsky? He was certain that was it; she had married and turned herself into a Klotsky. In Brooklyn? Terrific. Though could it conceivably be the Eleanor he had known? He would soon see.

A woman answered the phone and he said, "Are you the former Eleanor Hausman who went to Public School 67 in the Bronx? Ah well, too bad. Because if you were, I just wanted to tell you—this is a legitimate call, I assure you—I wanted to tell you what exquisite thighs you had." It was as far as she let him get.

Sandy Shell, he decided, would be in Long Beach under her own name, and sure enough there was one listed. He identified himself and Sandy Shell, who sounded like a bored surfer, said, "Oh sure, you're the jewelry salesman."

"I don't think you've got the same Jonathon Cutler in mind," he said.

"How many Jonathon Cutlers can there be?" she said, "—who sell jewelry."

"You're right. You're always right, Sandy. Sandy of the beauteous feet. I adore your luscious feet, do you know that?"

"Jonathon, you're far out. What are you on?"

"I'm on your trail. And I'm not Jonathon. At least not the same Jonathon."

"That's even better. But whatever you've been taking, honey bun, you're not going to sell any earrings that way. Only I can't talk to you now. Will you call me on Monday?"

"No, you call me. I'll be waiting for your call."

"All right, I'll call you."

"You promise?"

"I promise."

Rhoda proved a blank so he dialed another number. Naomi, his first love when he was a freshman and sophomore at NYU. Naomi had married a lawyer and he knew her married name. And how he knew.

He had never been able to have the last word with her. Now he had a chance. Not only to contact the past but to alter it, set it aright at least somewhat.

The year he met Naomi he was living in desperate poverty. He had one of everything. One shirt, one pair of shoes, one sports jacket, one pair of chinos, one love. He got fired from his part-time job because his one shirt had a tear in it and his boss told him he wasn't presentable. Three times a week he walked from 112th Street where he lived to 70th Street where his brother-in-law had a bakery. His brother-in-law gave him a loaf of rye bread and some danish pastries and he walked back. He ate one meal a day, almost invariably rice with a can of peas and carrots thrown in. Some days he had only the rye bread and danish. But he had Naomi so he lacked for nothing.

Naomi had two things. She had him. She also had a fiance.

But his life was better then, he thought. He had oneness, unity, wholeness. It was still what he was craving. He had not changed at all; he was still the most hopeless of romantics. After Naomi broke off with him he had ended up seeing a psychiatrist who accused him of massive self-destructiveness. Why would he go after someone who was already engaged? Jonathon said because he was in love. "So you finally did it to yourself," Dr. Benson said after he had described his misery. "No," he had answered, "it happened to me."

Naomi's phone rang and rang and on the tenth ring she answered it, sounding a bit out of breath. "I was in the shower," she said. The moment he spoke she recognized his voice.

"This is a serious call. The reason I'm calling," he said, "is because I could never get the last word with you. Like it was written in stone: Thou shalt not have the last word."

"Only you," Naomi said.

"It's no joke. Remember the time we were walking up Broadway and you turned abruptly on 114th Street? No, of course you don't remember. Well as you turned I rammed my knee against a fire hydrant, and just so I wouldn't look foolish in front of you I continued calmly walking up Broadway as though nothing had happened. The minute you were out of sight I dropped to the ground and started yowling. Everything between us was like that."

The moment he finished recounting the incident he remembered an almost identical one that happened with Alice in Chicago. These rituals of pain and stoicism were the constants of his relationships with women. The time with Alice he was left rolling on the ground, bawling like a baby.

"So tell me," Naomi said, "did you write?"

"Write," he said. "For the papers, articles."

"My husband's not a lawyer anymore. He's finishing up a novel. Isn't that ironic?"

"Your husband, outside the law?"

"*Flick Your Bick*, it's called. About a divorce lawyer named Bick. Lots of sex."

He could not think of anything to say. He told her he had another call and would phone her later and hung up.

On the way out he ran into Perlberg showing another apartment to someone. All of a sudden there was a run on apartments. What can you do, he thought, what can you do.

"So, how's it going? Get hot at the machine yet?" Perlberg asked.

"Getting warm," he said, "getting warm."

Jonathon was in the apartment two months when the phone rang one morning at about five. A woman's voice, sounding very faint, said, "I need you." He was certain it was Alice.

"Do you want me to come over?" he asked.

"Yes," she answered, her voice coming from far away.

She's taken pills, he thought, alarmed. He dressed hurriedly and took a cab over to Alice's.

"Just a minute." she said in a groggy tone in response to his repeated ringing, "let me put a robe on."

The moment he heard her speak he knew that it was a mistake; it was not she who had called. The door opened and she stood looking at him angrily. A few feet behind her was her newest lover, a dark lowering shape in the background.

"I thought you called," he said.

"Why would I call you?"

"I got a call, I thought it was you."

"Why would you think that? Do you know you're crazy? Somebody calls at five in the morning and you come here and ring my bell."

She slammed the door and Jonathon walked back out into the street. He felt cold and helpless. It was just a wrong number. Yet somewhere out there in the electronic void was someone who needed him, a woman who was waiting, sinking fast. A woman whose voice he thought he had recognized.

When he got back to his apartment he made a pot of coffee. It was Tuesday and he would have something new for Dr. Griggs. A small breakthrough. He remembered reading that it was the realism of the city that had brought about the end of the middle ages. No more cloisters or unicorn gardens. Hail the real. For the first time the apartment felt like home. He belonged there. So what if he was not Saul Bellow. Who needed Bellow? It was Herzog's place by rights, and his life had gradually turned into Herzog's. His mistake all along had been to suppose that he was a person and not a character. And that being the case—he took a sip of coffee, which was bitter but very bracing—maybe now at long last he could ask Dr. Griggs for a Life Saver.

James Park Sloan

WHAT WE LEARNED IN VIETNAM

(from *Other Voices*)

"**D**idn't we learn anything?"—spoken by an American female noncombatant.

Huk couldn't understand why the guy had called *him*. He was nothing to the guy. He was just somebody the guy had seen on a panel. "My name is Willie Stallings, I saw you at the veterans forum," the voice said on the phone. He spat it out fast like a salesman who was afraid of being cut off.

The guy had called Maggie first. How had he gotten that number? Who gave it to him? Maybe he had an old phone book, Huk thought. Maybe one of Virgil's people had Huk's old number. Maggie wanted to know what was up. "Who's this Willie Stallings? Where do you know him from?" She had that tone she got in her voice. "He said it was an emergency. He said it was urgent. He didn't sound right."

He didn't sound right to Huk either. "I'm calling because I thought you could help me out," he said. "As a fellow veteran. Veteran to veteran."

His father had just died, the guy said. He needed two hundred and twenty-three bucks for the flight home. It was the cheapest flight available, with a change of planes in St. Louis. When he went to his bank, they said he had a balance of one hundred eighty-six dollars and fourteen cents. He gave the exact number. He needed forty bucks, he said. So he could visit his mother. He would give his promissory note.

So why didn't his mother pay for the plane ticket? What about that? Maybe she couldn't, though, Huk thought. Maybe he knew she couldn't afford it. Maybe he couldn't bring himself to ask her. It *was* the end of the month. Huk figured there was about one chance in three the guy was on the level. "Can you help me out?" Stallings pressed. "One veteran to another."

"When?" Huk asked. "Where?"

The flight was at twelve-thirty. A friend was driving him to the airport. He worked at the university hospital. Huk could meet him at the emergency room.

Huk was thinking fast. It was the end of the month. He was short himself, but forty bucks he could swing. Forty bucks was about exactly what he could swing. The guy must have known he could swing it. A con man could always tell that kind of thing. Why didn't his friend who was driving him to the airport give him the money? Maybe he didn't have it either. One chance in three, maybe four. Huk was damned if he was going to do it.

"Okay," he said finally. Fuck it. "Tomorrow, eleven o'clock, the emergency room."

Liz had been there in the room when he took the call. "Who was it?" she asked. "An old army buddy?"

"Nobody I know," Huk said. "I never met the guy. He says he saw me at the veterans forum." He repeated the guy's story.

"Well, I guess you can't say no," she said. "What if his father really did die?"

"That's what I told myself," Huk said. "I figure there's about one chance in five, but it's better to be wrong four times than so say no the one time it's on the level."

As soon as he spoke, Huk realized that he was lying. The man caught him off guard, was all. He wasn't ready with a reason for saying no. The man had known how to make it hard to say no.

"Did I do wrong?" Huk asked. "Am I a sucker?"

"Of course not," she said.

"Do you think I should actually go?"

"Of course," she said. "But be careful."

Women, Huk thought. Jesus. He got up to drive her home. Fuck it. He would sleep on it.

When he woke up, he called Maggie. Maggie thought he should be cautious too. He asked her for her impression of the guy. "He didn't say much," she said. "He was on the phone for about thirty seconds. He wanted to speak to you. Then he wanted your new number."

"He told you it was an emergency?"

"That's right. That's all he said."

"You said he didn't sound right."

"His voice was strange, that's all."

"His father just died," Huk said. "He just learned his father died."

"Does he have this address?" Maggie wanted to know. "Where do you know this guy from? I'm thinking of the children."

"I don't know him from Adam. He's just some veteran who saw me on the panel."

"Wasn't there anybody else he could call?"

That was the thing, Huk thought. Maggie had put her finger on it. Maggie, always reasonable. "He didn't have anybody else," Huk said. "That's his story. I figure there's about one chance in ten he's telling the truth, but if he is, Christ."

"You better check him out," Maggie said. "Think of the kids."

What Huk couldn't figure was why the man had called *him*? It wasn't as if he was some kind of professional veteran. He didn't march or go to veteran's meetings. He hadn't gone to see the Wall. He hadn't even gone to see the half-size mockup when they put it up in Grant Park. There was just that one panel he had been on, for Virgil. Virgil. He was who the guy should have called. Before he knew it, Huk was dialing Virgil's number. Who answered was a housesitter. Virgil was out of town for the week.

"In Washington, I bet," Huk said.

"That's right," she said.

"On veteran business?"

"I expect that's it," the housesitter said. She sounded a little wary of him.

"Well, just tell him Huk called."

Washington. The fact was, Virgil was getting ready to run for Congress. Everybody knew it. It was obvious, in some sort of way. It was obvious to everybody but Huk. He had heard these two guys talking about it while they were milling around after the panel. "Do you think Virge will run?" one said. "Obviously," the other said.

Obviously. Nothing was obvious to Huk any more. When Virgil called him to do the panel, he had said, "Listen, Huk, I'm putting together this group of Nam people, it's sort of a Lessons Learned packet. What We Learned in Vietnam. It can help a lot of people. I think you should be on it, Huk. I think you have something to say." Huk had stammered around for a minute or two, but Virgil was always able to get him to do things. Virgil knew how to put things so it was easiest just to say yes. Yes was the path of least resistance.

The panel had helped Virgil. It drew about four hundred people and got Virgil's name in both the newspapers. Virgil seemed to know exactly what we learned in Vietnam. It was the wrong war at the wrong place at the wrong time with the wrong enemy, Virgil said. He was quoting some politician. We must never have another Vietnam, Virgil said. I was just a grunt soldier, Virgil said, but I know that much.

If he heard Virgil say he was just a grunt soldier one more time, Huk thought he would puke.

Virgil once told him he wanted to call his book *Grunt Soldier* but the publisher made him call it *Viet Vet*. Huk wasn't quite sure when Virgil had started to be a big shot. Was it the book that did it? So why hadn't Willie Stallings called Virgil? Virgil kept index cards on Viet vets, he was president of the organization, he was the man to call. Did Virgil know something about Willie Stallings?

Maybe Willie Stallings knew better than to call Virgil. Virgil could sometimes make things happen at the VA, but he wasn't likely to come up with forty bucks cold cash. That was Huk's opinion. Virgil told stories in his book, but Huk knew something about at least one of those stories. According to the story, Virgil had gotten himself nicknamed VC. It was supposed to have happened during the big fuckup at Ban Me Thuot. That's where Virgil was supposed to have gotten nicknamed, except he hadn't. Nobody had ever called him anything but Virgil except for one TAC sergeant at AIT who called him Virgil Clarence. Nobody ever called him VC.

It was Huk who had almost gotten nicknamed VC. It happened because of the fuckup at Ban Me Thuot. He had been on point, and Virgil had been in the 2d Platoon. The VC had come in from the flank, 124th Main Force, and their right flank had moved right past him, on top of him before he knew it. There was some shooting on the right. About six VC walked right past him about a foot and a half away, he counted six, and when he realized they didn't see him, Huk held his breath and then breathed shallow so the bush wouldn't move. He hid like a rabbit. From behind the bush he had seen Truck go down. Truck was this big colored guy from Watts. "Oh, mama," Truck yelled. Was he calling his real mama, or was it the way he used mama to mean any woman? "Oh, mama," Truck kept groaning, "they've shot my butt off." Truck just kept saying that over and over. Huk wondered if he was really shot in the butt or what.

In the middle of the shooting Huk had popped straight up from the bush and shot a VC in the back. The man was no more than ten yards away, but he was looking in the other direction. Huk jumped up, zap, and the man went over head first like a rabbit. Then Huk popped back down again. It felt terrific, like bowling a strike. A few minutes later he saw another VC with his back turned and popped up again. Up, whack, over. Splat on his face. After the shooting stopped, when the VC were long gone, Huk crawled out of the bush and walked over to check them out. They were center shot and dead as doornails. They were the only two men he shot in the whole war. He flipped them over with the toe of his boot. They were heavier than he had thought, but their eyes were closed. For a minute he thought about breaking out his bayonet and scalping them. What the fuck was the matter with him? He saw Truck lying not five yards away with his mouth and eyes open and bugs already around the blood on his mouth. He couldn't bring himself to turn Truck over, even though he was pretty sure they hadn't had time to booby trap him. He just stared at the bugs crawling around Truck's mouth.

Some guys in the 2d Platoon had seen his up, zap, thud. A sergeant-major from MACV came out to interview him for the after-action report. "When an American unit takes a licking like Ban Me

Thuot, we like to learn something," he told Huk. "We put together a Lessons Learned packet. Now why don't you just tell me about it?"

Huk described everything he saw. He didn't see the point in it. He didn't see how it would be of any use to anybody. He told how he heard shooting on the right, saw six VC go by, and saw Truck go down. He told how he hid and shot two VC in the back. The guys from 2d Platoon corroborated his story, and the sergeant-major said they would probably put him in for a Bronze Star.

"He popped those suckers," one of the 2d Platoon guys said. "Just like a fucking VC his own self. Blap. Down. Blap again. Hey, VC!"

"Don't call an American soldier VC, son," the sergeant-major said.

"That's what he was like," the guy said. "Just like a fucking VC. Up he jumps and blap! Hey, VC!"

"Not a VC, son," the sergeant-major repeated. "Maybe a Huk. Same thing, but we made our peace with them. They had them in the Philippines, Hukabluks, we called them Huks. We whipped them, but they were tough little bastards. Your man here popped up like a Huk."

So he was Huk. He liked the sound of it. Like Buck. Like Hulk. Like Fuck. He had new name tags sewed on his jungle fatigues and wrote it on his steel pot where guys put things like, "Yea though I walk through the valley of the shadow of death I will fear no evil, for I am the meanest motherfucker in the valley." Huk.

Liz thought he was nicknamed after a character in a story. Liz thought it was for being some kind of barefoot, freckled-faced kid. He let her think that, except for telling her he spelled it without the c. She probably thought he couldn't spell it right or spelled it wrong for the look of it. He let her think whatever she wanted to.

He was dialing the number of the hospital. They gave him nursing, which gave him nursing personnel. "A male nurse, I think," he said. "We don't have any Willie Stallings," she said. "Just an old army buddy," Huk said. "I thought he worked there."

The telephone rang and it was Maggie again. "What did you find out?"

"Nothing," Huk said.

"Was he a Negro? It sounds like a Negro name."

"He didn't sound like a Negro," Huk said.

"He had some kind of accent," Maggie said.

"Not a Negro accent," Huk said. A Negro: Maggie had once marched with Martin Luther King. "He's not a Negro," Huk said.

"Check him out," Maggie said. "Think about the children for once."

Huk hung up. Goddamn Virgil. Before the panel he had intro-duced Huk to the other panelists. "This is Huk. He shot two VC in the back at Ban Me Thuot." Virgil laughed when he said it. What was funny about it? In the book it was Virgil who popped up and shot VC, but not in the back. One of the other panelists was a social worker who counseled vets. When it was his turn to talk, he said that ground soldiers had a different experience of the war than sailors and airmen. He said that analytical guys tended to analyze their experience, while stupid guys drank and beat their wives and acted out. He said that what you did coming out depended pretty much on what you were going in.

The social worker that Huk saw had reminded him that Maggie was not his enemy, that marriage was a negotiation, that you had to live with the other person after the negotiation was over. Okay, all right. "I was just a grunt soldier," Virgil said. Then he called on Huk.

Huk didn't know how to start. "I don't know what I learned in Vietnam," he began. Then all of a sudden he started talking about Maggie and his job, his folks and her folks. Shit. He told about four hundred people the complete story of his life, as much of it as he could tell in ten minutes. You could hear a pin drop in the auditorium. He wanted to stop, but he couldn't seem to find a stopping place. When he got to the divorce, he looked over at Virgil as if to say, Stop me, stop me, but Virgil was nodding, Go on, go on. Virgil *wanted* him to talk like that. He had his Virgil purposes. He had *expected* it.

"You were great, Huk," Virgil said afterward. "You were terrific. You were perfect." Perfect for what? Huk still didn't know what had gone wrong with Maggie. It had gone wrong right from the start. She had made him suck up to her mother. Instead of a honeymoon, they had taken a week at her family's lake cottage, so they wouldn't be too far away. Then her high school friends had turned up. They had been in the wedding party. The guy was headed for Vietnam. They had no place to go, so Maggie said they could stay in the living room in sleeping bags. When he woke up in the night, he couldn't even go to the bathroom. He had to be careful not to make a splashing sound. It turned out the friend got pregnant, right there on their honeymoon cottage floor. He should have said no. He should have put his foot down. He had mishandled it. What he did was drink Jim Beam straight from the bottle and sit outside on the little balcony banging his head against the concrete. After that, things were never right.

When Maggie asked him for a divorce, that was the first thing that popped into his mind. He should probably have been a lot tougher. Then again, maybe he should have been kinder and more patient and more understanding. There was no way to know. The honeymoon set the pattern. Maybe he should have tried harder to listen to her. Maybe they should have gotten marriage counseling.

Maybe he should have all out kicked the shit out of her. There was just no way to know.

He tried dialing Liz, but there was no answer. Liz had her friends, Liz had her little ways. "Look at me, look at who I really am," she was always saying. "Reveal yourself, let me see who you really are." Liz believed in Peace and the Sanctuary movement. She was afraid we were going to invade Nicaragua. "Haven't we learned anything?" she said.

"What about Hitler?" Huk said. Liz was Jewish. "Should we just let that kind of stuff happen? Should we have said prayers and given daisies to SS troopers?" Even as he said it, he felt bored and tired. More Hitler shit. "What about the Iranians? We should have creamed the bastards. We should have bombed their churches and schools and libraries like we did the Germans. We should have burned up their statues and paintings. We should have wiped out everything that makes an Iranian an Iranian, the way we did the Germans. We should have killed their god." Liz looked at him with an expression that said he just hadn't got it yet. He was messing up again. He changed the subject, and when it got late he took her home. He always took her home at the end of the evening, way the hell out to the far south side. The phone rang and rang, but Liz didn't answer. What would Liz know about handling a Willie Stallings anyway?

Huk opened his top desk drawer and took out his bank book. He had two-hundred and twenty seven dollars and thirty-nine cents. Just a little more than Stallings. He was paid up on child support and had no credit card balance. He could make it. He could swing forty bucks. So what if it was a scam? Forty bucks he would go for and not a penny more.

But what if Stallings was after more? Maybe Stallings was a crazy. Lots of guys came back from Vietnam with their brains scrambled. Maybe Stallings was somebody who knew him from somewhere, or thought he knew him. Huk's eyes fell on the bottom drawer. One thing was sure, he didn't know Stallings. Stallings was an unknown element. He eased the drawer open and pulled back the cheese cloth. Underneath was the Colt .32, oiled, maintained, and unregistered. He picked it up and held it in the palm of his hand. What the fuck was the matter with him? It was more dangerous to run around with a piece than without one. What was he thinking about?

He wiped the handle a little with the cheese cloth. What if Stallings was a certifiable loony? What if it was some kind of setup? He would feel more comfortable with a piece, was all. As long as he had a piece, he could take care of things. He popped the cylinder and spun it. It was empty. He looked down the barrel. There were five rounds in an open cartridge box. He couldn't remember when he had fired the rest of them. He had two other cartridge boxes, but they were unopened. That was okay. Five rounds was enough. Five from a Colt .32 were enough to blow any motherfucker away. He picked them up and put them in his pocket. He looked for something to put the piece in. There was a Saks Fifth Avenue bag that Liz had brought over sandwiches in. He stuffed the pistol in. Then he wrote out a check for a hundred bucks. He could make it to the end of the month on sixty.

While he waited at the drive-in his mind was racing. He wondered if anybody had ever robbed a bank from the drive-in window. He wondered if the glass was bullet-proof. It was a weird kind of thing to think. Having a piece in the car made him feel weird. He took his time getting to the Edens. It was no time to get pulled over for a moving violation. He didn't even swear at the construction people. It was like L.A., he thought, if he felt like it, he could roll down his window and blaze away at any motorist who gave him any shit. What the fuck was the matter with people anyway? He turned onto the Ike, gave an eighteen wheeler the finger, turned off at Racine, and pulled over to put the rounds into the cylinder. He made sure that the first one was in the firing chamber. Lock and load, he thought. He put the piece back in the Saks bag and started cruising the area, looking for the emergency entrance.

When he saw it, he knew he had a problem. It wasn't one of those semicircular drives, like he had imagined, like the one at Rush-Pres. It was a dead-end fucking L. He had imagined himself driving up there slowly, casing the setup with the piece in the Saks bag below window level, ready to pull away like a helicopter aborting an LZ. But there was no pulling away here. There would be no way to abort. It wasn't laid out that way. If he went in, he went in naked, on foot. He hadn't pictured it that way at all. He hadn't even thought about walking in the entrance with a pistol. What if there were metal detectors? What if there was a security check? There were two cop cars parked in the pivot of the L, a university cop and a city blue and white. He decided to circle the block again. While he circled, a new idea crept into his head. What if the cops were part of a setup? Forty bucks. What if Stallings was copping a plea and he was the pigeon? He would hand over forty bucks, Stallings would drop a packet of cocaine on him, and cops would come rushing out of every direction. If he was carrying a piece, well, that would just ice the cake.

Where was Virgil in all this? He was off in Washington where he couldn't be reached to reference the guy, getting ready to run for Congress. Supposedly. Maybe Virgil was in on the setup, for one of his Virgil purposes. Huk checked the dashboard clock: a minute to eleven. A minute to jump off. He took the Saks bag and shoved it under the seat on the passenger side as far as it would go. He took out forty bucks and stuffed it back in the bank envelope. He wrote on the envelope: FOR WILLIE STALLINGS, AIR FARE, HAVE A NICE TRIP. Then he wrote the address where he worked: TO RETURN THE LOAN. He pulled over under the railroad tracks at the top of the L. He took in a deep breath, then let out about half of it. Okay, he thought, step off.

He walked fast, not toward the entrance but toward the side door he had spotted while circling. He wanted to come in on the room from the flank. He pushed through the outer set of doors. So far so good, no cops, no metal detectors. He could probably have brought the piece. There was just an old guy filling out a form and a couple of secretaries with their heads turned the other way. Okay so far, but keep moving, he told himself. There was another set of glass doors, and behind them, whatever. He popped around the frame for a look, then back again, like he had forgotten something. He caught a glimpse of somebody in the waiting room, wearing light green. There was a pile of books and stuff on the waiting room table. He thought it over. He could probably have brought the gun. Fuck it. He took a deep breath, let most of it out, and stepped through the doors.

Stallings was standing next to the table, looking out the front entrance with a thousand-yard stare. As soon as he saw him, Huk knew. He was wearing a pale green orderly's smock. He was short. He had sort of narrow sloping shoulders. He was standing like a man who had been pounded by a two by four every night for about twenty years. Huk was on top of him before he knew there was anybody else in the room. "Willie Stallings?"

"You came," Stallings said. He blinked twice and held out his hand. "I think I was a little late. Did you go back in there looking for me?"

"Yeah," Huk said.

"I appreciate this," Stallings said. "You being willing to come down here and help me out."

"That's okay," Huk said. He noticed the bullet crease on Stallings' neck. He didn't like to look into Stallings' watery eyes. There was something soft about Stallings. He was probably homosexual, Huk decided, or completely nonsexual. His eyes ran over the hospital smock. He didn't like to think what Stallings' body would look like underneath it. Guys sometimes insisted on showing their soft white bodies covered with knotty red welts and shrapnel scars. "I'm a P.A.," Stallings said, pointing to the smock. "Physician's assistant."

Huk nodded. Christ. They had killed the poor bastard over there and sent him home anyway. He held out the envelope. "Here it is," he said. "Have a safe trip. Are you sure it's enough?"

"It better be," Stallings said.

"Be sure," Huk said. "I could let you have twenty more."

"Forty is fine," Stallings said.

"Okay, then. Have a safe trip," Huk said. He started to hold out his hand for a handshake.

"Wait a minute," Stallings said. "Hold on, I want to give you something. It's right here."

Huk pulled his hand back. Christ! What now? He didn't know whether to hit the guy as hard as he could or run like hell. But Stallings was just rummaging around in the books and pamphlets. Huk could see that they were all veteran shit. The whole stack must have belonged to Stallings. "It's here somewhere," Stallings said. "You seen the Wall?"

"Yeah," Huk lied. He wouldn't visit the fucking Wall if they helicoptered him in.

"What did you think of it?"

"Think of it?"

"The Wall," Stallings said.

"I liked it," Huk lied again. "I basically liked it." He watched Stallings rummage through the pamphlets. No gun, no dope. Just veteran shit. The poor bastard, he spent his life wandering around with an armful of veteran shit. The war was going to be the only thing that ever happened to him in his life.

"Here," Stallings said. "Here it is. I want you to have this."

It was a post card with a picture of the Wall. Huk looked at it for a minute, then he looked back into Stallings' watery eyes. Stallings had needed to give him something. "Thanks, man," he said.

"I was Americal division," Stallings said.

"Thanks, and have a safe trip," Huk said.

"Good luck to you," Stallings said. He reached out to shake Huk's hand. "Say hello to Virgil, you see him."

"I will," Huk said. "Thanks."

They shook hands. It was like shaking hands with a corpse. They had killed the poor bastard over there. Thanks, he'd said. What the fuck was he thanking the guy for? What the fuck was wrong with him? He turned and walked out the entrance. When he got to the car, his hands suddenly started to shake. He reached under the seat on the passenger side and took out the Saks bag. He took out the pistol, flipped the cylinder, and removed the bullets. Christ. He had been ready to blow the poor motherfucker away. He put the empty gun back into the Saks bag and shoved it under the seat. He put the postcard of the Wall on the dash. What the fuck was the matter with people?

He turned on the ignition and the radio and the air conditioner and just sat there waiting for his hands to stop shaking. What the fuck was the matter with him? What the fuck was the matter with Virgil, trying to tell people what they had learned? They hadn't learned shit. They could shove their Lessons Learned packets straight up their ass. He pulled slowly away from the curb. In the rear view mirror he could see an ambulance three blocks away come tearing ass about half out of control. He hadn't learned shit. All he had learned was not to fight that particular war in that particular place at that particular time with that particular enemy. At least not in that particular way. Anyway, not if it was a Friday morning.

Laurie Levy

COMING BACK A STAR

(from *Chicago Magazine*)

Afrer Howard ran away with the topless dancer with the magenta snake tattooed across the back of her neck, Ruth gave almost everything he left behind to the Salvation Army. She kept the boots— they were fleece-lined and slid on easily over her tap shoes.

Tonight, Ruth was wearing Howard's boots over her silver-satin high heels, dressed up to see the great director, king of movie musicals, in person at the Orpheum. Howard once said she was obsessed with movie musicals. He said she was reliving her Las Vegas glory days and, if she felt that way, why in hell had they come back to Chicago? "I'll take my music and celebs in the flesh," Howard said; he missed the action. And the spotlights, and gelatin the color of ripe mangoes *see! the lady's flesh is gold rotating as her snake dips and coils and gongs ring over Ruth's right eye Look Howard! She's smiling at you do you know her? Howard?*

(No doubt he had returned to Vegas. Once a croupier . . . .)

Ruth was on her way to Broadway, zigzagging through slats of April sleet. Ice turned the young dead trees in the churchyard to Plexiglas. Mannequins with garnet smiles winced as the wind hurled sleet against store-front windows. Easter-egg colors ran together as Ruth streaked by, smooth as a moon ray sliding on glass.

A blond rinse disguised her gray hair.

Blue jeans concealed the black leotard and the Cyd Charisse net stockings, relics from her days in show business. Under a lumber jacket, Ruth wore a silver lamé T-shirt, no bra. Silk-lined, the T-shirt protected her nipples from irritation, but coaxed them to jut in youthful prescience. What else? Sunglasses to hide the theatrical make-up . . . . The diamonds! She checked before the traffic light turned green, found the earrings still hidden inside her coin purse. Someone, Howard probably, was turning a key in her side as if she were a wind-up doll, tighter with every step until she trotted round

the corner and saw the marquee just ahead, and he let go: sprack! The thrill ripped him stem to stern like a lightning bolt, for which good riddance. She hurried past Woolworth's. Through her green lenses, the neon tubes shimmered and wagged like wet pink tongues: O-R-P-H-E-U-M. From Orpheus . . . memory good as ever. Mama said it was ultraflexible femurs and where would you be without me and your God-given . . . but it was all those years of tap and tap-tap
SHUF-fle, Ruthie
KICK! and one-AND
Howard said that her memory compensated for her myopia. Howard was probably having a hell of a blast in Vegas, and welcome to all that glitz and crap. She was happier here, running her dancing school. All hers—her money, her reputation—and so convenient, just a few blocks from home. And what about the kids and their blessed parents who paid their bills on time, and the dentist on the floor below? Perfect landlord—stone deaf, but his heart was melted butter. Who else would offer another long-term lease, same rates as before, especially since the New Town folks had sent the rents to heaven? (Up there with Howard. "Died in his sleep of a bad heart," she'd told the dentist. Mama used to squirt liquid Ivory into her mouth when she lied, but the dentist sent a basket of carnations, red ones, big and lush as beefsteak tomatoes. Much nicer than the funeral wreathes when Mama died.)

She loved Broadway, Belmont, the old neighborhood. Chicago fit Howard like a tight shoe; she'd figured someday he'd get out of it. Exactly two months Tuesday since Howard waltzed off with his dandruff, bad heart, and the tattooed lady, the very day the school had begun to run in the black . . . .

She joined the crowd queuing into a line that snaked into the alley. Lumber jackets, jeans, boots. She examined everyone from behind the green lenses. A bald, scarred gentleman preceded her. *Film Digest* protruded from a pocket of his blood—or ketchup—stained trenchcoat. In front of him: a hulking *der Tod* apparition wearing a cloak like a shroud, her large buffalo head lowered as if about to charge. She was accompanied by a tall, fragile adolescent who now and then scraped the helix of his ear with a fingernail. Behind Ruth, two academics turned from analyzing a screenwriting course at Columbia to the Film Festival Tribute last night. " . . . That's why he's here. They say he'll get the Academy Award for *Mafia War.*"

"De Sade in the end zone, fans. No wonder he quit making musicals."

"Think he'll show, after last night? The VIPs?"

Ruth whirled, quietly severe. "Excuse me, but he went to this very theatre when he was a boy. The paper said he'd be glad to make room in his crowded schedule, a lovely honor like this."

The young men grinned. "His kind of town," one said. An air of festive edginess gripped the crowd as it neared the ticket window, music building in bodies rocking slightly in the liquid wind; small silent sobs of anticipation were in the wind. During the winter the neighborhood had gone shabby, but the tiny jewel-box Orpheum smarted with fresh gilt. Neon, blue-violet as a bruise, announced from the ticket window: AN EXPERIMENTAL THEATRE FIRST: COMPUTERIZED PERSONNEL***ARS LONGA, VITA BREVIS***—The Management . . . which possibly explained the fact that the woman behind the ticket counter was a waxen dummy, but Ruth was surprised.

The hulking woman's mouth emerged from the folds of her cloak. "A promotional gimmick," she told the adolescent at her side.

Ruth paid for her ticket and bobbed along as if carried in warm water into the lobby. The automated wax mannequin behind the popcorn counter dispensed "buttered" and "unbuttered" if one pressed the appropriate button. A man in the popcorn line hummed *I Wish I Were in Love Again* from *Words & Music*, and Ruth said quietly, "The Previn arrangement." His smile, all hot-milk teeth, thawed her icy fingers. She felt the satin slippers moving within Howard's boots, lifting her down the aisle. The lights dimmed. A muffled cloop-swish of spreading velvet and, on the screen, the opening of *On the Town;* she plunged into the sound colors—*New York! New York!* The audience exhaled, a collective jubilant sigh.

This was home. This was where she belonged. She opened her purse, exchanged her sunglasses for her clear lenses, reveled in chiaroscuro, and oh, the music. Bernstein! She knew every word. Moisture formed between her legs under the leotard under the jeans, Lord, like that stagefright lurch at the brink of a routine, waiting for the beat and the notes fell away like stars . . . heel and toe, now the spin and into *Howard's arms, a color wheel of flowers falling under him the warm fluid forms a puddle on rumpled sheets hey I could go round again you used to be able hell Ruthie you're getting too old to cut the . . .*

Tensing her thighs, she stared at the screen. Her favorite film clips, every one. Her silver-satin slippers, free of the heavy brown boots, moved in rhythm. (Surely she always had the talent.)

Kelly's *Singin' in the Rain; Get Happy* from *Summer Stock.* Astaire, Garland, Rooney, beloved frames. She began to cry softly— others cried out too from time to time; she longed to burrow into the thick scratchy wool of the old theatre cushion, hands (impeccably manicured nails) greasy with popcorn butter, the music sweeping into her throat. Her tears dropped from heavily mascaraed lashes, fell sweet and warm against the layers of foundation creme and rouge.

The screen colors ebbed. Ruth trembled when the lights began to flicker . . . house lights; they could *see* her. There was movement in the small theatre, several people fleeing to avoid interaction, faces averted. She too began to rise, but a rotund man had appeared onstage, arms extended to greet a tall man who hurried up the steps, across the stage apron, and Ruth sank back into her seat, frozen.

"Music!" roared the tall man, his endless mane of silver hair crackling in his vehemence. *That's Entertainment* instantly resounded from the loudspeakers. "Music will comfort you. Stay where you are! Don't be afraid!" The tall man's eyes flickered with laughter. A minute star danced on his upper left bicuspid. His nose and jaws were massive, as if carved from luminous rock.

The rotund man said, "I am Devane, California film historian, here in Chicago to field your questions to the greatest director of them all, and I'll begin . . . ." His tin voice played in small orange counterpoint to Lerner and Lane. The questions began. "What do you think of . . . ?" "What was she like?" The usual plea for the resurgence of the American Musical. The smiling man from the popcorn line rose: "Do you realize I have a niece out in Omaha who'll never see *Showboat*, other than on the hot screen? Never sing Kern's lyrics leaving the theatre? Never know the tragedy of Ava Gardner as Julie?" Several offered consoling hands. In spite of his syntax, they all understood. Ruth thought: We are together. I am one of them.

Devane attempted middle register. "The musical per se is dead."

There were groans. The hulking woman with the buffalo head raised a quivering hand. Ruth, across the aisle, urged her on silently.

"Yes, madame?" The voice of the great director was hot fudge but authoritative. *Love Is Here to Stay* oozed from the loudspeakers. The woman croaked, "Give us more musicals. Give us back our dreams." The adolescent pulled her into her seat, where she deflated like a huge gray life raft. When the audience cheered, she growled, "Cue!" and the boy recited: "Dreams are all we have." He began to dance on the narrow carpeted lane between the aisles.

"Down in front," someone said, but the others cried, "It's the music makes him dance" and "The young have no inhibitions."

"Give it all you got, Hermie," the hulking woman murmured, and Ruth remembered Mama. ("College! You crazy? You already got a trade. How many kids in your class get to be a Chez Paree Adorable?")

The questions went on and on.

"Now, the great director is ready to find one of you." The butterball historian wiped his face with a lacy handkerchief and trilled, "A once-in-a-lifetime screen test." The hulking woman stage-whispered, "*Go*, Herm," the director loomed, Moses on the mount, and Ruth was ready.

Hermie's feet flew in the aisle. He kicked higher and higher.

The great director thundered, "Who was Gene Kelly's co-star in *Cover Girl*? Name two hit songs from that film."

The thrill ricocheted through the silver lamé as Ruth raised her hand. "Rita Hayworth. *Long Ago and Far Away* and *Make Way for Tomorrow.*"

Several agreed, "Yes, yes, she's right."

"Sit down, Hermie," the hulking woman muttered.

"Who did the *Hat in Haiti* number in *Royal Wedding*? Who wrote the music for *Rich, Young & Pretty*?" And Ruth replied, "Astaire! Nick Brodszky did the score for *RY&P.*"

Yeses hissed in shared obsession rippled through the scarlet and gilt auditorium of the Orpheum theatre. Ruth clutched her empty popcorn box and waited, poised, oblivious of the world . . .[1]

"Who did the costumes and make-up for *Singin' in the Rain*? Who wrote *Treat Me Rough*?" Sparks single-filed from the great director's eyes like a sequined rope extending down the steps and up the aisle where Ruth sat tapping her silver slippers to the music she heard: "Helen Rose, costumes; Guilaroff, make-up. The Gershwins' song for *Girl Crazy.*"

Empathetic awe hushed the audience. She was their pilot, flying them home on Christmas Eve. Hermie stared at his hulking mother and then at Ruth, his mouth open, panting.

"Name the ringmaster dancing in *Carousel*. And Danny Kaye's leading lady in *Up In Arms.*"

"Jacques D'Amboise," Ruth said crisply. "And Dinah Shore."

"And the French co-star, male, of *An American in Paris*?"

"Georges Guetary," Ruth said to bravos, applause, cheers.

The director's pupils cast a single beam of light, narrowing the distance between them. The strings and harp climbed the scale fortissimo and fell away like drops of fountain water. She was flying down the bars of a song, no longer aware of the crowd, the chorus about her; she saw only her interrogator on the dais. Devane in his maribou boa giggled again in exultation

as Howard's undulating lady building
rhythm to finale blurs to writhing snake
and children's tops go spinning faster to
the drum-pulse brass crescendo at which
Howard swallows his gum . . . .

"And the final question," the director's voice was warm honey, throbbing with ardor: "Name the actor who played Jerome Kern in *Till the Clouds Roll By.*" A pause. "And who played Mrs. Kern?"

---

1 *not to mention Las Vegas, where Howard's left the roulette wheel, stopped taking bets. With feckless yearning eyes, he watches the woman on the stage, the magenta snake tatooed across the back of her neck, bumping and grinding into the first bars of a new Elton John number . . .*

(In the lobby of the Orpheum, circuits shorted in a sudden spraat. Wax melted, plastic cracked.)

"Take your time," the director urged.

(The munching mannequin behind the popcorn counter sank slowly under the avalanche of "buttered" and "unbuttered." No one would notice.)

"Robert Walker played Kern," Ruth said. "Dorothy Patrick was Mrs. Kern."

"Come," the director murmured, and Ruth threw off her jeans and lumber jacket, revealing the silver lamé shirt, the leotard, and net stockings. She removed her glasses, affixed her earrings,[2] left the boots and clothes in a pile under the seat. She was floating in her satin slippers and it was the way it used to be, the spotlight on her, down the aisle, while the audience sang a long protracted Oh of love and desire. She had a final sense of people rising, merged clusters, knots of lumber jackets and jeans, people backing slowly toward the exits . . . and the music played on, show music guiding Ruth toward the steps, where the rotund film historian had vanished.

The steps were slick with a soft, sweet substance—slippery butter or sugar syrup, and Ruth extended her hands, which the great director took, leading her slowly, lovingly, across the proscenium . . . he lifted her gently, as if through an iceberg, into and beyond the whiteness of the dead screen.

---

2 rhinestones, actually—(a one-time gift from Howard)

Hilding Johnson

LAST RIGHTS

(from *Other Voices*)

Now that he was dying, they gave him back to her. She slept in his room on a cot they brought in and placed beside his bed; it was cool and hard with clean taut sheets.

The first nights he had held her hand, seeking it out in the darkness, settling it hard against his palm like an amulet, but he had forgotten that now. He had begun to sleep hard and gracelessly, frowning, the breath catching deep in his throat in a webby snore.

He had awakened, startled, in one of the long evenings when the television set murmured and she did her needlepoint in the muted, still light.

"God. I wasn't snoring, was I?" He had wiped a corner of his mouth with his hand.

"No."

"I hate snoring." His hand trembled; he put it beneath the sheet.

"I know."

"I hate it." But he could not hold on to the thought. She could see the outrage, puzzling, linger after the idea, and then his eyes had lost their knowledge and he had slid into sleep.

In the mornings she would take the elevator several floors up and eat her breakfast in the hospital cafeteria. It was a bright room, sunny, with the cheerful air of a nice luncheon restaurant, the sort she had used to frequent with women friends. There were geraniums in pots, and through the windows a view of the city, which was pleasant from this height. The mood was ordinary and sensible, for no one here was sick. There were only the healthy who attended the sick—doctors and nurses and kin and friends.

While she ate, nurses prepared her husband for a new day. It was the one ritual for which they had not lost heart—the others, all the elaborate and arcane exercises which had been performed in hopes of killing his killer before it could kill him, having been abandoned. There was left only the advent of a new day and the necessity of addressing it: teeth to be scoured, the body to be washed and dried and powdered like a child's, hair to be combed, a clean gown. They did a day's maintenance, nothing that smacked of the future, and once, he had asked her, petulantly, to clip his nails since his keepers were not so inclined.

She had been afraid of her strength, unsure of her skill. She held his hand in hers too tightly or too lightly, she was not sure which, and the little crescents of white horn fell on the sheet.

He said, "They say they keep growing."

"What do you mean?"

"When you're dead. They keep growing."

"Stop it."

"And hair. Hair, too."

"I said stop!" She dropped his hand.

He examined his fingertips. "I think it's sort of interesting."

"It isn't."

"Yes, it is." He ran a finger down the inside of her arm.

"Don't."

"Kiss me."

"No. You're being vile."

He laughed. "Kiss me."

His breath was light and quick, his lips were dry.

It was not Doctor Stern who had shown her the pictures of his death. It was another man, a man she had not seen before, one who did nothing but photograph such things. He was young and very clever. They stood in a small room which was lit from all sides and he put transparent pictures on the bright walls in rows one after the other and he explained where death was in them, tracing it with his finger, snatching quick, oblique glances at her breasts and thighs as he did so. There. And there.

The cancer was grown up, pretty and branched like a vine, around the spine, putting out tendrils even now—she saw them, delicate spirals, pale and tender like morning-glory shoots—tease his jaw and tickle the base of his brain.

Here, the young man said. And here.

He took many more proofs of his argument out of a brown envelope and began to clip them to the bright wall.

No, she said, and turned away. I believe you.

Gregory would visit them in the early evening. When he was not going to be able to come, he would call. The telephone would ring at three-thirty—never more than a few minutes earlier or later—and she knew it would be Gregory. She did not know which she hated more: his coming, his appearance in the door, bumbling and apologetic in his perfect health, or his precise calls which were still more awkward and obsequious, all of it only the thinnest of covers for his immovable will.

She would pick up the telephone on the first ring, glancing, always, at her husband who never woke.

"Susan?"

"Yes."

"It's Gregory."

"I know."

"I can't be there today."

"It's all right."

"There's a client I have to see tonight. And dinner was the only time . . . ."

"It's all right. It's fine."

"I'm very sorry."

"You don't have to be sorry, Gregory." She would start to pace then, as far as the cord would let her, to the window and back.

"I could stop by later."

"You do not have to come, Gregory."

"If I took my client to one of those little West Side places, I could stop by . . . ."

"Please. Don't rearrange your evening."

"It wouldn't be hard."

She reached the window and leaned her forehead against the cool glass. "You are not under obligation to be here every day, Gregory. You are not under obligation to be here at all."

In the silence she could feel his hurt skittering out to her along the wire. She could see his pale brown eyes, wounded and blinking behind his glasses—which had slipped slightly—and then his finger, poking them up again. He said, "Well. I'll see you tomorrow then."

She pressed her face to the window. Perhaps it would shatter and her face would be sliced off like a piece of sausage in one of those machines, or a shard would pierce her brain and end everything with this moment.

"Susan?"

"Yes. Tomorrow."

Her husband's good times were in the early evening. The bustle of the supper meal was heartening. They would hear the cart coming along the corridor with its comfortable clink of cutlery and dishes, and there would be the homey, safe smell of gravy and stewed fruit and freshly brewed coffee.

She would put his tray on the table that extended over his bed (carefully, set so that nothing would press in any place against his delicate flesh), and take the covers off the little bowls and dishes of soup and eggs and custard.

And he would frown and say about the soup, "Ugh. Chicken again." But it pleased him to say it, it pleased her. It was so everyday, so ordinary—people were saying it at tables everywhere in the city at this moment; husbands in cars which winked far below in the dusky streets were on their way home to say just that.

She would say, "But you love chicken soup."

"Mm." He would not give up the frown but he would dip his spoon into the hot liquid quickly, the first swallows sipped eagerly. His hand shook, the spoon clanked against his teeth as though someone else were feeding him.

She would say, "It's good soup. They make good soup here."

"It's not bad."

Neither of them spoke of the fact that he ate less each night. He would slide the cover back over the bowl to hide the levels which rose inexorably like marks in a river's flood stage.

Gregory would come, breathless and earnest, as trays were being collected, just before or after the last red streak of day was pressed out of the night sky—it was all she knew of autumn this year, that it was darker each night he came and that he smelt of the cold, smoky twilight when he greeted her—and he would bring gifts. Large bags from department stores, parcels wrapped in paper and twine, small glossy sacks from exclusive boutiques: he came, always, laden.

"Look," he would say. "I saw this at Berger's." And he would unwrap a game, spilling cards and dice on the table and bed. "It's supposed to be interesting."

"Gregory," she would say. "You don't need to bring something every time you come."

He would shrug and go on unwrapping gifts: six perfect apples, a flask of lime-scented cologne in a cunning wooden box, a glossy book of photographs.

"This is ridiculous, Gregory. You must not spend this kind of money on such nonsense."

Her husband would laugh. "Don't be such an ingrate, Susan. Don't be such a drudge."

For her Gregory would take out from some bag a carton of little sticky pork ribs from a Chinese restaurant, or a damp, wax-paper-wrapped sandwich of spicy corned beef, and a handful of caramels—dark and nut-filled—which she loved and which could only be purchased at a distant confectionery. He would set them out apologetically on the table, the candy wet and melted a little from being held too close to his body in his jacket pocket. "I know hospital food gets tiresome . . . ." he'd say.

And she hated that he had known the day, the hour when she knew she could not bear one more dinner of the carefully plain poached fish and canned peach halves. And that, unasked, he filled her need, made up the shortfall. And she hated even more that sometime during the evening she would eat what he had brought. She would watch the two of them play whatever game it was they had decided upon this time and she would find herself with full, sticky fingers and with grease upon her chin.

Gregory would glance up, pleased. He would poke his glasses into place. "Is it good?"

"Yes."

Grinning, he would shake the dice and send them flying across the board. "I thought you'd like that."

He would not allow her to go hungry.

Sometime before the last card had been turned or the last move played out her husband would become distracted.

She and Gregory were together in it, their vigilance for the first dropped die or syllable, the two of them taut and prepared. A counter would miss its mark, would shoot from her husband's fingers onto the floor, making a little rackety shiver.

Alert, she would look at Gregory and he at her. Then she would put down her needlework and bend to retrieve the game piece.

"God. Just leave it, will you?" Her husband would shove the board away, and bits and pieces of brightly colored wood and pasteboard would fly out over the coverlet and floor. His voice would be high, shaded with what seemed to be petty crankiness.

"Darling, do you want . . . ?"

"Just leave me alone. Leave me . . . Oh, God!" And he would turn suddenly, flopping like a fish with a strength she would not have believed he possessed.

Gregory would take him in his arms then, hold the snapping, weightless body to his own strong, dense one, and cradle it. They rocked together like some monstrous pièta. And Gregory would say, "Get her, Susan."

"Oh, God . . . ."

"Get her."

She would run, silent on the rubber tiles, and, in the bright glass cube at the end of the corridor, they would not be surprised to see her. "Please come."

A nurse would nod and pick up the little tray with its vial and syringe and they would speed back together—everyone knew their parts now; it was wonderful and amazing how deft were their hands and feet, how well they knew the steps of the dance.

They would come through the door and Gregory would turn her husband, would shift him, would jerk up the thin cotton gown to expose the white, sunken flank with its joints bulging like unnatural growths—and she would always know a moment of terror: where had they gone, those strong, beautiful thighs which had held her, had commanded and driven her?—and then the needle would slip, sly, beneath the loose skin and squeeze peace into them all.

They would put him then beneath the coverlet, his body with no will or opinion of its own. And when he was settled she and Gregory would pick up the room—shove uneaten food and used napkins into the trash pail, arrange games in their boxes, close books.

She would stand with him for a moment in the darkened corridor outside the room. He seemed very big in his heavy winter coat, clumsy; his hands were always jammed down into the pockets. He would say, "I think the new stuff they're giving him is better, don't you?"

"I guess so. Yes."

"It's faster."

"Yes."

He would glance at her—not head-on, but from the side—and his eyes would have a sad, anxious cast to them which, with the shade of his long lashes, made them very pretty. "Would you like some pâté? I thought I'd bring some."

"If you like."

"It wouldn't be hard. There's this new little restaurant near the office . . . ."

"All right. Fine."

"Tomorrow."

"Tomorrow."

And he would go and she would watch him. It was so easy for him! The line from his nape to his heels so fluid and sure—he never thought about his walk, his steps—and he would stand in the brightly lit elevator car and just before the door closed he would wave—a small, tentative flicker, too late for her to wave back.

When she went back into the room her husband's eyes would be neither open nor closed but slits of hard-boiled white beneath the lids. His breathing would be noisy, loosely spaced. She would move about the room, restless, not able to resign herself to sleep.

Occasionally he would speak, his voice startling, his speech clear. Once he had said, "What would we do without Gregory?"

She had not replied.

"He's a good man, Gregory." There was a long pause, minutes, everything seeming to have gone by, been forgotten, then: "I suppose you'll marry him."

"Don't."

"Our Gregory. Him."

"I won't marry again."

"Our Gregory."

"Stop." She put her hand over his, and she could feel that she was beginning to lose herself. Tears dropped in fat, hot splashes on their fingers, and they must be hers. "Please don't do this."

"I hate him," he said, and slid away from her into sleep.

Doctor Stern began to come once again more frequently. He would stand at the foot of the bed and watch her husband.

She would say, "He seems less wakeful," and the doctor would nod. They had crossed some frontier on some night not long ago: where once they had wished, on his behalf, consciousness, now they wished oblivion.

On his way out, the doctor would touch him, would put her husband's hand on top of the sheet if it had been under, tuck it in if it had been out. It was an odd gesture which she herself had begun to perform, and whether it satisfied some deep need to help the helpless or only the compulsion to pretend animation on the part of the unmoving, she did not know. But they did it, all of them: they rearranged him.

In the evenings, Gregory would bring food for her that was soft and creamy, as though she too had become an invalid—rich, pale yellow vanilla ice cream, thick, eggy milk shakes. He played solitary games with cards or plastic cubes.

Sometimes, she would go downstairs to the hospital chapel. It was not what she would have wished; it was a silly, sterile place muffled in thick, beige carpet. At the front hung a softly back-lit blonde wood cross—not suitable for crucifixion. A pointless cross.

And sometimes Gregory would find her there.

He would creep into the room, carefully easing the door closed, and slide into the pew in front of her, his broad shoulders obliterating everything else.

She said once, "Why do you do this? Why do you come?"

He shrugged miserably.

"It doesn't mean anything to you."

He hunched forward; the muscles across his shoulders flexed and swelled against his jacket.

She knew those shoulders, knew the taper from shoulder to waist, knew the secret, sweet swellings in his flesh and how they felt beneath her hands. She had seen him raise his arms over his head to pull off his shirt, and her eyes had followed that hem as it retreated over his bright, taut flesh, and her hands had followed her eyes.

She remembered that he always took his glasses off last, that the first time she had laughed at how long he had waited—until nearly the last moment before removing them and folding them gravely and carefully and putting them, glass up, on the sill—and when she had seen his eyes she had known why he had waited, so guileless they were, so beautiful and gently flawed, with none of the defenses an adult is expected to maintain. His eyes tempted her to protect him. Or hurt him.

In the spongily upholstered pew, she had started to weep. She said to him, "Why do you come here? You don't understand anything at all."

It was the day before Thanksgiving that Doctor Stern came four times, and when Gregory arrived he took him aside to speak to him in the corridor.

Gregory told her he would stay the night and she said no, but he did not listen and sat in the uncomfortable chair by the television set, his legs stretched out in front of him, his head nodding against his chest.

She sat, Indian-fashion, on her cot. The moon moved slowly like a cold, gauzy ribbon across her feet.

In her hands she held a gold foil box Gregory had given her that evening. Very early in the morning she opened it. Inside there were four chocolates. They were molded in the shapes of leaves and shells; they were very pretty and costly.

"How could you do this?" Her voice was loud in the night room.

Gregory awoke quietly, coming to himself at once as he always did.

She said, "How could you bring such things here? Now?" And she began to weep, and this time she could not stop.

He came to her and wrapped her about with his arms and legs and they sat, one within the other like Chinese boxes, on the narrow, hard bed. Beneath her cheek his heart beat in a simple, exact rhythm which never stumbled.

Angela Jackson

FROM TREEMONT STONE

(from *TriQuarterly*)

I grew up in a neighborhood, a block of time frozen like dry ice
from which a heat arises. A drugstore and mailbox stood on one
corner. A paperstand on the other. A cluster of churches completed
the block, while down the street men and a few women wandered in
and out The Butterfly Inn. We peeked through the dim windows of
that place during daylight and saw night, the only constellation a
neon sign saying "Hamm's. The beer refreshing." Where the big
brown bear splashed into a lake of blue (it must be) beer. Hamm's.
One time Junior said the drunkman on the block was one of the
"children of Hamm's." Mama had to smile, but told him don't be
so smart.

Everyone had a place on Arbor Avenue. Mr. Rucker who was
the drunkman, Uncle Blackstrap who was the junkman, Miss Rose
who was Eddie's mother and no one's wife, Miss Wilson who was
the head lady, my father who was the good man you better not mess
with his kids, my mother who was the sun. And a host of women,
men and children.

From the drugstore Mama bought medicine on time. Everything did not come in a package. And people knew how to open
things, like their hearts and conversations with strangers.

Summer nights Mama and Miss Rose brought their kitchen
chairs outside to circle the stoop. Passersby could eavesdrop on
parental melodies, "bring me some ice-cold water," "run upstairs
and get me my crochet bag," and "y'all get off that curb before one
of the cars go out of control and come up on the curve on you."
Passersby could eavesdrop and ease up on the tension of walking
unfamiliar streets because our block sounded like home.

In the absence of elders we children would sing aggressively to
the women walkersby who interrupted our double-dutch rope tricks,
who broke into our Red Rover lines, who zigzagged through our
Captain May I, who wore a certain style—tight skirt, skinny heels,
and bracelets. Gold-hoop gypsy earrings. We'd sing disapprovingly,

gleefully, to their posteriors which were roundly outlined by the skirts fitting like stretch marks. "Shake it. Don't break it. It took the good Lord a long time to make it," we'd croon to the women who were no-one-we-knew's mothers.

"Nine months, Baby," a lady would sass back at us. This was a traditional call and response. A childish repartee. Harmless and endearing. More than likely it was a memory from the hamlets and towns of the South, something learned and transplanted to the City by the Lake. Something carried from Mimosa, Letha, Alligator, Greenwood, Leland, Indianola, Meridian, Monroe, Pine Bluff, Little Rock, Birmingham, Tuskegee and Tougaloo. In cars loaded down with children, luggage and survivals, our parents with hard hands and dreamy eyes and mouths thick and heavy with country colloquialisms followed the rivers to the booming factories, yards and tenements in the North where the dwelling places buffeted back the huge wind that took off from the lake like a plane or a giant bird. The wind called the Hawk, who tore the skin off your bones and set the bones to knocking on the street corners while you waited for the bus or a dream to come by.

They settled in the rambling houses on two wide boulevards setting off a part of the South Side, a mile or so from the lake, on the edge of a university and the surrounding posh section inhabited by well-to-do whites. The Black section small and contained for fifty years or more was called Bronzeville. Bronzeville in its earliest days was the home of the Blacks who served the wealthier whites and the factories and yards of industry (especially when the unions struck and owners opened their doors to Blacks).

Trains then were the veins and arteries of the nation, not a free-floating circulatory system of the sky; and dapper men of color with quick, quiet tread skimmed the railed ropes to the heart of the country, which was this City by the Lake where the Hawk, who did not then have a name, blew and tore the skin off people and the hordes of farm beasts routed there for dying. The Hawk tore the bowelly stink off the cows and pigs and spread the odor over the Irish section, the Jewish section, the Black, and then the Central European sections. The traveling men who came with the trains made homes in Bronzeville. Places for quick loving, good food, fast women and shuffling cards. Out of those places came music that captured the mood and pulse of a people. My daddy told me about that music, while he hummed it under the kitchen sink as water ran down his arms and the stubborn pipes moved under his hard turnings.

My daddy was always fixing things in that house he bought from the widowed white woman who moved to Florida. All the houses on our street were obtained from fleeing whites who scrambled to escape the expansion of Bronzeville when the post-World War II farmers and laborers came from the too-unchanging South to the city they had heard about from cousins and kin who came down with stories of plenty and progress. But by then the houses of the European escapees gave off peculiar odors, mice, roaches and calls for repair. And my father was always answering those calls. The absentee landlords of the tenement that took up half the block turned scarce and the building began to die while the people in it thrived and multiplied.

In our house there always seemed to be a baby and a babysitter. I wonder if my mother found her own swollen stomach friendly? When she was round with Anne, Earnestine and Shirley climbed into her high, big bed and drew a big smile and button eyes in red ink across her belly. Mama mostly slept lightly, but not this time. They stroked so softly it was like being tickled. The baby was curved, full and content inside of her. When Mama woke and discovered the drawing she laughed and laughed, until she found it would not wash off so easily. Over a stretch-mark design it stayed a face for more than a week.

I thought that red mouth those smile-closed eyes were friendly, hilarious. When Mama brought Anne home from the bright Catholic hospital because the colored hospital, ill-staffed and broken down, had served her bologna that stuck in her chest when she lay after having given birth to Earnestine and Mama said nothing should be born there until they cared enough to make it a decent place for human beings—when Mama lifted the soft green blanket from Anne's face, exposed, it seemed to me, was the same face my two sisters had written on the round, outer ceiling of the ancient birth cave. Everybody had a laugh, thinking Ernee and Shir had seen into our mother's womb and translated who and what was hidden in nutritious water. Translated before its time. Or, their wish, perception, of such a joyous face was drawn into Anne Perpetua's humors. Anne is the funny one. They molded her into the sister-person of their desire. They founded a friend.

I began in the morning. Katherine Pearl was born around midnight. Sometime around the midnight train going by. Before or after the train whistle blew, she coughed out her birth. Which came first, the whistle or the scream?

Anne Perpetua was born laughing. When the doctor slapped her bottom she looked like a sweet clown or a saint with egg on her face. And she giggled to be here. She was given to appropriate and inappropriate laughter.

Once Earnestine dropped Anne. Anne began to laugh. Sympathy and panic were on my face, stamped in Anne's eyes reflecting me. Anne began to cry. She learned her pain from other people. Just as I did.

Honeybabe said she was retarded. Honey said that I was retarded too. Honeybabe says we all retarded. She is the oldest girl, and disdain is built into hierarchy.

Sometime in my preadolescence the double-dutchers began to sing a new song about disposable babies born with no certain sex and brutal destinies. They sang and I sang with them a song that came from out of the air:

> Fudge, fudge, fudge, boom, boom, boom
> Call the judge, boom, boom, boom
> Mama got a newborn baby
> Not a girl, boom, not a boy, boom
> Just an ordinary baby
> Wrap it up in toilet paper
> Kick it down the elevator.
> First floor, Mrs. Carter.
> Second floor, Mrs. Carter . . . .

On and on the baby flew, thrown away, sexless, a brown mistake. This was near the time of the birth of the ice-babies. The weather grew colder after the summery seasons of our early dreaming in the city. Expressways cut out memories that ran through the place once known as Bronzeville until even that name was forgotten. Families knocked against each other in the tall housing units thrown up by the city like dams to hold the deluge of Blacks who swelled past the limits of the town inside the city reserved for the darkest children of the American Dream. The old Southern gestures mutated and the young men learned new walks that leaned against the Hawk. These young men dipped in their knees. Boys gritted their teeth at an earlier age. Much of the game went out of the flirt, and girls no older than me or my sisters raised their skirts, babies fell out with gritted teeth and tears of ice.

Packed together in the frozen compartments of the public-housing projects that soared into the cold reaches of the Hawk's nest, children came out like clear, separated cubes of ice—hard and harder. The row of tall buildings that speared the sky, sparing no blue space, now (as if under the influence of a comic god) threw people away as used, spare parts.

There was a dog named Calypso. A terrible albino Doberman pinscher with long white teeth. Calypso chewed through wire that caged him and chased children's legs that moved like fascinating pistons just out of reach of his sharp face. One day he licked my calf and the fear made me break the sound barrier. My scream must have excited Calypso, who pursued me with greater zest. He was happy and evil; if he caught a child he would eat it. He could not catch me.

If you think of cruelty, think of albino haunches, fleet movement and white fangs. Cruelty is a colorless dance. Malice is a certain kind of motion that chews through wire and chases you and chases. It is not to be explained, and so fascinating that you must look at it. Look at it from over your shoulder, from behind a scream of terror and self-sympathy.

From our father, Sam Grace, Littleson learned to beat wood rats with shovels, then flip the earth and fold them in, furry, fat and poisoned bodies. Littleson caught roaches and stuck toothpicks up their tails and held them over the front stove burner, watching them crispen and curl while he laughed and I was appalled.

For Littleson these small acts of sadism were practical. I agreed with the intent, but hated the style and the delight that Littleson took in the pest-penalties. I refused to learn cruelty because I could refuse. Littleson efficiently grabbed the stray cats that lurked over the back stairwells to leap on the least suspecting. He took hold of the spitting, clawing beasts, and swung them by their tails, beating them against the back porch railing, then sent them sailing to the ground below. The cats hit the ground like terrified, but instinctual trapeze artists who know how to land on their feet. Centuries before cities had taught them this. Then they gunned across the ground like bullets with Littleson's special notch etched on their sides.

Littleson would dust his palms and stomp down the steps. Fearlessly. Without a swagger, more a glorified practicality. He was, in the moments after his raids on the roaches, the cats, and the rats, heroic. Larger than his still-boy self. He had mastered a degree of cruelty; he had triumphed in the hunt. He could walk in the company of men. He acquired new height.

The other boys, who were mostly the sons of renters, who had no place to protect, no territory to stalk and watch for, turned their cruelties elsewhere. They *boiled* into manhood. The liquor of them overflowed from their bodies and touched their fiery environment and their liquor smoked and steamed into a stench or a lingering musk that drove girls wild. Their aromas arrogant and chokingly alive. Promissory and profane. They could smell themselves.

The Watermelon Days belong to them. They pulled a plug out of summer and tasted their futures. They tapped and knocked a melon and heard the hollow fates. They tore their thirst from sweet, red meats and swallowed the black and brown seeds whole. They washed each other's faces in the green and pallid white rinds during the Watermelon Wars. After the battles they piled their flaccid weaponry in a garbage arsenal guarded by flies, and went back to the houses cursing each other, and wiping the wet from their faces before it syrupped in the sun.

They were the sons of men and women who owned nothing or little besides broken promises. They could grow up to be dangerously unfettered. They could grow up to be cart men who walked the streets and alleys like refugees from a war-torn landscape. They could be devil-may-care like young Uncle Blackstrap, or delirious like older Uncle Blackstrap.

They would always be happiest in summer. Every warm and shining summer day they'd drag their tow-cart lives over the divided avenues, carrying summer ice and various flavored syrups, a hunk of ice that they scraped, scooped and stuffed into triangular paper cones, then drenched with fruit tonic.

In winter they would pile rags and refuse (metal, paper; and porcelain toilet stool, face bowls and kitchen sinks) into the same wooden-wheeled stall and wheel it all to a yard to be weighed.

Money-things were plucked from garbage cans. Hands that delicately shoveled for wealth among the filthy odds and ends, in early fall touched the wet fruit remains of summer and remembered the feel of boyhood.

One summer day Littleson and I were eating watermelon. Our cheeks rimmed inside crescent watermelon moons. Littleson raised his foot and smashed what he thought was a roach. When he lifted his foot we did not see a roach-corpse or milky-white roach guts. There was nothing to despise; in the changing light it had been a trick of the eye. There was only, before us, an adult watermelon seed like a flat polished worry-stone perfect for the palm of a child's hand. Something to fondle the sensitive nerve. Something to touch.

It had been a magic trick of sunlight. Littleson had thought that the innocent seed that came with the sweet fruit was his natural enemy. A common mistake.

"Crawl, nigger. Crawl, worm. Crawl, dog. Got shit in yo' pants."

"Want me to put yo' nose in shit? Huh, fly? Roach? Worm."

"Stuff yo' mouth with it."

They beat him until they felt the texture of his muscles change. His head slick, syrupped over with his blood. His arms and legs limp as rubber tubing. His tongue a strap with no buckle, hanging out the side of his mouth. Mouth unhinged.

In a glistening, gritty pool of his own waste they left him where Uncle Blackstrap found him. Curious, casting a cursory glance in the basement window, a constant eye open for junk and refuse. The sight of the boy had made him sick. He took his gloves off. He wiped his mouth with the back of his hand. Erasing the scream before it was born there in the vacant basement. Soothing the vomit-reflex. Blackstrap was a man who had travelled in war-lands, where it rained shrapnel and stray pieces of human flesh. But World War II before atom bombs and death camps had been a kind of clean war. Hadn't it? That's what they'd said: A War Against Evil. In any case what he had seen was nothing like *this*. A boy who could have been his son. Ruined in this way.

The boy was so flaccid and still that Blackstrap was afraid to stir the rummaged organs. So he stumbled from the basement empty-handed, called an ambulance, the police, alarmed the Grace household, and carried something terrible on his tongue to Eddie's mother, Miss Rose.

What happened to Eddie was the first true clue that I had that the worst thing that could happen to a boy or a man was *not* to be unemployed.

Such cruelty, narrowed kitchenette whippings, wars of protection, sister fights over clothes, and hunting to nothing. The hate was too large to go inside us. It lurked, touched us, licked at us. This was the first news heard of the birth of the ice-babies. No one ever knew who hurt Eddie or why. But we knew they belonged to winter, and they were subject to tricks of the eye. They could fall on you like bandits, but they were not bandits. Because they were the ones who had been stolen from. They and Eddie, who did not die in the days after the beating, although all the doctors knew that he would.

Winter yawned in our faces, licked our hands and feet. Caroline would tell us stories of foolhardy boys who went outside without earmuffs, who'd lost their ears to the winter, as if the city winter were a war. The Hawk a guerrilla that ambushed across the boulevard.

Rising before the sun, our Littleson pulled a sled loaded with newspapers in the light that the moon sent over its shoulder, the first glance of sunlight.

Eddie was in the hospital all through winter. We were too young to visit him. Only Miss Rose saw him every day. But once or twice I went, and Littleson went twenty times and stood below Eddie's window so that he could see him. Eddie would look out through the frost-frescoed windows. He appeared to us, a shrunken head on a pointed stick-body, smiling like an angel. Blessing us.

In spring, when Littleson (who insisted on being called Lazarus more and more) stalked before our eyes, we made new markings on the doorframe to measure his growth. Eddie, out of the hospital, had come back old, walking on wobbly legs. Like a sailor who had been lost at sea too long. His legs folded up unexpectedly under him. Littleson would catch him and hold him tenderly like an autumn leaf that he refused to allow to touch the ground and be gone.

Littleson, now known as Lazarus, who he had always been, would not let Eddie mark off his height on our doorframe. He hustled him away and gave him comic books and oatmeal cookies. Eddie soon forgot the notches on the wall, at least I thought he did. But I stood staring at the spot where he had been standing unsteadily. I have an eye for detail. I knew if Eddie had walked and stood against the wall, in that doorway, the top of his head would have come to the same etched line that he had made the year before. He had not grown, when everybody else was growing.

This knowledge, which Lazarus protected him from, was known

to him. He glanced up from the gaudy pages of the comic book and stared at the doorframe.

It was a doorway he would never go through. I went to the kitchen and took a fresh batch of cookies from the oven. Oatmeal cookies were the only sweet thing that I could make alone. I gave Eddie a whole plateful for his private consumption. Littleson, who was Lazarus by then, did not complain.

Every two weeks Eddie went to the clinic with his mother. We'd see them walking down the street. Eddie with his pinched body and Miss Rose with her pinched eyes. Miss Rose told Mama that Eddie couldn't hold his water. Mama told us that Eddie's clinic visits made her think of her Uncle E.W. and the Writing Clinic.

Later that spring there was so much rain that the eaves were tipsy and the gutters were swollen and drunken, spilling over. Trash tightened the drainage. Yet in places gasoline and oil made murals of the gutters, and Lazarus, Eddie and I would watch our faces shifting in a rainbow when we found one. Such pools could be like the house of mirrors wherein faces would seem huge, gathering comic perspective. We laughed together for a while.

Before the announcement of new watermelon, before the beginning of summer, Eddie died.

Littleson let me hold his hand for two minutes at the funeral in Star of Bethlehem Missionary Baptist Church. This was when Miss Rose rocked from her spine, gathering momentum like a dark, black-breasted bird, stretched out her arms like great sepia wings, sent up one shout that she didn't own, that panicked her, and let grief try to fly above itself, above her body. Her sorrow was magnificent; ours was so quotidian, so humble that we were ashamed and even more afraid that she would pull some of the same overwhelming magnificence out of us. We were Roman Catholic and did not shout in church. Yet our mother and the sisters in white seemed to know exactly what to do for Miss Rose.

Lazarus wiped his eyes and gnawed his bottom lip. Fascinated, I craned my neck to stare one last time at the boy in the coffin in the immutable trance of death.

It was all a mystery to me. We never learned why the ice-babies had beaten Eddie. They were never caught, although some people said that a boy who was sent to the reform school for stealing a car bragged behind the barbed wire that he was "a killer." They said that he had shrugged. Said it had been something he had had to do. They told us who he was and we looked for him in the parade (named after an imaginary white-man benefactor) that wound its way down three miles of boulevard. He was in the St. Edmund's Drum and Bugle Corps that turned out the annual end-of-the-summer parade. He was a standout musician, in a troupe of gut-grabbing, finger-popping music boys. We all said that you had to respect a bad boy. He could blow a horn with incorrigible style, and his drumbeat was the rhythm that sent a wild freedom through the crowd. We pulsated with the beat they sent out. It was alive.

I remember feeling bouyed up in the crowd. Like someone who cannot drown. This was a mysterious feeling. Lazarus had climbed a tree and was poised like a lookout for a pirate ship. There were policemen all around. They looked displeased with us, as if we were breaking the law by being so happy. Secrets ran through the air. I eavesdropped under the music. Perhaps the boy who'd killed Eddie was *there* in the street, making powerful music that jarred our bones and our teeth. Maybe Eddie was listening. An angel now leaning attentively on a cloud.

Suddenly, I wanted to not be sure that the killer boy was blowing a horn. His sound, delicious as it was, could only carry germs. Cold is contagious, and soon we could all be frozen in the attitudes of ice, like whole generations playing "Aunt Dinah's dead." Oh how did she die? Oh she died like this. Assuming some bizarre position and freezing there for an endless time. Catching cold and giving it.

Richard Stern

NOBLE ROT

(from *Chicago Times*)

Christmas Eve, Chicago was dressed in its climate of martyr-dom, deep freeze. Thirty-five years ago, Mottram's internal navigator had brought him to gelid Lake Michigan. Every winter since, he'd cursed the choice. A man's defined by his errors. Mottram came to Chicago with the worst of his, Adelaide Haggerty. He'd not only picked the wrong place but the wrong companion. (He'd managed to shed the companion.)

This Christmas, Chicago felt right to him. It was the right place, and freeze was the right climate for his solitude. Solitude, more, the sense that he'd been abandoned, was, in a way, his present to himself. He and Adelaide—ten years after their divorce they were friends, had waved their daughter Deirdre into the Alitalia flight to Milan. Junior year abroad. The first Christmas in twenty years without her. All in all, a relief. He need go through none of the Christmas hoops.

Mottram's father was an Anglican clergyman. For him, Christmas was the hardest day of the year. Even atheist and skeptic parishioners often let nostalgia bring them to the Christmas service. "They come to recharge their contempt," he said. His Christmas sermon was a frightful weight, especially—Mottram learned this when he read his father's diary—as old Mottram was himself a hive of doubt: self-doubt, religious doubt, polymorphous sexual doubt. Some of this young Derek had sensed. At Christmas, it settled into the rectory; it was in the holly and the mistletoe, the Christmas goose, the wrapped books, socks, gloves, and sweaters the three Mottrams exchanged before Father carted off his sermon to St. George's.

Self-doubt was a Mottram trait. That and hatred for its generator, the Infernal English Class Machine (scoring off the skin of inferior, degraded Englishmen). More than anything else, it sent Mottram to America. It didn't matter that Mottrams weren't near the bottom of the pyramid: Clergymen and successful tradesmen could snub as well as be snubbed. Three generations had gone to Oxford, they were certainly not bottom drawer, but this didn't mean insulation from jokes, looks, ironies, exclusions, and, worse, implied, required inclusions. After Oxford, Mottram was apprenticed to a cousin's wine firm. He spent a year in Bordeaux—where an even creakier Machine ground out points—then grabbed the chance to come to America with the firm. Whom should he meet his third month in New York but one of the relatively few American girls savaged by the Machine.

Daughter of a chauffeur to one of the First Irish Families, Adelaide Haggerty grew up feeling invisible to those she'd been taught to believe were everything. Pretty, she felt ugly, smart, she felt stupid. Timid, sex-starved, stuttering Mottram made her feel beautiful and wise. If he stuttered, it was in Oxbridge English. That signaled social superiority to the Southampton chauffeur's daughter. She fell for his phonemes, he for her falling for them. Two months after they'd met at a New York matinee, he was offered a job in Chicago with Sellinbon Wine Imports.

Driving back alone to the South Side—he'd refused a dinner invitation from Adelaide and her husband—Mottram prepared for solitude.

At Mr. G's he bought lamb chops, grapefruit, HäagenDazs, and Constant Comment, at the Chalet a slab of brie and two bottles of Bushmills Irish, at O'Gara's a sackful of paperback novels.

Martyrdom did not include starvation or mental blank.

Christmas Eve. Three-thirty. In his snug bay window, Mottram sat with the first whiskey of the evening. His apartment was the second—top—floor of Harvey Wallop's hundred-year-old brown shingle cottage. Pinewood Court's two—and three-story bungalows had been put up for workers who'd built the Columbian Exposition buildings in the 1890s. Like Harvey's, some had been modernized or enlarged, others were molecules away from collapse. Harvey, a contractor, had modernized, renewed, remodernized and re-renewed every inch of his place. The floor gleamed, the ceilings were freshly painted, the porch was solid, the heat and plumbing superb. Mottram was Wallop's ideal tenant: no wife, no young children, few visitors, and a polite sufferer of alterations and repairs. The rent was low, the living easy.

Mottram watched night fall into the street. Lamps shaped like guillotines exposed cruel humps of ice; now and then shadowy, thuglike nonthugs passed by, homeward, wayward. Some were leashed to dogs, some carried Christmas trees or sacks of packages. Here and there, tapered bulbs were strung on trees and wreaths; but mostly, on Pinewood Court, Christmas was invisible. Which suited Mottram. When the doorbell rang, it was as shocking as a fire alarm. (He hadn't seen anyone coming up the street.) There was no speaker system—Harvey mistrusted them.

Mottram kept the brass chain linked in its slot and opened the door. It was a tall, bearded man in a knee-length black overcoat. He carried a blue denim laundry bag.

"Yes? What can I—?"

"Derek. It's me."

Mottram looked closely and recognized him. "So it is," he said. "Denis. What in—? Come in."

"I walked from the Greyhound Station."

It would not have surprised Mottram if he'd walked from West Virginia. "That was intrepid of you, Denis. I couldn't imagine who it was. Santa Claus skips this house. I'm glad," he lied, "to see you. Give me your coat." He took the denim bag, then pointed to the coat till Denis got the idea, removed and handed it to him. It weighed a ton. He hoisted it over the brass knob and led Denis up the carpeted stairs. Denis had wiped his feet on the doormat. "You remember the way. What a surprise. What would you have done if I hadn't been here?"

"Waited for you."

Of course. Denis would have waited a month. The coat was probably full of peanut butter and Fig Newtons. "Well, we'll celebrate, tea for you, booze for me. Herbal, right? There's probably some left over from last time. It's what? Four years? Maybe there are some Fig Newtons. Petrified by now. We'll see. We'll scrape something together."

In the living room, Denis plonked himself in the red leather armchair in which he'd spent most of his last visit. "What's that?" he asked. *That* was Mottram's newest acquisition, a five-foot-high ficus tree in a lacquered rattan basket. "It wasn't here last time."

"It came a week ago. From Deirdre. She said she wanted something alive around here."

"Trees should be left outside," said Denis.

"I hope you don't mind if it stays inside."

Denis regarded its thin braided trunks and emerald leaves. "It belongs outside." But there were other enemies in Mottram's apartment. Indeed, he sat where he did to avoid seeing the painting over his head. It was Mottram's prize, a de Kooning-like swirl of rose and violet, in which lay a spread-eagled nude woman. Mottram had paid more for it than he'd ever paid for anything. "How is little Deirdre?"

"Not so little."

"She's a dear little girl."

Denis did not register much contradiction. "Where had you come from this time, Denis?"

"Missouri. The Lotus Foot Ashram. Outside Kirksville."

"Things didn't go well?"

"Things went very well. A fine place. Could've stayed a long time. No desire to leave. Had to. Not sure why. They gave me a bus ticket. Yesterday. Pulled me down."

"Pulled you?"

"I'd climbed up. A gazebo. Gold weather vane. Held on to it. They got a ladder. Took me off. The bird came too. Bad business. Nothing to do. I took the ticket. They knew I had friends in Chicago."

"Friends? Oh, yes. Of course." On a planet of five billion, somehow he, Mottram, had the privilege of being *the friends* of this pathetic gilk.

It was the third time in seven years Denis Sellinbon had come to him. The last time he'd stayed almost a week, the first time nearly as long. That first time, Denis's father had warned him Denis was coming. Walter called from L.A., where he and Eileen had moved after selling the business. "Denis is loose, Derek. I'd told him—I hope you'll forgive me—that in an emergency he could go to you. I'm afraid he might show up. He was with some Arkansas swami. If you could possibly take him in for a day or two I'd be very grateful. Or just get him to a hotel. If he has no money—he usually has some—advance him a few bucks. I'm sorry as hell about this, Derek. I wish—."

Eileen's trombone snort filled the earpiece. "He's no trouble, Der. A good boy. Basically. You know that. Different, maybe. A stubborn bugger, but he doesn't need much. Place to sleep, the floor's perfect. He's used to floors. He eats anything, stale rolls, beans, whatever, it'll be better than what those monks give him. And he's a world-class faster. Let him clean up the place for you. If I know you, it needs it. He's good with brooms. Just watch out for lice in that beard. Get him to shave it. We're off to Tucson for a few days. If you have a problem, put him on a bus. He'll be fine. Look, he may not even show up."

Of course, he showed up. Eileen had told him to. Mottram got that from Denis. Denis had asked her if he could come back home, told her he wouldn't be any trouble, No, she'd said, no way, Dad's heart was on the fritz, Dad couldn't take any excitement. "I won't make any excitement." "You *are* excitement. You go to Derek Mottram. He owes your father everything." That's how Denis reported it. Whatever else he was, he was no liar.

Which, considering his life, as Mottram did, was odd. How could a child of Eileen Sellinbon not become a liar? But instead of small, constant lies, Denis constructed a labyrinth of which only he was Ariadne.

For years, he'd been able to live in two worlds. The Sellinbons sent him to a Montessori school. At age ten, he'd brained a girl with a block and had to leave. From then on, he always had to leave.

Eileen wouldn't hear of a shrink; Boylans and Sellinbons didn't go to medicine men. For loose screws, there were seminaries and monasteries. Priests existed to mop up spilled milk. Walter—the free-thinker—had made a mistake not sending the kid to the nuns from the beginning.

In his first Chicago years, Mottram had known the Sellinbon household well. Walter did a lot of business at home, gave tastings and dinners for customers, salesmen, vintners, advertisers. Those first years, Eileen was under wraps. Even when she showed her crude stuff, Walter's kindness and courtesy compensated for it. But why had he ever taken up with her? Was his inner navigator as punch-drunk as Derek's or Denis's?

Like Adelaide, Eileen had been a sort of beauty. A big woman, but in those days, both slim and voluptuous. Her hair was the brilliant red of danger signals, her eyes were ice-blue. In those days, her mouth didn't look like hell's gate. The thing was she didn't talk much in those days, though when she did—just saying Hello, taking your hand and welcoming you—you sensed her discomfort and aggression. Mottram didn't sense her genius for other people's weakness, her hater's need to display it. The first time she set eyes on him she'd said, "I didn't realize your Englishman'd be such a dumpling, Walter."

In time, her vulgarity became a domestic Van Allen Belt against which Walter's kindness and gentleness shattered. Denis would have had to have the thrusting power of a rocket to break through unharmed. How terrified he must have been of her voice. Not that Eileen knew she shouted. She didn't even want to talk; it's just that she couldn't bear others talking. She hated other people's ease. (Why should they have what she didn't?) After those first, submerged, apprentice years, her tigerish self emerged. She interrupted, she contradicted, she overruled.

Only Walter escaped her tongue. Walter was the best of men, a wonderful lover, husband, father, a brilliant businessman. Eileen had been raised in a household of female deference. That part of her which didn't imitate maleness still deferred to it. So when the wine men—they were all men in these years—came to the house, Eileen buckled herself into her notion of femininity. That she had no taste for dress, make-up, charm, decoration, cuisine, or—Derek guessed—amorousness did not seem to bother Walter. That his Eileen tried so hard, that she went against what he must have known was her grain, moved him. Only when she brought out what had been fermenting beneath did he realize that the business was imperiled by it. Her terrible voice blasted the old give-and-take of vinous dinners.

The acme of her ruinous interference came the night a representative of Chateau Mouton-Rothschild, Alexandre de Bonville, came to the house. It was the night before the signing of their first contract with Sellinbon Imports. An arrangement with the firm of Philippe de Rothschild was very important to Walter. Perhaps it was this which roused Eileen. "I prepared for weeks," she said after. "Read my eyes out. I had Baron Philippe down cold, knew everything about him." No sooner was Bonville in his chair than she let go: "In this house, Alex, your boss is God. *Preemyay nay poos, second nay dikne, Mouton soos.*" This was her version of the famous motto, *"Premier ne puis, Second ne daigne. Mouton suis"—I can't be first, I scorn being second. I am Mouton.* Hearing it in her special brass, Bonville reeled, which was but prelude to her recitation of the rise of Mouton, its rejection by the Bordeaux vintners as a *premier cru* "after Phil took over," its acceptance in 1973. She went on to the annual labels, the change of name after "Paulette died, what a gesture," the rivalry with "your cousin's brew. You Jew boys know quality, just like us Sellinbons." Bonville was about as Jewish as the pope, but shriveled in his chair as if he'd been an eight-year-old *shtetl* boy before a storm trooper. A red trumpet of flesh, Eileen ended with "That's why we love doing business with you boys. Now, let's put on the nosebag."

They did not put on the nosebag. Bonville excused himself, and after five minutes in the bathroom, emerged with regret: Jet lag had caught up with him and was advancing a flu with which he did not dare endanger them.

The contract was never signed, and from that night on, Sellinbon Imports began to sink. Walter, awake at last to his domestic swamp, began shifting all entertainment to the office. Too late. Three years later, Walter sold most of the business to Felicien Trancart and moved to Los Angeles. Mottram turned down Felicien's offer to handle Italian, Spanish, and Portuguese wines and retired on his share of the sale and the small means of his father's estate.

The day after Walter and Eileen had called, seven years ago, Denis had shown up. Gentle, polite, he asked little. Much of the next days he spent calling lamaseries, monasteries, ashrams. It was astonishing that there were so many, you'd have thought the Midwest was Tibet. (The month's phone bill suggested a hot line to Lhasa.) The rest of the day, Denis sat immobile in the red armchair looking into space. Two or three times he went off to St. Thomas's for mass. The fifth day, after an epic call, he told Mottram he'd be off, he'd found a halfway house for alcoholic ex-clergymen in Ashtabula. Mottram walked him to the IC—the Fifty-ninth Street station, as Denis refused to believe there was one on Fifty-sixth. When he got back to the apartment, he found Denis's present, a book of poems and essays by modern Russian poets. Who else in his life would have found, let alone given him such a book? It was inscribed, "For Derek, who, beneath his shroud, is pure. From Denis. See Page 74." On that page, Denis had underlined sentences of an essay by one Khlebnikov.

*The word can be divided into the
pure word and the everyday word.
One can think of the word conceal-
ing in itself both the reason of the
starlit night and the reason of the
sunlit day.*

* * *

This time, Denis had brought a present with him. "I painted a
picture for you."

"How kind of you, Denis, I didn't know you painted."

"I paint well. It's to replace—" and he tilted his head to indicate
the painting over his head. I don't think you want little Deirdre
exposed to such a scene. And you may have other young visitors."

"Little Deirdre isn't little, Denis. She's twenty, and off on her
own. To Europe." Almost adding that she might be revealing herself
to some Italian contemporary in just the manner of the offensive painting.

Denis had removed from his denim bag a wrinkled square of
paper which he unfolded, then shook out like a wet towel. He took it
by the corners and held it up. "The wrinkles will iron out. But you
can see, can't you?" What Mottram saw was a mess of tepid color,
silvery blue with some reddish sticks leaning this way and that.
There were also some grayish oblongs against what in a realistic
painting might be a stormy sky. "I see you like it. I painted it last
week, thinking of you here. Of course it's abstract. I take Exodus: 20
seriously."

"Exodus: 20?"

"'Thou shalt not make graven images or any likeness of anything in heaven above or the earth beneath or the water under the
earth.' I believe one is permitted to suggest. Do you see Rockefeller
Chapel, the ice skaters on the Midway? I knew it would please you,
and I've used the colors of your rug. It's the size of—this thing." He
held the water-color above the splayed nude. "I see I misjudged it a
few inches each way, otherwise we could just slip it under the frame.
We'll have to tape it now. Have you got Scotch tape?"

There was no point in fury, but Derek was suddenly furious.
The colossal nerve of this intruding nut. How dare he? His mother's
son. Still, he managed to say, "I paid more money for that than I've
ever paid for anything, Denis. And I've been offered five times the
amount I paid. I have an art historian friend who thinks it's a master-
piece. Deirdre appreciates it. It has pictorial value. I'm afraid if we
subscribed to Exodus: 20, there'd be no artistic culture anywhere in
the world outside of Isfahan and Damascus. It is not something out
of Hustler magazine. Not that I'm ungrateful for your painting. It's
very pretty. I don't have room for it here, but I'll find a place for it

somewhere. I'm grateful to you for thinking of me."

"If you had Scotch tape, I'd show you how nice it looks here. I remembered the colors of the chair and the rug. You see how I've used them, red and pink. Give yourself a chance. You'll learn to like them much more than . . . ." Voice trembling as the demonstrative pronoun died in his throat.

When Mottram got up for his six o'clock pee, he saw down the hall Denis's immobile profile by the emerald bush of the ficus leaves. He wore the black sweater, pants, and shoes in which, last night, he'd gone to his room. Perhaps he'd slept in them. Or did he sleep? "Sharks," thought Mottram, "don't." Instead of standing up, Mottram sat down on the oak toilet seat. What was he going to do with him?

One thing he was not going to do was spend Christmas watching Denis watch, or not watch, him. He had an invitation he'd planned to ignore, had even mentioned it to Denis last night. His "out": "Felicien and Valerie Trancart's. He used to work for your father."

"Blond mustache, brown eyes, three cheek moles. Like Orion."

"Amazing, Denis. You can't have been more than ten when he left this business." Was there a smile-flick on Denis's hairbordered lips? Yes. But were Felicien's eyes brown? Were there moles on his cheek? He'd check that out. "He got your father into those Perigord dessert wines. Montravel, Bergerac, Monbazillac. We put them into Chez Drouet, Maxim's, the Ambassador. Cincinnati, St. Louis. We had a good order from New Orleans, the Commodore's Palace. Monbazillac alone did half a million dollars for us. Then Felicien tried making it himself, got some Semillon and Muscadet cuttings and planted them into an Ozark hill. They never grew the right mold. *La pourriture noble*, they call it, the noble rot. That was a few years before your Dad threw in the towel. Felicien took over half the business. He asked me to work for him."

"Why didn't you?"

Mottram was surprised. Denis was actually curious about him. It was as if the wall had said Good Morning. "Fatigue. Sloth. *La pourriture ignoble*. My father left me a little money. I'd put it in the market, done all right. And I had the share of Sellinbon your dear dad gave me. I thought I could just make it and I have. Biggest expense is Deirdre, and that won't be for long.

"Little Deirdre," said Denis.

* * *

Eileen's call came as he was serving Denis a poached egg and an English muffin. Nine o'clock, 7:00 A.M. in Westwood, she must have been prowling the floor all night after Denis's call. "Merry C.,

Derek. I hear Santa arrived. In the St. Nick of time. You boys having a nice time? Did he bring you a present? Besides himself." And *sotto voce*, "Selfish little bastard." In normal roar, "A relief I got him settled. I take off tomorrow."

"I'm not sure what you mean by settled."

"We don't want him riding the rails on Christmas, do we? By the way, you can take him to Felicien's today. I called."

"What?"

"Valerie, that little rat, began some French nonsense, I cut her off at the pass, reminded her what her little hubby owed the Sellinbons, so you boys won't have to be alone with each other."

"Very thoughtful of you. Where are you off to?"

"Paradise. Want to come? Tahiti, Moa-Moa, Samoa, Go-Blowa. Six weeks in a white boat with, please God, rich, rich white men. If I come back with the same moniker, I'll have blown thousands. Two weeks on the fat farm, a suction job on the boobs, I was stepping on them. You should see me now." Mottram shut his eyes. "Young tourist at the Brentwood market asked me if I used to be Kim Novak."

"Were you?"

"Too bad you're such a poor rat, Derek. Well, give that thief Felicien my love. He must be rich as the pope, I'm surprised he wasn't on the *Forbes* list." So, thought Mottram, she's scouting the world's four hundred richest; she's as deluded as her son.

"It's Mother?" said Denis.

"Right. Off on a cruise."

"Off," said Denis. "Always off."

That afternoon the two of them walked a slippery half-mile to the Trancarts's Kenwood mansion. Mottram had given Denis a blue tie, otherwise he remained the arrow of death.

At Trancarts's, a mob, neighbors and friends of the parents and three children. There were log fires, holly and mistletoe, champagne, punch and Glühwein passed round on silver trays; hams, roast beefs, cakes, and cookies were on the huge dining room table. Denis faded into a curtained nook where he sat in a golden armchair, his black-sweatered arms hung down its golden flanks. The bearded head was tilted, as if receiving messages.

Every fifteen minutes, Mottram checked up on him. People seemed to nod or talk at him, he seemed to respond, but blankly. He was not a social creature. The space around him grew as if people had discovered he was a George Segal figure of fleshlike material. Mottram felt a twinge of something. "But why? Let the bastard sink."

Mottram spotted a bottle of Monbazillac you couldn't get outside of Perigord and made it his own. He drank glass after wonderful glass. This was Paradise. Pretty women with red cheeks floated in the room on Bach cantatas. Faces, dresses, silver, mirrors, chandeliers, chairs, curtains, couches, the odors of good food, what a fine party. Mottram talked to a wine salesman, an obstetrician, a pretty professor of chemistry, the wife of a football player. The martyrdom of solitude leaked away. "Thank you, Eileen," he thought. "May you find your match in the South Seas, say a nice killer shark."

A woman's terrible scream speared through the jolly haze, followed by silence, as if the whole house had been hit in the stomach. Then another scream, and shouts, laughs. Mottram knew; he could not budge. "Get 'em down," he heard. "Right now." The "r" of "right" was French, the voice, Valerie Trancart's. Mottram took four deep breaths, then managed to walk through people toward the curtained alcove.

There was Denis, beyond Mrs. Trancart's outstretched arm, high up the curtain, bearded head touching the ceiling, arms and legs gripping the golden curtain. Men had moved chairs and were not reaching for his legs, but he kicked them off. He was implored, tempted. There was also laughter, hearty and nervous. Everyone found some way to deal with what you were not supposed to deal with Christmas—or any other day—in Kenwood mansions. "Derreek," called Valerie Trancart. "*Ou es-tu? Viens vite. Mon Dieu. Le fou est en train de detruire la maison.*"

He was at her side. "Denis, it's Derek. Would you mind coming down, old boy? We've had our joke now. Very good. But we'd better get home. I'm tired." For a moment, he thought Denis responded to him, but if so, he was just one voice among spectral others. "Maybe we'd better get the firemen. Or an ambulance. We'll take him to Billings. Or maybe—do you have a ladder?"

He'd been anticipated. Felicien and a houseboy carried one in and propped it up, a yard from Denis. Felicien pointed to the houseboy and gestured toward the ladder. The boy shook his head. As for Felicien, he had the physique of a cauliflower; even if he could get up, what would he do? People looked around. Where was the football player? Not here. Mottram felt the heat of attention.

"Hold it steady for me," he said to Felicien, who held one strut while the houseboy held the other. Mottram, breathing hard, went up one, two, four, five rungs, till his bald head was within two feet of Denis's beard. "Denis," he said quietly. "Look at me, old fellow." And Denis, eyes enormous with fear, did look, and seemed to see. "Could you manage to slide down, old boy? Then we'll just go home. We'll walk back to the house. Could you please do this?"

For a moment, comprehension and agreement seemed to be in Denis's face, then this small social contract ruptured, and he was back in the wild place that had sent him there. Mottram heard a small buzz-saw sound, then saw what it was. Behind Denis's head a rip opened in the gold fabric and suddenly, like a terrible laugh, it went. Denis swung like Tarzan on the gold curtain, swiped Mottram, knocked him off the ladder and crashed on top of him.

* * *

Three days later, Mottram walked around Promontory Point. He'd been pampering his aches long enough. No breaks, no large bruises. Luck and thick Trancart carpets saved him. And Denis, too, had broken nothing of his own. (He'd had not only luck and thick carpets but Mottram.)

And he'd signed himself into W-2, the psycho ward. "To spare you," he told Mottram. "You'll have a ready-made explanation for them" (*them* being the Trancarts, the party guests, all who couldn't understand the "higher reasoning" behind his behavior).

Mottram had been too furious to listen to the higher reasoning (it had something to do with inner and outer facts), although it seemed that he was one of the few people capable of understanding it. Aching, angry, and humiliated by Denis, exhausted by the ambulance ride and hospital processing—thank God, Denis had Blue Cross—Mottram was in no mood for Denis's loony flattery. Wheelchair to wheelchair, they waited for X-rays in the emergency room, and Mottram lectured. "There's no acceptable explanation, Denis. You ruined the Christmas of a hundred people. You ruined five or ten thousand dollars worth of drapery. You're a troublemaker."

"I am. I have been. I may always be."

"You need help."

"All do."

"*You* need medical help. *You* need to-to-to-" For the first time in years, Mottram stuttered. "Get closer to the world in which you-you-you live."

"I wanted to get out of it. That's what I was doing."

"Up curtains? Through ceilings? Did-did you-you think you w-w-were Santa Claus?"

"I couldn't remember where the door was. People stared, expecting something. Wanted me to leave."

"S-S-So you were s-s-s-supplying a demand? N-N-No. You created one. They didn't want you to go till you d-d-did what-what you did. You harmed people. You harmed property. People will have to pay real m-m-money for the d-d-damage you did. You can't."

Beard against his chest, Denis sank in the wheelchair. A study in contrition. No, thought Mottram, he's not contrite, he's working out loony explanations, I can feel the heat of his concentration. It insulates him.

Denis had ruptured his solitude, forced him into—well, pleasure, and then had made him pay through the nose for it. He couldn't disavow him, he'd brought him. (As the hunchback brings his hump.)

"They can hold you forty-eight hours, with or without permission. Sign in yourself and you can sign out when you're better."

"I know these places," said Denis, quietly. "But I'll sign. You'll have peace of mind."

Home, without Denis, was indeed peace. Beloved solitude. Nothing to supervise, nothing for which he was responsible. Bliss.

The third day of it, he treated himself to the walk up Fifty-fifth Street to Promontory Point. The sun was brilliant, the air frigid. Ice quilted the tiered boulders of the shore. The lake had carved itself into a zoo of almost-animals. Dazzling, beautiful, solitary. Occasionally a jogger ran by, huffing smoke. Six miles north, the black and silver cutlery of the Loop lay on the white sky.

Mottram was still stiff, but it was the stiffness of years. Age stiffened the cells as it loosened the moral seams. Bit by bit, it seduced you into carelessness till you died in a heap of it. Care-less. You didn't care. You took care—of yourself. Loosely: It didn't matter how you looked, what—within limits—you did. You weren't punctilious, weren't dutiful. Want to change a routine? Change it. The only boss was your body.

Mottram's father had been dutiful to the end, had asked the right questions, displayed ministerial concern. His collar bound him to obligation. Essentially, Mottram knew, his father was a cold man. He'd read his diary. Again and again, the old man beseeched the god in whom he hadn't believed for decades for belief, warmth, feeling.

Mottram had, for years now, felt himself turning into his father. First his looks, the baldness, the gray eyes, the pinched nose, the long cheeks and jowls. Five times, seeing himself in shop windows, he'd said with surprise, "Dad!"

And now he felt his father's inner chill. (The burden of obligation. Martyrdom.) Coldness had sneaked into him, like ice into water.

* * *

In the mailbox, a postcard, from Italy. SCAFFOLDING OVER THE LAST SUPPER. Deirdre. He poured himself a glass of Bushmills and read it in the bay.

Dear Dad,

Exhausting flight. Milan freezing. Hotel horrible. Still, I'm, here!! I guess there's no point in going to see this!! The Domo is white. Crazy. Merry Christmas. xoxoxo.

Signorina D.

ta figlia

The girl who owned his father's eyes, her mother's hair, and his two thousand dollars, the person who'd inherit his couch and carpet, armchairs, kettle, paintings, every material thing including what she'd have to see into the earth.

Light from the street lamps slashed Pinewood Court. Four-thirty, the dark was holding off. The door bell rang. Startling. What the hell? Down the stairs—legs aching, calling through the door, "Who is it?"

"It's me, Derek. Denis."

"Go way. You can't come here. You've given me trouble enough for a lifetime. I don't want to see you again." This is what Mottram wanted to say, came close to saying. Instead he opened the door, shook Denis's hand, took his coat, hung it on the brass knob, and led him upstairs.

And here he watched him, slumped in the red chair by the fizzy green crown of ficus leaves, almost hammer-locked in the legs of the rose and violet nude. Denis dunked Triscuits in peppermint tea and recited, quietly, his "escape from the medicine men of w-2."

For all the blips in his genetic matter, Dennis was as intrepid as Caesar. He'd pulled wool over a battery of psychiatrists, told them he wasn't used to alcohol, had had too much to drink, and then, before he'd known what he was doing, had pretended to be Tarzan to impress a pretty girl. He actually had been sliding down when the curtain ripped off its rings. Many people there had been amused by him, but not he—virtuous, sensible, Denis—he was embarrassed and ashamed. Felicien had been his father's friend and employee, he'd never in the world have done anything to harm him. And he would pay for the damage he'd caused, if it meant sending the Trancarts fifty dollars a month for the rest of his life. (Slipping soppy Triscuits into his mouth, bits befouling his black beard.)

"You surprise me, Denis. So-so manip- worldly."

"I know such people inside out. If God stepped out of the Burning Bush, they'd use him to light their cigarettes. If I told them the inner truth, I'd be locked up for a year."

"I don't h-h-have your spiritual resources. I'm ordinary. I live among the ordinary. Why don't you accommodate to us? You understand us."

Denis thoughtfully rotated a Triscuit in his fingers. Part of it fell on him. "It's only those who understand who count for me. My teachers. You."

"I can't teach anyone anything. My life's modest, even poor, but I have a right to it. You have no right to change ordinary people. Even if you're saving us. Okay for Je-Jesus to bring swords instead of peace, but there's been only one Jesus. Maybe one too many."

"You're afraid they'll put me away. You're doing your duty. In *loco parentis* for me. You're a good person, Derek." He sprang from the chair. Mottram, frightened, got up too. "I'm going to show you something." He raced downstairs, Mottram, still fearful, started to follow, but then he was up, carrying a white cube. "Here," he said. He handed it to Mottram. "My book."

That night, Derek read himself to sleep in Denis's book. Or rather, he read at it; the most dogged reader couldn't have read it straight. There were eight hundred small pages—Denis had folded and cut ordinary eight-by-eleven bond paper into quarters—every other one of which was covered with tiny script. Denis had explained the arrangement. "It's a workbook. Every reader's a collaborator. Across from my ideas, his ideas. Next to my experience, his. It'll be a great success.

"So you have commercial ambitions for it?"

"Why not? Money's filth, enlightenment isn't. Everyone can be reached."

"I thought you only cared for *cognoscenti.*"

"I don't know that word."

"People-in-the-know. Special people."

"The idea's to make everyone *cognoscenti.*"

The modest title was *The World's Mind.* The dedication read, "To my teacher, Satyandi Purush, at whose Blessed Lotus feet I lay thought and life." (Under the dedicatee's name, another had been crossed out.)

As for the book itself, it was written in short, clear (and clearly borrowed) sentences. It began with the human progenitor, "Four-and-a-half feet tall, muscular and black, Eve, traced via mitochondrial DNA. 200,000 years B.C." Millennia were skipped, and the author descended for a sentence to the pre-Paleolithic. Then the Lower Paleolithic: "The Clactonian worked with rough flakes. The Levalloisean worked with large ones." Mesopotamia: "4000 B.C. The Al-Ubaid period features simple agriculture and painted pots." That did it for Al-Ubaid. Asia Minor, Persia, India, Turkestan, China and Siberia took another two pages. Ancient Egypt, "known as *Kemet,* the Black Land," was given a page of its own.

Modern history got personal. So the French and American Revolutions were important because Sellinbons had "come to tame the Indians." The famous mixed with the unknown, the private with the public. "The most important person in Nazi Germany was not Adolf Hitler, but my teacher Herman Schlonk." This was the only reference to either Hitler or Schlonk. An account of Philippe de Rothschild's life took up four pages.

Here and there the book burst into reflection. So there was a discussion of leisure, an appeal to tycoons and politicians "to take more of it" so that they would "have less time to make trouble for the rest of us." Some pages were just lists of names, "Einstein, Mendel, Darwin, Faraday, Dr. Peabody, Whistler, Hudson, Chevrolet, Mayor Bradley."

"A history?" thought weary Mottram. "No, a listory."

He was too tired to turn out the light, but when he woke hours later in the dark he thought, "Odd, I could have sworn." He stumbled to the bathroom, not noticing what he did when he awoke again at eight-thirty, that Denis's book was neither on the bed nor on the floor. He looked under the blankets, beneath the bed. Nothing.

The explanation was that Denis was gone too. Mottram found his note on the kettle.

Derek. Was tempted to wait for goodbye, but the bus leaves at nine and it's a ninety-minute walk to the station. What is goodbye between friends? I'm off to Brother Bull's Lamasery, near Oconomowoc, Wisc. Long talk with him last night. Seems right for me. A black man. (Blacks are the only Americans who still feel.) You're one of the few whites that has a good black heart. I want your opinion of my book. It will be a useful guide for school children, and high school students can use it to prepare for the SATs. I put the ficus plant outside. Denis

Mottram, part of whose frost had melted at this letter, finished it in fury. His plant. Deirdre's gift.

And that was nothing to his rage when he saw Denis's horrible watercolor Scotch-taped over the nude. "I'll kill him." He tore it off and stomped on it. That filthy, cretinous Eileen-spawn had bombed his life. Where did he get the goddamn nerve? Taken in like a crippled dog with nothing in the world to recommend him except the memory of his father, and he repays with destruction. Bitch son of a bitch mother, crawling in like the hound of death, and pawing my sacred things. Where had he put the plant? Good God. Talk of exploitation, talk of power plays. These innocent killers, tuning up their harps while they rifle the eyes from your skull.

The ficus tree was freezing on the porch. Mottram ran down in his slippers and carried it in, the cold pouring off its bright leaves. The monster had killed it. "My poor ficus," he said. "I'll never forgive that bastard."

* * *

Two days later, the day Mottram did the laundry, he went to get Denis's sheets. Ripping them off—Denis had made the bed—he saw something fly into the air. It was a hundred-dollar bill. Incredible. The fellow couldn't even hang on to his few dollars. "I'll send it to Deirdre." Serve him right. But of course he put it into an envelope for Denis. When he got an address, he'd send it on. (Not to Eileen, she'd confiscate it.)

When a letter did come, four weeks later, he'd almost forgotten it.

The Lodge
Melvin, N.D.

Dear Derek,

Snow is part of my nature, but there's too much here at The Lodge. We're vowed to silence. At meals, the thoughts of Swami are read. So quiet. You hear the riprap of the river over the stones. Good for this restless soul of mine? Brother Bull's was good, but irreconcilable differences. I wish I had money to send you, but have only seventy-seven dollars. (Swami asks for the rest.) Please share it with Felicien. The author of Ecclesiaticus, Jesus, son of Sira, says (approximate reading), 'The world is a composition of fury, jealousy, tumult, unrest, fear of death, rivalry, and strife' (the Jerusalem Bible.) I read the Prophets, Bantam Shakespeare, and Kahlil Gibran (a Lebanese man who loved strong coffee, cigarettes, never married and eked a living from sketches and writing). If you need music, train your ear on wind. Practice drawing the light coming through the frost. One day you and I can tour the U.S. like Steinbeck and Charley. It interests me to know if it is all there.

Your friend,
Denis

Mottram was a poor dreamer, but that night he dreamed vividly. He was going into a church with Adelaide, but was stopped by a powerful detergent smell in the nave. "Varnish?" he asked. "No, it's george," said Adelaide. So, they waited outside, but inside was a full congregation. There a child cried. It was little Deirdre. Who was also Denis. He/she ran outside into his arms, weeping, and he told her/him, "I'll never leave you." In his body, he felt her/his sobbing relief.

When he woke for his six o'clock pee, the dream was with him. He asked himself what "george" could have meant. It was somehow important. As the yellow stream clattered into the bowl, it came to him. "George" was his father's church in the country which, so many years ago, Mottram had left for good.

James McManus

JAMES JEANS (NOT JAMES DEAN) AND THE JIFFY LUBE MAN

(from *Formations*)

Linda had made herself smaller than life. She was nervous. She was drawing her face in a mirror in three-quarters profile, shifting her weight on her work-bench, and smoking. She wanted to know what a penis felt like deep inside her, to be clenching it tight with those muscles. She glanced at the mirror, the drawing. She had made her lips fuller than they actually were, but they still looked like hers. She could do that: she was capable of such an effect and it was also considered permissible, in some cases even desirable. She was trying to make her eyes glint using very dark lines around where the light would come off. It was working. She felt pretty proud of herself. She was also a little bit drunk. Technically this was called chiaroscuro, but Linda preferred to think of the unnervous flicks of her hand that produced these nice glints as a kind of negative capability, hers, a term she had learned just last week in Aesthetics and Physics. Some poet named Keats (not that other one, Yeats) was the guy who had coined it. He had died very young, she had learned, but not before he'd come up with a bunch of great poems, or great odes, and that term.

Her Life Drawing teacher, Chuck Nash, had a penis. She never had actually seen it, but she always assumed it was there. Chuck Nash was married, or at least wore a ring, but did that make that much of a difference? He was standing right next to her now, helping Sasha. Linda could not see the front of his jeans, but she could see the back. There were smears of dried ultramarine on his pockets, the size of large thumbs. The paint was no more than a shade or two darker than the almost new denim, but when light hit it right you could see it.

She put out her cigarette, licked the dull point of her pencil, and squinted across at the mirror. Her face looked okay, but the one on the paper looked better.

She blew her blonde bangs from her eyes and kept drawing.

Penises were much in the air that semester at SAIC. In Linda's LD class, a sleek straight erection had been stylized as a red, white, and blue MX missile: the Peacekeeper. A graduate student who signed her work Siouxsie had painted a museum-scale portrait of John Wayne Gacy in his clown suit holding a lariat (or maybe a whip) in his right hand, his little pink dick in his left. One of the commonest lines of the resident graffitists was POWER TO THE PENIS: HARD ON! And, as if to illustrate this motto, the wall by the Kotex machine in the second-floor john now featured a six-foot-high model inscribed—in various inks, handwritings, and sizes— with dozens of names for that organ, of which some of the more original included Holmes, Daddy, dipstick, tootsie roll, throoper, boinker, trouser trout, hot pork injection, Mr. D, Mr. C, gizzpistol, Rodney, bazooka, snatchsnatcher, thang-whanger, gashhammer, muffstuffer, Trubba, meat, moonbeam, puppydog's tail, puddingpop, pearlpusher, clitstinger, tuskmusker, and a half dozen others that Linda could either not decipher because of the handwriting (or spelling) or ever begin to imagine. It was also a list to which Linda had nothing to add.

Hanging downstairs in the undergrad sculpture gallery was a humorous little contraption entitled *Ronnie and the Purple Penis*. It consisted of two latex figures dangling by strings from opposite ends of a hanger: a miniature Ronald McDonald and a grinning purple penis with a Reagan-style wave on its head. (It made Linda wonder if penises really got purple.) The artist was the notorious Jiffy Lube Man, who was actually a guy named Hank Rendeck who also just happened to be in her A & P class.

This Jiffy Lube Hank guy was also one of the founding members of a mini-anti-movement within the School that called itself Vas Deferens. Linda, in fact, had just seen a picture of *Ronnie and the Purple Penis* and read about Vas Deferens in that week's issue of *F*, the SAIC student paper. She pulled it out of her purse, sat down in the lounge, and reread it.

The headline over the story said VAS DEFERENS: AT WAR WITH ART. "Know your enemy: art" was their "rallying cry for the coming apocalypse." The article was accompanied by two black-and-white reproductions: *Ronnie and the Purple Penis* and a piece by Chester Treasure called *Jesus On A Tray (Part One of a Series)*, which was the face of an African-looking Jesus painted in goopy acrylics onto a cafeteria tray. There was also an interview with Vas Deferens' four founding members: Chester Treasure, Mr. Electricity, Artist With No Name, and the Jiffy Lube Man.

F: "Why is Vas Deferens 'at war with art'?"

Chester Treasure: "Because, okay, the attitudes prevalent in contemporary art are groty."

Mr. Electricity: "It's our duty as artists to make people realize what we have discovered."

Artist With No Name: "I mean, the whole art scene now is really pretty lame."

F: "Lame?"

Jiffy Lube Man: "Yeah, lame."

Mr. Electricity: "Well, pretty lame."

Artist With No Name: "Lamer than last year, at least."

F: "I've noticed that *your* art isn't all that exceptional."

Artist With No Name: "If you had any clue you would realize how good our art is. You can edit that out if you want to."

F: "So you don't believe in art for the people?"

Jiffy Lube Man: "Give me a break."

Chester Treasure: "If they can understand it."

Mr. Electricity: "If they can appreciate it."

F: "And you don't think that's taking an elitist attitude."

Chester Treasure: "If a person can't comprehend my art, he's not worthy of my attention."

F: "What, in your opinion, makes for a successful art piece?"

Jiffy Lube Man: "A successful piece of art is penetratingly executed, titled, and signed."

Artist With No Name: "Good use of media to get across an idea."

F: "You are at war with Art, yet you make art. Why?"

Jiffy Lube Man: "We are at war with contemporary art. After all, the old masters *are* the old masters. We do art in order to change contemporary views about Art."

Artist With No Name: "Art today has gone astray. Pun Intended. We must forge a new direction for artists."

Jiffy Lube Man: "Pun intended."

Mr. Electricity: "My art is a statement on the validity of other art."

Chester Treasure: My art heralds the fall."

F: "The fall?"

Chester Treasure: "The downfall of Art. It's already happening. As the quality of art gets lower so do art standards. It started with dada—turning non-art objects into art, stuff like that."

Artist With No Name: "As art gets worse it appeals to less people. It will quickly reach a point where no one, not even other artists, will like it."

F: "So Vas Deferens is trying to stop that from happening."

Chester Treasure: "No, we're trying to *help* that happen. When Art reaches that point it will cease to be art. Thus we will have brought about the downfall of Art."

F: "What will you do after that?"

Jiffy Lube Man: "We will begin to rebuild it using new, more rigorous and sophisticated principles."

F: "And those would be . . . ?"

Jiffy Lube Man: "Can't tell you. You would try and stop us."

F: "Fair enough... You equate the fall of contemporary art with an apocalypse. Would it actually be all that major?"

Jiffy Lube Man: "Maybe worse."

Artist With No Name: "Only one way to find out."

F: "In the meantime, however, what gives you the right to judge someone else's work?"

Jiffy Lube Man: "The same thing that gives them the right to call it Art."

F: "How do you feel about other people judging the worth of your own work?"

Artist With No Name: "No problem."

Chester Treasure: "Fine."

Mr. Electricity: "Fine."

Jiffy Lube Man: "It depends."

F: "Do you as Vas Deferens have any common themes in your work?"

Chester Treasure: "All our art work's for the downfall of Art, but we still don't allow our solidarity to get in the way of our artistic freedom."

F: "So you believe in individual freedom while at the same time working toward a common goal."

Jiffy Lube Man: "Sorry. End of interview."

Chester Treasure: "Good-bye."

F: "Good-bye."

Jiffy Lube Man: "Pleasure talking."

Apparently it went without saying that everyone knew what Vas Deferens meant. Linda assumed it was German, as in *Vas iss going on arount here.* And deferens sounded German as well. Wrong again. Her biggest mistake, however, was to casually ask Sandra, the mulatto hepster she sat next to in Intro to Lit, what it meant.

"How you mean?" Sandra said.

"You know," Linda said. "Like what's 'vas deferens' German for?"

Sandra winced like she couldn't believe it, then replied much too loud for the supposedly private conversation they were having: "Would you listen to her talking 'bout German! Are you kidding me, girl?"

Unfortunately, she was not.

"The vas deferens's the thing that carries the sperms from guys' balls to their cocks. I mean, girl, where you been?"

Well excuse *me*, Linda thought. She could feel herself blushing. "I guess I've been examining just a few less vas deferenses than some folks round here."

"Well I *guess*," Sandra said.

They both laughed.

"I mean, you know, as in vas-ectomy," said Sandra, forming scissors with two of her fingers and snipping the two blades together.
"Gotcha," said Linda.
"As in Vas-eline."
"I gotcha," said Linda.

When she got home that night she broke out some gin and looked up vas deferens in the dictionary. Where else? she considered, thumbing back to UV and then carefully turning the pages. She found it. *A spermatic duct especially of a higher vertebrate forming in man a small thick-walled tube about two feet long greatly convoluted in its proximal portion.* Say what? Greatly convoluted perhaps, but what's this about two feet long?

Her other dictionary had it as *the deferent vessel or duct of the testis that transports the sperm from the epididymis to the penis.* Okay. Getting warmer. Looking up deferent, she found *conveying away; efferent,* while deferential, just below, meant *respectful,* the very illogic of which led her (somehow) to understand that there was indeed a vas deferens between a man and a woman. Ha ha.

Sipping more gin, she looked up epididymis, which turned out to be *the elongated organ on the posterior surface of a testis that constitutes the convoluted beginning of the vas deferens,* which led right back to—what? The issue, or tissue, she thought, was getting more and more convoluted and certainly less and less sexy. It reminded her of the time back in high school when she'd discovered, purely by accident, while paging through some architecture magazine, that the curved edge formed by the intersection of two vaults was called, of all things, a groin: rather useless information perhaps, but something that she would remember. The irony, however, was that six months later a problem involving the groin of a vault had turned up on the math portion of the ACT test she was taking to get admitted to SAIC. Some facts were funny like that, Linda guessed.

She lit a cigarette and turned back to vas. In addition to vas deferentia, the plural, there also were vascular bundles, vascular cylinders (in Boston they'd be vascula cylindas), vascular tissues, vasoconstrictors (found deep in the Amazon jungle), vasodilations, Vaseline, and vasectomies. And while she was at it, she figured she may as well look up erection: in the event that she ever happened to come across one in the course of her studies, she wanted to be able to distinguish it from, oh, say, a vascular bundle. What an erection turned out to be was *a: the state marked by a firm turgid form and erect position of a previously flaccid bodily part containing cavernous tissue when that tissue becomes dilated with blood, b: an occurrence of such a state in the penis or clitoris.*
Hmm.
She blew a small smoke ring, watched while it billowed and

warped, then tried to blow another one through it. They simply destroyed one another.

Ho hum.

Definition *a*, she decided, could be her contribution to the list in the second-floor john. Definition *b* she'd reserve for some other, less public, contingency.

She sipped some more gin and kept reading.

The next time her A & P class met, on Tuesday, Linda, on purpose, arrived about ten minutes late. That way it would only be natural for her to slip unobtrusively into one of the seats by the door near the back of the room, where the Jiffy Lube Man always sat. And it worked. He was still sitting two seats away, on her right, but there was nobody else in between them.

Jonathan Strobe, the professor, had scratched four barely legible words onto the blackboard

POSSIBLE

PROBABLE

VIRTUAL

ACTUAL

with a short violent arrow slashing down on their left and a shorter, even more violent one, slashing up, on their right. "And so," he was saying, "for one *ve-e-ry* brief instant . . ."

A few of the students, including the Jiffy Lube Man, started laughing. They were supposed to be discussing "In The Mind of Some Eternal Spirit," an essay by some Sir named James Jeans. Linda had skimmed it that morning coming down on the el but had not really gotten too much of it. She pulled out her copy and wrote down the words from the board at the top of the first xeroxed page, then drew both the arrows. Okay. This was the last time the class would be meeting before they went on the field trip to Fermilab Thursday. According to Strobe there was some just incredibly fascinating connection between what Sir James Jeans had written and what they would see on this field trip, although Linda'd forgotten just what.

Rendeck was not taking notes. Linda hadn't actually *looked* at him, but still: she could tell. She figured that to stop taking notes now herself would tip off the fact that she'd noticed.

"Sir Jeans's central proposition, then," Strobe was saying, "is that God is a mathematician." He repeated this, paused for effect, then went on. "That mathematics, in fact, is the poetry of logic. So that whatever pictures or metaphors we may be able to come up with to help us to visualize the way the world works, however insightful, however poetic, that any or all of these non-mathematical pictures will turn out not only *not to be accurate*, but that they will in fact lead us one step further *away* from the truth, i.e. from an accurate understanding of the way that the world really works . . . "

Linda wrote *G. = mathematician and math = poetry logic.* She heard Rendeck's lighter click open, then five seconds later smelled smoke. She wrote *pictures or poems never work.*

Strobe had gone on in his usual ebullient, jittery, fast-talking manner: " . . . just as in Plato, where we sit imprisoned in the cave of our senses with our backs to the light, so that all we can see is what amounts to reality shadows—as Sir Jeans now points out, a position which Plato developed in response to his own age's tendency to interpret physical reality, or nature, in purely anthropomorphic terms, gigantic gods and goddesses hurling thunderbolts about at each other . . . "

Linda was dying for a cigarette now. She had her own pack in her purse, but what she (sort of) wanted to do was to get one off Hank. The best way, she figured, would be to coolly and subtly get his attention (whisper his name? just say yo? clear her throat? wait till he happened to look at her?), then nod toward his cigarette while holding her two cigaretteless fingers up to her lips and say with her eyes what she wanted. But of course she did not. What she did was write *Plato,* then *thunderbolts (anthropomorphic).*

" . . . until a thousand years later or so, after Descartes had taught us to mistrust the evidence presented to us by our senses, Bishop Berkeley hypothesized that . . . "

Hank cleared his throat rather loudly but did not look at Linda. Linda was writing *Descartes,* but she stopped and looked over his way. He was staring at Strobe with his right hand half raised, not really making that much of an effort to get the hand noticed, and was exhaling thin plumes of smoke. It was the first time she'd seen him, really looked at his profile, up close.

By now Strobe had glanced at Hank's hand more than once, but he had not acknowledged it yet. Linda looked back and forth between her notes and the board and the two of them as Strobe kept on talking.

And talking.

Her original impression of Hank had been that he looked like James Dean, only harder and smarter and darker: less pretty. Same wicked eyebrows, however, same swept back hair, pretty much the same blasé attitude. He also looked older (twenty-five, twenty-six) from this close than he had when she'd watched him from farther away. In spite of his general rep and his grease-stiffened Jiffy Lube jumpsuit, he looked very clean, and she liked that. She also noticed that his earlobe was pierced: but no earring. The longer she looked at him the more he reminded her of Stuart Sutcliffe from the Beatles'

Hamburg days: artsy, mysterioso, and handsome—a beatnik grease-ball but without all the grease or the beard—and bound, above all, to die young. Same high white cheekbones, same black-on-black plastic shades. (Although Hank didn't wear his in class, he did almost everyplace else.) Linda had been a fan of Stuart Sutcliffe ever since she'd come across his pictures in her mother's old fanzines (and then, after that, found her own). There was this one picture in particular, taken just before he died, at twenty-one, of an aneurysm or brain tumor, or something like that, in which he had—

"Yes, Mr. Rendeck?" said Strobe. He seemed slightly less pleased than he usually did to be entertaining the Jiffy Lube Man's impudent but (usually) intelligent questions.

Hank took one final drag off his cigarette then dropped it in front of him. It was clear he was making Strobe wait. "Yeah, well, this business about God, or whoever this eternal spirit guy turns out to be, about him being a mathematician . . . ?"

"Ye-e-es . . . ?" said Strobe, oozing mock-patience. He clearly was kidding the length of Hank's question.

Linda watched Hank grind out the butt of his cigarette with the sole of his boot. *Would Sir James Jeans's jeans look the same on Stu Sutcliffe, she wondered, as they would on the Jiffy Lube Man, or James Dean?*

"Anyway," said Hank, sort of smiling, apparently acknowledging the appropriateness of Strobe's bit of sarcasm, "isn't all Jeans is doing is getting ready to admit that nature, whatever, *is* quite a *bit* like a musician who's writing a fugue or a poet composing a sonnet? I mean, he says so right—"

"As a matter of fact, Hank," said Strobe, continuing his mock-patience schtick, "he *is* getting ready to say something like that, just as *we* are just about ready to get there ourselves, if you'll be kind enough to wait for the rest of us."

There were whistles, applause, and some laughter.

"However," said Strobe, suddenly changing his mind, "since Hank here insists, why don't we all skip a few pages ahead to . . . "

Hank had already started reading aloud from the article, but Strobe cut him off, speaking to the class as a whole: "Second-to-last paragraph on page eight, three lines down."

Linda located the paragraph, read a few words, looked at Hank. What she wanted right now was to ask—but he suddenly looked right back at her. His eyes were surprisingly green, but Linda could make out no signal before he turned back toward Strobe.

She could feel herself blushing and hated herself, hated Hank, hated the way—

"Have we found it?" said Strobe.

She calmed herself down, found the place.

Strobe started reading: "'To my mind, the laws which nature

obeys are *less suggestive* of those which a *machine* obeys in its motion than those which a musician obeys in writing a fugue, or a poet in composing a sonnet. The motions of electrons and atoms do not resemble those of the parts of a locomotive so much as those of the dancers in a cotillion.'" He took off his glasses and put up his finger. "Notice here that Sir Jeans is making a relative comparison between a poetic or musical picture and a more mechanistic way of looking at things and finding the former to be *somewhat less inadequate*, but that—skipping ahead now to the end of the very same paragraph—he says, '. . . then the universe can be *best* pictured, as,' um, 'as consisting of pure thought, the thought of what, for want of a wider word, we must describe as a mathematical thinker.'" Again he looked up at the class. "In other words, understanding nature as music or poetry, or dancing or painting, may be *somewhat* more adequate than understanding it, as our nineteenth-century forebears did, as some vast machine, and it is certainly a clearer picture of things than gods tossing thunderbolts, but that the best of all possible ways, according to James Jeans at least, is to think of reality as pure mathematical thought."

"In the mind of some eternal mathematical spirit," said Hank.

"Exactly," said Strobe.

Five or six hands now went up, but Strobe had stayed focused on Hank, the main reason being that Hank had just taken the desk next to Linda's and was rattling it against the tile floor.

Then he stopped. "As in, say," he said, "the pure mathematical *thought* of this desk here?"

"Exactly," said Strobe. He was grinning. (Was he pleased, Linda wondered, by Hank's strident counterexample or relieved that he'd stopped shaking the desk? Maybe both.) "As difficult, or perhaps impossible, as that idea may be to conceive of via one's astonishingly feeble human brainpower."

He was clearly referring to Hank's. There was laughter.

Strobe went on. "Because a hard metal desk and the noise it makes when it's rattled are merely the thrice or so removed *extensions* of what is primordially a mathematical idea."

Linda briefly considered writing *primordially* down, but did not.

And even as Strobe had been talking Hank had been fishing around in his briefcase. He now produced a Dunkin' Donuts bag, reached inside it, and pulled out a half-eaten longjohn. "As in, for example, the original, virtual, primordial, and *pure* mathematical thought of this baked good," he said, then proceeded to take a big bite.

This ploy apparently amused Strobe even more: he was visibly struggling to keep a straight face.

Linda, for her part, could not.

Hank grabbed the desktop again, but this time he chose not to shake it. Instead, still melodramatically chomping the longjohn, he said, "Wha *I* wu li to su'ges—"

Strobe interrupted him, making his own chomping noises while drawling out "Ye-e-es . . . ?"

It was weird.

Hank, having swallowed, continued: "Is that it makes just as much sense to think of this, this primordial creator as a baker—" and he raised what was left of the longjohn, "or a carpenter—" and he knocked on the wood of the desktop, "as to think of him as this prodigiously talented sculptor working in all kinds of forces and waves . . ."

"In other words," said Strobe, taking a few steps toward Hank, "that what God does isn't necessarily mathematical, but rather something that pretty much fits the description of what Hank Rendeck does."

"Now that you mention it," said Hank. "Yeah, that sounds about right."

Much groaning. Even Linda was a little dismayed at the extent to which the discussion had (or at least seemed to have had) degenerated.

Strobe seemed delighted, however. "Now we are getting somewhere," he said. He was back in the front of the room. "Because if you've been paying attention these last several classes, you'll have noticed that most if not all of the theories we've looked at can be seen, at least to a certain extent, to be little more than egocentric extrapolations by each of the theoreticians. Tribal warriors posits systems in which warrior gods make things happen. Indian gods look like Indians, African gods look like Africans. Along comes Plato, the idealist philosopher, and posits an abstract reality in which the ideal *forms* of all things are really what matter, any disputes about which to be settled by—who else? Idealist philosophers. Then there's Spinoza, then Berkeley, the bishop, who both posit God as the primordial essence of nature. James Jeans and Einstein, the math wizards, posit pure mathematical elegance. Just as Hank here, the sculptor, is positing sculpture as the basis of all our reality . . . . Do you see what I mean?"

Linda did and she didn't. And the rest of the class? From where she was sitting there was no way to tell. They were silent. Even Hank had no comment, though she sensed he was working on one.

"To put it more simply," said Strobe, "things have a way of turning out to be pretty much what we will make of them."

What?

"To which Jeans would say 'horseshit,'" said Hank.

"Not really," said Strobe. "To which Sir Jeans would probably attach the proviso '*mutatis mutandis*.'"

The proviso *mutatis mutandis*. Linda had written it down before Strobe had gone on but did not look it up after class. She was pissed. She had wanted to follow along, but after a while she hadn't been able to keep real close track of who was replying to whom, let alone what the issue still was. The discussion—Hank and Strobe, for the most part—had continued until people from the class after theirs had arrived, which was the way most of these debates ended anyway.

Anyway. There had not been a chance to say even one word to Hank, or for Hank to say one word to her.

She was pissed.

For the drive out to Fermilab Thursday, Linda somehow got stuck riding up front with Strobe in his Volvo along with a pink infant carseat. There were three other students in back: Gordon and Paul and Suzette, none of whom Linda was friends with or even knew very well. The remaining eleven or twelve of their classmates were following the Volvo in three other cars. They had met in the lobby at ten and waited around almost forty-five minutes for Hank and another guy, Tim, who Strobe then found out had just called in sick. So they left. Hank simply never showed up.

They headed west out of the city on the Eisenhower, through Maywood and Broadview, then picked up the East-West Tollway— "the official tollway," according to Strobe, "of our illustrious sister school, East-West University"—and headed south-southwest toward Aurora.

Linda had set her alarm for 7:15 (a couple or three hours earlier than she usually did) to give herself plenty of time to tart herself up, to deal with the pimple that had (inevitably) emerged on her forehead, then make it by ten down to school. And she had. What she hadn't had yet, though she'd been up now for almost four hours, was a cigarette (her hard and fast rule was never to smoke before noon). To make matters worse, her period was just coming on. She was groggy and bloated and ornery. She also was sure there were parties in the three cars behind them, or at least the opportunity to just yawn and stay silent, whereas in Strobe's goddamn car you may just as well have been sitting in class. In addition to his running commentary on the "visual environment" of Chicago's West Side, the point spread in that Sunday's Bear game and ways of "disguising the forty-six blitzes," he was treating his fortunate four student-passengers to a bonus introductory lecture on antiproton debunchers, Doug Plank, colliding charmed quarks, and the differences between bevatrons, boosters, and tevatrons.

Christ!

Yet in spite of her mood, in spite of the captive conditions, did Linda not have to admit that what Strobe had to say about where they were headed was interesting?

Categorically, unequivocally, absolutely, most definitely *not.*
Ah ah.
No way.
Not a chance.

Strobe stopped the car at a tollbooth and tossed in some coins. They were now out by Oak Brook. Could you hitchhike from here back to school? Linda wondered. Or walk?

The tollgate went up and Strobe shifted gears and accelerated. "Please let me know if I'm getting too technical," he said. He was only half kidding.

"Oh no-oo-ooo," said Gordon, who apparently felt pretty much the same way as Linda. Paul and Suzette, though, were writing things down in their notebooks, merely the idea of which made Linda feel carsick. And as if that weren't bad enough, they were actually asking Strobe "follow-up" questions in order to make him talk *more.*

Linda sipped her black coffee. She stared out the window a while, but the tollway-side scenery could not have been too much more boring: vast shopping plazas surrounded by still vaster parking lots, complexes of *trés moderne* condos, between which lay flat brown dead nothing. She did not feel like chatting, however, even less like attending a lecture on charmed quarks and Bears while seated right next to the lecturer, let alone taking notes or "participating." What she did feel like doing was (literally) puking. Because all of a sudden she had started to feel pretty carsick. She opened her window a little and took some deep breaths. Very carsick, in fact. Whatever James Jeans (whose essay she'd finally read Wednesday night) had to do with all of this technical stuff, or the Bears, or Enrico H. Fermi's damn lab, Strobe hadn't gotten to yet. But Linda was sure that he would. Would have bet the whole rest of her life on it.

Would have lost. Because by the time they turned north off the tollway at the Eola Road exit, Strobe had at last lightened up and the air in the car had begun to do Linda some good. She was hungry, in fact. Even the scenery had improved: it wasn't the ocean or mountains of course, but at least there were trees around here, changing colors, and every so often a pond or a barn or a river.

Ten minutes later they arrived at the Fermilab entrance. Strobe said good morning to one of the guards, was corrected with "good afternoon," and drove through. James Jeans's theories had still not been mentioned. Just as amazing, perhaps, was the fact that the other three cars were still with them.

Linda was doing her best to get pumped: any place with an official security outpost manned by uniformed (albeit female) armed guards could not be *all* boring, she figured. But the first thing she saw, as they came round a bend in the road, was the last thing she'd ever expected: a medium-sized herd of—what?

Buffaloes?

Yup. (Had she seen one before in real life? Aside from a pair in the Lincoln Park Zoo, she had not. And that had been when she was ten.) There were five or six dozen, it looked like, grazing quite nonchalantly on a green sloping pasture, and in all shapes and sizes to boot. The largest—the bulls, Linda guessed—were truly gigantic, the size of at least two large cows, with magnificent humps on their shoulders and thick chocolate manes surrounding their horned massive heads. They looked like a cross between lions and rhinos and bears, ass-backward throwbacks of some sort, but gorgeous: beautiful strange shaggy monsters from another whole age. Linda loved it.

Strobe slowed way down as they drove by the pasture, though his tour-guide routine was now very much back in fifth gear. He even had taken to waving and shouting to the students who'd pulled up behind them. Linda was content to just look and so managed to phase out his spiel. It was still sinking in that she'd come all this way to watch quarks get collided in tevatrons and but here she was gawking at . . . buffalo.

The Fermilab cafeteria was on the ground floor of an atrium that featured her two favorite colors and textures: mottled gray staggered-board concrete hung with patches and streamers of ivy. It was enclosed on two sides by glass and on the other two sides by vaulted twin towers rising up over the treetops then coming together several more stories above them. In all her born days she had never seen anything like it. The State of Illinois Building's was larger, she figured, but this place was somehow . . . sublimer.

Gordon was sitting across from her at the end of a long empty table. He had already wolfed down a burger and was talking non-stop about school. Was he flirting with her? Yes he was. He also was managing a better than fair imitation of Strobe's lecture manner: beaming, beneficent, talking five words a second about six things at once—hard not to like but still more than a little ridiculous.

Linda assumed the effect was intentional, so she shook her head, nodded, and laughed. Gordon looked baffled, then pleased, and she knew right away that meant trouble.

She concentrated now on her food. She had ordered the special: potato-tomato-and-green-pepper omelette, onion croissant, and the medium drink of her choice (since Bombay-and-tonic had not been an option, she settled for New Dr. Pepper). After three bites of omelette, however, with Gordon still blabbing and staring, her appetite somehow had vanished.

She lit up a cigarette, her first of the day, and stared through the trees and the plants and out the glass wall at the sky.

"Cats," Gordon said.

Huh? Linda thought, but said nothing.

"You look sort of just like the chick who was playing the lead in the, you know, the white one. Grizabella. In *Cats*. Did you see it?" She suddenly felt very dizzy. The sky was so blue. And she hadn't.

"Awkward silence," said Gordon.

Though she still felt real dizzy, she took one more drag. She hadn't a clue what to tell him. The sky—

"This is your captain," said Gordon. "Your captain says we are going down . . ."

She refocussed back on the concrete, still dazed, and then up at the point where the vaults came together. "Do you know what you call that?" she said—God knew why. She felt like she was going to vomit, or faint.

"Big Science?" said Gordon.

Or vomit *and* faint. Or faint *and* then vomit. Or maybe—

"Call what?" Gordon said. "You mean—"

"Nothing," she said. She breathed out and in very slowly.

"Call nothing?" said Gordon. He looked toward the top of the atrium. "You mean what do you—"

"Yeah," Linda said. What else could she say? "Where the two concrete vaults come together."

"The chancel?" said Gordon. "No, not the chancel. You mean there, at the top of the atrium?"

"I don't think the chancel," she said.

"So what do you call it," said Gordon.

"The chancel?" she said. Then she shrugged. It was lame but the best she could do. "I don't know."

"Not the chancel," said Gordon. She was touched he was trying so hard. "It's . . . shit. It was just on the tip of my tongue." And he stuck out his pink tongue to prove it.

More awkward silence.

"I just thought you'd know what you called it," said Linda.

The tour Strobe had promised commenced at 1:30 sharp, as he'd promised, in a room with a screen in the front. Linda sat down near the back, by herself. She sipped Dr. Pepper and breathed. The woman conducting the tour welcomed the class to Fermilab and introduced herself as Helga Fife. She was right around Strobe's age, late thirties, still blonde, a little more handsome than pretty. But pretty. She was wearing a plaid pleated past-the-knee skirt, a bone-colored turtleneck sweater (cashmere, it looked like, from where Linda was sitting), and a navy blue blazer with a small purple iris sticking out through the lapel hole. Somehow she just didn't fit Linda's image of a middle-aged female nuclear particle physicist.

But, hey, there you were, Linda thought. And then: Maybe she's really Strobe's lover, his excuse for the trip in the first place.

Helga Fife passed out a stack of white folders with a (competent) line drawing of Enrico Fermi on the cover. Inside each folder were five or six stapled (long) articles, photographs of a pagoda and a geodesic dome, and a six-inch-long sample of what was labeled as niobium-titanium alloy.

Oh boy.

Somebody switched off the lights. There was silence for five or six seconds, then whispers. An unfocussed slide then appeared on the screen. Helga Fife focussed the slide—an aerial photograph of the Fermilab complex—and started her lecture by asking them to stop her if things got too technical, at which point old Gordon yelled, "Stop!" There was laughter. When it stopped she restarted by stating that the facility was funded by the U.S. Department of Energy, that construction had begun in 1973, and that the project was completed at a cost of some very large number of dollars.

In the light from the next several slides, using her black micro Uni-Ball pen, Linda gave Fermi more hair, sweeping it back off his forehead and filling the sides in a little. Positive capability, she noted. With a few more deft strokes she added some slant to his eyebrows and took away some of his smile. Then she wrote down the last thing she thought she heard Helga Fife say: *earthen berm.*

The slide show took twenty-five minutes. The next stop on the tour, for which they had to leave Wilson Hall and walk through a parking lot, was the pre-accelerator area. Strobe and Helga Fife walked ahead, close together, Strobe (as always) talking and gesturing with great animation, Helga Fife nodding her head. As a couple, thought Linda, they didn't look half-bad at all.

The inside of the pre-ac building, as Helga Fife called it, was the first place that Linda had seen on the field trip so far that looked like a place where scientific experiments would actually go down. There was a hum, a low buzz, in the background, and much shine and dark all around: meters, beepers, gauges, CRT screens, lots of small flashing lights and dim corners, with strange words and figures—the weird hieroglyphics of ultra-high tech—stencilled in black on smooth metal. There was even a sign that said CAUTION: 480 VOLTS. Another said RADIOACTIVE.

"This is your captain," said Gordon. "Your captain says we—"

Someone shushed him, and Linda thanked God half out loud. Gordon blushed.

The actual pre-ac itself was housed in a thirty-foot pit lined on its top and its sides with red bricks, with a single glass slit of a window too small for more than two people to look through at once.

"This is our Cockcroft-Walton Pre-Accelerator," said Helga Fife. "It is capable of producing . . ."

Okay, Linda thought. This is a little more like it.

When it was finally her turn to look, Linda moved front and center and took the whole window. Below her, glinting in silence in a glowing white room, was a huge soft-edged cube, about eight-feet-by-eight-feet-by-eight, very smooth, very shiny, supported by four thin black legs and with five or six arms protruding in different directions. It was stark, vaguely scary, and massive. Both the legs and the arms were ringed at two-foot intervals with the same gleaming metal that the cube was made out of. It reminded Linda of a headless (though still very smart) metal X-Oid in the secret control room of some alien starship. Or something like that. She had never liked sci-fi stuff much, but she had to admit that the Cockcroft-Walton pre-ac-whatever impressed her.

After the pre-ac came a better lit, more spacious area manned by technicians and doctors and nurses in pressed sky-blue lab coats with plastic ID cards clipped to their pockets, together with what were apparently—because of their pale tufted scalps—cancer patients. Correcto. Because according to Strobe's low-key whisper, they were now in the Neutron Therapy Facility. Once again they had come round a corner and suddenly found themselves in what amounted to another whole world.

Helga Fife was explaining—even tone, normal volume—that the second step of the process, the linear accelerator, spun off some extremely fast neutrons as by-products; after being ricocheted off a special beryllium target, the neutrons could be used to treat hypoxic tumors. The stages of this treatment were illustrated in the gruesomest trio of before—, during—, and after— pictures—all color, all close-ups—that Linda had ever laid eyes on. There were oohs, groans, and gasps from her classmates. Two guys were already sketching the pictures, one on the back of his Fermilab folder, and Suzette had unscrewed her lens cap. The first picture showed the lower back portion of what was clearly a woman. Bulging out over one hip was a tumor (a "sarcoma" was what Helga Fife called it) that looked like a large baked potato, only bluish and veiny and millions of times more grotesque. It had stretched the pale skin that contained it to a transparent thinness that gave Linda the willies and then some. In the next picture—"Seven Weeks Later"—the tumor looked more like a jumbo blue egg, and the hip had what looked like a very bad sunburn. In the third picture—"Fifteen Weeks Later"—all that was left where the tumor had been was the sunburn, which Helga Fife assured them had eventually disappeared, too.

Linda swallowed.

They moved on in relative silence. They were shown through the central control room, then two more rooms of computers. After that came the booster accelerator. Gradually things lightened up. Linda, however, could not get the tumor, or whatever it was, off her brain, just as nobody else could, she figured. Goddamn.

The next thing she knew they were outside again in the parking lot with some very bright sun in their eyes, being herded back toward Wilson Hall.

From the east-facing side of the fifteenth-floor observation deck, by looking as far to her left as she could, Linda could see the buffalo pasture. She could even make out, though just barely, some buffalo. She had eaten a chocolate-chip cookie while riding up in the elevator, so she now felt a little less woozy.

Even from only fifteen floors up, you could see for what looked like forever, since there were no other tall or even medium-sized buildings for miles. It reminded her of looking out over the Loop from the top of Sears Tower: from fifteen stories or ninety, the view was still quite "panoramic." The only thing was, when she tried to look down she got dizzy.

To the east, right below them, was the four-mile-long ring of raised earth—Helga Fife's "earthen berm." Eleven feet under this earth were the rings through which protons and antiprotons were zooming along at 99.995 percent of the speed of light.

Helga Fife snapped her fingers. "Fifty thousand times," she said. Then she made a very quick loop with her hand while snapping her fingers again. "Fifty thousand more times," she said. She paused for effect. "Every second."

"Which is three times faster than anyplace else in the world now," said Strobe.

Helga Fife said, "In effect."

"In effect," said Strobe. "Right. But so inside that ring is the place where E comes the closest to actually equalling $mc\ squared$."

Some of her classmates were still taking notes. Linda wasn't. Others were staring down out at the berm. Linda wasn't doing that either.

"There are two rings, actually," said Helga Fife. "Protons in one going one way, anti-protons going the opposite way in the other."

All of a sudden Linda was hungry again. As a matter of fact, she felt like she was going to faint. She knew that she actually wouldn't, but still: she was thirsty, bored silly, and starving.

"A series of superconducting pulsed magnets suck them along through the aperture," Helga Fife was now saying. "When we decide to collide them together they produce almost two trillion electron volts of energy, which gives us three times the luminosity of the second most violent collisions now being—"

"For what?" Gordon said. "I mean, you know, what for?"

"That's a good question," said Helga Fife.

Gordon glanced over at Linda.

"That's a *very* good question," said Strobe.

"One of the things that we're looking at," said Helga Fife, "is what amounts to the angle of ricochet as the hadrons get broken apart into their constituent quarks, from which we are able to draw certain conclusions about what's come to be called the Big Bang."

"Excuse me," said Strobe. "That's certain quote unquote, correct?"

Helga Fife surprised Linda, and apparently old Strobe as well, by simply ignoring his question and saying, "The scintillation detectors in the spark chamber are able to sense when the hadrons have managed to—"

"So then what's a hadron?" said Gordon, inducing high school-style tittering from the three guys around him.

"*Another* good question," said Strobe, who was grinning, as ever, at Helga.

"A hadron," she said, unperturbed, "is either two or three quarks, quarks being the smallest particles we now are aware of, bonded together by what we now call the strong force."

"Things do be getting more and more interesting," said Gordon.

Linda half-rolled her eyes in disgust. As she did there appeared, just over Helga Fife's shoulder, Hank Rendeck. Though she tried hard to hide it, Linda now did a literal triple-take. Because standing with Hank was a tall crewcut guy with bad acne: Chester Treasure, she knew. And between them, much shorter, was a beautiful Japanese woman.

Oh boy.

"We got sort of a little late start," Hank said to Strobe.

Chester Treasure said nothing, apparently content to just stand around looking sullen as humanly possible.

"Sorry," said the Japanese woman. Her voice was like porcelain sculpture: from just the one word, Linda deduced she was smart, self-assured, and terribly terribly sexy. The other thing was, she really did seem to be sorry. Then to top it all off, in response to Strobe's welcome, she smiled, letting her big white teeth shine straight into Linda's crazed brain.

Helga Fife had continued her lecture. They had turned one more corner and were examining a scale model of the tevatron system in cross-section. Linda had positioned herself so that she could face Helga Fife and pretend to be paying attention, but could also keep one eye on Rendeck and friends (they *were* just three friends, were they not?) and figure out who was with whom.

Hank was now listening to what Helga Fife said with what seemed to be great fascination. He was wearing a wrinkled gray raincoat and bluejeans in place of his Jiffy Lube jumpsuit. Chester Treasure was talking to one of the guys from the class. The Japanese woman still was positioned between them but was nodding at something that Strobe had just said. She was wearing a scarlet wool blazer to go with her glossy black hair, which she wore in a braided chignon. Her skin was a flawless white gold flushed with pink stretched tautly across what were, from Linda's perspective at least, some truly astonishing cheekbones.

Linda was certain she wasn't from SAIC: if she had gone to school there, or taught there, Linda was sure she'd have noticed her long before now. She also was certain that the woman was older than Hank was. Her best guess was thirty, though perhaps she was even much older . . . but so what was she doing with Hank then? Weren't these Japanese women supposed to be—what was the word for it? Chaste? What a laugh. The longer she stared at her, the more she reminded her of a sleek stunning version of Yoko.

Helga Fife was describing how liquid helium kept the niobium-titanium magnets cooled down to three degrees Kelvin, or four hundred fifty degrees below zero, and how the magnets were "trained" by a series of pulsed excitations and quenches.

"Coldest stuff on earth," said Strobe, "surrounding the smallest and fastest and hottest."

Though she wished she had not once she had, Linda asked Gordon, "Who's that just showed up with what's-his-name?"

Awkward silence.

"Do you really want to know," Gordon said, "or are you just praticing for one of those *performances* of yours?"

Fair enough, Linda thought. Then she smiled—exposing, on purpose, her snaggled and off-white bicuspids. She did not even care any more if her bangs were still hiding her pimple.

The next stop on the tour was an arrow-head collection from what had once been the Indian camps on the site. The stop after that was a mock-up of the scintillation detectors inside the spark chamber. The stop after that was the north view, from which the buffalo pasture could be more clearly seen, and at which point Helga Fife asked if any one in the class wanted to adopt a baby buffalo, since lately the Fermilab herd had been getting "a bit *too* successful." A joke.

Linda was no longer paying too much attention. It was almost 3:30. She'd been up for eight hours but had still hardly eaten. She was dizzy, exhausted, and beyond-hungry queasy. She did not even feel like a cigarette. And she still had to face the hour-and-a-half drive in Strobe's car back to school, plus the ride on the el, then the bus. She did not want to think about that. She did not want to think about Hank. She did not want to think any more.

Home, in bed, after midnight, when she tried to recall what the Japanese woman had looked like, she was unable to get her face to stand still. It would either start shimmering in and out of focus or flash off and on very quickly. Sometimes it just turned away, frame by frame, in slow motion.

She did not think at all about Strobe—in whose car she had finally puked—or James Jeans. She did not think about antiprotons. The sarcoma, or whatever you called it, on the wall of the Neutron Therapy Facility kept flashing back to her. Spooky light blue. Shine and dark. All that cancer.

And Hank. Just what was up with that guy, Linda wanted to know. She was frantic for five or six seconds, then calm. She was sick, but the room was not spinning. Her eyes were wide open. Her guts felt swelled up. She was bleeding.

She got up and went to the bathroom and looked at her face in the mirror. One pimple. Her eyes were all bloodshot and puffy. She was neither real stunning nor grotesquely ugly, she figured.

And then: She was crazy. She glared at herself till her eyes stung, then blinked. Was she crazy or wasn't she? No, she decided. Just ugly. Not stunning, just stupid.

She opened the medicine cabinet and her face disappeared, just like that. She was wasted and sick. She was thinking.

She leaned on the sink for a second then held on with all of her might.

Somehow she knew that her face was still there.

Puffy and shining and dark.

In the mirror.

PAPAGENO

(from *Playboy Magazine*)

I always come out here after a job, because no one knows where I am. It's like being on the moon. The dry lakes and cinder hills and Joshua trees stretch for hundreds of miles. The jeep is parked in my cave on the high ground and all I have to do is wait for the signal on the short wave. While I wait, I live off the land and play my cassette and write in my diary and watch time pass with the shadows on the ridge line.

Most people would tell you that deserts are sterile places, but that is not true. There is water here in every cactus, and there is life wherever you look. There are insects, rabbits, hawks, lizards, coyotes, snakes. You just have to know where to find things.

I killed a rattlesnake this morning. It was curled very close to my face as I woke up. I suppose it had settled near me for warmth during the night. When I opened my eyes, there it was, not three inches from me, eye level, and as I stared at it, I could hear its tail start to shake like beads in a gourd. If I had blinked, I would be dead now, but I rolled over, fast, and the rattler struck the back of my sleeping bag. I jumped out and grabbed my entrenching tool and smashed its head. I will make a belt out of its skin and a choker out of its rattles. I am lucky in the desert.

It is a good life out here and sometimes I think about staying forever.

"Your Mexican connection is screwing you," I said to Giordano. He had sent his bodyguard away and we were alone in his kitchen. The tax forms were spread on the table and he was squinting at the numbers. We were trying to decide what had to be laundered and I talked about his options.

"The IRS is probably going to write up a reciprocal agreement with the Bank of Mexico," I said, "and if that happens, Skipsey won't be able to help us. OK, do we go through Bueno, then?"

"I don't trust him," Giordano said. He stood up to stir a pot of sauce on the stove. He wiped his hands on his apron—yes, he was wearing an apron.

"I don't trust him, either," I said. "But the Nevada skim is supposed to show up in Cuernavaca."

"Change it," he said.

I wanted him sitting down, so I kept talking. "OK, we'll work the Bahamas harder."

"Yeah. Good," he said.

I put the new signature cards on his place mat. I knew he would have to sit down to sign the cards. He did, slowly. I took out the calculator and turned it on. He checked it with a flick of his eyes. Then he went back to reading the cards while I talked.

"Murdoch is short-weighting all of the silver, even the dollars, but the receipts don't check with the totals. I think that's happening south of the border. Now all we've got to do is keep it out of domestic income, so I'll open a chain of offshore accounts for shell corporations. The IRS can't find that. And we'll change the Nevada route completely; different pilots, different flight plans. I think we'll be OK."

"We better be," he said as he leaned forward. He signed the cards slowly. He was breathing like an asthmatic. It was five days before he was supposed to testify and his nerves brought on his illnesses.

I held the calculator in my hands and pointed it at his right temple. I pushed the safety. Then I shot him. I shot him six times, once through the roof of his mouth, because I had to make it look right and proper, a family hit, and it was the method to deliver a shot through the mouth if it was the mouth that caused the concern. Giordano was about to testify before Congress re our Cuban connections, and that was reason enough for many of his own people to want him quiet.

"*Ca va mieux?*" I asked his corpse. I could hear Mozart in my head as I pushed the trigger mechanism back into the slot. I was singing to myself while I dusted the table, the glasses, anything I might have touched. It is not that I was happy, but I needed to stay calm, and Mozart did that for me.

I ran out the back door just as I heard the bodyguard come in the front door.

Falcone met me with the taxi in the alley. I hopped in and we took off. I talked to the back of Falcone's head as he drove me to O'Hare.

"You need more insulation for the barrel housing," I said. "It got hot in my hands." I studied the calculator and wondered who had invented such a thing. "The silencer baffles rattle. Somebody should fix that." I was shaking and I could not hear Mozart anymore. I tossed the calculator onto the front seat.

"Glad you liked it," Falcone laughed. He was smoking a cigar, but I could still smell his lime after-shave. He stopped the taxi at the edge of the forest preserve and threw a regular .22 pistol into the woods. Not too far. Someone would find it. People would think what we wanted them to think. The .22 had been pre-fired. Its barrel was identical to the barrel in the calculator. The fingerprints of the bodyguard had been carefully etched into the weapon. It was all very cute.

"We'll let you know when it's cool. OK, Gene?" Falcone asked me as he let me out on the airport ramp.

"OK, I'll be listening," I said.

"OK, man. Good job, hey." Falcone offered his hand out the window. "So where you going to be, huh?"

I did not shake his hand. "See you," I waved. I turned my back on him and went into the terminal and flew to Palm Springs by way of Los Angeles.

When I came out to the desert that time, my jeep got stuck in a gully during a flash flood. I stayed under my shelter half and wrote in my diary and waited for the sun to bake the mud. I did not like being out on the flatland, where people might see me. It was very quiet after the storm. I trapped a wild rabbit. I know how to do things like that.

Last night I drove south across the lava flow that lies east of the Bullion Mountains. The Marines were firing illumination rounds toward Mesquite Lake. The flares looked like burning seeds while they were hanging from their parachutes. I sat up on the ridge line and watched the fireworks: 105s, 155s, high explosive and white phosphorus, barrages that sounded like God's own thunder. After it was over, I drove back here to my cave and I played my cassette and sang like a madman:

"Der Vogelfänger bin ich, ja
Stets lustig, heissa, hopsassa!
Der Vogelfänger bin bekannt
Bei alt und jung im ganzen Land."

I pretended that I was in Vienna for the first time, a young kid with stars in his eyes hearing Mozart and eating chocolate at Demel's and making love with the streetwalkers who gathered near the cathedral. I was 19 then. I had spent the summer in East Germany on French papers. I was supposed to assess how the young people felt and thought in Magdeburg and Leipzig and other forbidden places. Then I was to come out through Eisenach and take a vacation in Vienna, write up a report, talk to debriefers. In Vienna, I went to *Die Zauberflöte* every chance I got. Then I talked to our people and told them what they did not want to hear: that there were 22 Russian divisions in-country, that there were no young people to meet, because they were all in government service, that the state was highly organized and that you had to run machine-gun nests and guard towers to get back on the autobahn. Revolution? Not hardly. But that was in

1956, two months before the Hungarian Revolution, and our people thought that all of Eastern Europe would soon be in flames. They heard only what they wanted to hear, and then they asked me to drive the Simca back to Paris and sell it for whatever I could. They called it my honorarium. I did not know what the word meant.

The desert is a community of energy. Its rhythms are as neat as Mozart's. There is a sense of order here: Lizards eat insects: rabbits eat vegetation: hawks eat rabbits: coyotes eat anything. Everything works until people arrive. When the Marines come up from Twenty-nine Palms or when the bikers ride out from Los Angeles, then things start to go wrong. I wish the desert were always empty and I did not have to worry about people.

I had to kill an old man three days ago. He was a prospector and he stumbled past my cave in the early morning. It was my fault, I suppose, because I was not being careful, and if I had not been listening to the short-wave, perhaps it would have gone differently.

I pretended that it was good to see him. I gave him a full canteen from my water bags and we talked: of homesteading, mineral rights, weather patterns, gold mines, silver speculation. He smiled like a toothless monkey. We watched a Cessna flying over Kelso Peak and the prospector nodded at my jeep, which was covered with camouflage netting.

"You think that son of a bitch knows we're down here?" he asked.

"No. Not unless he's got special lenses," I said.

"I'll bet he's a revenuer," the old man laughed.

It was his last laugh, even though I would not have chosen death for him if I could have helped it, even though I could tell that he had survived great chaos in his life and probably deserved to live. But it was him or me. Possibly, Falcone sent him. How was I to know? I used to trust Falcone, but now I don't trust anyone.

"Say, there, buddy," I yelled after I had gotten upwind of him, after the atropine injection and the cloth over the mouth and the deep breath that I held while I shot the cartridge straight into his face when he turned toward me again. He looked very surprised, as if I had spit at him. The VX sent his heart into fibrillation and he died immediately with all the symptoms of a coronary: purple face, blood in the mouth, eyes frozen open. There was music coming from somewhere and it stayed with me while I drove to the Barstow road and dumped the body, leaving it for vultures, knowing that if someone found him, there was no way an autopsy could reveal anything. Coroners do not run radioimmuno assays on old mule skinners. They do not go to Washington for the reagents or to England for the glass-refractile index. And if that old bastard was a plant, and if Falcone sent him, then whatever they ran could not be published.

The East Germans still work with curare, but I find that too clumsy. You have to scratch the skin, which leaves evidence, and it takes a brush contact to deliver it. When Mulking died down by the docks in Istanbul, our doctors found a small welt on his hand. So we knew what had happened. The method left nothing to appreciate. It was obvious, direct, unsubtle.

Method is everything. You must learn to match the method. Hit men have their M.O.s. Fashions change. You learn to bend with the times like a rice shoot in water. You try to be as graceful as a birdcatcher.

I am letting myself grow a beard out here. With my track shorts and shoulder holster and .45 and running shoes and sweatband, I must be quite a sight. No one knows where I am, and that is OK. My answering service tells people I am in Istanbul again on loan to British Petroleum for an audit. Why not? Sometimes I dream that I am sitting in Bebek with the Bosporus lapping at the sides of the restaurant and the raki curling like smoke over the ice in my glass. Nedim and I argue again about Chekhov and in my dream I am eloquent.

"You don't understand," I say, "that death is an aid to art. *The Cherry Orchard* is Chekhov's best play. It is also his last play. He died shortly after he wrote it. He sensed his death, Imperial Russia's death, and it gave him more reason to work well. Death helps. Mozart wrote his best opera just before he died." In my dream, Nedim's eyes cannot handle that thought and they go blank; but even in my dream, I understand that Nedim has been scarred forever. His own father was hanged alongside Menderes. All of our money could not save him.

People do not seem to accept death the way animals do. For example: I caught a chuckwalla this afternoon. It was sunning itself on a rock near Cadiz Lake. It was more than a foot long, and when it heard my steps, it ducked into a crevice and blew itself up like a balloon.

"Hello, chuckwalla," I laughed. "Do you think I can't pull you out of there now?" I reached in and cut its throat. Blood and air rushed out like steam from a casing. There was no struggle, no histrionics. The chuckwalla and I understood the terms. Everything was neat and simple between us.

Tonight, if I build a fire, I will roast the chuckwalla and the sidewinder and I will toast yucca fruit and make tea with juniper leaves. I will eat cactus berries for dessert.

No one can touch me. I could live here for years. If people will just leave me alone.

I think I saw a light tonight in the valley north of Danby Lake. There were thunderheads over the Piute Mountains and it is possible that it was raining on the dry lake bed. Maybe someone down there had to use lights to survive. The thing I do not like about it is that I did not know anyone was there. I must be getting sloppy.

"We are now sleeping with the Devil," Madden had said. "We want you to join us."

We were eating steak in that small restaurant in Florence. Madden had come up from Palermo to see me. He was on sabbatical. He knew everyone in the Italian labor movement and he spoke of the organization we were infiltrating.

"They're a fact of life," Madden said, "like dirt. They are there under all of us. We've needed them since World War Two. We still need them. Very badly."

"I don't see where I come in," I said. The white-tile walls of the restaurant gleamed like mirrors of milk.

"You have the credentials," Madden said. "You're clean. Ivy League. Marines. They like that kind of thing. You bring a certain respectability with you."

"It's good for country clubs," I said. "But that's about all."

"You'd be surprised," Madden said. He was eating meticulously. He did not know that he was going to die in a cell in Cienfuegos years later.

"What do you want me to do?" I asked.

"Let us know where their money is going, who they're working with. That sort of thing. We'll never use you for anything but surveillance. We want to use them, not prosecute them. Trust us, Gene. We'll even feed you information, to make you look good. You'll be the best damned accountant they ever had. Just trust us."

I sat there drinking wine. I did not speak for a long time. Then I said, "Machiavelli lived right across the river. They kept him under arrest most of the time. You know what he had hanging over his fireplace? The handcuffs he'd worn in prison. How about that?"

Madden saw no connection. He was tired. He wanted to wrap me up. "We think you could do the job," he said firmly.

"You remember how you recruited me the first time?" I asked. "'You don't learn to pick locks at Princeton.' Remember how you used to say that? 'You don't learn to jump out of airplanes at Princeton.' Sound familiar? My own Renaissance and Reformation professor. Putting stars in my eyes. And you're still trying to do it. You got me to go into East Germany twenty years ago. You used me in Laos and Turkey. Off and on. Contract work. Little moments. Lots of dollars. Now you want me to go do the books for some people in silk suits?"

I spoke with conviction, but secretly I was wavering. The price of exertion was climbing. My energies were being newly metered by me. Something inside me was burning out, like a lamp in a mine. I was bored; bored with my family, my colleagues, my life. There was an itching inside my head, as if a thousand cockroaches were running through my brain, and I was wondering if my middle years would be spent playing golf with fat men. Madden was offering me an exciting life again. A voice whispered to me, "Take the job. They won't use you for much. You'll have a good-looking secretary and a lot of money and things will not be dull."

Madden saw my eyes shift. He did not say anything directly. He simply moved on with the proposition. "We need a C.P.A. we've worked with. One we trust. We think we can get you inside. They admire sound financial advice. Your track record is good."

"I can make people money and I can save them money," I said. "I used to think that was the most exciting thing in life."

Madden began joking with the waitress. It was very late and we were the last people in the restaurant. The waitress did not know that Madden liked slim young boys with cute butts, and for a time she thought he might go home with her. When he turned abruptly cold, she smiled at me and made the sign of the horns.

"*Finita la commedia*," she laughed.

"Not quite," I said under my breath.

So I went to work for Madden and Company again, and I began to counsel aging *padrones* about real estate, stocks, commodities, Liechtenstein incorporation, exotic investments, daring dodges. I became known as a man who could save millions. I established the reputation of a guru, a clairvoyant, and my work was so good that it seemed miraculous, as if I had access to grand-jury testimony and IRS memos and Justice Department sitreps. Which I did.

I have a copy of the new tax code in my jeep. When I get bored, I read it and laugh and laugh. The people who wrote that are the best comedians in America.

My cave is near the top of Old Woman Mountain. It is like a fortress. I have laid trip wires down all the paths. They will set off flares if anyone tries to get up here. There will not be any more accidental run-ins with prospectors or anyone else. I have transmitters wired down the slope and I have my Starscope and my grenades and my .45. I am good at my work, a renaissance man. I can reconnoiter or figure an itemized deduction.

Only the high ground is safe. That is what Pulaski used to say. "Love the high ground—hate the low ground," he preached. "Don't let nobody get above you, Poppa Gene," he said. Pulaski was the first one to call me by that name. He thought the way I played *The Magic Flute* to myself all the time was funny.

Pulaski was an old Southeast Asia hand who had worked with the French at Dien Bien Phu and then stayed around for the next war. He worked under AID cover out of Vientiane. I was attached on temporary duty to his office from the Marines. He taught me a great deal, and he was a talented man who deserved more than he got.

"Everybody down the slope from you is a pissant," Pulaski would lecture me on patrol. "But don't let nobody get on top of you, understand? Everybody above you owns you. OK?" Pulaski talked like a coal miner, which is what his father had been, and he kept his bad grammar like a badge. He liked to say ain't in the presence of generals. The fact that he also had an M.A. in Asian studies from Columbia was not something he mentioned much.

One time, after we had seeded the trail with special transmitters that were disguised as animal droppings, a technician flew out from Travis to examine what we had done wrong. He was picking up incredible noises on his monitor and he was ordering air strikes that produced no joy. "There's something out there," the man said, shaking his head. He wore yellow shooting glasses and a tan canvas hunting jacket with a bird pouch in the liner. He looked like an ad for a sporting-goods store.

"There ain't nothing out there but a bunch of monkeys," Pulaski laughed.

"That's not what the print-outs show," the technician said. He talked as if his mouth were full of cheese.

"We know where the Pathet Lao is," Pulaski sighed. "Our people tell us. Your transmitters must be hearing things."

"There's a large concentration of troops out there." The man pointed at the overlay on the map. He was studying an area southeast of the Plain of Jars, down toward the panhandle of Laos.

Finally, to shut him up, Pulaski and I choppered in and rappelled down through the trees. We lay on the forest floor for two days, on our backs, pointing in different directions, nibbling salami and salt tablets. When the jungle got used to us, we saw the monkeys. They began throwing the transmitters through the trees again and bouncing them on the deck.

I started to laugh. "Foxtrot Six," I radioed back, "what we got here is a baseball game."

"Say again?" the handpiece crackled.

Pulaski grabbed the mike. "The best laid plans of Sperry Rand gang aft a-gley," he said.

There was a long silence, and then the thin voice of the technician asked, "Uh, is that a mayday?"

"Negative," Pulaski smiled. "You got monkeys throwing your shit around. That's what you've been hearing. Do you copy? Mable-Omaha-Nancy-Kilo-Easy-Yankee-Sugar. Monkeys. Is that a Roger?"

"That's a Rog," the voice said quietly. "Easy-Yankee-Sugar."

When we got back to base camp, the technician was already gone.

The monkeys are not there anymore, so do not go looking for them. Between Agent Orange and saturation bombing, they have all gone bye-bye. There are not any leaf monkeys or squirrel monkeys or howler monkeys or Tonkin snub-nosed monkeys. We wiped them out. We did not get rid of the Pathet Lao, but we sure took care of those monkeys.

Pulaski is gone, too. He plowed into a hill near Pakse. I was on the radio with him, coordinating close air support, and Pulaski was flying air observer for the Royal Laotian Air Force. He brought his Cessna down for a look-see, but he cut it too close. "Uh-oh," he said to me just before he hit. "*Sayonara*, Poppa Gene."

"*Sayonara*, buddy," I said after he disintegrated in a bright ball of fire.

All of that happened very early, before there was any perception Mainside that we were at war. I flew back to Vientiane that evening and resigned my commission on the spot. There was nothing they could do, because I knew too much, so they let me go. I packed Pulaski's footlocker and shipped it to his wife in Indiana, and then I went back across the shining sea and decided to make a lot of money and forget where I had been. I went to business school and got a C.P.A. I got married and had kids and went to the opera when I could, and I watched everyone around me, including me, start to get fat and bored. Then Madden came along and showed me a way out. I left my family and found excitement again. It was a fair trade.

There may be a nest of coral snakes in the cave next to mine. They look like Egyptian jewelry, all black and red and gold, and I think I will try to net them tomorrow morning. Their venom makes excellent contact toxin. It will be a game between me and them, and I will have to be fast. Accurate and fast.

Poisons interest me. The sting of the scorpion, for example, is highly overrated. I have tested that on myself with the *Superstitiona* scorpions that I keep in the jar by the radio. The *Superstitiona* has two eyes on each side of its head. I wonder what that is like. Quadruple vision.

My thoughts are getting scattered because the wind is picking up. It is hard to concentrate on my diary. I heard something about an hour ago that turned out to be a desert dog running the ridge line. That animal does not know how close it came to being blown away.

I write these thoughts, and then I burn the pages when I am done. It is not a waste, any more than talking is a waste. It is a way of keeping myself company. I would not say that I am lonely, exactly, but I do know that I am tense, and I wish I could trust Falcone more. He asked me too many times where I was going. He talked a little too kindly, smelled too lime-sweet, and I find myself wondering if he followed me out here. It is a paranoid thought, but it is there. I hated Miami and I hated that job.

Falcone was in my Marine basic class. He was one of the few there who had not gone to college. He set the obstacle-course record and he fired expert in all weapons and he was battalion honor man. We thought he was being groomed for great things, but then he disappeared and no one knew much about him. There were stories that he set a free-fall parachute record at Fort Benning, that he was seen at the Navy's Seal School, that he had been killed at the Bay of Pigs. Somebody told me just before I flew out of Kadena for the final time that Falcone had been stationed on Okinawa and was looking for me. That was the last I heard of him until Madden mentioned that Falcone would be my case officer.

"I don't think I want him," I said slowly.

"He's the best we have," Madden smiled, "and, besides, you do not have the luxury of choosing your superiors." Madden held up his hands before I could say anything else. "Gene," he said, "believe me, this is the man for you. He's done it all: pit boss, Teamster, delivery boy, driver—he's been there and back. He'll help your cover, believe me."

"I remember your lecture on the Medici," I said to Madden. "Do you feel like you're working for them now?" It was a wiseass question and I did not expect an answer.

But Falcone did have their trust and he did get me introductions to the right people. Without him, none of this could have even begun. So? Do I owe him? Or does he owe me?

Miami was more than I bargained for. It was almost a month ago, but it seems like it was this morning. I did not want to go through with it and I told Falcone.

He shrugged. He was not impressed. He knew—I think he really knew—that there was something in the work I liked, and that if he waited, I would eventually do what had to be done.

"Take him out any way you like," Falcone told me. "Nobody will find him. Just cut him up a little, like the locals would do. You know the Cubans. Make it their M.O."

"Why don't you do it?" I dared him. We were sitting in a bar in Key West. Falcone smelled like key-lime pie. He was wearing his standard shaving lotion made out of aloe cactus and limes.

"You bring him to me, I'll do it," Falcone said. "But I can't get to him first, remember? That's your job." He was speaking with a smirk on his face, as if the conversation were a matter of form, a discussion to please my conscience, the way a pimp might talk to a John.

"They're going to put all this together sometime," I said. "Somebody will figure out that I was the last one with both of them."

"No way," Falcone laughed. "They already offed the bodyguard on the last hit. We made it look like him, didn't we? Huh? Poppa Gene, what's happening to your nerves, man? We'll take care of things. You are Priority One, baby. You're the tax man, remember? You wear three-piece suits and talk nice. Blue blood, Ivy League, Continental, all that shit. Just do your thing and we'll cover for you. We'll make you look good. Just take him out."

I tried to argue, but Falcone knew my brain was itching with cockroaches and my arms were ready to work and there was something about killing that pleased me. Falcone knew that I had felt alive and powerful only a few times in all my years and the addiction was there, the exciting moment when I could play God. I think that is why I hate Falcone most of all. He had killed before, I was sure of it, but he could walk away from it. I needed it.

Rizzoli was sitting by his pool when I walked in. He was alone. He had his scams that only I knew about, and he did not want his people hearing too much.

"We'll do some commodity spreads," I said. "Butterfly spreads." I raised my hand like a boy scout. "I swear they're almost legal," I tried to joke.

He did not laugh. He was eating caviar on toast, egg and onion on the side, white chianti bottle in the ice bucket. He did not offer me anything. Sitting in his canvas deck chair under the awning by his private pool, he looked like a fox, like a dead silver fox. He was on the docket for subcommittee examination within the week.

I put some commodity-price charts in front of him on the table. "Here's how it works," I said. I was talking very calmly. "You put a silver spread on. One side is this year—it's the loser. You show a big loss. You deduct it. But what the IRS doesn't know, see, is that you've covered yourself by taking an opposite position, same commodity, same pit, the next year. We branch you off into lots of Subchapter S corporations, and they each take the maximum deduction. OK? You can defer year after year after year. Big losses that aren't losses. You can roll over profits ad infinitum."

Rizzoli smiled at my high language. He reached up and patted my cheek. "Bravo, Professor," he smiled. That was all right. He did not know that his street snobbery toward his accountant was going to be the death of him.

I moved behind him while I talked. I wanted the high ground. I talked of false dating and forged trading cards and deals off the floor of the Board of Trade, and with my pen as a pointer, I showed him gaps in the chart action while I was shifting my weight.

There was a moment of frozen time, like the eye of a hurricane, and then I kneed him in his kidneys. He gasped. His spine arched like a bow. I cracked his Adam's apple with the edges of my hands, and then I held his windpipe, his carotid arteries, and nothing moved for a minute or two. When I knew he was dead, I let him go. He slumped to the ground. I picked him up in a fireman's carry and dumped him into my car trunk in the garage.

As I drove off Key Biscayne, it started to rain. There was something dirty about the rain. It had smoke and chemicals in it, like the breath of sewage and dogs. I whistled Mozart as I drove along. I tried to find him on the FM, but he wasn't there, so I sang to myself and let the music make order for me. Life was not plastic and bitter then; it was not overcrowded and cheap; birds sang like flutes; parks were green and empty and trees were 1000 years old.

Falcone was waiting at the canal with the oil barrel. He was holding an Uzi under his raincoat. He looked like a Borgia with the rain dripping off his nose.

"You do the cutting," I said. "I'm no butcher." I posted myself as an outlook while he wrapped the wrists and ankles in chains and made the proper incisions. I had a headache and I tried to hum to myself to make it go away.

When Falcone was finished, I helped push the barrel into the canal. It did not sink completely.

"They'll find him," I said.

"I don't think so," Falcone said. He was breathing heavily.

"He may sink a little, but he'll be gassy within the week. He'll come back up," I argued.

"Let him," Falcone laughed.

"They'll think what we want them to think?" I asked.

"Exactly."

"Revenge within the Syndicate?"

"Yes," Falcone said, and then he pulled on my arm. "Come on, Gene, let's haul ass," he said. He ran to the car and we drove to the Everglades. The rain followed us. The interior of the car smelled like a lime tree.

I tried to nap, but there was no music in my head. After an hour, Falcone turned off the main road at a sign that said MONROE COUNTY ROAD CREW. I did not know where we were going.

"Back in the Dark Ages," I said, "when Madden first got me to take this on, I was supposed to be used strictly for surveillance. Nothing black." We were passing Quonset huts and a generator. The rain had stopped. A Beechcraft Bonanza sat in the heat at the foot of a red-dirt airstrip.

"You should've seen this place in Sixty-one," Falcone laughed. "Then we had business."

When I got out of the car, I thought I could smell dinosaurs and coal deposits. Everything seemed ancient and slow. I felt very old. I knew I was supposed to hurry, but I could not hurry. The prop wash from the Beechcraft blew moisture out of my eyes.

"Where you going this time, Gene?" Falcone asked me again.

"Same place," I smiled.

"Really?"

"Really," I said. "It's my little secret."

"You want to share?"

I looked at Falcone's face. I did not like the smile on it or the thoughts behind it. "No," I said.

"I was just wondering," Falcone shrugged. "You know, in case we got to get in touch or something."

"Use the short wave," I said coldly.

"OK," Falcone patted me on the back. "OK, Gene."

"*Es siegte die Stärke*," I smiled.

"German?" Falcone asked.

I nodded. "'Strength is the victor,'" I translated. "Mozart wrote it. Hitler perverted it. Now everybody uses it."

"You're a very cultured man," Falcone said as he helped me open the cockpit door. He waved at the pilot and threw my briefcase on the seat.

The engine noise was high. "Culture?" I yelled in Falcone's ear. "It doesn't mean a thing anymore. The *Kommandant* of Buchenwald loved Mozart. So what?"

Falcone was waving his forefinger in a circle. He wanted the engine revved higher and me out of there. "Don't miss your plane," he shouted to me.

"Any one of us can kill anything. Better we should leave it to the monkeys," I said. I climbed in beside the pilot. He was a young blond man who looked like a clerk at an insurance counter.

"Let us know where you are when you feel like it," Falcone shouted through cupped palms. The edges of his hands were dark with callouses.

"Yeah, Sure." I gave him the Sicilian high sign. "Or, better yet, why don't you come find me?" I smiled "It gets boring where I go."

"I might do that," Falcone yelled.

I closed my door and tightened my seat belt. The plane bounced down the runway, pulled up over the trees and banked hard toward the west. The pilot paid no attention to me. He was flying me to New Orleans, and then I was to be on my own, which is the way I wanted it.

It is dawn now. I have written all night. There have been no sounds on the speakers. Maybe my transmitters washed out. A rainstorm hit about three A.M.

The light disappeared on Danby Lake. All the lakes around here are dry lakes and sometimes people camp on them. To the west are the Ship Mountains. Cadiz is beyond them. I will have to go into Cadiz soon for more gas. I carry four extra jerry cans, but nothing lasts forever.

The air is fresh and clean. Even now it is warm in the early-morning sun. I know that this is going to be a hot day. That is all right. The wind has died down. I am safe here.

There are jet contrails in the sky over Turtle Mountain. I will watch them break up slowly like smoke signals. What else is there to do now? It is boring sometimes, but I know how to occupy myself. I will live off the land, drink cactus water, eat berries, listen to Mozart, sing, talk to the snakes, smell the limes.

Reginald Gibbons

THE VANISHING POINT

(from *Saints*)

Ayoung man with very bad teeth and a wall-eyed gaze, holding some poster boards on his lap, where they sagged at each side, and drawing on the top one with an old chewed ballpoint pen.

It was a severely rectilinear highway scene: a powerful exaggerated vanishing point puckering the empty horizon, lanes of cars coming on—as yet only outlined—and lanes of big trucks going away, already finished. One after another, all alike, semi-trailers with company names on them, and all the perspective acutely correct. It all looked to have been drawn with a ruler, strictly and slowly; but he was doing it freehand, each stroke of the pen absolutely precise. Or rather, as imprecise as the human hand, but with an authority that could convey and even create precision in your eyes as you looked. Even the lettering he was putting on the side of the last, closest, largest trailer was as if painted by machine, and he never paused to consider proportions or angles, but simply kept drawing and darkening the shapes with the blue pen, as if he were tracing with quick uncanny dash a faint design already there on the white floppy board.

This was at Chicago and State, in the subway station.

A woman happened to come stand near him, and watched as he worked with his intent rhythm, his head bobbing and sometimes with his face low to study his work closely with one eye at a time. She watched, and he noticed her and smiled a wreck-toothed wide blind man's smile at her, and said, more than asked, "Nice work, idn't it!" She put her right thumb up and smiled back at him, and said nothing, and he lifted the top board and showed her the finished one underneath, for an instant—another roadscape, in colors, filled in and alive, the whole huge white board crammed with convincing and convinced detail.

"Nice work, idn't it!" he said again, and showed her the one underneath that one. Again, thumb up, and she too smiled happily— a wholly natural acknowledgment of him, an unsurprised understanding of his talent. She didn't act as if it seemed strange to her that he was sitting on a worn drab bench on the subway platform, next to the tracks, working in the dim light while commuters and others stood around waiting impatiently for the next train. It didn't seem to strike her that he was crazy and half-blind. That his work was driven, obsessively scrupulous, uninhabited, repetitive, brilliant, rhythmical, depthless, spiritless, useless.

"Nice work, idn't it!" he said to her each time, and he showed her—and me, because I too was standing there—six or eight more drawings: the Sears Tower, the skyline along Michigan Ave., traffic in the streets, not a single person. The long lines were perfectly straight but when you looked at them more carefully they zigged with freehand force across the board in spurts. And her thumb went up to each in turn, and she smiled and each time she did, he said, "Nice work, idn't it!"

"I do nice work!" he said. "I did *all* these, and not a *single mistake!* Nice work!" he was saying as the train came in like sandpaper, hissing and blasting. She walked away toward it, without saying goodbye, and he looked at me, then. "Nice work, idn't it!" he said, as cheerfully as a man could ever say it.

"It's beautiful!" I said. The doors to the train opened a few feet away and everyone was stepping inside. "It's nice *work!*" he said, smiling, and I moved to the train and stepped in, with the great force in him holding me to him still, and with part of myself I wished that it would win, but I did get in, the last passenger, and the doors shut at the same moment the train jerked and began to roll out of the station and away.

Anne Brashler

HE READ TO HER

(from *Iowa Woman*)

She locked the bathroom door, sprayed the small closed room
with lemon odor, then removed her robe. The colostomy bag
was full and leaking; brown stains seeped down her belly and across
old scars, new scars, old stretch marks. Her stomach looked like a
map of dirt roads. "Crap," she said. She cupped her hand under the
bag, holding it like a third breast, then held her breath long enough
to break the seal, remove the bag and quickly tie its contents into a
white plastic container. Her colostomy resembled a brown puckered
rose.

The bathroom filled with billowy steam as she stayed under the
shower. When her husband rapped on the door, she said, "I'm fine.
Leave me alone." As she stepped from the tub, refreshed and clean,
the puckered rose exploded with bile, shooting brown stinking liquid
over the sink, the mirror, the toilet bowl. Doubling up her right
hand, she smashed the mirror to smithereens. Her husband removed
the bathroom door and, gagging from the odor, placed her on the
sofa bed on the porch, cleaned her off, then dressed her open wound,
positioning a clean bag over the plastic rim that held it in place.
"There," he said. "Everything's going to be all right. You're going to
be just fine."

"I was brushing my hair," she said. "My hand slipped." He
pulled mirror slivers out of her fist with tweezers, swabbed the cuts
in her hand with witch hazel, saying, "There. That's better."

"Nothing you say or do will make me feel better," she said. She
smelled the bile; tasted it at the back of her mouth. She ran her
tongue along her teeth, convinced they had turned green. "I want
my red bed jacket," she said. "Not this raggedy thing. Why didn't
you bring me the red one?"

"I'm fixing tea," he said, running from the room. She heard
him gag in the kitchen.

"I don't want tea!" she shouted. "Just leave me alone." The
kettle whistled, playing an organ strain from Bach, sounding nerv-

ous. She knew he'd bring the tea, the doublecrossticks' book, the reference books. She'd looked up the Down answers of the puzzle he'd been working on so that when he got stuck, she'd be able to provide the correct solution, shorten the game. He'd made a cherry wood bed tray, carved flowers around its edges and was carrying it in, its legs splayed like a little dog flying. "Tea," he said. "Lemon slices, sugar; a rose for my beautiful wife."

"You creep," she said. "That's not going to do any good." She watched his face pale, contort, then smooth out like a person beautified. "I have something different today," he said. He held a book behind him like a surprise.

"Oh yeah?" she said. "It's a quote by Thomas Wolfe from *Look Homeward, Angel*. The definition for Number One Down is 'geometric progression.'" She wished she could hurt him but didn't know how; doublecrossticks was the best she could do.

"You looked," he said. "But that isn't it. I did that puzzle after you went to bed last night." He puffed pillows into shape, then tucked them under her head, ignoring her when she made her body stiffen. The bag gurgled as liquid hit the plastic.

"Why don't you just leave me alone?" she said and was instantly sorry. Lord knows it wasn't his fault. Lord knows. A joke. Lord, Lord, have mercy. Outside a squirrel chased a blue jay up a willow tree; blue and gray among silvery leaves. Their porch was over the garage, so in summer, with trees filled out, it felt as though they were in the branches of a forest. Their daughter had insisted she recuperate here, in this room, her favorite.

He sat down, ignoring her, then opened the book and began to read in a soft clear voice: *"Call me Ishmael. Some years ago—never mind how long precisely—having little or no money in my purse, and nothing particular to interest me on shore, I thought I would sail about a little and see the watery part of the world . . . ."* His face was intense, as if he'd turned into a priest since she'd been away.

"Are you going to read the whole damn book out loud?" she asked. She wondered if she'd be angry for the rest of her life. She'd hoped she'd be able to laugh again, say something nice once in a while.

"I thought I might," he said.

A breeze picked up leaves, turned them over, making different shades of green. The children had guests; they were racing with inner tubes in the pool. Her son had found huge truck tires at a flea market, hosed them off, patched the inner tubes with colored swatches. Her daughter had taken over the household chores while she'd been in the hospital. They'd kept the family running, shipshape. Her husband, too; he'd had a shock, nearly losing her, going out of his mind with guilt, with self-loathing, the worst kind of pain. "I'd like that, Darly," she finally said. The tea was cold but she drank it anyway.

"Say that again."

"Say what?"

"What you just said."

"Darly? I stole it from some story," she said. Her bag filled suddenly and she thought how convenient it all was.

"I like that. Call me that. Will you call me that?" he asked. He leaned forward, his gray head nestling in the hollow of her shoulder.

"But it's not mine," she said.

"I don't care. I like it."

"Some man said it to his wife. He called her that before they divorced." Was she threatening? Lord knows.

"I don't care," he said.

"Darly," she said, sighing, "Read to me." They'll sort it out later. When cheers for the winner of the inner tube race rose from the pool, she pretended the cheers were for her; she pretended she was a star.

"*. . . Whenever I find myself growing grim about the mouth; whenever it is a damp, drizzly November in my soul . . .*" She lay back and closed her eyes. His voice was music; he became Ishmael, telling her a story.

Charles Dickinson

RISK

(from *Atlantic Monthly*)

Owen is the host tonight. Washing glasses, he flips them in the air until they are just winks in the light. Catching them again takes his breath away.

Frank is the first to arrive. Then Nolan. Frank wore dirty clothes that afternoon when he took his laundry down to the big machines in the basement of his apartment building; with the load in the washer, soap measured, and coins slotted, he added the clothes he was wearing and made the long walk back upstairs to his apartment naked. He paused to read the fine print on the fire extinguisher. Noises in the building set birds loose in his heart. Frank takes the red armies when they gather to play the game of world conquest.

They hear Alice arrive in a storm of gravel. She has moved herself stoned across twenty-two miles of back roads in just under twenty minutes. She lives with a man she has known for seven months, in a rented farmhouse on a hundred acres of land. The man is good with a garden and with his hands, a warmhearted, full-bearded man who plays the banjo professionally, an amicable host when the game is at their house. He loves Alice, but still she meets another man on the sly. Half her appointments and reasons for being away from home are fabrications. This other man treats her like a child, making fun of the gaps in her knowledge, hurting her feelings, which she perversely enjoys. It is a counterpoint to the sweet man at home. Alice plays black.

The world is arranged on Owen's kitchen table. A strong yellow light shines down through the night's first gauzy sheets of smoke. The game's six continents—North and South America, Africa, Asia, Europe, and Australia—are not entirely faithful to the earth's geography. Each Continent is formed from territories, and between these territories war will soon be waged with armies and dice.

Owen pours Frank a beer. Owen hosts as often as possible; he would play three or four times a week if he could. The gathering of his friends soothes him and fills dark spaces in the house. The smoke softens edges. He tries to get Eileen, his wife, to play, but she refuses. She remains in the other rooms. None of the players press on this point of awkwardness.

Owen shuffles through the game cards, a glass of beer at his elbow, a cigarette in an ashtray. Alice comes into the kitchen and shades her glassy eyes. "Hi," she says.

"Speak for yourself," Frank says.

Nolan, who has arrived in a sour mood, says, "The nation's motorists are safe for a few hours."

Alice hangs her coat on the tree by the door. She takes her makings out of her purse and carefully arranges them by her place at the board.

"Wine in the fridge," Owen says. "I'll get it for you in a second." He shakes the white dice and throws them across the face of the world. A pair of fives and a six.

"Oo," Alice says. "Hot."

"I'll take that all night."

Frank asks, "Who's late again?"

Les is late again; he makes a point of it. He never offers to host, nor does he ever bring beer or food. He feels that his presence is sufficient. Les always rolls good dice. It is something he demands of himself. He wins more often than the other players. From early March to early December, he drives a 1,000CC motorcycle without a helmet. The others allow him to continue to play despite his cheap habits because he is so good; to bar him would be cowardly. But Frank has dreamed of Les hitting ice on his cycle, his unprotected head bouncing sweetly on the highway.

Les and Pam arrive at the same time, though not together. Les's hair is swept back like Mercury's wings. Where Les is allowed to play because he is the best player, Pam, the worst, is invited back because she is so generous and so good-looking. She has large green eyes, long curly pale-red hair, and heavy breasts tucked into a loose sweater. She is usually the last to arrive and the first to lose all her armies and be eliminated. She has been playing for a year and still does not have a handle on the game. She tries to have a sense of humor about this. She always brings a large bag of pretzels and two six-packs of Dutch beer. She is always welcome. She plays pink.

Pam is in love with Nolan. She tries to catch his eye from across the room as she hands Owen her sack of food and beer. She has been with Nolan just that afternoon. It is stitched in her memory in dim light. The run through stinging branches to his basement, their time there, their almost being caught by his wife. They met at one of these gatherings and have known each other a year; Nolan's presence kept her coming back after she learned that she was not very good at the game and probably never would be. She liked his lean frame and dark-blue eyes and the clever look his glasses gave him.

But he is married, to a woman named Beth. Pam has met her once, a shy, tall woman with a plain face—she played the game a half-dozen times, even winning once.

Pam knew from the first she appealed to Nolan. She learned long ago she appeals to most men. They had a cup of coffee out in the open, later a lunch in the shadows, then a drink that afternoon and a sly sneaking into his house from the rear basement door. She takes her seat at the table. Nolan won't look at her. Her head swims in dates and half-remembered cycles. She had thought she was between lovers and was using no contraception. Her calculations told her she was safe but she is not absolutely sure.

Getting settled, Owen shakes the dice, sips his beer, smokes, observes. Frank has his twenty red armies in five neat rows of four. Alice has rolled a joint thick as her little finger and touched a match lovingly to one twisted end. Blue smoke flows upward. A seed explodes and Pam jumps, laughs. Nolan grimaces.

Les counts out his twenty green armies. He is serene. The night, so clean and cold out on the highway, has purpose. He won the previous two times they played. He smiles idly around at those soon to fall. He asks Owen, "Did you buy that stock I told you about?"

"I don't have the money, Les."

"Get it. I went in at three and a half and it's seven already." He pauses to decline the joint Alice offers. "It's a great place for your money."

"I like banks," Frank says.

Les proclaims, "Banks are for suckers."

"They're insured," Frank says.

"So? You've got to go for the big return in this economy. Most people aren't chickenshit like you, Frank."

Owen, who as host strives for player equanimity, says mildly, "I still don't have the money."

Les shrugs. He can only do so much. He says, "Let's get this carnage under way."

Two red dice go around the table, each player rolling to see who goes first. With six players, the world's forty-two territories will be divided evenly. But the player who starts will be the first to have three cards (a card earned each turn if a territory is conquered), which he or she might be able to cash for extra armies. Nolan's throw of ten is tops. Owen smiles and deals out the cards. They diverge from the rules in allotting territories. Each card represents a territory that a player will soon occupy with armies. Luck is involved, and time is saved. The players bring the cards up off the table, fan them in their hands, try to plot.

Les has been dealt New Guinea, and that is toehold enough for him on the continent of Australia. He deposits every available army there.

"A clear signal from Down Under," Nolan says. "Les is going for his continent early."

Les smiles beatifically.

Alice's seven territories are spread all over the world. She smokes her joint and studies her options. She knows that with six players, one or two will be eliminated early. A player without a firm base will be picked off a little at a time. Four of her territories are in Asia, which is much too large to try to hold as a continent. As she thinks, she feels herself float out of her seat; she feels her heels tap the chair seat as she rises clear. When she is on the ceiling, she lets out a laugh that is like taking on weight and drifts back down. Nobody has witnessed her brief ascension. They are too engrossed in the coming war. She sips wine and comes to a decision. She doesn't like Les very much when they play, and she owns Siam. It is the doorway to Asia from Australia, which Les will inevitably control. She puts all her armies in Siam.

Les looks over at her. She loves it when she makes his eyes go mean and flat. Les has green eyes, not as green as the color he plays, but green like dirty dollar bills. His eyes are always so cool and rich and calculating. He expects to win; this attitude rankles Alice no end. He may win tonight, but first he will have to fight through her.

Nolan has been splitting his armies between Central America and Greenland, preparatory to a run at North America. Seeing Alice's troop placement, he announces, "A bloodbath on the horizon in Siam."

Alice says, "I'm ready." Les drinks his wine.

"Les may want to invest in body bags," Frank says.

"I'm ready," Alice repeats.

Through all this, the only thing Owen hears is his wife moving in the room next to the kitchen. She has gone in there to get a book or the night's paper. She makes soft flutterings like a bird caught in the wall. He wishes she would come in, watch the game, have a glass of wine or a beer. An hour before the players arrived, they talked about having another baby. More than a year had passed, they were both in their early thirties, a better time would not arrive. But she could not give him an answer. Her willingness and her sadness remained locked together inside her.

Through the crack beneath the door he sees the light in the next room go out. He hears Eileen move deeper into the house, away from him; he thinks he hears her moving away long after the sounds have been hidden by the war around him.

Owen has Egypt, North Africa, and Madagascar, and he is delighted. He will soon control the continent of Africa. He won't be one of the first players eliminated, the host forced to sit and top off drinks and think.

Frank says cheerfully, "It's a gas to have the Middle East," and loads it full of his armies. He has nowhere else to go. His other armies are scattered in every continent, and worthless. He says, "The Middle East is the territory around which the world revolves."

"Frank's trying to sell himself a bill of goods," Les says.

"The poor jerk has nothing *but* the Middle East," Alice says.

Frank replies, "It's oily yet."

Pam owns Brazil and Venezuela, the doors in and out of the continent of South America. She divides her armies between the two territories.

"A bold move," Nolan announces. She looks to see if he is making fun of her, but his eyes trip away from hers.

The world is full of colored armies soon to contend. Nolan begins. After placing his three free armies, he attacks Les's lone army in the Northwest Territory, loses an army before advancing, then loses another getting Owen out of Alaska.

"It's never easy," Nolan says. But he now controls the three routes in and out of North America. He takes his card. The game moves to Frank.

"Am I in danger?" Owen asks.

"Possibly," Frank says. He puts his three free armies in the Middle East.

"Because I want to go to the john."

"I just want to go for a card," Frank replies.

Owen leaves the kitchen. Let them wait for him if he can't get a straight answer. Eileen is in their bedroom. She sits against the headboard reading; she looks up almost warily when her husband appears.

"Who's winning?" she asks.

"Just started. Why don't you come out and say hello? Have a little wine."

His wife shakes her head. Her hair is a thick caramel wave that runs in and out of the light like surf. Her face is delicate and oval-shaped. He reads in her eyes that she expects the worst possible news at any moment. "I'd have to get dressed all over again," she explains. She's ready for sleep, in a flannel nightgown buttoned up the front and tied with a ribbon at the base of her throat. He kisses this spot, then uses the bathroom before returning to the game. Making his way down the shadowed hall, he glances into his house's second bedroom, but forces himself to think about getting hold of Africa instead.

Frank has darted into Southern Europe, taken his card, regrouped back in the Middle East, and stopped. Les has taken Australia. His armies wait in a clot in Indonesia, across a strait of blue-green water from Alice's Siamese force.

"The world is taking shape," Owen notes.

"Les suggests everyone invest in philatelic devices," Frank says.

"They're illegal in this state," Alice says.

Owen says nothing. He won't sit down just yet; not until it is his turn. He is unable to lose himself in the game. This has never been a problem. Tonight, though, he is itchy.

While he gets wine and beer and opens Pam's pretzels and pours them into a bowl, hosting the event in all earnestness, Pam takes South America. She and Les have continents, though they are the two continents easiest to win and hold, and hence worth only two bonus armies per turn. Still, they are continents. Les and Pam won't drift rootless over the world.

Alice's three free armies go into Siam. She looks at Les, her left eyebrow cocked, a question asked. He meets her look blankly. She sees that he has pushed his anger down. His cash-green eyes have reclaimed their arrogance.

Not yet, she decides. She attacks Nolan in India for her card, then pulls back into Siam.

"Buy body bags," Frank urges one and all. "Buy stock in the Red Cross."

Now Owen takes his seat. "Who has hot dice?" he asks.

"Nobody, really," Nolan reports. "Still too early. I think Alice should go after Les before his heat up."

"Les suggests we invest in numismatic tools," Frank says.

Owen rolls the dice against Pam and takes the Congo. His armies advance down through South Africa and up into East Africa. Just like that, Africa is his. He is spread too thin to hold it, he supposes, but he has a continent.

Nolan's turn again, and he can't remember what he wants to do next. Beth's face swims up to him, fitted on Pam's lush body. He stirs in his seat and tries to concentrate. He must fortify North America. One minute he was having a beer with Pam and the next he had come to this dangerous decision and they were parking her car a block over from his house. Cutting through the lawns, the darkening spaces between the houses, he could think only of the lack of cover. All the leaves were fallen; this was an affair meant for summer. He pulled the girl along by the hand. They went into the basement by the back door and undressed in the failing light. She tasted of flat beer when he kissed her for the first time. Chimes went off upstairs; he counted with them to five as he kissed her belly—an hour before Beth was due.

"Whose turn is it?" Les asks pointedly. Nolan's attention jerks back to the game. The world spreads before him. The girl keeps looking at him; she will give him away if she isn't careful. He is playing blue. Her sexual presence hit him the first time he saw her: a chemical lust. She never had to open her mouth. In fact, he preferred that she didn't. The peeling back of layers of existence that was life with Beth was never a factor with Pam. She was not very good at the game, and he knew nothing about her life otherwise. At their early meetings he filled the silent spaces talking about himself. He never thought about Beth at those times; she existed on a different plane. He found it remarkably easy to ask Pam to make that run to the basement with him. It would be the extent of what he wanted to know about her. Only when they were out in the open and on the run did it strike him what a wild chance he was taking.

And after they had been in the basement only twenty minutes, as they were finished and sitting in an awkward envelope of silence, a door opened above them and Beth's heels cracked smartly on the floor over their heads.

"Nolan," Les snarls, "it's too early in the game for such long thoughts."

Frank says, "It will be the rumination of your soul."

Nolan looks at Pam, then his eyes fly past. She waited with him in his basement like a canny burglar. Her ripe body had become an unwieldy burden he must transfer out of there for his own safety. His wife moved about upstairs, and the sky outside darkened. Then they slipped out the basement door and back to her car. She drove him to where he had left his car. They did not say a word, moving on those dark streets, as though his wife might yet hear. He took deep breaths to calm himself. Leaving, he had looked back up at the house, and in the rectangle of light of the upstairs bedroom window he had thought he saw a woman looking out. But he had lost his glasses in the rush of adultery. He was flying blind. He had to be careful driving. At home he put on a spare pair and made a quick, surreptitious inspection of the basement. Nothing. No glasses. They were buried somewhere like a land mine. He might step on them at any moment and blow himself up. Beth, happy to see him, undressed and pulled him into bed with her. He said he didn't have time but she insisted; he noted no strangeness in her behavior, no knowledge of what he had done, of what he had become.

Owen gravely says, "As host, I'll have to rule you either move immediately, Nolan, or forfeit your turn."

Nolan slaps his three free armies down in Alaska. He conquers Les in Quebec from Greenland, then takes his card and sits back. Pam is a little disappointed. After such long consideration, she had expected something grand from Nolan.

"Bold," Les sneers.

"Jam it."

Frank drops more armies into the Middle East. Les says, "You can't let Owen keep Africa."

"Always fomenting trouble," Owen says good-naturedly. The possibility of attack hurries his blood, though. Frank moving on Egypt or East Africa is strategically sound. By the next turn, Owen

will be better fortified. If he survives here, Africa will be his, probably for the entire game, with its three bonus armies per turn. Frank
has the manpower at the moment and Owen's dice are rarely better
than fair.

Frank attacks Owen in East Africa. Africa falls in six rolls of the
dice. Les says, stirring more trouble, "You're poised to cut across
North Africa and take South America away from Pam."

"No, thanks," Frank says. Too many armies wait in North Africa
and Brazil. There is nothing in it for him. "I am content, not conten-
tious," he says, and moves half his force back into the Middle East.

Les shakes Alice's shoulder, pretending she has fallen asleep.
"You with us?" he asks in a loud voice. "Enough brain cells still
alive to finish the game?"

She purses her lips as if to kiss and blows blue smoke in his face.
"I am ready," she says carefully, from the ceiling. These three
words falling down to Les pull her after them like anchors. She
wraps her leg around a leg of the table for balance and the table leg
convulses. Les shrieks theatrically, "God! She's trying to get me
sexually aroused so I'll go easy on her in Siam. But it won't work!"

He untangles his leg from Alice's. She grabs the table edge lest
she float away again. A balloon of nausea rises in her. She puts her
hand to her mouth and concentrates.

"Looking pale," Les says to the others, pointing at Alice.

"No fair throwing up on the world," Frank warns. "If you don't
like your situation, be a man and live with it."

Les puts three armies in Indonesia, two in the Ukraine. He
decides he is in no hurry. Let things build. He rolls the dice and
there is a six. He gets a card from another point on the globe.

"Uh-oh," Frank says.

"Very efficient use of that six."

"Thank you," Les says modestly.

Alice smiles at them all. "It's early yet."

The world comes to Owen and it goes away. He is a fine host,
and breaks out corn chips and roast-beef sandwiches, empties ashtrays,
opens beers, pours wine. He spills liquids into the oceans and across
the plains of Asia. The players groan and protest. A whale dives in
the Mid-Atlantic. To the south, a tall ship moves under sail. He
excuses himself. The light is out in their bedroom. It is 1:00 a.m.,
and Eileen sleeps in blankets wrapped tight as a premium cigar.

He passes the second bedroom going back and decides to go in.
The crib had been dismantled right away. Even a year later the four
indentations remain in the carpet where the casters pressed, stake
holes for a precise parcel of ground. The baby had been so weightless, and home for such a short time; he is always amazed that she
could mark the room so indelibly.

A night light remains in the wall socket. His wife might have overlooked it when she was cleaning out the room. She might have been afraid to look down. He kneels by it and snaps it on. A mouse's head, a glowing white face, round black ears, cartoon-rodent eyes. It's kind of unnerving: the head of a tiny ghost floating above the floor. Not the sort of thing for a baby girl. Had she been scared to death?

Owen returns to the game. Without Africa he is nothing, and the game has become a chore. He will be eliminated soon. Frank is gone already. Les took him out with the force he built in the Ukraine, using the secondary force to win cards and let some of the steam out of the situation brewing between Siam and Indonesia. Frank waited too long to take this Ukraine army seriously, and now he has gone outside; nobody knows what has happened to him.

Pam is pinned in South America. Owen's last armies block her in North Africa. Nolan has a major force in Central America. He will march on her in Venezuela.

The bloodbath between Alice and Les approaches. "You've got to come through me pretty soon," Alice taunts. "Nolan's getting too strong."

"This is a fact," Owen says. He desires resolution of this conflict so he can send his guests away.

The door opens and Frank is back.

"Where you been?"

"Standing naked in the dark," Frank says.

No one pays any attention. Nolan is attacking Pam. He goes after her in Venezuela, because it is the sound move at that point in the game, and also because he wants her gone. She usually leaves after she has been eliminated. Nights past, he was sorry to see her go. Now she embarrasses him. He expects her to slip up and start crying. She keeps looking at him.

Nolan rolls the dice and Pam waits. If he would look at her they might reach some understanding, but his eyes are fixed to that spot on the board where her dice will fall.

"Come on, come on," he says impatiently.

She rolls and loses two armies. Alice says, "Don't let him badger you."

"It's OK," Pam says softly. She thinks she will cry. Everything is wrong.

"Would you roll the dice?" he asks sharply.

She flings the dice across the board. She keeps them in sight through filmed eyes and sees sixes come up, which on closer inspection are really fours. Her tears make the pits shiver and drift. But fours are enough to win a pair of armies from Nolan, who rolls nothing higher than a three.

"Get him," Alice cheers.

But they are only dice; only Les has learned to tap their souls. Nolan's superior forces pick implacably away at Pam. Her armies fall like threads in a garment until they are all gone and she feels naked and stupid. Out of the game again. She turns her cards over to Nolan. He cashes them for extra armies and moves without a word against Owen in Africa. Pam watches this action blankly. She could open her mouth and tell everyone of the time she spent with Nolan in the recent past. She wields this knowledge like an ax on her tongue and is larger within herself for not using it.

She takes her empty glass and washes it out in the sink. At her back, Nolan eliminates Owen.

"You'll pardon me if I don't stay for the end," she says.

Owen stands, wipes his palms on his trousers. "I don't blame you for leaving," he says. "I'm bored myself."

"The pitiable whine of the previously conquered," Les observes dryly.

Owen smiles and takes Pam's coat off the tree and helps her into it. He walks her out to her car.

"Thanks for coming," he says. He likes being outside, away from the smoke and the bloodlust. The white gravel of his driveway gleams. The air feels like it wants to snow. He takes Pam's keys gallantly, and after she shows him the one, he unlocks her car door. Owen leans in and kisses her good night. She hands him a pair of glasses.

"They belong to the guy playing blue," she says. "I saw him downtown today and we had coffee together and he left them with me by mistake."

These words break over Owen in a rush; he can only say, "OK."

He stays outside after Pam is gone. Nolan's car is unlocked; he puts the glasses on the dash. He has no interest in the truth of their coming into Pam's possession. He returns to his house through the front door. He hears the voices of the players in the kitchen, the labored buzz of an old digital clock turning a minute over. Through the dark passages of the house, moving with a freedom bestowed by his guests' believing he is still outside, Owen glides into the bedroom. His wife lies wrapped and asleep. He understands now why the night's game offered him nothing; it was an event out of order of importance. Eileen comes half awake at the way he pulls the covers and makes a space for himself in the loose, warm cylinder. He gets her nightgown unbuttoned and untied and fights through the clumsy hands she throws in his path. He plants a long kiss on her sour mouth. She utters a word into his mouth that he ignores. She will kill his desire if he lets her.

"Where are your friends?" she whispers, warm in his ear.

"In the kitchen. The world will fall soon."

"You aren't being a good host." He is stirred unimaginably to hear teasing in her voice. Her hands have opened against his back.

"They think I'm outside," he whispers. "This way, I can be two places at once."

She kisses him on the neck. They move on together, Owen careful of dark chasms of memory he must transport his wife over. She proceeds along a fine edge that her husband slowly widens.

Les says, "Siam from China."

"Hand me the bones, please," Alice says. Frank gives her the white dice. "Like skulls," she says, "with twenty-one lance holes."

"Siam from China," Les repeats.

"Pincer movement," Nolan announces.

"Pinch her movement and she'll follow you anywhere," says Frank.

Les has swept his second force into China so he can attack Alice's Siamese armies from both north and south. He rolls dice the same way from first to last: three shakes of his left fist, then a gentle, coddling tipping of the dice out onto the board, as though they might bruise. It is his secret that he treats the dice well so they will reciprocate. He once revealed this secret while drunk and voluble, and seven straight games of cold dice followed as punishment.

He beats on Alice from China: a softening action. Alice is poised for defeat. He can see in her slack face that she has had enough: enough grass, enough of their company, enough of this game. She is tired and anxious to go home.

"Where's Owen?" Nolan asks.

"He walked Pam to her car," Frank says.

"That was a half-hour ago."

"So?" Les asks, impatient at this break in his concentration. "Go look for him if you're so concerned. But shut up."

"Gee, Les, you're such a charming guy," Frank says.

"Eat it."

"Come on, Les," Alice complains. "Roll the dice. I wanna go home."

"The night is breaking up in a sea of bad juices," Frank says. "Why does it always have to be this way? Like love."

"Shut up, Frank."

Nolan is at the window, cupping hands around his eyes to see through the light reflected on the glass. Chrome winks from the handlebars of Les's motorcycle. He can see Alice's car, his car, Frank's car. Not Pam's car, though.

"They left together," he says.

"Who did?" Frank asks.

"Pam and Owen."

"No way," Alice says.

"Intriguing, though," Les admits.

"Her car is gone. So is Owen. You put it together."

"He's married," Frank says.

"Frank, you're such an innocent," Alice says.

Frank says, "And his wife is in the other room. Who'd have the nerve to go off with another woman under those conditions?"

Nolan says, "Maybe she's asleep. Maybe he figures she figures he's still out here. She never checks on him. Maybe he figured it was worth the gamble."

"Are we still playing?" Alice asks Les. He is startled; he has been thinking about Pam. The dice feel funny in his hand, as though the corners have been shaved fractionally, or the pits rearranged. They feel cool at being ignored in the midst of their performance for him. He is afraid to roll, and when he does it's all ones and twos. He rolls cold for the next five minutes, losing armies, losing confidence. In time his China force is wiped out, and Alice still exists firmly in Siam. Outnumbered, she nonetheless has the hot dice that ordinarily are his province, as though they have taken another lover. Fives and sixes roll languorously from her hand. Alice licks her lips, wide awake now. Hot dice get everyone's attention. Les awaits her exclamation of disbelief in her good fortune, which will drive the dice spitefully back to him. But it does not come. He loses armies in pairs. By and by, they are evenly matched, Siam and Indonesia, and Les stalls to count armies, trying to cool her dice this way.

Nolan says, "I feel uncomfortable without a host." He opens himself a fresh beer. He begins to look through bills that Owen keeps stacked on the counter next to the telephone.

"Jesus, Owen has $1,108 on his Visa," he informs the others.

"Stop that," Alice scolds.

Les likes this unexpected turn; Nolan's rude exploration has taken Alice's mind off the game.

"Many people are faced with serious and potentially catastrophic debt," Les says.

Nolan goes on. "A phone bill for $79.21."

"What if Owen comes back and finds you doing that?" Alice asks. When her head is turned away from Les, he blows gently toward the dice in her hand to cool them.

"He's with Pam," Nolan says. Saying this makes it a fact; makes him feel released.

"Roll the dice," Les orders. "I want to get out of here before daylight." He is certain that the dice have come back to him. Alice has lingered too long between throws. She has lost favor by ignoring the good fortune that the dice were eager to bestow. He reminds her, "I'm still attacking."

Alice rolls, thinking of Owen. He had telephoned her when the baby died, the phone seeming to explode with compressed tragedy in the middle of the night. To this day, she can't talk to Eileen without seeing grief encasing her like an invisible jar. Only lately has

Alice seen her smile. Would Owen go off with Pam at just such a time?

Les wins two armies. Then two more.

Nolan says, "A bill for $177.44 from People's Gas."

Alice wishes Owen would return and discover Nolan and banish him forever. But the house is silent except for the click of dice. Maybe Owen has left with Pam; maybe it is the only response to this time in history. The man Alice meets on the sly is married to a sweet woman who he claims has nothing of interest to say. And Alice has never considered herself fascinating. The man she shares the farmhouse with had a marriage end years ago when he was caught in a hammock with another woman. She thinks this might make her safe, that he might understand if he ever catches her.

Les rolls and Alice falls. He was right: the dice have come back. When he clears her out of Siam, he still has ten armies in Indonesia. He takes the four cards Alice holds, and with the cards already in his hand cashes twice for forty-five armies, a huge green force he places with care to battle Nolan while his dice are running hot. It takes another hour to finish the game. The dice are at home in Les's loosely cupped fist and at two minutes to four o'clock in the morning he is the winner for the third consecutive time. Alice and Frank sit quietly and watch.

"Dear Les," Alice says, standing and stretching. "You do go on."

"And on . . . and on," Frank says. "Like a fungus." He shakes Les's hand. He folds Owen's board, puts the cards away, puts the armies in their containers.

Nolan asks, "Did Owen take his key?"

"I couldn't tell you," Les says.

"If we lock the door," Frank says, "and he has to knock to get in, we could be inadvertently exposing him to exposure. Or exposure. A guy like Owen could die of exposure."

"He should've thought of that," Nolan says.

"He can just say he forgot it," Les says. "He could say he went to breakfast after the game and forgot it."

Alice puts the wine in the refrigerator and washes out the glasses. She leaves a small light on over the stove.

Birds stir outside, though it is still dark. The four of them stand, corners of a square, in the driveway.

"Somebody mentioned breakfast," Nolan says.

Frank pats his pockets. "I'm broke."

"I'll buy," Nolan says. "The vanquished will buy with the reparations they receive from the victors."

"Ha! You'll get nothing from me," Les says.

"I'll still buy."

"I think I'll pass," Alice says.

"You'll pass on a free meal?"

"I don't feel so hot."

"Suit yourself," Frank says.

The other three turn from her and make their plans. She does not want to be alone just then, though a sleeping man who loves her awaits at the end of the drive home. Nolan and Frank start their cars and drive off and she is left standing there with Les. He sits astride his motorcycle, pulling on his gloves and watching her.

"Come with us," he urges.

She moves to his side. "I'm tired of Nolan and Frank." She kisses Les. "Can't we go somewhere?"

He laughs. "That might be difficult to explain. I've been coming and going at awfully odd hours. She thinks I play this game at all hours of the day and night."

"Coward."

Owen is awakened by Les's motorcycle starting. Unwinding himself from Eileen, he feels her stir. She loops an arm around his waist when he sits up on the edge of the bed. His friends will be going for breakfast at this early hour. It is a tradition of the game. The night's war will be replayed. Stories will be told, rumors will be spread. Owen would love to go with them, but he doesn't dare.

GALLAGHER'S OLD MAN

(from *TriQuarterly*)

W hile we're on the subject of work, James, it's as true a fact as there is that when Alpha Company—us grunts—would hump back to our base camp at Phuc Luc for a couple days' rest (stand-down, we called it), Lieutenant Stennett got so he didn't much care what we did just so long as "every swinging dick" made morning roll call. We never much told him, and Stennett—finally smarting up—never much asked. Some of us would sneak off to Tu Duc Phuc's #I Souvenirs and Car Wash in town and get laid. Some of us would dawdle around the company nursing our diarrhea, bored out of our fucking skulls and homesick to boot, drinking anything we could get the top off of, writing letters home and play- ing penny-ante poker. The walking wounded among us would gobble our Darvons and antibiotics, resting up as best we could for the next move-out.

But Paco and Gallagher and Jonesy and Jigs, the medic, and some of the rest of us, would troop down to bunker number 7 on the east perimeter—that bunker, James, about chest-high and as big as a two-car garage—where we could sit and drink our beer and smoke our dope, shooting the shit, in peace. We would smear that foul- smelling insect repellent on ourselves, and still we would swat mos- quitoes all night. It was a constant motion of heads and hands, James, quietly slapping at them or brushing them away, or mildly scratching. Jigs would bring the makings for the jays and a three- legged stool he snitched from the medics' hooch. Paco would bring this shit-for-nothing lawn chair, and would sit so deeply in it, with his knees way up, that he looked as though he were sitting in a barrel. Gallagher would sit on a wooden ammo crate as if it were the bottom step of a porch stoop back on the block, and would lean against the bunker and let the cool of it soak into his back—those sandbags fucked up with mortar hits and near-misses. And Jonesy would sit directly above him on the edge of the shallow-slanted roof, with his legs dangling over and his back to the rolls of concertina wire, and the marsh bubbling with slime and the beat-to-hell woodline a hundred meters opposite. Jonesy had to crouch almost double because we talked in hissing whispers.

If you stood back from those two, James, you'd swear that Gallagher and Jonesy looked like a totem—lots of guys said that: Jonesy's ashy, caramel-colored skin, pink nails, and bright black eyes, astonishing eyes; the livid scar along his jaw and under his lips; the lumpy razor rash; the well-oiled 12-gauge shotgun laid across his lap, and a pair of blacked-up, well-tended jungle boots ("Man's got to have some prideful fuckin' feelin' about some goddamn thing," he'd tell you). And literally between Jonesy's knees would be Gallagher's stubby face and pug ears, his bull neck and short thick fingers ("Golden Gloves motherfucker," we'd tease him, and laugh; "Fuck *you* up, boy," he'd tease right back, and grin, knocking his knuckles together, his eyes twinkling). He wore a green towel draped around his neck and his .357 Magnum packed in his shoulder holster, his feet flat on the ground, and that Bangkok R & R red-and-black dragon tattoo on his forearm from his wrist to his elbow shining like a trophy in the moonlight ("Got this here in a tattoo parlor," he'd say, bragging his head off, "that was part opium den, part fag whorehouse. That old papa-san must've had *thousands*, and I picked through them and finally took this sucker. It's a honey," he'd say, showing it around).

One night Gallagher had a bottle of Johnnie Walker Red. "Me and my man Paco scrounged this here bottle of John Dub-ya," and Gallagher shook the bottle in all our faces, "scrounged it from that goddamned Goody Two-shoes Captain Culpepper." Gallagher jerked his head up the hill toward Culpepper's tent—the captain's silhouette stooped over his famous Scrabble game—"Letting *him* drink this shit, why you might as well knock the neck off with a claw hammer and pour every last fucking drop down that Bravo Company piss tube across the way there!" Gallagher pointed over at the Bravo Company tents, then waved his hand in front of his face, making a pass or two at the mosquitoes. He cracked the seal, took a healthy swig—it *was* his bottle, James—and passed it on. (As the night wore on, the bottle emptied sip by sip, and you could hear it slosh more and more; the ring of it more and more mellow.)

Paco passed out the beers, and Jonesy and Jigs made the jays and passed them out. Then we sat quiet and absorbed in that small circle for the longest time, drinking and smoking—ruminating.

Gallagher slouched back against the bunker more and more, grumbling and muttering. If you listened close you could hear him repeating, "Shit. Fucking shit," growling with a deep, sharp voice. A couple days before, a Bravo Company man got his arm shattered in a mortar barrage, and it was this incident that Gallagher brooded over. Gallagher had seen it happen by the oddest chance, but it was not the actual event he picked over—the man's arm the last piece of anatomy pulled into the bunker, that 60-mm round hitting right near with a hard *crack* the way they always ripped, leaving a crater that wasn't much more than a boot scuff. No, Gallagher wasn't thinking about that—"Seen that plenty, Jack!"—but rather, the funny, dumbshit look that came over the guy's face when he raised himself up and took a good look down where the stump of his arm was—just below the elbow—as shaggy as a buckskin fringe. Or, as Gallagher later told Lieutenant Stennett, "just the same as you'd shove a rolled-up newspaper into the business end of a roaring room fan, *sir*," looking right at Stennett as though it was he that done it.

Paco watched Gallagher slurp foam from his beer and stare at the smooth impression the whiskey bottle made in the pillowy, dusty dirt between his feet. Gallagher was mulling all that over, Paco knew, but then suddenly he shivered all over like a horse chasing flies and changed the subject on himself. He whipped out a cigar (he was smoking Antonio Y Cleopatra then) and lit it with his famous "Fuck you up, boy" Zippo lighter—the cigar tip soon cherry red and his head enveloped in billowing smoke; the air still, the smoke rising with ease and glowing strangely in the clear, undiminished moonlight.

(Almost everyone in the company had a PX Zippo lighter, James, and many of us had it inscribed with that parody of the Fourth verse of the Twenty-third Psalm:

> *Yea, though I walk through the valley of*
> *the shadow of death, I will fear no*
> *evil: for I am the meanest mother*
> *fucker in the valley.*

But Gallagher—the company killer, the company clown, a man both simple and blunt—had his Zippo engraved with his all-purpose response:

> *Gonna fuck*
> *you up,*
> *boy.)*

Gallagher looked at Paco as though the two of them shared a secret, and said, "I think about my old man sometimes. You?" And Paco, whose father was long dead, said, "Yeah." Gallagher swigged at the whiskey as it came around and cleared his throat with a growl. There was no melancholy in his voice, same as the night he told us about one of his older brothers killed in a car crash—*raining* like hell, *side-swiped* an abutment.

"My father drove a Chicago city bus—Chicago Motor Coach, CTA; drove streets like long Western and Lincoln, Kedzie-Kimball-California and Lunt-Touhy, Broadway and Sheridan Road. And I remember he used to come home nights ass-whipped tired, just *draggin'* his ass. My brothers and my ma and me would be sitting at the dinner table and we'd hear him and his goddamned galoshes coming up the front porch steps, and then he'd burst in the front door. We'd all look over our shoulders and see him in this big mirror that hung over the davenport in the living room. The copper weather stripping on the door would always twang—Ma kept it that way so that no matter how easy you tried to sneak it open it would always twang (it'd make your eyeballs just squeak); there'd be no comin's or goin's in her house *she* didn't know about. It'd be the dead of fucking winter, see, so he'd be wearing his huge, heavy coat with the stiff, thick collar, something like those big lumbering pea-coat-looking things that railroad men used to wear—only with more pockets and *much* heavier—and a pair of ordinary garden gloves. I tell you aside, I don't think my old man had a decent pair of gloves his whole fucking life.

"Everyone else went back to dinner, but I always watched him undress. First he'd pull off those gloves, one finger at a time, and lay them palm up on this squatty radiator we had by the front door. By springtime the fingers would curl into claw-looking things, and the cotton would fray at the fingers and they would unravel to the knuckles. Next'd come this gray scarf my great-aunt got him one year, that thing looped around his neck and tied like an ascot. Then he'd do the coat buttons—big as silver dollars, they were—and haul that coat off and hang it, and the scarf, on a side hook at the back of the closet. A big brass thing you could hang a side of beef on. Then he had two sweaters—one a thick, loose, golfer-looking thing, and underneath *that* was a close-knit, navy-blue V-neck he'd had since God-knows-when and had patches and darned places aplenty. And all that while he'd be standing there in these big-ass, ugly, fucking galoshes—big as coal hods—unbuckled but with his thick serge trousers shoved down into them, real sloppy. He'd pry those fuckers off, and if it'd snowed or rained, there'd be melted show or mud sprayed all over Ma's prized paint job. The galoshes went on this big baking sheet behind the door.

"Well, then he'd start with his bus-driver gear—punch and changer and watch—and the big leather belt they hung on. That fuckin' changer was as big as the cast-iron bulldog that held open the kitchen door. There was a penny slot, two slots for nickels, one slot for dimes, a couple slots for quarters, and one slot for halves. I'd guess thirty-five, forty dollars. There was a slot for silver dollars, but he never used it. Bad luck, somehow, he told me once. Then would come the punch he had in a leather holster engraved with his initials— DDG—and kept clipped to the belt. The punch was real hefty, German-made, and would give you a star-shaped hole. He set the changer and punch on Ma's gateleg table, which was all ruined with gouges and scratches, and gray with water spots. Then he'd pull his pocket watch from the shirt pocket where he kept his pencils—that watch as big as your hand, 17 jewels, with Roman numerals and a sweep second hand as thin as a sewing needle. He put that down with the changer and punch. I remember, too." Gallagher said, snorting and grinning, "he used to pull that fuckin' thing out at Thanksgiving and Christmas, and bullshit my uncles that it cost him a month's pay and took food out of our mouths. He had it on a braided leather fob about as long as your arm, which drooped into his lap when he was driving, and he had a habit of running that fob through his fingers, stroking it—the same as you see old women working their rosaries at church—ticking off the stitches. He laid down the watch with the changer and punch, coiling the fob around it like a Sunday sailor coiling a deck rope." And Gallagher coiled that fob in the air so we could all see it, as dark as it was.

Gallagher poured some of the whiskey in his beer, stirring it around a time or two, and took a slug. "Then he'd haul off that belt of his, and I tell you, Jack, you could hear that fuckin' thing snap through every loop. You sure could tell what kind of an evenin' it was going to be by the sound of that fuckin' belt. If anyone was counting on a lickin' that night, you could see him flinch but good. My old man would coil that sucker around his fist, set it down on the gateleg, and drape the buckle end of it over the coin slots of the changer. I swear to God, Jack, he could count money by the look of the stack it made, by the heft of a handful of it. So may God pity the poor fuckin' fool who snitched as much as a dime, he would know. I remember many a night going up to bed and looking down around behind at the bottom of those stairs and that gateleg, and there'd be that fuckin' changer, chockful of coins, with the buckle end of that wide fuckin' belt laid over it just as easy and casual as you'd put your hand on somebody's shoulder from behind. That was the belt we got our lickin's with, you understand? I remember many a night curled up as tight as a fist under my covers, listening to one or another of my brothers getting a whipping—them hopping around downstairs on all fours like a damn crab—my old man stompin' after them, shoving furniture aside and thrashing at them with that fuckin' belt—bellowing, *screaming* angry. Shit, bub! You could stuff a blanket and an afghan and a pillow apiece into your ears and you could *still* hear that goddamned belt rip and whistle through the air. My brothers and me got scars from that fuckin' buckle, which was one of those ordinary, square-looking, nickel-silver affairs with a thick crossbar.

"Anyway," Gallagher said, taking a moment to draw on his cigar and blow smoke rings up into the still night air, "my old man would stand in front of that closet—'putting away his work,' he called it.' Some nights he'd come right in to dinner and some nights he'd go straight upstairs, but some nights he would stagger into the living room and slump into his easy chair. He'd crouch nearly double, his head in his hands, half blinded by headaches, squeezing his scalp for all he was worth, with those cold, rawed-up fingers of his, and his eyes'd be red and milky, shining—and sometimes those fuckin' headaches went on all night; years later he told me he could feel his face droop like a gob of warmed wax.

"My ma and my brothers and me'd sit around that table, looking at him, and I'd look the longest—me being the youngest had something to do with that, I expect. And every once in a while he'd stand there in front of that closet for a *long* time—that closet where everything hung, don't you see: football gear and mechanic's tools, Monopoly and croquet, the flashlights and *Reader's Digest* and Lionel trains, the coats and boots and shopping bags. He'd stand there in those galoshes and that big heavy coat of his, stinking of fuel oil and diesel fumes, and this look of pale and exhausted astonishment would come over him, like he just woke up and couldn't bring himself to believe where he was and what he was looking at.

"Fuckin'-A" Gallagher said, disgusted ("Goddamned drunk," as Jonesy would say). "My old man busted his ass all his life, and all's he got out of it was his beat-up hands, bad eyes, and a bend in his back.

"And you know what else," Gallagher said, sniffing and laughing at the discovered irony, then taking another heavy swig of his boilermaker. "That was the same look as come over the poor fuckin' fool from Bravo Company a couple days ago when he drew himself out of that bunker and took a good long look at what was left of his arm. Then the pain worked itself up his arm and into his face, and after that he never stopped screaming." And we all had to shiver then, remembering the screams.

"Fuckin' Bravo Company," Gallagher said, brushing at the mosquitoes in his hair and sitting up—as good as done with that bottle of whiskey—"How you gonna have any pity on those geeks?"

William Brashler

CITY DOGS

(from *City Dogs*)

T he port went down like milk. It was lukewarm and bitter, running over his teeth like rain over moss, and he shook himself. He found a rumpled pack of Camels on the bed and lit up the last scurvied survivor. A speck of tobacco clung to his lip and he tried to spit it out, failed, then left it hang there like a fly on flypaper. The darkness of the room, the shade drawn shut, door closed, the single light bulb and the picture tube dark, brought back the bleariness, gummed with new wine, of the night before. He leaned back and stung the knob of his shoulder bone on the curved iron bar of the bed. He rubbed it and sank into the depths of his mind, his eyes closed trying to see himself in Wrigley Field, where he always had dreamt of being, all in green and sunshine, gamboling in the outfield with Hack Wilson, losing himself in the vines after a screaming liner, the leaves and the cheers and the uniform all in him and of him, Harry Lumakowski of Milwaukee Avenue and the National League.

If he could have frozen his life at any point, it would have been in 1932. Not that life was particularly good then; in fact, it was the thick of the Depression and Harry was lucky to find work unloading groceries from trucks at a food store. But life for Harry in 1932, and it was etched in his memory, was the Cubs, the fighting, scratching, winning Cubs. Harry virtually camped out in Wrigley Field, usually after only a few hours' sleep after work, sitting in the grandstands or the bleachers and rooting like a maniac, more fervent than if he were at a religious revival, with his gods wearing blue pin stripes and baggy pants.

He was devoted to the likes of Riggs Stephenson and Kiki Cuyler, Charley Grimm, and Billy Jurges, and he knew the weaknesses and the tritest characteristics of Gabby Hartnett and Babe Herman. Yet his real hero, his alter ego, his do-no-wrong tower of strength and glory was the Arkansas Humming Bird, the tall, gangling right-handed pitcher Lon Warneke. Harry saw most of Warneke's twenty-two victories and agonized through the few times Lon lost that year. It was an awesome, overpowering spectacle, Warneke going through lineups as if they were highballs at a Polish wedding, and Harry cheering past every batter; even if he was sitting alone and curling his program he yelled as if he were leading the crowd. Or if he went with Billy Mrozsinski, the two of them would bet on how many strikeouts Warneke would get, or the counts he would run, the hits he'd give up. With each victory, not Harry's or Billy's, but always Warneke's, the two of them would stand up and beat each other on the back, hollering, whistling, catcalling. And during the show, as Long whiffed through batters and fooled power hitters, Harry alone or Harry and Billy would sit back and smile smugly, purring with satisfaction over their personal righthander who was the cream of the league.

At midseason Harry was so starstruck with Warneke that he began to use him, to flaunt him, to ward off his enemies with him. If Pittsburgh or St. Louis or Philadelphia got uppity while the Arkansas Humming Bird was on the bench, while Pat Malone or Burleigh Grimes or Charlie Root was throwing, then Harry would cup his hands around his mouth and hex the enemy with the specter of Warneke. It was a long, rolling catcall, three syllables usually bellowed in the silences of the game, not *War*-neke, like everyone else said it, but with the emphasis on the second syllable: War-*nek*-i! That way the Arkansas Humming Bird acquired a distinctly Polish heritage, War-*nek*-i, with all the gristle and *kapusta* and snort of Milwaukee Avenue, or at least as much of it as Harry could give him.

After a while it became a part of his vocabulary, a word he used as a threat in almost any situation. It ran through his mind, gaining speed and power like an overhand fastball: War-*nek*-i! as if it could somehow put out the fire of the moment, the impending danger, the uncertainty. He said it so much and in such odd circumstances that people began to look at him sideways, wondering if they heard right, not bothering to ask. Only Billy Mrozsinski really knew, for he had seen Harry lean forward countless times, tighten his eyes, and croon it like a midnight owl: War*nek*i.

Harry headed for the Ron-Rick Cafe for a cup of coffee, the worst drip in Uptown, or all of town, black and filmy, bitter because the pots were never cleaned. It settled in his cup, the steam swirling, reminding him of the gasoline rainbows he used to see in the puddles on the street.

"Raaaaa-haaaa," he spat, echoing his phlegm-coated distaste throughout the place.

Sully, the counter man, the white-aproned hash clerk with no upper teeth, rammed Harry's coins into the cash register.

"You don't like it, pour it in yer nose."

"I'll drink it, don't you worry about that. But sure does remind me of something I ate yesterday," Harry said into the cup. The coffee burned his tongue, awakened the buds, scalded the layer of wine dew.

He held the cup with both hands to keep it from shaking, letting the steam curl around his eyelids. Sully walked by with a plate of eggs rimmed with a range of sodden hash brown potatoes.

"Hey, how's about that Billy Williams?" Harry barked, but Sully ignored him, sauntered back to scrape the grill, tip his paper hat on the rear of his head.

"The sonofabitch could hit a fruit fly in a hurricane."

Harry felt his pockets, a bit of change, his roll now down to three dollars, green and crinkled but capable of smiling if he wanted, and sixty-five slipper cents. That would have to do, have to be morning, noon, and night, the salad and the dessert, until October, days away, when he would hound and chew out and bug his welfare worker for his $171.05 of general assistance, in this case most generally and generously accepted by Harry Lum. But he had to do something until then to get some money. Something. The coffee dripped over the cup and down his chin, a drop held on his stubble, then he wiped it into the patch of leather on the back of his hand. He looked through the haze of his thoughts and saw Leo across the counter, good old Leo, plowing through the hash browns and sunny-side-ups like a thresher through wheat. Harry stuck a finger through the thick handle of his cup and slid off the stool.

Leo looked up, stared over his lower lids, the reddish-pink, glistening lower lids, saw Harry, twitched, a stream of egg yolk winding a river through the cactus of his chin. He grabbed his fork with all five fingers and shook it at Harry like a cleaver.

"Away. Get off 'cuz I ain't got nothin' here," Leo growled. He stuffed a piece of bread in his cheeks, muffling his baritone rasp. His fork continued to waver, his head cocked at an angle, bobbing slightly and shaking the stiff hairs of a brown-green toupee he wore on the top of his own hair like a hat. The wig came from one of the trash bins he picked through each day, lying there like a ratted, wild lily, and he took it and wiped it off and kept it as a treasure even though it was stained and matted, minute clods of hair, like fairway sand traps, dotting his head.

"Where'd ya get the money for the meal?" Harry asked.

"Girl gave it to me from a car," he mumbled, searing the egg into his face like yellow dye. "A dollar."

"Jesus, brought your appetite up from the dead, it sure did. You ain't ate like that since Christmas."

"Not since Christmas," said Leo. A meal to him was like a bath, something he didn't expect and had learned not to look for, working the streets, stumbling around all day for quarters, grinning blankly, trying to get the words out before the windows cranked shut and he was breathing exhaust. When he was desperate he pounded car windows, drubbing and jabbering a hoarse, thunder-gibberish at cars captive at red lights, until a squad car came along and chased him off. Leo was somewhere in his fifties but wrinkled like lettuce, bleary, pink-faced, with sphincter muscles that had died and gone on to their reward and left him with a soaked crotch at the mere sight of a drinking fountain. He had to hide his mossy inseams if he wanted to sit at a diner, or hope a waiter like Sully didn't know, or didn't remember, or just didn't have the nose to smell it or see the steam rise from the stool.

"What you got, Harry?" Leo said. "You got something up?"

"Something big alla time. The roof, the sky's the limit, yessiree bob," Harry said.

Leo shook his head, as if he understood, a bulge in his cheek, then he choked on the potatoes and coughed into his plate, lunged at it as if it were the only thing keeping him from spitting up his throat. Harry sucked on his coffee.

"Clobber the bum, will ya!" Sully yelled from the hot counter.

Harry reached around and swatted Leo on the back, clopping him a couple of good ones, but Leo coughed until he began to gag. Then he suddenly stopped, looked up with a googly-eyed expression on his face, as if the blood had drained into his eyeballs, then went back to the slop on his plate.

"Somebody got it last night," he said.

"Yup," Harry said.

"Over at the hotel on Vicklen."

"How you know?" Harry hardly heard him, knew the wino's mind was as alert as his liver. The silt at the bottom of Harry's coffee cup came at him.

"I seen it," Leo said.

Harry put his cup to the counter, thunking it so that Sully looked up, and watched Leo chase the last bit of yolk around his plate with his fork. Failing, watching the yellow glop paint a streamer in the grease of the plate, Leo put the fork down and finished the job with his two fingers, both black with dirt caked pores, one with no nail on it, pushing them around the plate like tugboats, then sucking them. He did it over and over again until the plate was smeared with the finger grime, each time sucking them as if he wanted to eat them too, two bungy, egg-flavored lollipops.

Harry got up and left.

He jaywalked across Wilson over to Broadway. The sun was out, a ball-playing sun, flat and warm, the Cubbies not around to enjoy it, and Harry opened his coat and let it beat into his wool plaid shirt. He walked with both hands in his pockets, part of the motion of

Broadway, the wide sidewalks, the open doors of the daily pay halls. He ran his fingers over the change and the three dollar bills in his left pocket. Monday, he thought, the dog day, and he was almost broke, dragging his ass on the concrete. He thought about hounding his caseworker for an emergency check, he was an emergency, Harry Lum, right now, you can sit there and give me guff but I got to eat, I'm a human being and I pay taxes and I'm hungry, right now, not yesterday. But they would make him wait in the goddamn office for three hours just to tell him to get lost, wait until the first of the month, didn't have to be a genius to know that himself. They didn't tell Harry nothing new.

At Cullom he stopped in front of the Archway Liquors, a circus of blinking bulbs, windows boarded over and covered with hand-painted specials, sub-buck six-packs, Guckenheimer, Amigo wine. Regulars passing pints huddled in clusters, jabbering like politicians in caucus rooms, swigging the sting of the juice in noisy gulps, belching. Maybe another, a pint, Harry thought, a burgundy to chase the coffee out of his gut. He took a step toward the door; joints like this seemed to have tilted sidewalks, so much so that Harry for years had lost his balance, as if caught in a thirsty undertow, until he was slack-jawed at the counter. But he caught himself, what the hell, mouthed the words as he thought, I ain't no wetpants Leo, ain't no goddamned alky wino on the street smiling for quarters. Not your Polish Pride Harry Lum, with a heritage stronger than any one of those bums, yessiree, feeling those vines in Wrigley Field, passing the sour cream, and he turned around and ambled past the Archway. It was will power, you better believe it, he said to himself, will power two winos tucked into the foundation sucking muscatel just didn't have. He kicked rocks and empties across the vacant lot.

I got to get something up, he told himself. Got to.

On Winthrop, he walked a block until he came to a large red-brick rooming house with a four-by-five hand-painted sign advertising transient rates. He followed a concrete walk around the side and down to a basement door, kicked it three times, waited. Then he kicked it again, three dull thuds with the side of his foot. But the door didn't crack, no music, and he scratched his elbow bone and looked up the street. The apartment belonged to Frank Tulka, a squatty booster who wore pouch-lined sport coats that could absorb watches and pizzas, radios and pork chops. Once in a while he let Harry fence for him, hawk a zircon on the street for a few bucks, hop a bus to Maxwell Street and bargain with the niggers, or pass it off to his vendor at Wrigley Field. He hadn't seen Frank for a couple of weeks, no one had, but Frank couldn't have skipped, he wasn't that hot, wasn't that much of an operator. The cops had his address, nagged him, but didn't lay on him.

It was a good idea, Harry thought. The middle man, it appealed to his sense of merchandising, a salesman who could swap the ass of a hooker. Maybe he should wait for Frank; the two of them could pull something off. Like before.

But it was no good to hang around somebody's place. Like hanging crepe paper on the joint, bullhorns, inviting the cops and their wives. He would find Frank somewhere around; he had his ways, Harry knew. He felt for his cigarettes but they were a memory, like the morning. He had no bottle, he had only the change and the three bills, which were crumpled and smothered with his fingerprints because he was mussing and pulling and wadding them in his pockets. Things were loose; he tried to yawn but couldn't, felt the thirst, his stomach, then twitched, shook his fingers, saw them shaking.

Then he spotted two heads in a car parked along Winthrop, not coppers but skinny, greased heads, and he walked toward them. He picked up the pace when he recognized Donald Ray Burl and Jimmy Del Corso slouched in the front seat of a '61 Chevy. He got to the curb on Burl's side, about a foot away from Burl's hand, which flopped limply on the car door. Burl was a hillbilly, still young, about a dozen lean years out of Kentucky and looked it, citified but still a shit kicker, his thick, hill-country brown hair combed around the sides of his head like Elvis Presley, a glop of curl hanging against his forehead like a hook. Burl had two lower front teeth missing, one left on the floor of a bar in Kentucky when he'd gone home for a visit, one he lost in a bar in Chicago. But, to take attention away from his pink gums, he had a pair of eyes with lids that drooped, lazy lids that made him appear tired or hung-over or strung-out even when he was sober as a stone.

"Got something up, Don?" Harry asked.

"Get the livin' hell outta here. We're busy," Donald Ray said.

"Don't give me the brush. I want in."

"The only thing yer gettin' in is my foot when I smash you one good."

"Gotta big mouth for a hillbilly. If you was thinkin' you'd know I could help yuse. Keep you out of the can."

"Shit on a bun. You ain't ever done nothing. Talk like yer some gangster and you ain't nothing' but an ol' winehead." Donald Ray twanged the words out of the side of his mouth, coating them with beer and barbecue.

"Never drink when I work. One of my rules of order," Harry said.

"Never work, either," Donald Ray said.

Harry stood there, staring at the car, shifting his weight, not wanting to lean over the roof to give Burl a poke at him. He put his hands on his hips and spat on the curb.

"Shut up now, fucker, and mow your ass outta here. Corso got his old lady run through this morning and we ain't in the mood for you."

"I'm around if you need me. On top of things," Harry said. He shook his head and looked seriously at Burl.

"Bums like you are always around," Donald Ray said.

That night Harry succumbed to the tilt of the Archway and paid for his pint of elderberry. He stuck it in his waist, not wishing to share it with anyone, wanting to drink in peace and quiet, maybe with a cake. He turned and went for the vacant lot, but just outside the door, from the shadows beyond the blipping of the Archway's obnoxious bulbs, someone called to him.

"Hey, winehead. Mover yer ass. We got something for ya."

For days they had cased the jewelry store, eyeing it from above and below, through the glass of a laundromat across the street, from a car, once from the platform of the elevated train a half block down the street. They watched and timed, drooling as the jeweler leaned into his window every morning and night picking and plucking his wares like children off stools. But on the third day, as they watched and bored themselves, trying to figure how much they knew and how much they had to learn, they were given an opening that whapped them in the face like a shaving-cream pie. They chided themselves for not thinking of it sooner, for not scraping their heads for television tricks. It was the plates that first hit them, white on maroon from Michigan, Water Wonderland, then they saw the case, the lovely leather, smooth-grained, unfillable, samples case. It lit up in front of them like a cashier's drawer, yet so much more real, so much more accessible.

Donald Ray saw it from the bar, threw back his stool as if he'd seen his woman rubbing up against a pair of strange thighs, and hustled down the street. He breathed it to Jimmy as Del Corso sat in the car, then both in the front seat, and they pulled from the curb as the Michigan plates passed them.

The salesman was a good one, patient, smiling like an undertaker, the bands, the casings reflecting in the lenses of his eyeglasses. He made four stops a day, returned to his car with the bag swinging, his keys, sat on the seat, made some notes on a sales pad and drove off. He was doing well, metal is forever, diamonds longer, and it didn't dawn on him to check out the '61 Chevy with Bondo on the fenders which was shadowing him at a religious three car lengths to the rear. Jimmy drove. Donald Ray sat with his fingers drumming against the dashboard, Nashville lovin' sounds in his head, trinkets for the baby.

They followed the Michigan plates and their light-blue '69 Ford sedan company car over to Lincoln Avenue. It was late afternoon and the sun bit into the windshield from the west, over the treetops from where it would sit in some cornfield. The car turned north on Lincoln and followed the diagonal route through the neighborhoods, the crowded shopping districts with their kids and paper vendors, until he hit the strip of motels on the edge of the city. It turned into Quality Courts, bumping over the high drive, jiggling the samples after a hard day. The '61 Chevy continued past on Lincoln, two pairs of eyes cutting swaths into the motel lot, then doubled back and around the rear of the motel.

They chugged up a side street about to hit another entrance, to swing through and around to cover the angles, when Donald Ray sat up and slapped Jimmy on the arm.

"No sir!" he shouted, then hurriedly, "Keep on! Go on!"

The look on his face was dull and scared and expedient, his eyes tightening, hands furtively slicking back a loose string of hair, looking down at the trash and scuz on the rubber floor mats. For a while it hadn't registered, the short time that it took Jimmy to prepare for the crank of the wheel, the turn into the lot, then it hit him like a stab in the armpits, as if his daddy had cashed in a Dr. Pepper on his skull, and his mind clicked the shutter and he told Jimmy to hit it. He alone knew that private moment of panic, cooped inside the front seat, blessed, that's what I am, he said to himself, and he told Jimmy to drive on, get out and keep on going.

The next day Donald Ray Burl, in his best criminal intentions, decided to call upon the dimming, cirrhotic abilities of Harry Lum.

"Listen here, now. Listen, you ol' fuckin' winehead. We got this here thing all set up like you wouldn't believe. Me and Jimmy been working on this for a long time but we got to lay low on account of me being on probation and Jimmy just at the cops on account of his old lady. So we're gonna give you a little trial and see if yer really worth a puddle of piss or if yer just an old winehead who's worthless as shit.

"Now listen here. We got this here salesman, see. We got his whole route mapped out better 'an he knows it hisself. He's in town right now, see. Works the North Side, especially around Lincoln. Now we ain't gonna touch him, you know. We got enough shit for guns last time and this is gonna be simpler, anyhow. He's got this case, see. It's full of watches and rings, and bracelets and shit. About ten grand worth, I figure it. He don't sell it; he shows it and takes orders.

"So we been follering him, right. Driving all to hell watching show that shit. But he always come out with that case, see. And it's always full up. Good stuff with no numbers, no wear or nothing. Get rid of it in an hour.

"But here's the thing. Listen to this. He stays in this motel on Lincoln Avenue. He takes the case with him inside and sleeps on it. That is, *sometimes* he sleeps on it. Sometimes he gets juiced up and is leavin' it in the car trunk right out there in the middle of the parking lot.

"Now yer saying why didn't we go and grab it when we sees him do that, and I admit we should a done it. But we had some trouble and couldn't get to it, and the next time we tried it weren't there and he had it with him.

"Now this is where you come in. We knowed you used to be a hotshot at punching trunks and things. We watch him, see, and when he leaves it in his car we come and picks you up. We drop you off about two in the morning and you get on over there and punch it. If yer any good it'll be like breaking into a candy bar. We pick you up in back of the run and get on out. Split it twenty-forty-forty on account of we set this thing up and this is your first time in.

"Maybe some other jobs and you'll get more. Shit, this is more dough 'an you seen in a year on welfare. Keep you in wine for a year.

"That's the way it's gonna be. He's got a '69 Ford, light blue, parks it near the side of the building in a corner. Dumb shit thinks it's safer there. You can't miss it cause it's got Michigan plates on. You can read something besides them wine labels, can't you?

"Now don't give me no shit on this, 'cause we got it set up and that's it. We'll be by every night by that store where you buy your juice at about one. If you ain't there you ain't going and you just blowed your chance for good. Could be tomorrow, could the day after next. We don't know.

"And don't be gettin' loaded up and shouting all this to yer wine head friends on Wilson Avenue or in the Salvation Army or wherever yer shakin' out yer ass nowadays. You blow this, Lum, and we'll take care of you good. I ain't got nothing to lose no more because I done time and the fuckin' cops know me on sight. Some old winehead iced out here and there don't mean nothing to me. I'll just blow your fuckin' head off and go back to Kentucky."

Harry shook his head up and down, up and down, like a kid or a gofer, feeling the linings of his pockets and the itch on the ends of his fingers. He'd go through a month of cold turkey to stay straight on this one, this one time, even as Donald Ray Burl, the hillbilly kid who hadn't shaved and smelled like rotten Old Spice, mapped it out for him as if it was Fort Knox and he was Yellow Kid Weil. He sat in the back seat of the Chevy, parked in an alley off Magnolia, nodding his head up and down, up and down.

Donald Ray's words were like the supplications of a priest, words that called him home.

Fran Podulka

COMING AROUND THE HORN

(from *Other Voices*)

T he tour was becoming a passage of some kind; he felt it as a small disturbance in the soft days and as an annoyance with Ross, the Sun Tour's tireless guide. He felt like a child at camp, over-scheduled, protected from risk and reality. After a week of island hopping he staged a minor rebellion and refused the shopping trip to Lahaina, saying he had better things to do although he had nothing particular in mind.

The trip had been Germaine's idea. "I don't need a vacation," he'd told her. "I've been on vacation for six months."

"Retirement isn't vacation," she had reminded him.

But it felt like it and already bored him. He felt himself flailing about in the free fall of time, losing his edge and initiative. Agreeing to the trip proved it. Germaine meant Hawaii as therapy for him, a forced march into a *joie de vivre*, but the experience depressed him. That morning at breakfast with his fellow Sun Tourists, among all the gray and white heads bent diligently over continental juice and rolls, medications and admonitions against drinking caffeine and taking salt, he had thought of dying his hair. Combing through it the vaseline product he saw advertised on television so that, day by day, slowly, with no one the wiser, he would be transformed. When he walked into the dining room they would show him to another table where he could at least pretend to be himself again.

While Germaine and the others shopped he moved his discontent to the Whaler's Inn bar, had a gin and tonic, and browsed through the place. In the old days it had been a sailor's rest, a brothel, and looking up at the tiers of rooms opening onto balconies over the inner courtyard, he imagined what it would have been like. Christ, the times they must have had coming around the horn, horny. He studied the old photos on the bar wall. The men, some only boys really, their faces sea-dark, posing crazily, bursting with life. He would have given a hundred Sun Tours for one night there in the old days, in a room with shuttered windows that looked out over the dazzling harbor, a nut-brown maiden on each knee, a fan turning slowly in the ceiling.

He decided to stay for lunch.

The courtyard service catered to transients who didn't seem to mind that there was only one waiter. Half the tables were littered with breakfast remains, and the small swimming pool looked thick, rather green, and was choked with palm fronds. He ordered shrimp, another drink and watched two young women sip something that had apparently been injected into pineapples. After while, he wanted to join them. He liked the way their faces glowed in the pink umbrella shade of their table and the way they approached the ridiculous pineapples and sipped their drinks through tiny straws. One of them wore an ankle bracelet with a glittering shell dangling from it.

On the way out he tested a harpoon which stood in a dim corner with other tools of the whaler's trade: a vicious blubber lance, a blunt headed club-like instrument for what use he didn't know. When he tried to lift the harpoon something pulled in his hip and he couldn't raise the harpoon from the floor. A fine film of rust coated his hands and he went to the men's room to wash it off. Then he strolled toward the main square to wait for Germaine in the immense shade of the banyan tree.

The sun barely penetrated the high leaves of the tree; he thought it must be ten degrees cooler. The branches threw almost a half-acre of shade. Nothing grew beneath it but its aerial roots, hanging everywhere, searching down for a place to root. Where they met the red earth and took hold, they thickened and served as props to the older branches. Even the concrete sidewalks criss-crossing the square had been invaded, split open. Such ingenious fecundity pleased him and when someone thrust a broadside into his hand, a notice of celebration, the banyan's one hundredth birthday, he decided he would be there. "Would you mind?" someone with a camera said. He moved out of the way and saw Ross, Germaine, too, with the others heading toward the bus. They were all laughing at some story he was telling them. Germaine wore a long, flowery dress, something new. "Like it?" she asked as they settled into the air-conditioned bus. He did and took her hand, held it loosely all the way back to the hotel. Both of their hands folded together in the flowers spread wildly in her warm, open lap.

Germaine was in the bathroom doing her eyes when he brought up the banyan tree. She smiled at him in the mirror, her eyes wide as she applied a final brush of mascara. "What was that about a tree?" she said.

"The one in town, in the park where I waited for you. There's going to be a celebration, a kind of birthday party." She pressed by him on her way to the closet. "You know how those chamber-ofcommerce things are, Cy. They don't usually come off. Besides we're leaving for Waikiki tomorrow. It's all set."

"We could catch the tour later. What does Ross care?" She backed toward him, holding the dress in place and he zipped her up. "You look wonderful," he said and kissed her shoulder. The dress, a sarong, flattered her full body, rode easily over her hips and exposed one slim calf and ankle. He thought of the girl with the glittering shell as Germaine fastened the tiny straps of her high-heeled sandals. He sat next to her on the bed. He ran his hand up her calf, under the inviting slit to her thigh and rested his palm against the slick crotch of her panty hose. He felt her press her thighs lightly together, felt a soft quiver.

"We have to be downstairs in ten minutes," she said after a quick kiss.

"We can be late."

"We won't get good seats for the show." She eased away from him again, apologetically, without passion. "Cy, really, the timing is wrong." She plucked the dinner tickets from the mirror frame and studied his disappointment a moment. "There'll be time later," she said turning around, spritzing perfume over her neck and shoulders.

"Well, Christ," he said softly. "Later, we'll both be tired as hell."

He wondered at the inconsistency of it all as he followed the sway of her long skirt to the elevator. A lush tropical print, flowers and vines, exotic, formalized, promising; like the sailor's rest, seductive, memories and fantasies that would never be realized. *Coming around the horn, horny.* He smoothed his jacket, checked himself in the narrow glass between the elevators and felt foolish. What a fool, going down to carved ice swans and crab souffles, candlelight, chef's caps, with a hard on. On the elevator someone asked him what time the baggage had to be in the lobby. He tried to be pleasant. "I suppose Ross would know about that," he said.

In the morning, the bellboy interrupted the flow of their lovemaking. After the third ring, after trying to ignore the persistent rap on the door, he came. He was disappointed for Germaine. "It's all right," she said. She told him to consider it a gift from her. "There'll be plenty of time, later," she said.

The boy came back again while he was putting on his shorts. They rushed the packing; he hadn't shaved yet and kept the kit out. He would have to carry it in his lap to Waikiki. When the bags were gone, they were told they had time so he took his binoculars, also left out on the dresser, and went onto the narrow iron balcony to watch the sea.

A sailboat moved away from shore into open waters. The sails suddenly caught the breeze, ballooned out and pulled the boat into the bay. He could see the people aboard, their hair blowing, their faces wet with spray, strolling up along the bow. He scanned the bay for signs of whales. They had seen four or five one afternoon. First the spume above the water, then the black, enormous backs and fins breaking above the blue before the dive; the flukes rising, languid, graceful before they slipped away. Humpback whales, he had learned, the ones that sing, are recorded, mysterious. But today there were no whales.

On the beach, a young woman flattened herself onto a mat and reached back to undo her top. The straps fell away. Her back shone with oil. Then an old couple crossed his line of vision, walking side by side with towels over their arms and he followed them as they looked for a good spot near the water. He hoped he and Germaine would look as well put together in ten years or so. He guessed the couple might be in their late seventies but both were trim, straight-backed. After spreading their towels side by side, they walked hand in hand into the light waves.

The surf broke its main strength on a sand bar a distance from the beach. He could see the dark blue line of a drop-off some twenty feet out in the direction they walked. Could they see it? There were no lifeguards on the beach before nine. Well, these people certainly weren't kids; they had seen a beach before, and you don't reach your seventies without learning caution. They had stopped wading out anyway and the man turned his back to the breaking surf while the woman gingerly splashed about, then ducked into the waves letting them spill over her. Cy followed a surfer for awhile, watched him race along the crest of a breaking roller beyond the drop-off, then traced the binoculars back to the couple. The woman had gone down, was spinning around in the push and pull of a series of big waves while the man struggled to reach her. But suddenly he was in trouble. He was being pulled out in the backwash.

Cy turned and rushed to the phone. "Someone's in trouble on the beach, get a lifeguard out there!"

Without explaining, he ran out and heard Germaine shouting, "We have to check out. For God's sake, Cy, what are you doing?"

By the time he got there, the surfer had already pulled the woman out. Cy waded in after the man who was on his hands and knees. A slight undertow tugged the sand from beneath his feet as he forced his way through the water. He had forgotten to take his shoes off but their weight worked for him, gave him more stable footing. He reached out to the man, lifted him to his feet. Together they made their way back to the beach. The old man felt light, his arm like a bird's wing. People rushed at them from all directions with blankets, oxygen, a stretcher but the old man waved them off. "Take care of her," he kept saying, "take care of her."

Cy stepped away to let the rescue crew do their work. The woman, wrapped in blankets but still pale and shivering from fear and cold, sat gulping air from a mask. Her eyes fluttered, then opened wide, wildly searching for her husband in the confusion of strangers. They embraced and sat together, holding each other close for a long time. Cy wanted to be with them, close, his arms around them both, saying something encouraging, hopeful: that it was just bad luck, a tricky current; that it could have happened to anyone caught by surprise. But they were being led back to the hotel; he wasn't needed. As he walked up the stairs from the beach, people stared. He knew he looked wild, crazy. He pulled off the wet shoes and socks, tossed them casually into a trash bin, and in his bare feet and sandy, heavy slacks walked into the lobby and didn't give a damn.

Germaine stood with the tour group and he went to her. She obviously had no words to cover the situation. She kept looking down at his feet, at the wet sand falling from his cuffs as he shook them out onto the gleaming terrazo.

"There was an accident," he said. "Someone almost drowned out there."

"Ross has been looking for you everywhere. The bus is waiting," she said.

"Let it wait."

Ross came up smiling, holding out a boarding pass.

"Quite a morning," he said. "I'll get your bag so you can change. Good as new and off we go." He grinned good-naturedly until Cy refused to budge, would not be guided to the men's room and insisted Germaine's luggage be taken off the bus.

"We're not going anywhere at the moment," he said.

"Cy, are you ill?" Astonished, Germaine turned to Ross. "He looks terrible," she said.

"I'm just fine," Cy said. "I'll be even better when we get off this goddam tour. No offense, Ross. We'll handle things ourselves, that's all. I'm tired of seeing the world through tinted glass."

"You're kidding," Ross said. "No one has ever walked out on a Sun Tour."

"Well, we are," Cy said.

Germaine sat down in a lounge chair. A boy brought the luggage and placed it around her. She shrugged wearily when Ross looked at her and seemed clearly puzzled. "We owe an explanation," she said.

"Personal reasons," Cy said and pressed some bills into Ross's hand. "Have one on me in Waikiki."

"You're the boss," Ross said," but this beats the hell out of me." He turned and walked toward the bus, then hollered back. "You call Chicago, tell them you got sick or something. Maybe they'll refund."

He had no intention of calling his travel agent in Chicago; he didn't care about a refund. Instead, he changed into dry clothes and took Germaine out onto the terrace for lunch. He would try to calm her, charm her over to his side, try to explain. He began with an apology.

"Sorry I ran out like that but when I saw the old couple going down . . . they had looked so happy and then, well, the look on their faces . . . " Germaine leaned forward, waiting for him to finish. His throat tightened and he looked away. The lawn beyond the terrace blurred, became a haze of green.

He heard Germaine saying, "You did the right thing. Lucky for them you saw it all."

He couldn't explain the tears welling in his eyes, wetting his palms as he tried to press them back.

"What was their name?" she finally asked.

"I don't know. It doesn't matter, does it?"

Things came into focus again and Germaine seemed to brighten. "They shouldn't have been out there alone," she said.

"No dammit, that's just the point. They should have been. I mean should feel free to be. Now they may not ever try again."

Germaine sat very still, a piece of melon poised halfway to her mouth on a delicate silver fork. She put it down and placed her hand over his. "Why has this upset you so? You said yourself the surf is tricky."

"But you have to keep moving, watch for the unexpected."

"So we had to leave the tour?"

The waiter slid plates of grilled sea bass between them. The breeze shifted and clacked through the palms. He could smell the sea more sharply. Germaine studied him carefully, waiting for more but he could do no better. The feeling of urgency and alarm that had turned like a knife in him that morning on the beach, now seemed vague. He couldn't explain himself. "Let's have wine with this," he said, and later when they were both lightheaded, giddy with the minor excitement of a change in plans, he said the reason he wanted to stay was, after all was said and done, she must remember, he had told her about the Banyan tree. He really wanted to go the festival.

"Why not," she said. "Why not?"

They rented a seedy beach studio for the rest of the week in Lahaina, all they could find on short notice. But there was a wooden fan turning slowly in the ceiling, which pleased him immensely, and a small refrigerator. The patio was shaded by a sea-grape tree and had a grill, a few faded deck chairs and a rough wooden table. A steady breeze blew through the wood shuttered windows, cooling, fresh, not like the dank and disagreeable air-conditioning in the hotel which required everything to be closed up tight, where plastic flowers decorated the chilly hallways. He felt himself again.

In town they picked up a bottle of gin, some mixes, fruit, sinfully expensive macadamia nuts, and brochures: what-to-do-in Lahaina. When they got back to their room there was a bowl of fiery red hibiscus on the coffee table. Germaine tucked one into her hair, then placed one behind his ear and after closing the shutters stepped out of her muu-muu and stretched out naked on the couch like the girl in the Maja painting. They made long, lazy love and drank gin, sleeping on and off in the shuttered light, like children put to bed in the heat of the afternoon.

He woke and noticed the light had changed. Germaine still slept, turned on one side with her legs drawn up. He got up, pulled on his shorts, and went out to the patio. The sky and the sea seemed one, fluid lavender and rose. A boy was moving along the line of rooms lighting torches that pegged the path around the motel. In the dark that came all at once the effect was exciting. He had forgotten the noises of a tropical night, tree toads and insects sounding off everywhere. No one in the world knew where they were and the anonymity pleased him. It was the way things are, in their naked age as they say. They were like the old couple pulled from the sea, at risk, on their own. One never knew.

Years ago, in Jamaica, he had felt the same gut anxiety that he had felt on the beach that morning. He remembered it was Easter Sunday, the hills and soft bluffs above the sea had been dotted with bright, diving kites. He and Germaine had been on their way to Dunns Falls on a cruiser arranged by their hotel. Halfway to the falls, he realized something was wrong. The cruiser rolled and wallowed. Leaning over the side, he saw the bilges were riding below the water; they were taking on water. He had made a panicky count of life jackets in the cabin. Not enough; overloaded.

"No problem, mon," the captain said. "Only going over there." But over there, the white dock shaped like a cross, seemed too far and he had felt sick, tricked into a perilous test. The rest of the passengers seemed unconcerned as they threw back free rum drinks. Later, he couldn't bring himself to climb the rock slick path up to the falls, even with a guide. Later, he had felt too embarrassed by his fear to report the incident to the hotel. In a good many places things were done that way. You had to look out for your own skin. He had taken a cab back from the Falls and kept his mouth shut.

"Almost cashed in, in Jamaica," he would say telling the stories to friends, and end with a crack about the easy-going young captain who ate raw conch cock as an aphrodisiac. He still wondered now and then if there might not be something in that, and went in to take a shower.

Germaine, her face shiny and flushed, sat on the bed with her knees drawn up, her breasts rounded against them, startlingly white above the tanned, freckled knees. The hibiscus was crushed against her hair. She was looking around the strange room for a clock. "What time is it?" she asked.

"I love you," he said quietly, and went to the dresser to look at his watch.

In the morning they decided to try snorkeling and signed up with a guide from a dive shop not far from the motel. He promised an easy place, well-marked, and assured them there was nothing to it. They parked the jeep in the shade of a palm grove which curved precisely around a small cove suspended in light. The guide, a burly Hawaiian, patiently demonstrated the equipment. Germaine seemed apprehensive. She stood in the shallows, the skirt of her bathing suit floating like a flower around her waist, and said she didn't want to spit into the mask.

"Is it necessary?" she asked.

"That's the way we do it," the guide said.

He showed them how to handle the snorkels, clear their masks, and supervised a turn around the shallows; then gentled them into deeper water where they couldn't touch bottom although it seemed within a hand's reach. The reef, a vague ridge of blue-gray, lay just ahead. A light surf broke over it but inside the cove was calm and easy. Here and there a marker with a flag bobbed on the surface to mark the way. Cy reached out and took Germaine's hand and they kicked together, the sound of their breathing rasping through them as they followed the guide.

Then the guide was beneath them, the bubbles of his sudden dive trailing behind him. He signaled toward a tall bed of grasses and dove deeper, flushing out a turtle, jewel green, the width of a car tire. He struggled to hold him, rolling over and over, the turtle's underside showing one moment, then its jade green carapace, then he was free, his scaly flippers beating up a hard current they could feel against their bellies.

The guide popped up beside them but Cy had kicked off after the creature which headed straight to the reef. Using his arms free-style, kicking hard, he managed to keep up but as they came up on the dark wall of the reef, he began to tire. His legs burned, his breathing became uneven, but there was more life, amazing color on the reef and when a cloud of minnows burst around him in a silvery explosion, he felt a rush of energy. Water spilled into his snorkel. Salt stung his throat but he hadn't lost the turtle. It zig-zagged just below, confused by the dead end, searching frantically for an escape.

The cold reptilian eyes glanced up, sized him up, as the turtle turned sideways just beneath him. He felt the dull rasp of its shell along his thigh and grabbed at the ridge just behind the head. For a moment he was able to hang on but only for a moment. He was tossed about, then shaken off as the turtle scrambled through an opening and disappeared into the open sea.

A light chop brushed him against the rough outcroppings of the reef, the only sounds, his own deep breathing, his heart, the sound of himself, of life and oceans. He sculled away and lifted his head to get his bearings. Several hundred feet away he made out the seal-dark head of the guide, his arms waving, calling back. Germaine bobbed beside him, her mask flashing sun like a beacon. He raised an arm, thumb up, and when his breathing settled down, put his face in the water and kicked slowly, arms trailing, concentrating on the life below and all around him. He felt filled with warmth. The light bounced off the bottom sand, shot through the grasses and seemed to be passing through him, pouring through his back, arms, and legs with an unbearable heat and energy. He moved easily, rhythmically, toward the beach, taking his time, recording the wonders of the cove. He didn't want to miss anything. He felt as if he could go on forever, circling, scanning, spreading his light everywhere.

"I can only recommend the shrimp and gin," he said. Germaine glanced up from her menu, surprised.

"I had lunch here. It's all right." He had brought her to the sailor's rest against her better judgment, arguing for the atmosphere, the history of the place. He thought it looked better at night in the primitive torch light. The pool had been cleaned and more waiters improved the service.

"I'm not very hungry," she said. "I think it's the sun. We're both burned. Look," she said, reaching over the table, pressing a finger on his forearm. "Too much sun." The skin turned white under her touch. "I heard you can get a terrible refraction burn from snorkeling."

"What?"

"Refraction. The sun magnified by the water. It's like holding a magnifying glass over a leaf, I suppose."

The dinner, grilled Mahi-Mahi, came almost immediately because there were so few diners in the courtyard. Germaine found bones and fastidiously picked them out until they lay in a grisly curve around the rim of her plate. The effort seemed to exhaust her. He felt obliged to make up for her patience, to make the evening more entertaining, and told her about the old days. "They didn't have metal here when the first ships came and ship nails became very valuable. The sailors used them for barter with the natives, with the native girls."

"Really?" Germaine spooned up a dollop of coconut ice cream and offered it to him, held up the spoon while he ate it.

He told her, "Nails for love. The sailors pulled them right out of the ships until the damn things were falling apart." Germaine laughed as he painted a verbal picture: a ship separating board by board, miles out, men diving off in all directions. "Cursing the nut-brown maidens," he said. "But without regret."

"Certainly some regrets . . . I mean drowning for love . . . for sex. Really Cy, you are a hopeless romantic."

"Well, I hope so," he said, "I really hope so."

On the way out he thought of asking her if she would spend a night there, just take a look at one of the rooms over the harbor. But she came back from the ladies' room without having used it. "Let's get out of here. You can't imagine . . ." and the moment passed. If only she saw things the way they really were. Not there for any particular judgment, just there, to be seen or ignored as one felt like it. To be captured, he thought, held for a moment, bad or good. Lately, everything seemed so fleeting. All the good moments were like mayflies on a summer pond.

He followed her out. Across the street the square was full of workmen. Ladders leaned against the banyan tree, reaching up into the highest branches. Thousands of tiny Italian lights were being draped and twined above and down along the aerial roots.

"How old did you say it was?" she asked, taking his hand.

"Over a hundred. Still going strong."

"They're overdoing it a bit. It's going to be garish."

As they crossed over to the square for a closer look, the lights suddenly went on. Germaine gasped and stopped. They stood a long time together, not saying anything, looking up into the bright canopy of light and leaves.

20 QUESTIONS

(from *Chicago Magazine*)

When the phone rang Miranda knew it was Bradley. He always called at the most inopportune moments: when she was halfway through hanging the bathroom wallpaper, or just as she reached a melting point in a new beau's arms, or now, as she maneuvered a French massage glove guaranteed to slim her thighs.

She picked up the phone. "I'm in the middle of massaging my thighs."

"This will just take a minute," Bradley said. "How do you cook a lobster?"

It was to be expected. They had been divorced for two years, yet still Bradley called with questions.

"How do I iron my batiste shirt?"

"How can I stop the kitchen floor from yellowing?"

She held more conversations with Bradley now than in all their three years of marriage.

"You drop the lobster into a large pot of boiling water," Miranda said, though she had never cooked a lobster herself, "and when it stops scratching on the sides, it's done."

"It's already dead."

"Oh, Bradley, don't eat a dead lobster. You'll get food poisoning."

"Frozen, for God's sake, frozen. Annabelle left three lobster tails in the freezer when she moved out."

Annabelle came after the divorce. And after Michelle, Jill, Marian, and Teresa. With each new beginning for Bradley, Miranda's hopes had risen: Now he will learn how to wash his black corduroy pants.

Then the calls would start again.

"Miranda, could you tell Teresa how you make lasagna?"

"Miranda, could you explain to Michelle why you did my income-tax deductions that way?"

She finally accepted the fact that no matter how often she tossed him off, Bradley, like a boomerang, would always return.

"Doesn't this lobster tail come with instructions?"

"Does a tomato come with instructions? It's just there in the freezer.

She gave up then and went for *The Joy of Cooking.*

He was impossible, she knew, but when it came to questions that could be answered in concrete, measurable terms ("Heat two quarts of salted water to a rippling boil . . ."), Miranda tried her best. It gave her a sense of order and definition—things she had originally left Bradley for.

But lately Miranda noticed a new, almost evanescent direction to Bradley's questions.

"Remember that sandwich shop in Old Town?" he said in one three-a.m. phone call. "It's not there any more—it's a bookstore or a pinball gallery now—but remember when we were there, I was wearing my suede jacket from college, and this guy at the counter was arguing with these Mexicans. Well, what was the argument about?"

Another time he called to ask the name of the song he had danced to in a Paris café the night he was lost. Miranda hadn't been there but Bradley had told her about it. Surely she remembered?

Pointless details, long and best forgotten, but he seemed to feel an urge to track them down and hold them.

Miranda felt no such need, but set off by Bradley, the questions hummed through her mind. They infiltrated her dreams at night and by day diffused her energy at work.

She worked at a local radio and television station where she sold blocks of advertising to sponsors. There, among the expanses of time measured on grid paper, Miranda found a sense of peace. Bradley, too, was fascinated by the job. "Miranda sells time," he told anyone who would listen. "How much do you need? Twenty minutes? A couple of weeks? Enough years to outlive your wife?"

It was a thinly amusing joke to some people, but time was no joke for Bradley. He liked to ask Miranda if she couldn't sell him some time, not in the future, but from the past, in particular another 1968. He was fond of saying that he hadn't been happy since 1968. Now that they were no longer married, Miranda didn't take it personally.

When the phone rang it snapped Miranda out of her dream: She had been painting a staircase. Up or down, she tried to remember as she fumbled for the receiver.

"Why didn't we ever have a kid?" Bradley asked. "Or a color TV?"

"We had a cat and a dog and you said they took up too much room."

"A black-and-white cat," he said with a snap of triumph. "Even our cat wasn't in color."

From the moment Miranda had brought the stray cat home, Bradley had disliked it. "I've always thought cats were really some kind of alien beings from outer space spying on us earthlings." When she refused to debate this, he had stoked his case. "Haven't you ever noticed that Mars looks like it's full of fur?"

What she did notice, one day, was that Bradley was becoming more disturbing than charming. Not being him, she had no interest in trying to track down the exact moment when she knew she would have to divorce him. She remembered the day she had asked him to leave. He piled his legal briefs in the shower stall, packed, took a shower, and left. When the briefs were buckled with mildew, Miranda threw them out.

Now Bradley lived downtown in an apartment with a bed, a color television, a Tensor lamp, and a view of the lake. He told Miranda his pantry shelves were filled with a month's supply of staples: Scotch, Pepperidge Farm cookies ("the kind that look like playing cards, not the kind you always bought"), and peanut butter. She believed him.

He had always cultivated the culinary tastes of a child: no salads, no vegetables ("Are you trying to make me sick?" he practically shrieked the first time she cooked turkey divan), and a passionate devotion to certain brand names. Once when Miranda bought Oreo instead of Hydrox cookies he split them in half and left them laid out like checkers on the kitchen counter. The dog jumped up, ate them, and then got sick on the living-room rug.

These days Bradley thrived on a diet of ham-and-cheese sandwiches on plain bread (butter also made him sick) and chocolate malts. He mixed his own malts in a blender, his only purchase since the divorce except for the color TV and a video tape recorder, which he used to tape and replay programs that filled him with great melancholy: grainy reruns of *Sergeant Bilko, 60 Minutes,* and stark, sinister movies like *Badlands.*

Miranda, on the other hand, was now free to cook dinners consisting of steamed vegetables, grapefruit, and Ry-Krisp. She ate granola bars and Haägen-Dazs ice cream for breakfast, kept the coffee table pushed to one side so she could exercise, and, in *her* blender, whipped up honey, almond, and raw oatmeal body masks. She also dated men—they were usually either sexy or nice, but rarely both—for as long as they seemed reasonable, calm, and not possessed of too quizzical a nature. Often they were merely boring.

When the office phone rang Miranda picked it up and heard Phil Silvers's voice from far away, as if he were barking orders into the wrong end of the receiver. Her first urge was to hang up. It was a bad day; a major sponsor had just pulled out its account and Miranda's current man, James, was in Toronto on business. The thought of now adding Bradley to her problems gave Miranda's voice a flat, rigid tone. He caught it immediately.

"Come and have a drink with me," Bradley said. "It'll be pleasant. I'll be amusing and you can relax."

She doubted this. At his best Bradley would be asking her how to sew on buttons and get rid of lint; at his worst he would badger her over the name of the usher at a movie they had seen three years ago. But his coaxing won.

When they met in a bar near his law office, they were awkward and strained. Bradley turned suddenly shy, as if this meeting had been arranged only to humor her. With little to say to each other, they ordered a bottle of wine and drank steadily.

Miranda noticed that his hair was turning gray. He wore new glasses frames, probably having been lured from his misshapen wire-rims by some woman who used her wiles better than Miranda ever had. She thought he looked very crisp and sharp, full of angular intelligence.

But then she had always thought that. Miranda remembered the day that she and Bradley, still married, had gone to the zoo. Their favorite place was the ape house and that day they had ended up in front of an African baboon's cage, transfixed as the male with the painted muzzle stared them down. Bradley finally broke the moment by saying that baboons stared because they were trying to memorize people's faces. Your face would be imprinted on the baboon's mind, Bradley said, and if it ever got out of the zoo, it would try to find you.

Several people within earshot took their children's hands and moved away. Bradley didn't notice. As he continued to talk about the possibility of waking up one night and finding a baboon staring at you—just like now—Miranda thought that as soon as her personalized stationery was used up she would leave him. Then, to her dismay, she realized that she was starting to think like Bradley.

She hadn't, of course, believed the baboon story even then, but she had once believed that Bradley was the smartest and most endearing person she had ever known. Remembering this now, her voice broke as she tried to answer one of Bradley's questions.

"Oh, honey," he said, seeing tears in her eyes, "it makes me so sad to see you like this. Don't cry," he murmured, patting her hand. "Don't cry. Say something to cheer me up."

This captured her attention. "What do you have to be depressed about?"

"I don't know," he said, visibly glad that she wasn't going to cry. "Maybe I should quit being a lawyer."

"What else would you do?"

"I'd like to drive a Federal Express truck."

She exhaled a puff of air, exasperated that she had been suckered into this exchange.

"I'd love to drive packages out to the airport," he said, "and watch planes take off and land."

She knew enough to pay no attention. Years earlier he had pined for Colorado, though he had never been there, and life in a log cabin. "I could write people's wills," he had said, "and close their A-frame deals for them." He finally took a trip to Boulder when his brother got married. Later Miranda had asked how he liked it.

"There are mountains in Colorado," he had said in a tight voice, as if he had been tricked. The subject never came up again.

"You know all about takeoffs," she told Bradley now. "What you've never learned is how to light."

They relaxed now, laughed over old jokes, and drank until there was barely enough time to catch the last trains from the North Western station. Miranda wanted the North Line home, Bradley the western train to visit some new sweetheart. So with a flurry of drunken energy they gathered their coats and hailed a cab.

In the back seat Bradley slid close to her and Miranda settled into his arms. Kissing him was exciting, forbidden, and surprisingly familiar. Once he murmured something that sounded romantic but Miranda, her ear pressed against his camel's-hair coat, couldn't hear clearly. She didn't ask him to repeat it.

They parted at the station, running for separate terminals.

By the next week Miranda's memory of the taxi ride was fuzzy around the edges, just like her voice when she drank too much. She didn't hear from Bradley but she really didn't miss him. James returned from Toronto and she knew she liked him enough to probably end up living with him, though not enough, at the moment, to go to the zoo with him. She spent most of her evenings now with him or in a new exercise class, so perhaps Bradley's calls were just missing her.

When Miranda got the wedding invitation she felt less surprised than irritated at having to give up a lunch hour to shop for a present. Sibley McLellan, Bradley's bride-to-be, was not registered at Marshall Field's, so Miranda cruised Field's Afar, Crossroads Market, and any other department with a relevant name, trying to pick a present that would suit Bradley.

She settled on a small pink-and-white machine that made peanut butter out of peanuts. It seemed to have the vaguely scientific aura of a blender and a video tape recorder and it would keep Bradley out of Sibley's way. A stopgap measure, to be sure, but Miranda knew that every little moment counted.

To buy it she had to stand in line behind a woman returning a multipurpose kitchen machine. "I bought this when I was stoned," the woman explained to the saleslady. When it was Miranda's turn, she had the peanut-butter machine gift wrapped and sent.

The next time she heard from Bradley it was not through a phone call but a post card from Ocho Rios. "Having wonderful time. Lee is too marvelous for words. Thanks for the present. Will have you over for peanut-butter sandwiches and chocolate malts when we return. What is the name of the music I like so much? I mean the theme in *Badlands*."

Miranda paused for a moment over "Lee." Was that just a nickname of Sibley's or had Bradley run off to Ocho Rios with someone else?

Deciding there was nothing better to do that weekend, Miranda went to the reference room of the downtown library and from there to Rose Records on State Street. The library had been unable to pinpoint which Erik Satie compositions were played in *Badlands*, so after careful consideration, Miranda bought *Danse gothiques, Aperçus désagréables,* and *Sports et divertissesments*. All of those sounded like possibilities for Bradley.

At home she played them through once and then again, but she couldn't concentrate. The music made her nervous. It was exactly the kind of sound she was sure would run through her brain if she were having a nervous breakdown. Even her cat seemed jumpy when the records were on and Miranda decided the music could stunt her plants. Not bothering to match album to cover, she packed up the records and put them in a closet. She waited a week and found that she felt little loss. Several weeks later, she gave the records to the mailman.